# T⬥KEN PHANTOM

FROM INTERNATIONAL AWARD WINNING AUTHOR

## KIA CARRINGTON-RUSSELL

CRYSTAL
• PUBLISHING •

# DEDICATION

To my readers,
Thank you for keeping the dream alive. I wouldn't be here without you and your
support.

To my friend, coffee,
Thank you for supporting me through the long days and late nights.

To the dreamers and believers,
Keep doing what makes your heart sing, and don't give up just because you're having
a restless day. Believe in the magic and process of the journey, not the end result.
Your time will come.

# PHANTOM

*Exist, but only for destruction.*
*Don't be heard, until whispering intimately into their ear interment death.*
*Do not fight the chains around your neck that anchor you to this world.*
*Nor argue the phantom-like stature you have been given to abide it.*
*Your rules are made only by me, a silent entity that guides you.*
*Fulfilling and permitting your most monstrous desires to come forth.*
*I am not your sin; I am your accomplice.*
*I am not your imagination; I am your Master.*
*I am not your quest; I am your only answer.*
*And with your hands, they shall get bloody.*
*If only to find mercy in this world where you have purpose once more.*
*Stick to the shadows, and do not be noticed.*
*Only when it is time to strike.*

# CHAPTER I

THE FULL MOON'S ominous glow splintered into the cave entrance like a line in the sand. A division of the world we might've once known and the world that was coming. For hours the humans had remained silent, comforting the small children and accepting our help rather than taking matters into their own hands. Most susceptible, this was outside their field of expertise, and the risk was their lives. Titan didn't leave my side and now had her small head on my lap, bundled and coddling into my waist as she slept on the floor. It was... uncomfortable to say the least.

I often received glances from the members who I'd once trained beside within the Human Compound. Few of them had even been there on the fateful day of their military leader, Sydney's demise. Chase had seemed like the big bad vampire that killed and ran off with his body, but in actual fact, it had been me. They would've had numerous questions after I disappeared under my alias, Ellie at the Human Compound. Jenn had lied and told them I was dead. That was during the time I was hunting down and retrieving Chase and Tythian from Fier's Council. And now they were looking at a ghost or a very alive Ellie. Surprisingly though, none of them asked questions. They focused on easing the hysterical children into a fake sense of comfort. Dire expressions filled the cave.

They were meant to have been on a short trip, exposing their youngest recruits to what it looked like beyond their wall. Six adults and four children, one being Titan. It was the first time any of them had ventured past the walls, and they were so quickly met with an implacable fate. I gritted my teeth, both in suffering for my tolerance to be so close to humans who had open wounds and were bandaging themselves, but also the calculating thoughts that consumed me, trying to figure out why their own humans would turn on them. I doubted they realized their own kind orchestrated the wolf attack. And I certainly couldn't believe it was because of chance.

I needed to speak to Yolo telepathically. I didn't often use my gift to speak with others, only with Chase. I often influenced their thoughts but speaking with them felt too close, too connected with who they were and all the raw emotion I didn't like to expose myself to. I was getting stronger, but as soon as I opened that gateway to speak with them, it was a barrage of lifetimes regrets, hatred, pain, and suffering and it took a lot of effort to keep it at bay. The only other person I'd spoken to telepathically had been Whitney, Tythian's familiar. It had been the final seconds of her life, and in that moment, there was no regret or pain, only serene understanding and acceptance. I closed my eyes for a moment in a will to refocus. Whitney wasn't relevant. Yolo and I had to figure out something.

Cramped in the tiny cave where we sat silently, ushering the children to sleep, it was the only way we could communicate. So, I gritted my teeth, trying my hardest to ignore the willful smell of their blood reaching my nose like a banquet of different flavors and treats. I took a gulp, pushing down that everlasting thirst that felt like it'd never be quenched. I made a point to focus on Yolo, and only Yolo. *It's happening. The human government is making a move on their own.* I'd filled him in on the interrogation of the human who'd been bitten by Fire when she'd attacked their group. He was already maddening or maybe he was like that before.

Yolo, still in Jenn's form was uneasy as he replied. He was fearful and cautious. Worried that as we spoke, I had the gift to also read his thoughts and memories. The latter I couldn't do, yet. But I was very aware of the heavy guard he constructed between us. He was trying his hardest to press down a darker part of himself, one I imagined to be orientated with his former lover and familiar, Jenn, who he'd loved and mistakenly killed.

*We need to help them,* Jenn replied simply. It struck me as odd initially when Jenn's voice was cerebrated back and not Yolo's. And although she boldly stated she wanted to help them, and genuinely so, there was fear there—of the unknown. The thoughtful terror of a monster that could turn human into wolf. I wondered if the vampires had feared the creations of hunters all the same those three hundred years ago when we were crafted. We originated from their venom, from scientific design to fight against them, and now the humans who had remained quiet all these years had created something else, of even greater magnitude, and what they pitched to sound more of a plague. We could only create other hunters by reproduction. It was one of the few things that kept us human.

*If it happens,* and what I meant by 'it' was if they did shift or turn or whatever was to come, *You can't be in here.* Yolo was a vampire, even though he was human in Jenn's form it wasn't a risk we could take. If he were bitten, it could be the end for him, just as the human had said.

*And what about yourself?* Jenn forcefully replied, not spitefully but calculatingly. She was attending to the last wounded soldier who'd been bitten on the shoulder. Jenn had stapled the wound shut and heavily bandaged it, blood still seeping through. Cole, who had once been a good friend and second to Sydney, stared at me silently. He was now in charge of this group and the last he'd heard I was dead.

If they reacted in any way as the human prisoner had implied, we could leave the humans in here, watching from the outer edges of the cave. The twins, Kora and Kasey, were still close by, under Lincon's orders to keep a shield over the cave and keep the humans in. I had been bitten by Fire myself, and nothing had happened since. But I had no desire to risk it a second time. Whether that was because of my naturally born nature as a huntress, I wasn't sure. Nonetheless, I wasn't willing to risk anything that could trail down my link with Chase and challenge his sanity.

But I couldn't stand by either if they decidedly began turning on one another and shredding each other apart. I looked down at Titan who lightly snoozed. If that were to happen, I'd make sure to at least get her out.

I felt that all too familiar nudge on the line that connected me with Chase. He was becoming impatient. *Where are you, my love?* he asked. It was all too soon. My hand glided into the bundled silk hair in my pocket. The lock of hair he and I had exchanged with our vows to one another. It saddened me that so quickly that moment would be tarnished. That already I was calculating if he would agree with my actions or if I had to keep this secret. A pain unfolded in my chest. That unfamiliar flutter of emotional suffering because I was so close to Chase. I didn't want to betray him in any way, but these people... I couldn't so easily execute them which is what would be deemed necessary. I knew that, logically I understood. And usually, I wouldn't care. But I looked down at the one reason why I did.

Titan was now lull snoozing, her small snore a hot breath flushing on my thigh. Tempted to brush my fingers along her hair, my exposed and outstretched fingers paused, my long nails pointed in hesitation to reach out for her again. *What was I doing?* I could sense Jenn watching me from afar, making sure it wasn't an aggressive handle or attack on the girl. I retracted my hand, abashed by my own provoked form of affection.

I wanted to tell Chase, it burned me to hold this from him, but as the coven leader, he had a responsibility to his people as well. He tugged on the tether between us. It would be only a matter of time until he found us, especially if I didn't respond.

*I'm okay, my love. What do they plan on doing with Fire tonight?* I asked. While I was stuck here, I wasn't there with her. And I had no ambition on moving this group anywhere closer toward the houseful of vampires who lingered in the institute. I could sense Jerimiah and Darcy hovering around where they could last pick up my scent. Lincon and the twins were enough of a deterrent for them to really suspect what was happening here. That, and they'd trapped us in here, deterring anyone's interest.

*We're locking her up in one of the rooms,* he said and paused. *She seems anxious without you here.* I felt the swallow of pride as he meant himself as well. It pained me that he knew I was avoiding his question purposefully.

I stroked over Chase's hair lock in my pocket once more as I looked over to Jenn in the illuminated cave. How it killed me to not tell him. But I didn't want any further attention brought here. I gracefully propped Titan from my lap, making sure not to rub against the bandage on her arm that had small puncture marks still bleeding through. It would leave a vicious scar, but at least she still had her life.

*I'm working on something,* I said to Chase. I could feel his reservations about my secrecy, but he didn't push any further. *I won't be back for a few hours.*

*Do you need my help with anything?* Though he offered the aid, I knew he'd be busy putting the coven into order. Cesar and him had much to go over with the others and what their next plan of action would be.

Before finding out what role I had to play in those plans, I had to confirm with my own eyes if anything was going to happen to these humans. And if not, then Yolo and I would guide them to safety before any other vampires knew they lingered so close. And if something did happen… Then we would deal with it then.

Cole looked up at me begrudgingly when I approached him, far from the extended hand he'd once offered me as I joined their ranks. I didn't blame him. Everyone thought I was dead. The coppery taste of blood filled my nose, but I focused only on him as I spoke, the first few words gritting out as I fought against the blood frenzy my body was tricking me into tasting.

"Your government has been working on a new virus that spreads through wolves to counter the vampires. We have reason to believe your team was bitten by one of those wolves tonight."

His face crinkled in anger. "And why should I listen to a dead woman?"

I sneered at him, the ungrateful human. I closed my eyes momentarily, counting to ten as my father had taught me to execute patience instead of caving in to my temperament. Jenn edged closer to our discussion. Though he had no reason to believe me, it was the truth. The others watched on, tired and wounded. Another man stepped to his aid. I shot him an effective glance that suggested he found his place seated on the floor again.

Cole continued, "Our government wouldn't turn on its own people." I could almost taste his fear for the lie that it was. Even he was aware that something was afoot and had lost confidence in his hierarchy after my simple suggestion. If they were to change into some monstrous thing, I decided it was best they know, a warning—something I had never been gifted when my own monster awoke, leaving me with only confusion and thirst in its wake.

"You don't believe that," I blatantly replied. "Or why else would you let Jenn help you? Why else would you be cowering in a cave with your young instead of retreating to the safety of your own walls?" His face twisted, angry and humiliated. "That bite mark could very well be a test to turn you into something entirely different much like the lab tests I'm sure you've heard about in your compound." He blanked white, horror shading his features. So many of their own never came back from their labs. Sydney had tried his hardest to protect them from the reality of that place, but I'd seen it firsthand. Seen the way they turned into sabers immediately when overdosed as live test subjects. And now that expectation was on this man, to protect his group. I doubted he could measure up to the protection Sydney shadowed them in. All fighting spirit left him.

"What will happen to us?" Ryan, his second asked, drawing closer to our conversation. He too mirrored the shades of horror that illuded their imagination. The six adults were staring at me intently, hinging their next breath on my answer.

"You could turn into a wolf," Jenn said, furrowing her eyebrows as she said it. Out loud, it even sounded strange. Almost impossible. And yet here we were, tucked in a small cave braced for the worst. Anything was possible in a world that was catered for monsters.

Cole and Ryan both opened their mouths but couldn't manage a word to escape. Jenn interjected, "If our intel is correct, apparently the shift is temporary, only lasting a full moon. But we've never seen this ourselves. We don't know what to expect, really."

"What do you mean you don't know what to expect?" Cole demanded.

"Remember we didn't do this to you," I seethed bitterly. His face red from anger, he went to stand. The moment he did, he winced back into place, clutching his wound. All anger vanquished from him and pointedly turned to desperation.

"How do we stop this?" he asked quietly. He searched the eyes of his team. They all looked at one another as if ripping their infected limbs might be the only way to detain the possibilities.

There was a silent pause before Jenn somberly replied, "We don't know."

"Well, isn't this your area of expertise," Ryan countered, furiously stepping forward, frantic to find a solution.

I pinned him with a look, forcing myself to physically halt before I engaged in any altercations that would suggest I was otherwise human. "We only heard of this recently. We didn't expect to come across your lot in the crossfires with the very same ordeal."

Cole was staring at Titan as if for the same reason that I had been earlier. For all that she stood for and the remainder of Sydney's legacy, that we so very much wanted to keep alive. He looked at me again and then spoke to Jenn. He didn't trust me any more than anyone else, but I could see the desperation in his eyes as he looked to Jenn.

"What do we do?" His throat bobbled. "How do we fix this, Jenn, please."

Jenn offered a weak calming smile, her elegance somehow brightening the dire situation. She was offering them confidence in her skills, and I found her all the crueler for it. Jenn was a monster as well, their enemy in reality. But here she was shining as if a beckon that could protect them from the darkness that was approaching. "Stay here, we've put in measurements where you won't be able to escape, especially if you're a danger to anyone else. And we just ride out the night, seeing if something is going to happen or not."

I could smell a small shift in the air, a perfume of fresh forest and pine. The cold cave began to radiate in heat. It was only a subtle change, but I could sense their temperatures were rising, much like a fever. The full moon had peaked for three hours now, and nothing had happened. But this was the surest sign that something was going awry.

"Jenn, we need to wait outside," I said. In unison, they all began to become aware of their sudden fever. Cole dampened his forehead, mortified when he pulled back droplets of sweat. I looked over to Titan who was beginning to stir restlessly awake.

"Jenn." I grabbed her arm and tugged on her in urgency. We had to leave this place.

"I'm sorry this is all we can do for you now," she said apologetically.

"No, Jenn, please don't leave us." Cole scampered and reached out for her.

"Who are you people?" one of the women asked. I recognized her. She'd been on the same team the day I'd killed Sydney. If memory served correctly her name was Angela. Jenn and I hovered on the entrance of the cave. I could sense Kora and Kasey's bubble diving to open for us as a sealed gate. The outside world swept through a cold and damp breeze into the cave. They all shivered from its abrasive nature.

"If you survive this," I said unempathetically. "We'll let you know."

Jenn gave me a side glance but didn't give anything away. I wasn't about to break Jenn's alias, and I certainly wouldn't tell them about how closely they were being kept near a houseful of hundreds of vampires. But I would tell them the truth. That if anyone could be their savior, then it was us.

"Wait, no, please!" Ryan begged, lunging for us. As we walked out of the cave and the barrier was closed behind us, he slammed into the wall. He desperately surveyed the invisible wall in a frantic. "No, Jenn! Ellie! Please help us!"

"Ellie, I feel hot!" I heard Titan's shaken and exhausted voice cry out to me. I looked back at Titan who ran toward the exit, trying to chase after me. Much like Ryan, she was thrown back from the force of the invisible barrier. "Ellie!" she screamed.

An unnatural pull toward the girl enveloped me.

"We mustn't," Jenn said. "Turn your back, Esmore." And it was said in a way that I heard Yolo's identity come through. "This is all we can do for them."

"What if they turn on each other?" I asked.

"Then that is the nature of their beasts. But we can't put ourselves in that ring. That cave is nothing but a prison now." I looked at Jenn abashed. She wanted to help them just as much, if not more than me. So why was I struggling to turn my back on them? A howl erupted in the distance, silencing everyone who scampered behind us. The clouds swept past the full moon, ominously and seemingly putting everything to a stop. "I want to help them too, Esmore. But right now, this is all we can do. This is their journey."

My gaze lingered on Jenn's beautiful colored eyes that glistened in the full moon's glow as the clouds cleared once again. But why was Jenn so desperately trying to keep them alive? This went against everything her binding loyalty to Cesar. Why was she risking everything, much as I was, in my way of lying to Chase?

"We're shifting into a new world, Esmore," Jenn said solemnly. "And I'd rather be ahead of the game, that includes knowing everything we can about this virus."

And then it began. The gut gurgling screams, panic and pandemic began. Jenn and I twisted in unison to face the monsters that were creeping into this new world. I clenched Chase's lock of hair in my pocket, and for the first time ever, I prayed that there was something bigger than our existence that could save us all. Because what I was witnessing was nothing but the damned.

# CHAPTER 2

"ELLLIIIEEEEEE!" TITAN'S DESPERATE scream begged for me. I gritted my teeth, unable to hold back. I lunged forward to help her but was blocked and pinned back by Jerimiah and Darcy who grabbed either side of my arms. I hadn't even heard them sneak up on me. As soon as they locked around me they solidified into their gargoyle forms. I thrashed back and forth trying to break out of their grasp, but I was cemented in by warriors who aged lifetimes before me and had the strength to keep me at bay. *Chase had sent them,* I realized.

I floundered on my feet, forced to watch as Titan's little hand stretched out to me, with tears streaming down her face. Everyone else's voice became nothing but an echoing scream in the back as I watched on in horror as Titan's little frame broke apart in front of me.

"Ellie!" she screamed and buckled onto her knees, scratching so deeply into her arms that claw marks remained. I focused on her nails that had elongated into thick and sharpened claws. Her wounds oozed so deep the blood loss alone might kill her.

"Oh, my god," Jenn said behind me as she watched on.

"Ell-" Titan's scream was cut off as another one of them barraged over her, pushing her further into the cave. I tried to jump in but couldn't pull out of the firm grasp I was captured in. The one now in front of her was screaming and holding his head as it began to split in size. Ryan's ribs moved beneath his skin like snapping vines, springing loose and reshaping limply, until they solidified into a bone size that outmatched the stretch of his human skin. But it only continued to grow and envelop him. His body shimmered under the moon in translucency as his bones broke beneath his skin. His face stretched, his nose becoming a snout, and his ears shifting upward into pointed fur ears.

How was this possible? His skin became inundated with masses of fur, his clothing entirely shredded on the floor as he backed up on his hind legs. His gut gurgling screams turned into whimpers and vicious snarls.

Moments later, the man who had once stood before me was a dull-colored brown wolf, twice the size of his human form. He snapped at those still in transit as if trying to make coherence of what was threat and who was brethren. I tried to look past him and focus on Titan, but his large frame blocked my view.

He snarled and licked his lips savagely as he turned on one of his own. The red-coated wolf behind him was circling him in the same way. I couldn't reach them physically but maybe I could with my gift. I hovered my mind over theirs, trying to catch on to any human or coherent thought. There was no such thing, only rage and fury entangled with an uncontrollable desire to let loose and hunt. And if they served their purpose correctly, they were thirsting to hunt down the vampires. When I racked my mind over the red wolf, I realized with clarity that it was Cole. Though I couldn't read his thoughts, it was much like the impression and feel I had of someone when first connecting with them telepathically.

"Oh, my god, they're going to kill each other," Jenn said franticly and stepped forward. This time it was me who interjected.

"No," I said, snapping my gaze to hers which was effective enough to halt her. They had no coherent human thoughts, or not that I could understand, but they were pure emotion and instinct. Something I could understand, if not better, than the emotion I felt around Chase. Primal urges and need. "They're fighting to establish the alpha." I searched further into the cave and realized the younger ones were now being pushed back against the wall and guarded by other wolves in this makeshift pack. They were creating a barrier around the fight, so the younger ones weren't involved. I jarred my neck back and forth trying to find Titan's little body, but I couldn't see it amongst the masses of fur and beast that protected her. I could sense her in there though, frantic and scared and still not entirely turned. Her mind was distorting into primal and human incoherency—and pain, there was so much pain.

"Alpha?" Lincon said behind me, inquisitively. I quickly swept my gaze over my shoulder, having been so enthralled in what was happening that I hadn't noticed him sneak up on us. He was perched on a nearby rock, utterly enthralled and evidently giddy as he watched on. Blood was dripping down his lips as he took another plunge into Kora's wrist as if watching a performance while on his high throne and snacking. Kora winced as he took another mouthful but didn't fight him off. A low snarl pitted in my stomach. Though I didn't like the twins, I didn't enjoy seeing them bound to Lincon of all vampires in such a pathetic way. They had been huntresses, like me, and yet this was the way fate twisted our paths.

The wolves launched at one another in the cave, drawing my attention back to them. The two males lunged for one another, snapping and ripping into the amounts of fur about their necks. Ryan was slammed against the invisible wall Kasey and Kora had erected, his back pushed into the unseen wall. He yelped as Cole bit into his shoulder savagely. Out of desperation, Ryan was able to overpower and flick him off. Dark red blood oozed from his wounds. The coppery smell of it hit my nose and I almost gagged, repulsed by the foul odor. They might've bled red, but that was far from human. No vampire would ever be so desperate to even attempt drinking that repulsive smelling blood.

The two snapped and snarled at one another, lunging and trying to rip at one another's jugulars. "Cole will kill Ryan," Jenn whispered. If that were the case, and if they ever awoke out of this nightmare, then he'd be the reason that his best friend was dead. The other wolves had their ears pinned back, growling as they watched on. They'd tightly formed and backed into the corner ensuring the safety of their young. A female wolf crept out from the shadows in the edge of the cave, circling the fight as she watched on with big blue predatory eyes. When she found an opening, and Ryan was pushed back momentarily, she cowered under Cole, as he snarled and snapped toward Ryan.

"Why is she doing that if she's scared?" Jenn said, sounding almost desperate for the wolf to return to where she first hid. I wavered over the wolf's mind, realizing it was Angela who'd spoken to us earlier asking for our true identity.

"She's not scared," I said, understanding her primal instinct. "She's guarding her mate's throat."

"That's Angela?" Jenn whispered, amazed. It took me by surprise, the immediate connection and overpoweringly instinctual connection the two had. It could only be described as that of what Chase and I had, the unconditional binding of two familiars. These wolves also had that. Maybe we weren't so different at all.

The two continued sizing one another up, the suspense lingering in the cave for who would lunge next. Ryan pinned back his ears and slowly buckled to the ground in surrender. Cole pounced, snapping and snarling in his face, testing to see if he'd stand against him once again. But Ryan remained with his head pushed against the floor, cowering. He whimpered, closing his eyes and then opening them again to see if Cole had stopped. When pleased by the established hierarchy, Cole's hackles lowered, and his attention narrowed toward us. He lunged, being caught in the invisible screening and rebounding into the wall of the cave.

The alpha female snarled at us but backed away to make sure her mate was okay. Ryan leaped for the barrier with a loud smack as he unsuccessfully tried to break through.

"Not very bright creatures are they," Lincon mocked. I scorned him with an effective look. He barked out in laughter, blood spitting from his mouth. His legs bounced with excitement as he pointed to them. "Well look at them, just animals. But so marvelously interesting."

I stared on, frozen and bound by the gargoyles that anchored me. What could I have even done if I'd given in to my urges and entered that cave to intervene? We watched on for what felt like hours as the larger wolves continued trying to bust through the barrier. I still couldn't manage to see Titan through the group who defended the pups. When I hovered my mind over theirs, I could sense they were aware we were a threat, and they were backed into a corner. So primal, a basic language I felt I understood more than deciphering human notions.

As dawn approached, Lincon, Kora, and Kasey evidently became uncomfortable by the rising sun. The fog density in the forest blocked the majority of it, but it still put Kora and Kasey in irritable dis-ease. They forfeited back into the shadows, though their barrier remained. They wouldn't release the wolves until Lincon ordered them too. And if still abiding by my say, that meant I gave the order. An exhausted howl passed through the wolves. One by one they answered the call in a tone that uniquely matched their new form. The sound became unhinged and curdled as it muffled out and turned into a very human scream. And then silence. Within moments, the crunching of bones and shifting from fur to skin revealed the very naked, still feverishly hot humans. And in the corner, with a woman's hand over her protectively, Titan was curled into a small ball, panting harshly in an unconscious state. Her midnight black hair was filthy as it sprawled around her.

Jerimiah and Darcy shifted into their natural forms. They took a step away from me as if disgusted by my involvement and what they'd witnessed.

"What are these monsters?" Jerimiah seethed under his breath. It was the first time I'd ever seen such an expression of horror on his face.

"Esmore," Darcy whispered, concerned. "This isn't right. We should kill them."

"No," I said defiantly. They would absolutely listen to Chase, but would that extend to me as well? I could feel a small tug from Chase, beckoning me to come back to the institute.

*Esmore, I need you. Something's happened.* The dire desperation in his tone had me shivering. He wasn't scared for me but something he'd just witnessed. With Fire locked up, I imagined they were studying the human who'd been affected just as I had this group.

"Can you look after them?" I asked Jenn.

"Look after-" Darcy said, astonished, but was cut off by Jerimiah's warning glare.

"I need to return to Chase. I'll see what supplies I can find and bring them back," I instructed Jenn.

I looked to Jerimiah and Darcy. "You two have a choice. You guard these humans from him," I said, pointing at Lincon.

"Me?" Lincon asked, exasperated with a hand on his black, miserable heart. I didn't feel comfortable leaving Jenn and the humans to be pegged down by Lincon's bewildered glare. But I needed him to ensure Kasey and Kora kept them locked up.

"Or, you can come with me and say nothing about this to anyone. Though I'd much rather and appreciate you stand guard here."

"We are ordered to guard you, Esmore," Jerimiah said simply.

"And I'm sure not much will happen in the time it takes me to reach the institute. Please." The mannerism felt foul on my tongue. They would accept me as theirs and listen to my orders, but that control was only spared by being Chase's familiar. And ultimately, they would listen to him. I wanted to slowly gauge what control I might have over them and to what extent how much of that power was mine.

"Chase has instructed us to guard you at all times," Jerimiah said once again.

"Or, how about this," Darcy piped up chirpier, trying to break the tension between leader and subordinate. "I stay, and you go with Esmore. That way we're doing both."

I placed my hands on my hips. I wasn't a woman who allowed compromise, but if it meant one extra vampire to protect them over none, then I was okay with it.

"No," Jerimiah said and looked at Lincon dead on. Lincon's smile stretched, elated as he began to stroke his beard thoughtfully. "I will stay, and you go with Esmore."

I looked at Jerimiah, trying to gauge why he wanted to watch Lincon instead of Darcy. Of the two, Jerimiah was definitely the leader of his elite group. I wondered if he was more capable of handling him than Darcy. I wasn't sure if even their entire team could manage Lincon if it came down to a fight. Lincon was a wild card and a danger to us all. I wasn't ignorant to the barred fangs that were always at my back by having Lincon follow me. Nor did I have control of getting rid of him. Lincon would only leave of his own accord, and I regrettably believed that'd be quite some time.

"Only Jenn is allowed to enter and leave this cave as she pleases," I instructed Lincon, but I knew Kora and Kasey were somewhere nearby, listening in. I neither trusted Lincon or Jerimiah in his revulsion for the human wolves. But I doubted he'd go solo to try and harm them, especially with Lincon in the way. They would both be babysitting one another in the act of trying to gain my favor.

"Esmore, the others can't find out," Jenn said gravely.

"Yolo," I replied, speaking to his true identity, so he was reminded of his nature and obligations to his coven, and consequently the betrayal he was placing on Cesar. "You and I both know this will not be our secret to keep for long. They deserve to know, but I have no intention of letting anyone harm them."

"But we could-"

I cut Jenn off. "No, Yolo. Remember who you are." Jenn looked shocked, and then with bundled rage, released it with a sigh. We were in the middle of a war that was about to break out, that was our reality. From now on, everything we did we needed it to be in numbers. It was like I was able to see clearly for the first time since seeing Titan. The riled part of me from last night had diminished, if only slightly. The hours of keeping this secret from Chase had destroyed me only further. I curled my hand in the pocket, brushing the softness of his locked hair.

We had to play this smart. They needed more protection than what Yolo and I could offer. And for that, I needed to convince Chase. He would be the only one willing to help me, and even then, it would be reluctantly. I looked back at the cave and the unconscious, sweaty body of Titan. My focus was locked on her predatory like. I couldn't explain my irrational pull to protect this child or the makings of her kind, but I would not fail where I had her father.

I didn't entirely understand my own reasons for wanting to blanket them, but what I couldn't articulate was why Yolo was putting so much at risk as well to protect them. I watched on as Jenn stepped into the cave, her slim shoulders folding as if expecting resistance from Kora and Kasey's barrier. They had extended it around her, so she had easy passage. No, what I couldn't understand was why Yolo was putting everything on the line to help them. Lincon continued stroking his beard and waved at me with delicate fingers. His smile didn't reach his cruel eyes. Lincon was easy to read. This was nothing but cruel entertainment for him.

"Let's go, Darcy," I said, not wanting to keep Chase waiting any longer. I tugged back on our connection, in return being flooded with relief. He'd been worried. I'd spent the majority of the night locked in my own thoughts, checking in on him absentmindedly. When my mind ever wandered, it inevitably always searched for him. It sapped energy from me trying to block him from reading my thoughts, something that felt unnatural to the connection we had and the fluidity between our minds and bond.

Something caught my attention. I looked to my right, and in that split second, Sydney was standing there for one moment and then vanished the next. I stopped in my tracks. Had I just seen a ghost? But there was no looming presence or slight of wind with a scent. There was nothing.

Darcy had stopped beside me and briefed a glance in the direction I searched. I continued walking, deciding to break into a run instead, just to flush some blood through me or something to distract my mind from what I'd just seen. That was the second time I'd seen Sydney. And I saw Whitney last night. Was I slowly losing my sanity? Was I now seeing illusions of the dead? Or maybe even worse, was Lincon tormenting my mind without me realizing it?

I ran faster, trying to outrun the curdling in my stomach that was now thirsty and deprived of blood. I was relieved to know I hadn't lost control, even when they'd been injured. But how long would it be until I lost myself entirely from this haunting and unnatural thirst?

# CHAPTER 3

THOSE POSTED AT the institute's entrance were reluctant to open the large wooden doors. The covens were in upheaval, arguing between themselves and attacking one another. The gargoyles who solidified the line between the two covens were intervening, pulling, shoving, and threatening anyone who dared cross the line, baited by the other coven's provokes. Those who remained loyal to their coven leaders' command abided by trying to pull their own back. Chaos had broken loose.

My gaze found Cesar who had just walked out himself, disgusted by what he witnessed. He was standing atop the stairs and looking down on his disciples.

"Enough!" he shouted, so fiercely that the entire room went into silence, including Chase's members. "Do you really want me to come down there and rip you all from spine to spleen? The situation is being handled." *Situation?*

The vampires were restless, anxiously eyeing one another tempted by their antagonists. One vampire was hunched over another, caught red-handed and ready to rip his head off. Another was splayed over the staircase, a knife poking from his stomach with black blood oozing around it. He continued fighting, unperplexed by how it affected his movement. He yanked it out, the clatter of the knife hitting the tiled ground, furthering the suspenseful ambiance. Everyone eyed one another as if weighing up the options to continue brawling anyway.

I coughed. The small noise was subtle but enough to evoke the attention I expected. Darcy twisted his upper lip, showcasing his fangs intentionally to any of those who might disrespect me. When Cesar spotted me, his face lit up with that fawning expression he often held as he looked upon what he pronounced his 'darling daughter.' I entered the room, walking down the invisible line that divided the two covens. Members parted way for me. I leveled with a large vampire, one of Chase's members, who refused to move. Where he favored in brawn, he lacked in wit. He looked down on me with a clenched square jaw, contemplating as his mind pulsed with his most animalistic of natures, already so riled from the fight.

I suppressed my own lavish desire to make an example of him. Everyone paused, watching in suspense as to how this would play out. I continued looking past my nose at the vampire who was half a foot taller than me. Right now, leadership and consequence were what needed to be reinforced.

"Best you move, mate," Darcy said over my shoulder. The foul oaf made no gesture at Darcy but grunted. His eyes were pinning back and forth as he narrowed on me again, measuring if I were weaker than him. That maybe, just maybe he could release his own wild nature, no longer caring for who I was or my placement within this coven. And evidently because of that, in this room, I was one of his biggest threats. His vampiristic urges blindsided him.

I let my beast spring to the surface, her nature so encapsulated in the dancing energy around her, and a soon to be fight. My fangs slipped out, and my vision hazed purple. I had to make him move, from intimidation or ending him as an example.

My vampire-self relished in the leash I extended it bit by bit, giving it a tether at a time so my dominance could radiate. But I could only give it so much before my control would waver. One small droplet of power at a time.

"Move." My command was eerily dark, a void in the room that was so certain, if it had a physical form, it would've split him in two. Suddenly, his green eyes seemed to register who exactly he was sizing up. He shuffled uncomfortably and stepped back ever so slightly so I could walk past him. Without hesitation I did, and he made sure not to touch me.

"Lapdog," the big oath seethed under his breath as Darcy brushed past him, their shoulders colliding. My hand reached the tip of the railing to ascend the stairs. I halted at the first step. Though we needed numbers in this upcoming fight, we also needed utter obedience and command. Anything that opposed that was a threat to our cause. A flash of Titan came to mind, and I halted my ascension. Especially if I was to protect Titan, I needed to ensure total obedience.

I idly looked over my shoulder at Chase's coven who watched on, frozen by the tension. Cesar's had already begun to back away slowly into their division, following his lead as he looked down on them. Darcy remained by my side, with little acknowledgment to the oaf's words. But that simply wouldn't do. To let it pass over was ignorance and could model into something problematic in the future. I had to ensure little stress reached Chase and plagued his mind. Anything could mount on him and turn him into a saber. And I would prevent that at all costs. There would be order, even if I had to move the hand myself.

"Kill him," I uttered to Chase's coven. And without a second glance at the big oaf, I ascended the stairs, my focus on Cesar. I couldn't read the expression on his face nor did I want to try and read his thoughts or feelings. He was either wickedly pleased that his daughter was as bloodthirsty as he was or worried about the taint that was guiding my vision and command. I'd begun to adapt to this new world that wasn't guided by the Guild I once strictly had to follow. Out here, in this new day, anything was possible. Titan and her people were a testament to that.

The coven hesitated, trying to figure out if they could act immediately or show restraint. Maybe it was a grander test I was putting them up for. Or maybe, I was being lenient and permitting them the one thing they were after this morning—bloodshed. By the time I reached the third step, the oaf was begging me for his life. The others sprung on him, and another brawl broke out. Darcy followed me, glowering up the stairs. The gargoyles solidified in the center again, ensuring that the covens wouldn't intermingle. I could hear the growls coming from Cesar's coven, satisfied with watching on.

There was a consequence in this coven for disobedience, and I had to remind them of that, no matter how minor the crime.

*A little strict wouldn't you say, my love?* Chase toyed with me telepathically. He sent through an image of him touching the top of my nose with a little 'bonk' sound. He pushed waves of his humor and joy that had me smiling. The purple haze of my eyes vanished as my fangs slid back into my gum, all tension relieved.

*If only you hadn't been so lazy to come and clean it up yourself,* I replied in dry humor. *You're not hiding away from responsibility are you now?* I could hear the chuckle vibrate through our connection, filling my core with the same amusement.

*And miss the chance to see you ascend a staircase looking like my badass vampire queen, no way.*

His amusement ceased on me when his words echoed similar to Fier's. *If Chase is considered a King, then that would make you his Queen.* I'd declined the notion, such a thing was unprecedented during these times. It irked me in ways I couldn't understand.

I followed Cesar down the unlit hallway toward his quarters and wing of the institute. This was uncharted territory for myself or anyone else in Chase's coven. Chase was down there and waiting already. A strange form of relief washed over me as I considered the two. They weren't necessarily getting along, but were becoming accustomed to comradery in the affairs that ultimately affected us all. We were all housed under the same roof, and if the two coven leaders couldn't get along, then neither would the members. It was already drawing on a very thin line. Cesar begrudged Chase because he didn't deem him worthy of me. And Chase stirred Cesar because... well, Chase was Chase, and although he had many reasons, he simply enjoyed riling anyone he could, especially a well-aged Scottish vampire with a temper. I supposed my father and I had a resemblance there, where others might entertain Chase's games, my father and I immediately rolled our eyes and tried to shut him down. I however, ultimately found him endearing. Cesar very loudly stated that he thought Chase was a brat.

Instead of leading me up toward his tower, Cesar led me downward. They'd moved the infected human from the center room that was positioned on even grounds for the covens and where we'd previously tortured him for information. Since, they'd dragged him down to the depths, where he was likely in shackles and being monitored.

We reached a staircase that vanished further down into darkness. I didn't hesitate to follow, sensing Chase was waiting, alongside familiar minds, such as Tythian, Balzar, Connor, and his familiar that he had no intention of truly claiming, Deemori. As I descended with an unnatural glide of ease in the swelling and cold darkness, I reached out to find Fire. She was still in my towered room locked away with my mother who catered for her. I was grateful to know they were still both okay and after whatever this discussion might've been, I planned to check up on them before returning to Yolo's side. Though Fire was evidently pissed off now from being pent up all night, she had an acute awareness that I'd returned. Her senses were focused on my smell, tracking me with that intelligent mind of hers.

I wondered what happened to her last night. They'd locked her in my tower room, and I was curious if she changed in any way. Did she try to break loose and hunt vampires as well? But that was a question that could hold, right now the curiosity that beckoned was what was at the end of this stairwell.

"It's a bit of a mess, you see," Cesar nonchalantly said, trying to make light chit chat with me. There was only one flickering flame lit, unflinching from the lack of wind or fresh air that reached this cold, damp room. On my right looked to be what might've once been a wine cellar. And on the left were three small, barred cages, the metal poles lining from floor to ceiling. *What kind of institute had prison cells in their cellar?*

*A sadistic one who punished students in cruel manners,* Chase replied to my rhetorical question. *Or maybe this was made after the great war, who knows.*

The space was rather cramped with so many already waiting in the room. Two sabers were stationed by, lulled on the ground at Deemori's side in peaceful slumber. It still rendered me odd as I looked down at the chaotic barbaric beasts, who she considered family. *The monsters were acquiring more monsters as pets,* I thought with Fire in mind.

"Where have you been?" Balzar asked, unimpressed by my apparent tardiness. He sat casually inside the middle cage, his back leaning against the bars. Across from him, in the third cage, was the same human I'd spoken to the day before. He was shaking from the same feverish heat the humans in the cave had experienced. I could sense his mixture of fear and fury. Dry blood stained his ears and nose. He was naked, with dry blood coating his body from where the others had enjoyed torturing him. His wounds however had healed.

"Missing out on the fun, apparently," I said, striking Balzar an effective look.

"Don't blast that shit with me," he tsked back. Chase casually shuffled, stretching a cruel smile to flash his fangs at Balzar in warning. Chase didn't need to intervene, but he enjoyed playing the part of hero. His gaze then shifted to me, his stare and smile turning into a completely different type of challenge as he raised a suggestive eyebrow. I looked away, trying to keep my composure. Damn him and his smoldering looks that had me hot and heavy in a heartbeat, especially in an inappropriate time like this, which is when he often ensnared me.

"Where's Yolo?" Tythian asked before Balzar could cause a scene. Balzar grumbled his complaint, though he didn't shift from sitting in the open cage, as if it was comfortable. He sat there pompously as if at an edgier angle to watch the human. The man still looked crazed as his yellow tainted gaze darted between us as an eerie onlooker.

"Why am I keeping track of your sons?" I asked Cesar spitefully. Tythian sneered at my response.

"Enough, we're not getting anywhere here," Deemori said, unfazed by intruding in what could be considered as 'family bickering.' She was now wearing someone's loose shirt to cover her usual nakedness. Her English was fluent now as if it had only eroded because she hadn't spoken with another person for so many years. Cesar surprisingly let her remark go. She didn't so much have a place with us, only because of her connection with Connor was she even allowed in here. Tythian and Balzar's pressing gaze remained on me, but they'd quietened after we'd all been chastised.

"Hi, Sweetie," Chase said, unfazed by the tension in the room. He grabbed my hand, intertwining our fingers, and pressed a feverish kiss on my lips, completely unapologetic for his display with such an audience. In perfect Chase fashion, I knew something had gone very wrong while I was gone, because he was resorting to humor in the space of a dawning conversation. He tried to pry a few more kisses from me, but I pushed him off, trying to keep the smile from my face. He was inappropriate on every level, but my body still responded to him wanting more than little butterfly kisses. I pushed him off for both of our own good, or it'd escalate quickly as it always did.

"What happened?" I asked, circulating my gaze around the room and resting my curiosity on the outsider. I didn't have a thirst or desire for his beating blood—the thought repulsed me. He smelt like the other humans, grotesque and unappetizing.

"We kept him chained up in the room where we'd been interrogating him, which turned out to be a mistake." Balzar began as his green snake-like eyes glowered at me in the dark. His short cut black hair glistened with what looked like vampires' blood. It was when he fully turned to face me that I noticed the splatters of black blood that was drying on his face. His upper lip lifted in a small snarl as he threw a piece of stone at the human. The human flinched and began to snort as if coming down on some deranged drug. Were the others acting like this now? Still wild and animalistic even in their human form.

"We had him chained to the chair, and as he so prolifically claimed, he shifted into a wolf, double his size. Obviously, the chains broke free and this *abomination*," Balzar seethed the word, deplorably facing the human, whose lips began to churn into a smile that was unbecoming, "went rogue."

"It killed twelve," Tythian chimed in, flicking off a small bit of dust that drifted onto his dress shirt. Despite the mess of the story, he was still perfectly clean. The others didn't have blood on them like Balzar. I noticed the splotches of blood on Chase's black boots. Presumably, Balzar went head on and risked his life to stop this wild creature, and Chase wasn't far behind him. I flicked my gaze from Chase's boots to his face. His hand firmed around mine in reassurance. *I'm fine.*

The reality hit me as I realized while I'd been out for the night, studying the others and trying to protect them, I should've been here so I could protect Chase. Anything could've happened. What if he was pushed over the edge and stepped closer to the saber within? *I'm fine,* he said again with a little more force.

"When it broke out of its chains, the three who were guarding it in the room were killed almost immediately," Tythian divulged. Connor's crystal blue eyes only watched on, remaining near-mute as always. "Instead of smashing through the glass and opting for freedom, it broke through the doors and leaped over the staircase. It flanked toward Cesar's side. By the time Balzar was able to mount it and angle its head away, Chase was able to gut it. During that time however it took out another nine. Its singular bite killed them all."

"It's not how it does the killing that's the scary part," Balzar said, looking up at me through his thick lashes, begrudgingly, as if I had been the person who released the wolf. "It's the bite. It's vicious, but can be taken down if mounted and stunned for long enough. It took us a while to drag it down here after we muzzled it afterward. The bite's the problem. Whether it's the saliva or whatever it is, within an hour those who had been bitten became feverish, delirious, began to turn on their own, and self-imploded. Literally, they're body exploded. But a handful of them died within minutes."

"The claws were ineffective, nothing but physical damage," Connor added, speaking for the first time. His gaze often shifted over to Deemori before he caught himself and looked elsewhere. They were standing close to one another, whether they realized it or not. The pull between them was magnetic as much as it was obvious to anyone else in the room. I couldn't understand how they so willingly ignored that unfathomable need and desire. They might've been the most controlled vampires in all of existence to deny that most primal calling.

"Not even I could control its mind. It's nothing like a saber," Deemori said in her thick accent.

Chase rubbed his eyes, irritated. "It's just unexpected. We need to figure out how we add it to the equation of what we were already planning on doing." He directed his attention toward Cesar, much to my surprise. There had been numerous conversations already about tact and this uprising fight and war, but this, this was another element and one that might far outweigh the immediate threat of Oppollo and the Vampire Council.

"Do you think others know?" I asked. Had other vampires found out about these shifting humans? How were they dealing with them? How could we use it to our advantage? How could I build a strong enough case to convince the members in this room that the humans I was currently protecting in secret were of value—if only to protect them from immediate extermination. I had to find a way to protect Titan.

"I don't know," Cesar said ambiguously. "I'll put out a few messages to other covens I trust, and when I say trust, I mean loosely believe won't kill me on site. This might've been a reactive response from the humans though. Maybe we're closer to their base than we realize."

"But they only released a few wolves by mistake," I added. That was what the human had told us.

"We have a bigger problem. It didn't just end at a few loose wolves," Tythian elected. "The Human Compound Yolo infiltrated was inundated last night."

My mouth went parch. "What?"

"We've been keeping tabs on their movement. They are after all, and as you would know, not far from here," Tythian added with a knowing gleam in his eyes. Did he know what we did last night? Did he know about *our* humans? "Half an army infiltrated their walls with wolves, who seemed to listen on command. Not like the little wolf of yours who strayed and ran away with her mate. These were wolves who sat, groveled, and unleashed when told. The fight went on for a few hours, flames were lit, and then our scouts returned when a few human officers began spreading out with their wolves."

"It was an orchestrated attack?" I said in a voice that came out much smaller than intended. I tried to piece bits of the puzzle together. How could the humans benefit from turning on their own?

"Why am I only hearing about this now?" I asked Cesar angrily. How did something of such a large magnitude go unnoticed? How had we allowed that entire compound to be devoured by monsters in the brink of night? It reminded me so much of when Fier led the sabers to my Guild, and it too went up in flames within minutes.

"Well, you might've known sooner if you weren't playing hooky during the night," Tythian sneered. Chase was fast to firm our interwoven fingers as he sent calming waves over me. Tythian was purposefully pushing my buttons.

"We might've pushed their hand in this," Cesar announced, weary of the tension between Tythian and me. "We need to send more scouts out, we might be closer than we realize and if any humans are roaming aimlessly in the wild then they might be infected, meaning next full moon they'll turn into this."

We all looked back at the blubbering human, who was staring into the roof, dazed. Had he gone mad in the process or had he already been like that? Was Titan left in a state like that?

I thought about the humans who were in the compound. They would've been trapped, and someone from the inside would've let those humans in. Someone permitted that attack to be orchestrated, and I doubted that even the scientists in there who were used to experimenting on others were exempt from becoming the new test. I could imagine the screams from the terrified humans, especially the children. Titan and her group were so close to escaping. It was sheer luck that they were out on a small mission at the time, but still one stray wolf had scented them out and found them. They probably had no idea what happened back at the compound.

So then was it sheer coincidence that Yolo came across them, or was he already watching the compound closely? Maybe even one of the scouts was working for him instead. But it was Yolo. He'd never betray Cesar in any way, would he?

"I want to see it for myself. Take me there." I had to confirm it with my own eyes.

"No one is going anywhere near that compound now," Cesar ordered.

"You can't dictate what I do and don't do," I revered angrily.

He flushed red, spitting as he spoke. "No, but I certainly can tell Tythian where he can and can't teleport." It was only the slightest of movements, but Connor and I both noticed the tightening of Tythian's fist. *Interesting.*

*If you go there, I can't come with you. I have to stay close to the coven, especially while they're in this state,* Chase telepathically counseled me.

*I need to see it, Chase. I won't risk you or myself. If anything seems amiss, I'll come back straight away.*

He deliberated on what he wanted to say next, and I could feel the raw emotion behind it before his words chimed in. *I never want us to part again,* he said honestly, sending me a memory of us exchanging vows. Like I carried his locked hair, he had mine in his pocket too. I played with the blue necklace at my chest. Chase had gifted it to me when I first infiltrated Fier's Council. It matched the same gem that dangled from Chase's ear.

*And I don't want that, but we both know, leading up to this, we might just have to.*

*You're hiding something from me.* The twang of suspicion pained me. I looked into his stunning gray eyes, remorseful for the crime I was committing. When I was with Yolo, not close to Chase or looking at him directly, I could usher him away. But being with him now, I struggle to keep up the ruse and lie.

*After this, when we have our privacy, I'll explain,* I said earnestly.

Cesar continued, "For now, we're safe here. I've concealed the perimeters so no one can smell or hear us. And on the edges, those who are guarding are remaining hidden, so we don't attract attention. We need to wait it out until we know how to squash it."

"But maybe we can retrieve more answers if we go straight to the source," I argued, flushed in irritation. I had to see it for myself. I had to witness Titan's home for myself and know that there was no place for her, other than the protection I could shield her with.

"Ridiculous, they could possibly still be there!" Cesar raged, flipping me with a shrug of his shoulder as if I was a spoilt child.

"If it went up in flames, it's probable they took them back to their own territory," Balzar spoke up. His green eyes locked on mine. He was… agreeing with me. "It might be worth a shot. If we get near the place and they're still there, then we pull out. But I know they have all those human experiments and stuff happening down there, from what Yolo's told me. Maybe we can find something about this. Surely the humans left something behind, they're not that thorough."

"Speaking of Yolo, where is Yolo?" Tythian interrupted and looked at me poised as he crossed his arms. I narrowed my gaze on him. He was testing me and making a point of it. I couldn't reveal that I was with Yolo last night and doing… what we were doing. For whatever reason, Tythian might've known and wasn't saying anything. I questioned whether seeing Whitney was my imagination or real. He had his secrets, and I had mine. Or maybe I was just going mad. Well, that I already knew.

"Can we just stay focused?" Balzar flashed angrily. "Yolo can catch up after doing whatever he's doing. You know what he's like," he grumbled at Tythian, oblivious to the unspoken under handing that was happening between Tythian and me.

"I said, no!" Cesar growled at Balzar.

*Call him Daddy,* Chase telepathically bemused.

*Ew, I'm not calling him such a thing,* I replied, abashed.

*Just do it. Trust me.* I was reluctant to eat my own pride. *Do you want to see the place or not?*

I cleared my throat and wavered a glance over at Cesar. He looked at me expectantly with his chest puffed and his arms crossed. His red beard was always oddly groomed despite the fact that he probably rarely showered. Not that vampires really needed to. "Please."

"No," he said, shaking his head.

I cleared my throat again. Why on earth was I begging for this? I swallowed my pride and encompassed my Ellie persona, who was slightly more approachable than my usual self. "Please, Dad."

He looked shocked, his eyes bulging. "What did you just call me?" he said in a quiet, tender tone. I could feel Chase's inner smirk push along our connection. Oh, how smug he felt.

"Please, let me just see it once. If it's occupied, I'll leave. I just have to see it for myself, and it's safer if Tythian teleports me than me running on foot." Not entirely a lie but I was angling this, so I looked like his helpless little girl. "Please, *Daddy.*"

Balzar covered his mouth with his hand, trying to hide his chuckle, and hid his face away so Cesar couldn't read his amused expression.

"Well, it's not safe," Cesar began, flabbergasted. But his demeanor had already entirely changed. His challenging pose receded into a harmless old man. "And I only do all of this for you, my beautiful daughter. I just want to protect you." He was pushing it. "And you know I don't like putting these rules down to upset you."

"Then don't." I held my irritation down on the last statement. I didn't need rules from him or anyone. But I let it slide, learning to deal with and manipulate his 'daughter infatuation' with me. "I'll come straight back if there's danger. It's not worth the risk. I understand that."

Cesar looked at everyone uncomfortably, realizing he might publicly have to take back all his gusto and argument to permit the happiness I so desired. "Fine. But from now on, everyone who leaves this establishment is to wear masks. We don't know what degree their technology is at. I don't want anyone being identified."

"Okay…" I said, looking at the others. Was he doing this, so he still felt like he was in control?

"And robes with hoods. Tythian, I'll leave it in your capable hands to acquire those before you head out. Take Balzar with you after he cleans himself up. I don't want you pent up in this room, staring at this crazed creature. And take Yolo with you. He knows better than anyone the boobie traps in that compound." He swept his gaze over us, puffing his chest out with final authority. "Your mother isn't going to like this much."

"I'll be sure to tell her myself," I said with a small smile that didn't reach my eyes. My mother was a huntress. Though she might not have agreed with the decision, she certainly wouldn't have tried to stifle me as Cesar had. Was this the affection of an overbearing parent?

"What do we do with this thing?" Connor asked, looking at the human grotesquely.

"We should kill it," Deemori said without hesitation. "This is not a creature that should be of this world. If I can't control it, then nothing can."

One might've considered her arrogant for saying so, but it was true to a degree. If the vampire who had control over sabers couldn't tame them, then who or what could? Or more importantly, how did the humans have such control over them?

"No, we'll see if it starves out and monitor it until the next full moon," Tythian said coldly. "And if we find any more humans that are showing the same symptoms, we should do the same to them." He looked at me pointedly. He must've known. But for whatever reason, he was keeping mine and Yolo's secret. For now. "Well then, I suppose I have some masks and hoodies to collect. I'll see you soon," Tythian said, unimpressed, and vanished.

"We should break for a while," Chase said to Cesar. "We need to think about our next moves and how this affects them. But for now, we need to get our covens into order."

"I agree," Cesar said in a grumbly voice, not as evolved as I'd taken his pettiness for. Cesar looked down at our intertwined hands and grumbled under his breath.

When four vampires crept down into the room, begrudgingly that they'd been selected to be on guard duty, we made our leave. Cesar left first. I glanced over at the human once more, not entirely ready to meet the conclusion that Titan and all the others like her might be in the same state.

"Esmore, that was cringe, *Daddy,*" Balzar said as he walked past me.

"Shut up," I said, slightly shoving him but finding an odd playfulness amongst it, being the only levity from the all-consuming situation we were in.

"Daddy's girl," Chase added with a chuckle. I squeezed his hand harder, crippling it as he winced in pain, still with a smile plastered to his face. I couldn't help but mirror his smug expression.

"Look what I got us," Chase said, pleased with himself. He pulled out a bottle of wine from behind his back. "This one has aged four hundred years, almost as old as me."

"That's disgusting," Balzar said. "Not your age, but don't you think wine has like an expiry date or something?"

"Wine gets better as it ages," Chase said childlike.

"Yea but-" Balzar's words were lost on him. "Whatever, man, risk it yourself."

"No, Balzar," Chase said, wrapping his arm around Balzar's neck forcefully. "You'll be trying it with me."

"Absolutely not." Balzar straightened like the soldier he was. This was a new side to Balzar I'd never seen before, especially with Chase.

Behind us, Connor and Deemori remained. Without anything else having to be said, we left the human whose eyes continued to scatter throughout the room, now darting between the vampires who looked on at the human with disgust.

So much suspicion was swimming around the human government's recent activities. Much like everyone else who was gravitating to this upcoming war, it looked like the humans weren't hiding any longer either. And they were yet again, just another obstacle on our board, as we tried to walk toward some paradoxical freedom.

# CHAPTER 4

"WELL, I'LL GO find Yolo," Balzar said, prying himself from Chase's iron grip.

"There's no need. I'll grab him," I announced, brushing off Balzar's suspicious glare. Small stars danced across my sight as we crept from the darkness of the cellar. Darcy was in his gargoyle form guarding the door and waiting for our arrival. It really was like having my personal guard.

"Well, Balzar, why don't we just start the party early?" Chase crooned, holding the bottle of wine like it was the most precious thing in existence.

"I'm absolutely not drinking that." Balzar's attention was caught by another scuffle that broke out amongst Cesar's coven. "For fucks sake, can no one act civilized anymore!" He jumped over the railing to punish those who were involved, using it as the perfect scapegoat to abandon Chase's bottle of wine. Lydia was already between the two groups of vampires, attempting to simmer them down. The residents were becoming angsty from thirst and being in one spot for so long. It'd been days since we were able to go on any real hunts, cautious as to how close the human government was, if they were at all.

Chase's coven snickered and encouraged the brawl. "Is something funny?" Chase asked in a low voice, but it rumbled amongst them. They lowered their heads, scorned, and dipped further into the shadows, hiding in the secondary room that was our side for claiming. Claudia was playing with a dead bird, entertaining Spungee. He was on his back with his head in her lap, looking up and toying with its feathered wings. He kept trying to grab it, but she'd yank it out of his grasp with lightning speed. Her cool eyes never left mine or Chase's as she continued to play the grotesque game, bored.

"Chase?" I said, preparing myself to tell him the truth.

"Yea, babe," he said, pulling out a knife from the interior sleeve of his jacket. I tried not to ogle at the way his muscles beneath his jacket flexed. I went blank for a moment, transfixed by his movement.

"I need to talk to you," I said, refocusing. Don't get distracted by the beautiful specimen, aka my familiar. With a fast and clean slash, he sliced the top of the bottle off. It cut through the glass with a clean swoosh. The top of it flicked over the railing and smashed at the bottom of the stairs. He winced. Everyone looked up at him with terror, as if they were about to be reprimanded for whatever lecherous thoughts they were having. Even Balzar looked back up in the silence, confused. He grimaced at the now open bottle and turned to reprimand members in his group once again, shoving them into separate directions in their designated side.

"Crap, that wasn't meant to go flying," Chase remarked. He shrugged his shoulder nonchalant. "Okay, let's wait until we're in our room before discussing secret squirrel business. We'll have some time. I imagine Tythian will be a while to gather the masks and robes. Hmmm, Tythian's like his personal shopper, isn't he?" He mused with delight. Cesar retreated to his personal quarters after our discussion. He was relying heavily on the order of his hierarchy taking care of the other vampires, just as Chase was dependent on Clarissa and the gargoyles doing the same for his own. They didn't seem to mind. In fact, they probably relished in being the chosen ones to inflict the punishment.

As we began walking toward our wing, Darcy shifted back into his normal form. Chase took a swig from the wine bottle and choked, pulling a horrific expression. "Oh, WOW. Mmmm." He grimaced, a tear springing to his eye. I rolled my eyes at his dramatic flair. Its bitter fumes enveloped my senses, and I swatted it away like a bad smell.

"I didn't even know vampires could get drunk? I've never tried," I admitted. We had once come across a few bottles of whiskey on a raid, but in this day and time it was used resourcefully as opposed to its methods of abuse back in the human era. Though I was certain a bottle went missing from the loot, but I never asked my Token Hunter, Drue, where it vanished. Stealing such a resourceful object was considered a crime within the Guild.

"We can, it just takes a lot more, and its effects don't last as long. I was quite the party animal back at Fier's. Would you believe this was one of his priorities? He has some distilleries in San Francisco through madness of methods. His preferred, vodka." Chase rolled his eyes. "But we won't start you on this either, we can find you something better." He turned to Darcy. "I dare you to have a mouthful."

"Why would I want to do that after seeing your reaction to it?" Darcy asked cryptically.

Chase beamed a childish smile and slowly raised his fist, tempting him with a fist bump. "But you're curious, no?" His fist hung in the air. Darcy, who looked the youngest of the group, with his red hair and freckles, fidgeted at his iconic fist bump waiting for him. He couldn't resist. He bumped his into Chase's fist and swiped the bottle from his hand with stifling speed. He threw back a large swig, spitting it across the floor immediately.

"Oh, my god, that's horrendous!"

"It's so bad, right?" Chase encouraged. I shook my head, amused. Some things simply couldn't be changed about Chase, this goofy, eccentric, unreasonable side included. Nor would I want it to ever change. I'd never met anyone like him.

"So, do you want to tell me what you two have been up to?" Chase asked as we approached the staircase to our wing. I side glanced Darcy who closed his unhinged mouth. His eyebrows furrowed in complex thought. I'd sworn him not to say anything, but Chase was his coven leader.

"It's okay, Darcy," I reassured him. I understood. "I'll explain everything soon, just wait until we're in our room. You might want this conversation in private."

Chase looked between us. "Well, that never sounds good." And he was genuinely concerned. I could feel the wave roll through him and down our line. I grabbed his hand, worried that this information would only strain and stress him further. I had to watch out for this disease that was spreading in his mind. My actions were selfish, but I couldn't just leave them.

*Don't worry about me,* he said sweetly, telepathically. *I'm sure you have your reasons. Though I don't know how I feel about you being more in Cahoots with Yolo, than me.*

I nudged his shoulder playfully. *Chase, I'm always in cahoots with you, for better or worse.* He smiled.

We reached the top of our tower, passing the bell. The door to our room burst open, and Fire leaped breezily, hammering into my chest. I fell to the floor with an umph. Darcy had already unsheathed his two swords on his back. Chase placed a hand in front to halt as he idly took another swig from the filthy bottle of wine.

Fire's fur was matted, and her back ankle had a chain wrapped around it. She licked at my face, her offensive breath flushing over me. I tried to wrestle her off with as much surprise by her greeting as my mother who stood at the door with a hand on her hip.

"Thank the heavens," she said, crossing her arms. She pointed to a spot in the wall that had been ripped out, trailing bits of cement as evidence. "She just busted from the wall where she'd been chained up all night."

"The wolf cares for her?" Darcy asked inquisitively to no one in particular.

"She's never acted like this," I said to my mother and Chase. Chase wasn't impressed. I could sense he was disappointed for giving me a creature to care for that turned out to be ultimately a threat to his kind. Where she was meant to stand for cute and fluffy she posed as terrifying. I only found the irony in it. His lip twitched into a small smile. And somewhere so did he.

"We don't know what kind of bond you two have after you injected her with your venom," my mother said. "I might've brought her back, but it was your venom running through her veins at the time. If she were a human, you would've been her maker. So, who knows what kind of bond you two might have." My mother looked like she hadn't bathed or slept in days. Her eyes still held a sharpness that missed nothing, but her eyes were shadowed in black circles. She was all huntress in her glory, wary and alert, ready for any attack. She was living amongst vampires, and even Cesar hadn't let his guard down, reminding himself of that factor. I could sense vampires within his coven, trusted members strategically positioned around her. Some of their scents I recognized from his elite team of twelve. My mother was as heavily, if not more guarded than me.

"What happened to her last night?" Chase asked, taking another bitter swig of the wine he hated so much. I shuffled Fire off, patting over her thick white fur, to keep her at bay. Her strength was formidable, and I could see now why these wolves were able to strike a killing blow to vampires. Or maybe that was because my venom had revived Fire, courtesy of my mother's gift.

"She went the way we thought she would. Cesar and I spoke and because she had already bitten Esmore, we have suspicions that maybe hunters aren't affected lethally. We decided I was the best option to monitor her overnight. We had to chain her up like you did with the human downstairs. Physically, she didn't change, but her nature did. She wanted to hunt. She tried everything to bust out of her chains, which is why I had to apply one to each leg, around her chest, throat, and mouth, which seemed enough to contain her." I looked behind my mother, where small parts of the wall continued to crumble. Nailed to various parts were the chains and muzzle she spoke of.

"So how did she get free now?" I asked. Her frenzy had dispersed, much like the humans.' They'd been left exhausted and weak. But now Fire was wagging her tail and nuzzling against me, baring her teeth at Darcy as he shifted uncomfortably.

"No," I said dismissively. "Darcy is our friend." She looked at me before forfeiting her gusto and laid her head in my lap.

"Oh, I'd been taking them off so I could take her to the toilet," my mother said, clicking her fingers at Fire. Her ears perked and she stood up obediently. "She busted through the last one when she heard you coming up the stairs."

"After last night do you think she can so freely walk around?" Chase asked. He was leaning against the small bell tower, having forfeited his bottle of wine. He looked mournful. No matter how many sips, it evidently didn't get any better.

"Like you, Cesar announced the wolf isn't to be touched. There are vampires strategically positioned around in case any vampires get a little too cocky. And besides, I'm sure we can fend off a few vampires, it was after all what we were built for." My mother's eyes glimmered with mischief though a smile never reached her face. Chase took a large theatrical gulp.

"Thank you for looking after her while I was gone."

"Yes, speaking of, where were you? You do realize you having nights away during current circumstances is stressful for everyone who is trying to protect you," she lectured. My back straightened out of habit. My mother had always respected me as an equal within the Guild, but there was also a tone that overshadowed me. I imagined it was something only a mother could do. Although part of me automatically wanted to challenge her for hierarchy, another part of me, one that I was grateful to still hold on to, didn't want to disobey or displease my mother. I had been so angry at her and lost so much respect for everything she had done to me, even though I understood it logically. But even now, it was nice to see her, especially after being told she was dead.

"I know. It's a long story. I need to talk to Chase about it, but afterward, I'd like to ask a favor of you." Her lips thinned into an unimpressed line. I hadn't quite narrowed down as to where my mother's loyalties were. Now having a familiar myself, I understood the constraints coerced into that relationship. I didn't want in any way to betray Chase, but I found myself sometimes making decisions that he wouldn't necessarily agree with. More than likely like the conversation we were about to have. And I wondered if my mother was the same. She'd already gone so far to protect me, Dillian, and the others. She was the only person other than Yolo and Chase I could trust with this secret of the wolves. And possibly the only one I could ask to help nurse them in Yolo's stead while we went to the Human Compound.

"Well then, I'll leave you two to it," my mother agreed and ushered Fire away. Fire was reluctant to leave my side, but I encouraged her to go. I couldn't deny the bond now between us. It was different to the one I had with Chase, and much more solidified than the one I had with Sydney after I'd turned him. It was a mixture of loyalty and wilderness. She wasn't human with coherent thoughts, but she understood that I saved her from the brink of death. And in that, no matter what form any species took, there was a bond of camaraderie and restitution.

"Darcy, can you please watch over Esmore's mother closely for the time being," Chase instructed. "Oh, and take this. Give this as a gift to the vampire you least like." Darcy's lips twitched into a smile as they shared a mischievous expression. He accepted the half-empty bottle with a fist bump. He then escorted my mother, who seemed indifferent to who's member of what coven kept her company. That was all vampire politics that as huntresses, we were still trying to come to terms with. We never realized there were so many different branches of rules and hierarchy. We had simply hunted them—no questions asked.

"Now, my little Huntress, what have you been up to in the dead of night?" Chase asked as we walked into our quarters. Claw marks were embedded into the cemented floor beside the chains that now hung where Fire had once been immobilized.

Chase took a seat nestled against the wall and closest to the door so he could listen out for anyone who might try to eavesdrop. Instead of telling him in so many words, I opened my mind to him, like a flood gate of information with everything I'd witnessed and dealt with in the last twenty-four hours.

He shot up out of his chair, infuriated. "Do you know how much risk you put yourself in?"

"I'm a Huntress, Chase, first and foremost before being your familiar," I reminded him, though I had a pang of guilt for saying it.

"Esmore, you could've been hurt. What if the others found them," he said, looking to the door. He hushed his tone into a whisper. "They aren't natural. You've seen what they can do to our kind."

"Who are we to claim what is and isn't natural? Look at us, both of us go against what is considered natural. Half of the creatures lurking in this world have already been condemned, so why should they be any worse?" I gestured with my arm, getting frustrated. Chase and I were a partnership of equal measure. But that didn't take away from the fact that we were both used to being leaders who often had the final word.

"Esmore, this isn't the time for a moral compass. We are dealing with so much already." Without him saying it, I could sense him regarding the disease Fier implanted in his mind, and the impending war that was coming, as well as throwing in the human government and my previous Guild that still wanted to kill me. "My priority is to keep you alive. We can't keep stretching ourselves so thin."

"But we can if anyone can manage the impossible. We can!" I needed him for this. I needed his support and brilliant mind. I was asking for his help in uncharted territory.

"It's foreign for all of us, Esmore. I love you so much. But this is too much. They risk everything we've been working toward here. What of

Dillian and your other hunter friends? I thought they were your priority to protect?"

A twang of guilt hit me, and I was infuriated that he'd use them against me. I took a breath, counting to ten as my father had taught me when I felt my temper rising. I didn't want to fight with Chase. We'd never fought like this, and I was overly conscious of the strain it might've been putting on him as well.

"You know I want to protect them more than anything, but ever since we escaped Fier's Council, right at the very start of our story, we've been thrown back and forth into the unknown of things we can't control. But maybe I can control this. These humans that turn into wolves, what if we can use that military power. What if it's something we can use in our favor for everything that's soon to come?"

Chase shook his head, disheartened that we disagreed. I could feel the peril and anguish it was putting him through. As his voice rose, out of a need to protect me, he realized it was only hurting me and likewise. We were both emotionally unstable and were one another's vices to fix that. We needed one another more than anything, but we couldn't see eye to eye on this. He saw them as monsters, and I saw them as something of unnatural balance and craftsmanship- something similar to me.

Pain flashed in his beautiful gray eyes, having read my last thought. "This isn't about using them for military or in our favor. That hadn't even crossed your mind until now. Tell me honestly, Esmore. Why? Why is it so important for you to protect these humans?"

I stared longingly into his gray eyes that were resolving into darkness like a wild storm, equally measuring my frustration. My natural instinct was to snarl at him, be angered and lunge, and figure this out in the best way I knew how—physically and unapologetically diabolical. But this was the man I loved, and it scared me how much my temperament wavered when I thought of these humans and Chase possibly being the one to come between us. I had to make him understand because if he didn't... I couldn't think past where that would leave us.

"Esmore, I need your transparency," Chase said, shaking his head. "This is more. What you're asking of me is to go against everything we've built to protect, not only you, but everyone in this institute." It was the first I'd seen him take responsibility fully for the safety of the others. To consider how his coven would be affected by this because of my selfish act and how he would measure it accordingly. That maybe I could end up as an outsider if I couldn't make him understand. Being indifferent to Chase scared me more than I'd like to admit. After all we'd been through, we had to see eye to eye on this. No matter what, it would always be me and Chase, everything else around us we had to maneuver, for better or worse, and to always be together. I let my guard down entirely, forfeiting the truth of why I so greatly wanted to protect them. Chase would see my weakness and vulnerability in a time where I wanted him to only be able to depend on me. I had to be strong for both of us because of his *illness*.

"Esmore," he said gently. "You don't have to worry about me. Honesty and equality in this partnership—forever." He leaned forward, reaching out for my hand. I hesitated, struggling to allow myself to be so irrationally weak, even in front of Chase. I wanted to be his pillar as he was mine. He had only ever been transparent with me, and I was filling myself with deals and lies in his absence. This much I could give him, in the hope that he would understand. I took his hand, intertwining our fingers. I could feel the tension ease from my body, only slightly.

"One of the girls in the group," I began. I would only share this vulnerability with Chase, but was frightened by his reaction. How would he judge me? Would he deduce me as harshly as I did myself? "I have an attachment to one of them. Titan, she's Sydney's daughter."

Immediate understanding dawned on his expression. His jaw tightened. "The human you accidentally turned?" His accusation filled the air with tension. *Yes, and the one who you killed for me.*

Chase turned away in disgust. *It had to be done. Please understand, Esmore, I only ever did that for you.*

"I know," I said abruptly out loud. And I did understand that. Chase had saved me from a lifetime of misery much like Clarissa and Spungee. But it didn't take away the absence of something that felt like it should've been in my life. Perhaps in a sense, my fixation on Fire had overtaken that position, in the way Chase had originally hoped, though his 'pet' choice might've been slightly off.

Chase looked at me hurt. He gently pressed forward. "Esmore, my love, we're not the heroes in this story. Protecting this girl only puts everything we're working toward in jeopardy. They're creatures that should not exist."

A fury bubbled through me, and it pained me to lash out at Chase because he disagreed. But I took it so personally. I hadn't chosen this path, and I'm certain if he and his mother had the choice, he wouldn't have chosen his path to be turned either. Everyone here who'd been turned into monsters all had tragic turnings and loss. We didn't decide to be like this, but this was the path we had to take and so it shouldn't be any different for them. I had to convince him. "They didn't choose this path."

"None of us did."

"So who are we to judge that they should be slaughtered for this misfortune?" I asked him, begging for him to see my angle.

"Esmore, they threaten everything we're building toward. We don't have the time to manage pups that will very well turn into monsters and slaughter half our coven every full moon."

"*Your* coven," I seethed angrily, whipping back my hand. It pained him, and I knew my words would cut through.

*Please don't do this,* he begged. *They are manufactured to kill our kind, Esmore. Manufactured to kill both you and me.*

I tried to keep my temper in check, reminding myself of how much I loved this man. I was still trying to deal with this irrational self-notion and understand this foreign emotion I could only experience when with Chase.

"But what if they're given a choice, my love," I said, taking his hand again, wanting to ease the tension I could feel plaguing over him; over us both. I couldn't risk stressing him any further. I never want to be the reason he would nearly lose control again. But this conversation was important. "Chase, my kind were crafted and designed to kill vampires as well, and yet here we are."

"It's different," he said, cupping my hand over his face, savoring the feel of my touch as if healing himself from the pain I was inflicting on him. It drove me insane just as much him, wanting to comfort him even though it was our indifference that was causing us both this anguish.

"It's not, Chase. They only come in a different form."

"Esmore, they physically turn into wolves. From human to animal. That isn't normal nor is that kind for them."

"Chase, we are no better than them simply because we wear the mask of a human," I said gently. "We're all monsters here. I'm a killer, Chase, and so are you." He evened his gaze on me.

"We're not killers, Esmore, we're predators, and this goes against everything in our nature. Against everything I am designed for, what you're asking of me…"

"And yet here you and I stand," I said, placing my hand on his chest. "As husband and wife. As huntress and vampire." His expression softened as his shoulders sagged, defeated.

"I do this to protect you, Esmore. I'll always do what I think is best to protect you. I don't care about anything else." He looked to the ground, deflated. My chest swarmed with warmth and love for this man who would protect me, and I him.

"Chase, let me try to be a hero for once. Let me try to protect the weak in my own way. One that isn't staged with duty in the Hunter Guild, or expectation of me as some new monster in the world of vampires. *Please*, let me make this choice to protect the little girl who lost her father because of me. Let me contribute to our arsenal in my own way."

Chase heavily sighed, not that he needed it for breath but to imitate a dramatic human response. He kissed the open palm of my hand. "Why did I choose to marry such a willful wife?" he grumbled under his breath. I pulled him toward me, uncomfortable by the tension between us. I just wanted to hug and protect him, as much as I could sense he did the same for me.

"How boring would it be if you didn't," I replied, staring into his beautiful stormy gray eyes that had softened in color. I pushed back a part of his black shoulder-length hair.

"But we need you to infiltrate Tracey's Council," he added. "And there are so many other things we've been discussing. This will only impact that."

"Then we'll figure out a way to do both." I rested my forehead to his. "As long as we have each other, we will get through this, Chase. We'll find a way." I would find a way to protect Dillian and the others, and now these humans who would turn into wolves every full moon. We would somehow find a balance between the two covens and the upcoming battles we had with Oppollo, so I could upkeep my promise with Fier, and he could remove this lecherous disease from Chase's mind.

He lifted my chin, brushing his lips against mine in a gentle kiss. "Together," he whispered, entirely absorbed in the motion of consuming me as he tenderly licked past my lips and savored the taste.

*Together.*

# CHAPTER 5

CHASE PROMISED TO watch our interactions from afar so they wouldn't see him. We were certain they'd recognize Chase from when he'd taken the fall for killing Sydney. Chase was a very memorable encounter all on his own, let alone when he tormented them with their leader's dead body. And now was too soon to introduce them to the vampire committee we were aligned with, if ever. I couldn't expect them to be as accepting about their predicament as I'd grown to be. My only comfort in this arrangement was the confidence I had in being able to defend myself. For them, despite their gifts and abilities to shift into wolves, I doubted they had the strength to overpower a handful of vampires.

After informing my mother and trusting her judgment on the matter, she followed us and agreed to replace Yolo. We carried whatever we could find from the institute, old shirts, skirts, and blankets—anything that might be considered a comfort for them.

This lodging could only be temporary. It was a risk having them so close to the covens, and although my mother could now conceal the cave they were in, and with Kora and Kasey keeping them locked in, it would only be a matter of time until someone absentmindedly found them. My mother, much like Chase, was reluctant. She didn't determine a positive outcome, but her overwhelming mechanics stifled her to protect humans. It was the sole reason hunters had been crafted, so it wasn't easy for her to turn her back on them, even if they weren't entirely human. As soon as I mentioned there were four children her mind was made up.

Darcy escorted us with a tower of items my mother had thrown on him, telling him to be useful. He looked at me almost scared of my mother. We'd even found some old food tins in kitchen cupboards. Whether they were edible was a completely different matter, but he promised me some of the things that were once crafted in the human age were meant to last forever. He idolized something called a Twinkie. He then added, 'some things were meant to last, well everything except maybe their race.' I hadn't found the joke amusing, though Chase approved with wicked laughter and fist-bumped him in congratulations.

Our leaving hadn't gone unnoticed by a few of the guards who were posted around the institute's fence. The elite team who were enunciated as my mother's guards were a little harder to shake. After a stern talking, we told them this was family business, and they weren't welcome. Boundaries and internal alliances were being made every day. I was certain the only reason they listened was because of the respect they held for me on that fateful day we charged against Oppollo.

Fire followed us, sometimes straying off the path with curiosity by something that caught her attention, but she never left for long. I struggled with the necessity to control and call her back but allowed her to run free as her nature permitted, although not too far so she wasn't under my protection.

We weren't far from the cave when snowflakes began to appear and distort my vision.

"What is this?" my mother asked, ready to drop the handful of clothes in her arms to reach for the sword strapped to her back. A circle of wolves surrounded us with their lips curled back, snarling at us. Fire who was by my side began growling, standing in front of me protectively.

"Lincon," I viciously said. I was all too accustomed to his illusions. His laughter swirled around us as a snowstorm took hold. It vanished as quickly as it appeared. To my left, Lincon stood on top of a rock as if it was his mighty tower. Chase sneered at him.

*I don't know why you allow him to stay. He's dangerous,* Chase grumbled his complaint. He certainly didn't have to tell me twice. I was aware of what Lincon stood for. But I didn't know anyone who could very well drive him away unless it was of his own accord. And he'd shown his reluctance to leave.

"Pray tell for how long we'll be looking after the little beasties? Me and my girls are famished. It's a little exhausting being the head of your security on this so important project," Lincon deliberated whimsically. His lips curled into a delightful smile. "Oh, bless your little hunter boots, you brought them a change of clothes."

He jumped down from his rock. "Oh, and you brought the momma, Esmore. How delightful. Can I take something?" My mother eyed him wearily, her grip tightening on the clothes.

"My mother can conceal the presence of the cave. I have to go somewhere, but when I get back, we'll look at relieving you from keeping them within the cave."

"Oh yes, isn't that a nice little trick? Is that how they hid your heart so well?"

Silence. Lincon's blue eyes locked with mine and then Chase's who readied himself to fight. I'd never seen Chase so defensive with anyone else. Often he'd toy with others, even under the most barbaric of situations, but Lincon he wouldn't make an exception for.

Lincon was the last person I wanted to have information on the whereabouts of my heart or the reason it'd been removed and the power that lay dormant in my gift once we put it back in.

"Oh, please," Lincon wavered off. "It's just casual chit chat, don't get so antsy. Speaking of antsy, would you believe your little friend hasn't taken his eyes off me ever since you told him to. Such a good little soldier."

I looked over to Jerimiah who was positioned above the cave in his gargoyle form. He looked like an ornament atop what might've simply been an empty rock.

"Anyways, just wanted to make my presence known and make sure I'm appreciated," Lincon said flamboyantly. "I'll leave you to whatever devices you guys plan on using to rein in the human-wolf killing machines." He pardoned himself with another smile and disappeared. He didn't stray far, and I could sense Kora and Kasey close by with him.

We briefed a glance at one another. Lincon was a hindrance, and though I had no obligation to help the twins, I wanted to find out how I could pry them out from beneath his influence.

"Okay, Esmore-" my mother corrected herself. "Ellie. Show me these humans of yours." Only my mother and I could go forward. Chase ushered Fire back into the bush where he could overhear and watch from afar. Once again, she was reluctant to leave my side. And he seemed equally hesitant to welcome the very beast that could kill him from one bite. She sparked no aggression and sulkily walked toward him. I hovered my mind over Fire's making sure she had no hostile intentions toward him. I'm sure he'd already done the same.

Darcy circled the cave and left the small mound of tins he carried to the side where they couldn't see him. It was a gamble bringing my mother here. I wasn't sure how they'd take to having a huntress intrude, considering they'd long ago cut ties with the order and protection from our Guilds. But desperation would serve them. And better being introduced to a huntress than a vampire.

I telepathically connected with Yolo easily. He was fluttering about as Jenn inside the cave with them.

*There's been a change of plan,* I said to her, and mind-dumped the conversations that had been had and why I was here with my mother.

*They won't trust her, Esmore,* Jenn said bashfully.

*We weren't given a choice, Yolo. Cesar was very specific that you had to come with us. And besides, don't you want to see what happened to the Human Compound?*

I could sense her curiosity piqued. Though her nurturing side wanted to look after them as the only person they somewhat knew, she also wanted to pry and see if there was any evidence she could collect.

We neared the cave when Titan spotted me. "Ellie!" she screamed and ran for the entrance. Cole pulled her away from the entrance, yanking her by the arm. The moment he saw my mother's bright orange huntress eyes his expression changed to resentment. "Is this what you call help, Jenn?" he seethed angrily. My mother looked down on him past her nose.

"The woman bringing you and the children blankets, food, and clothing? I would assume that as help," my mother said with little tact.

"Cole, it's okay. She can be trusted," Jenn said. "She's a friend of mine." He looked abhorred.

"None of this fucking makes sense," he seethed, throwing his hands in the air.

"Cole, it's okay," Angela said. "We need this." He didn't seem happy about it nor did he move aside as he blocked the entrance. Ryan watched us from the corner of the room, quiet and at a distance from everyone. I wondered if they recalled anything that happened while they were in wolf form.

They were all naked, their clothing torn from when they'd shifted.

"Ellie!" Titan said again as I walked over the threshold and ignored Cole. I felt when Kasey temporarily dropped the barrier, permitting us to enter. Titan pushed past the blankets I held and clung to me. My mother's expression didn't change, but I could sense she watched us with keen interest.

"Are you okay?" I asked her, offering the blankets to Cole. He crossed his arms arrogantly. Angela sheepishly took them in his stead. I pushed back part of Titan's beautiful black hair. She looked up at me, her eyes already filled with tears.

"Where were you?" she asked, her bottom lip quivering. My heart panged, and I felt Chase embody me with comfort as he watched from a distance. This nurturing emotion was different for the both of us.

"So what now, you're in cahoots with hunters, Jenn?" Cole seethed when no one gave him attention.

"You seem very arrogant for someone who's surely smart enough to have realized his current predicament. Last I checked, humans who shift into wolves should not be judging the first mastered creation from humans," my mother tsked with all the ferociousness of what made her a core member in our Guild. He was taken aback by her words. "Need I remind you that it was your own that turned against you and used you as a live experiment, one that you have no control of and have been left for dead. So perhaps you shouldn't be so cruel to those who are offering you a hand and chance of survival."

"They didn't abandon us," Ryan shot back defensively from the corner.

"Then why do you tremble with despair?" my mother asked. "If you'll excuse me. I have tins of food to gather for you." And just like that, she was done. No more needed to be said, in my mother's eyes.

Jenn and I exchanged a glance. I wasn't concerned about leaving my mother in charge of this group. I could give her a hundred more and still not be concerned as to whether she could keep them in check. If it weren't her way with words to cut a man down, then her overwhelming presence forced them into submission. But I wanted them to learn to trust her, it would make the process much easier. Instinctively, I was certain humans could decipher the difference between help and threat. My mother could be both.

"That lady looks like you," Titan commented. "You have the same hair." I pushed a fake smile.

"That's because she's my mother," I said gently. Jenn's eyebrows shot up, and I could feel Chase's surprise that I'd disclosed that information with them.

"What?" Cole snapped to attention. "You're a hunter?"

"Half," I corrected. Not that they needed to know exactly what the other half was because they assumed it was human. "Let's just say when my memories came back, I was in for a hell of a surprise and wasn't as 'blessed' with the full huntress scheme and power thing." It was a mixture of lies and truth. It hadn't been uncommon for hunters and humans to have children together. If they were born with fluorescent eyes it was an indicator they were birthed with the power and abilities of a hunter. If not, then they were mere humans. I wasn't in the mood to express how I was partly both the species they hated so much. One truth and a lie were enough for today.

Tears glistened in Titan's eyes. It felt like a hand grabbed my stomach and dragged it down into the unknown. She didn't need to explain why she was crying, I just knew she was thinking of her father. He too had been half. I lowered onto my knees. "Shh, it's okay. Everything's going to be okay."

She began to cry, a heartfelt sob that felt as if it wobbled the ground I was kneeling on. She threw herself onto me, rubbing her face into my neck. I was taken aback. Hesitantly, I curled my arms around the little girl who emotionally fell apart in my arms. My mother waltzed back into the cave, watching me with interest. Such gestures weren't something I was used to. And though I knew my mother loved me and my father often spoilt me with affection, it was never displayed in public where other hunters could see. It was considered a weakness.

*You are not weak,* Chase reminded me as if lifting me into a more positive resolve. I could hear the kindness in his tone. The waver of understanding as to why I wanted to protect these humans so much. This little bundle of what should've been innocence was now desperately climbing to survive in this terrible world. My instinctual side considered it being a better fate for them having been killed instead of this. *But here you are, protecting them from a worse fate with the shit hand they've already been dealt.* Chase said before I could feel worse about wishing death upon them.

"So, what now?" Angela asked. My mother held a mounted stack of cans. If they weren't edible we'd organize Darcy or Jerimiah to hunt on their behalf.

"I have to show Jenn something," I said.

Cole confronted me. "What, no, you're not just leaving us."

"If you would stop interrupting me and listen to what I have to say, you might think differently." He opened his mouth to speak, but Angela looped her arm with his. It seemed to silence him. The rest of the group tiredly listened. Their temperature was still feverish though none of them seemed bothered by the unnatural change. I could sense their heartbeats had rapidly heightened and I wondered if they were experiencing any other profound heightened senses because of the change. It only made sense considering when hunters were manufactured, everything was heightened.

"Last night, the people I'm accompanied by watched over the human who we'd captured, and I'd spoken to you about. He'd also been bitten by a wolf and *changed,"* I deliberated the word. "He comes from the place where they've crafted this virus. It is very real that your own human government turned on you. Out there, isn't safe for you."

"But it's safe for us to be sitting bait in here?" Cole asked angrily. It was out of desperation for his team. He was frightened, and he had every right to be. Titan clung to me hopelessly, and I doubted with human strength I'd be able to pry her small fingers from around my neck. So instead, I lifted her up with me as I stood, propping her awkwardly on my hip.

*I must admit, my love, you look as awkward as you feel,* Chase mused. I gave him a slight mental nudge. His laughter trembled down our line, washing me with solace.

"Your humans did this to you," my mother said grimly. "And from what I've seen they will further experiment on or kill you. We're offering assistance."

"What, you and your little Hunter Guild team?" Ryan sniggered.

"I wouldn't call it a Guild, per se. I abandoned my post for my daughter a long time ago," my mother said, grabbing their attention. No one heard of rogue hunters. "We're coming into a new era, and it's *only* because my daughter came to me and asked me to help you that I'm offering aid. If you step out on your own, I can guarantee you will die. And not a pleasant death."

A little boy in the back choked in a sob. Terror was written on his face. A woman hugged him throwing a scornful look at her. My mother showed little remorse.

"I cannot coddle your children or tell you what to make of this wolf shifting. But we will help you until we can relocate you to somewhere safe."

"What about the Human Compound? Maybe they don't know what happened to us," Ryan asked.

"You know about the experiments they conduct there. Jenn knows firsthand what those details were. Do you think you will be the exception to that?" I frankly asked. I wasn't going to inform them yet that the Human Compound had been compromised. Lies and truth.

"Connor," Jenn interrupted. Her usual poised self was tired and perplexed. "You know I wouldn't help you or restrain you from going back to the Human Compound unless I thought it was for the best. I'm caught in the same situation as you. I won't be able to go back either, but I believe everything has a purpose, and maybe I stumbled across Ellie that day for a reason. Maybe it was with the intent that they'd help us one day."

"You don't really believe in that divine timing mumbo jumbo stuff, do you?" Ryan sneered.

Jenn deflated. "I've always believed in science. And look where that has gotten us," she said pointedly to them. But if I can figure out a way to help you and protect you with the help of Ellie and her mother, then I'll accept it, and I'd strongly advise that you do the same, if not for the children.

They watched us carefully. Titan began to rub her eyes, tired. "Ellie, will you come back? I don't want you to leave," she said through a stifled yawn. Angela offered to take her from me. I handed Titan over. She clung to me desperately.

"It's okay, Titan, I'll come back for you. I'm not abandoning any of you. I understand what it's like to be an outsider more than you probably realize. Jenn and I will do all we can for you."

Jenn nodded in harmony. It was a roomful of lies but with good intent. Neither of us was truly who we said we were, and yet we might've been the only two on the entire continent who were willing to help them. The vampires who they hated and wanted to kill and overthrow were the ones who were holding out their hand in the hope of a better future.

"I don't like it," Cole yielded.

My mother pulled out a small knife and pierced the lid of a tin. "Good, because the feeling's mutual. But at least you'll live for another day." Though I imagined in her mind she was thinking *'ungrateful swine.'*

# CHAPTER 6

W
E INSTRUCTED JERIMIAH and Darcy to guard outside the cave in Yolo and my absence. Though I knew firsthand my mother was more than capable of protecting herself. The only initial threat I kept in mind was Lincon. For the time being, he was distracted by being a nuisance and puppeteer to the twins. But he was a creature who grew bored quickly. Chase was still reluctant to help them, but extended his aid because I'd asked it of him. This was important to me, and because of that, despite his own judgment and belief that they should be killed, he swore to secrecy to help me.

Chase, Yolo, Fire, and I waited for Tythian and Balzar in our personal quarters. We didn't have to wait long until our makeshift group was all in one place preparing for the expedition.

Tythian handed out the masks nonchalantly. Mine was what appeared to be a snow-white wolf's mask. I held my gaze with Tythian as he handed it to me with a smug and knowing gleam to his eyes. Of all the mask designs he could've given me, he found that of a wolf. I was certain he knew or at the very least had suspicions. I examined the mask more closely. The small slits angled like half-moons covering my eyes, the nose and lips covered into a solemn smile. I grimaced. I raised it to my face, not at all pleased with how much it felt like it limited my peripheral sight.

"This is silly," I anguished, watching as the others put there's on. Tythian's white mask bared an elongated nose with harsh black paint around his eyes that flickered down, alluding the nose narrower. His blond hair seemed to be slickened back by the mask neatly, and his blue eyes pierced through, reflecting from the small amount of light that shone through the alcove. His mask was eerily daunting and utterly suitable for his character in a sophisticated way.

"There are always means to Cesar's madness," Tythian berated, flinging the black hood over his head.

"It's smart. We need to start securing our identities now that we're moving around so much. If even one of us is recognized, it could jeopardize us all, especially our association with one another. They could source it back to here," Yolo eluded. His voice was somewhat muffled from the mask he wore of a red dog. Again, only tiny slits were cut out for him to see through, its eyes, lips, ears, and nose, encircled by purple. "But it is stuffy," he admitted as he shrugged his hoodie on as well.

"Yolo and I'll go first. We'll check the perimeter. If humans remain, we're not going in, and then you won't have to wear the mask that dissatisfies you so greatly, Esmore," Tythian taunted.

I eyed him warily. Though Cesar might've permitted this excursion under certain conditions, if there was any sure sign of humans being close by it'd all be for nothing.

"Let's go, oh and, Chase, I left one in the bag for you," Tythian said and threw the small half-unzipped bag at him.

"For me?" Chase perked excitedly as he snapped it from the air. He split the bag open, the zip springing to life as he opened it to peer inside. "No way!" He shoved his hand into the contents pulling out a red mask with bug eyes. "You got me a Spider-Man mask?!"

"A what?" I asked confused. Whatever it represented the utter joy on Chase's face beamed with elation. Tythian had a gleam of appreciation in his eyes for how it was received. He placed his hand on Yolo, and they vanished into darkness.

"Babe, look," Chase said proudly, gesturing to the red mask he'd put on. "Okay, let me explain. So, there were like these comic books, movies and stuff and one of the characters was Spider-Man, and he was totally rocking. And he was human, but he got bitten by a spider and then had really cool superhuman powers and then he became 'Spider-Man,'" he gushed with excitement. He pushed a hand through his shoulder-length black hair, combing it back so it wouldn't hang around the edges of the mask.

"You look ridiculous wearing that red mask in your leather jacket with no shirt and dusty old boots," Balzar said, rolling his eyes.

"You're just jealous because you didn't get one," Chase said snootily, placing a hand on his hip and popping it.

"Do I even want to know why this 'Spider-Man' was so great?" I asked, finding amusement in Balzar's reaction. I couldn't help but feel bubbling mirth as Chase's excitement twinkled down our connection that was often and loosely wide open between us.

"Good question," Chase said, walking over to me. "So, what he could do was shoot webs from his wrists, and he'd tangle the bad guys and save the city."

"Ridiculous," Balzar mumbled under his breath, restlessly playing with his white mask that had small green pointed horns from the forehead. He seemed just as begrudging to wear it. Maybe that's why Chase's excitement irritated him so much, considering Chase wasn't even coming with us. Fire huffed in the corner, grabbing my attention. The big wolf seemed bored with the conversation as she propped her head on her paw and closed her eyes to rest once again.

Chase ignored Balzar and Fire's reaction looking down on me, his red mask, irking my lips to twitch into a small smile. "And there was a scene where he saved the love of his life, and he nestled down on a thin web, upside down, and she kissed him." I could see the fantasy dance in his stormy gray eyes that contrasted with the red of the mask. My darling Chase who had lived four hundred years had seen many things, and instead of growing tired he was the embodiment of childlike energy— still.

"Well, I'm sorry, my love, but I can't kiss you upside down. Nor through a mask," I said, waiting to watch him sag in depletion.

"Lucky I'm willing to settle," he muffled under his breath, combing the mask atop his hair to reveal a cheeky smile. He dipped his head down with a fluttering kiss. His tongue licked the top of my lip, tasting me as he stepped closer. I wrapped my hand under his jacket, uncomfortable by the new weight of the hood I was wearing. I felt the coolness of his muscled skin, and stroked my thumb over it, comforted by his touch. He looked adorable with his hair pushed back, that childlike spark hardly ever leaving his eyes.

"You were meant to be finding me sexy," he growled under his breath. I smiled up at him, pressing another kiss to his lips.

"And I do. And we'll continue on that thought when I return because I *will* be coming back," I assured him. All of this, Chase's edginess was because he was nervous about our separation. His humor and idle chat all in play to stop his mind from going into overdrive with the possibilities of 'what ifs.' We'd lost one another before, and we weren't willing to do it ever again. Neither of us thought we'd be separated so quickly, but he had his role and I had mine.

I cupped his jaw, rolling my thumb over his cold, smooth skin, tracing his elegant bone structure. We wanted to stay together always, and I worried about him just as much. But this was something I had to see out myself. Like he had to deal with the demons of his past, such as his coven; I had my own, one of those being Sydney and his daughter, Titan.

He let out a slow sigh and nuzzled his jaw into my hand as if he were Fire lapping up in my pat.

"Did you just compare me to your dog?" he asked with a bewitching smile. Balzar rolled his eyes. Though he couldn't hear our inner dialogue, he knew that telepathy was one of our shared gifts. *You should start getting ready.* "Here, let's put this on, so you're ready for when they come back."

Chase twisted behind me to lace the black ribbon of my mask tightly. He made sure not to bunch my hair, instead rolling my plait over it. After a few yanks, a perfect ribbon was tied.

He stepped in front of me once again, admiring the handy work of the mask. He charmed a wicked smile and pulled his mask back down. His, however, was constructed with a rubber band instead, as if it were catered for a child.

"And now we're the same," he mused in his Spider-Man mask. The mask hid my smile so instead I held out my hand to him, embracing every second our skin touched as I waited for Tythian to return to collect us.

*Everything is going to be okay.*

"It shouldn't be taking them this long," Balzar mumbled impatiently as he paced back and forth in the room. I wasn't overly keen on the wait either. I was sitting on Chase's lap, my arms looped around his neck as we bided time. Fire had moved and now used Chase's boot to rest her head. I thought she was doing it purposefully, with an odd sense of humor. A wary tension strung through him. Though he identified her as my 'pet,' he still viewed her for the wickedness that she was. All it took was one bite. I could sense she wasn't a threat to Chase, but she was finding some amusement in toying with him. I sensed she was warming up to him because he was my familiar and mate.

Chase never accused me of being selfish for desperately trying to keep her. I'd lost control when I reacted to her death and was beyond comprehension. And because of that, I'd inevitably hurt Chase. I'd pushed him too far, and the evil that was spreading in his mind was pushed like an atomic bomb waiting to go off. I couldn't define why I struggled to hold onto Fire, but it was in the same pursuit to salvage the humans. Someone had to defend them, and that was why I had to see the remains of the Human Compound with my own eyes—to witness the cruelty of the human government to reinforce I'd done the wrong thing. To solidify that turning my back on my beliefs and duty within the Guild as Token Huntress was the right choice—was the *only* choice.

*Whichever path we walk down together is the right one,* Chase said, nuzzling into my neck. I could sense he wanted to go downstairs, but not until he saw me off. He had intentions to sift through his coven individually, to see what they were capable of and what he was working with. So much had happened since he took his rightful place and with the chaos that followed, he was unable to assess those he oversaw. And I had no doubt that he and Cesar were formulating their next advantage point. There were so many variables in their pursuit to overthrow the Vampire Council and ultimately removing their biggest obstacle—Oppollo.

With perfect timing and snapping me out of my spiraling thoughts, Tythian appeared alone. We froze. Where was Yolo?

Tythian coolly raised his hand. "Don't be alarmed, he's okay. He's waiting for us."

"What took you so bloody long?" Balzar impatiently walked over to Tythian. Tythian glowered at him, I could see even that much through the mask.

"Sometimes when the adults are out to play, inspections go longer than first thought."

"Don't patronize me," Balzar grumbled. Chase propped me out of his lap. I uncurled my hands from around his neck and brought his lips down to mine for one more parting kiss. A short and sweet one, to remind him that I wouldn't be long and we'd pick up where we left off.

"It was an entire compound that was over swept by human military in one night. Did you think it'd take two minutes to be cleared? Maybe that kind of thinking was what shadowed *you* even as a human," Tythian provoked. Balzar grumbled, reminiscing the time when he'd been human and fought the last war that they'd epically lost at one hundred and fifty years ago.

*Be safe and don't keep me waiting long,* Chase said telepathically. Our fingers were intertwined as I slowly stepped away. The mask still pushed back his hair, cupping his glum expression. Fire stood up as if to follow me.

"Not today, Fire, you have to stay with—"

"Daddy!" Chase tried to sound enthusiastic, but he was grimacing on the inside. "You get a whole day with Daddy." He crouched and hesitantly brushed his hand through her fur. It was for show, for me, in reassurance that she'd be safe.

"That sounds so disgusting," Balzar commented. A smile spread on my face, and although concealed by the mask, I knew Chase could feel my appreciation through our bond. *Don't do anything rash. Remember even with your Spider-Man mask, you're not invincible,* I teased. I took my position beside Tythian. The last thing I saw was Chase's lopsided smile, evidently not okay with seeing me go. Tythian pressed his hand to my shoulder, and the nauseous wave of being teleported dragged me from one location to the next.

We were peering in from our position atop the great wall to the Human Compound. At my back was the forest eerily covered by dense fog. For now, I couldn't sense anything or anyone, but I was doubtful the silence would remain much longer. Surely something was left behind. I was certain it would only be a matter of days, if not hours, until other beasts would find their way in here, searching for what might remain and what they could feast on. I doubted the mutated rodents were prejudice to what kind of scraps they could devour.

The dome was open, allowing us to spy into the massacre below. It had always been closed only opening temporarily for no more than an hour to let natural sunlight flood in, on those very rare occasions. Now much like the graphic scene below me, it looked as if it had been pried open and a bomb thrown inside. It was utter carnage.

The wind pushed apart my robe, letting the thick black material flick behind my leather pants and boots. My mask was stuffy to wear and did very little to block the stench from overpowering my sensitive sense of smell. It had been a blood bath with a mixture of human blood, the foul stench of the wolf blood, and a lingering gas that I imagined would've weakened those who were inside.

"It was a massacre," Yolo glowered beneath his mask. I angled my head to better examine him. His knuckles turned white with clenched fists. He'd worked and been a part of this establishment for years, and it was evident, especially because of his human persona, Jenn, he'd become attached.

I drifted my gaze to the edges of the wall where precise scratch marks lingered. The wolves would've poured over the edges when the dome had been opened, which could only be done from the inside. Blood was sprayed and bodies scattered amongst the individual sectors where humans trained, others plowed their vegetables, and the children had once played. Not everyone had been turned and taken—those who remained looked to be those who stood to fight with a few bystanders.

"Well, Esmore, this is what you wanted?" Tythian said with low merit. "You've seen—"

"We should look for traces of what directions the humans went while we're here and the tech's down," Balzar announced. His green eyes snaked from Tythian and fell on me. Though I left it unsaid, I was appreciative of his rational thinking. Tythian was trying to make a point that this expedition was a waste of time. But if we found something, I wouldn't simply look like a spoilt Daddy's girl in his eyes. Being outvoted, he had to comply or then it was too obvious his disgruntlement was personal instead of operative.

"Not everything is down. I checked before your arrival," Yolo interjected. "The way this compound's set up, particular sectors are depending on backup generators that'll last for decades. The cameras and scan system beside the door have been wiped, giving clear access, which is how it would've been easy for them to purge sections at a time. It's also why the dome opened once the security was overridden, everything opened up like a vulnerable flower. To have that kind of access comes from the top of the top. There was evidence someone tried to rebel and override them which is why they would've resorted to opening it entirely instead of periodically." Yolo shook his head. I could hear the acid in his tone. "So many resources and years of research all gone to waste."

"Yea, well while you're tripping down memory lane about your fake human life, I'm going to make this time we've been afforded productive." Balzar stepped off the wall and into the inner circle. I watched on, waiting for a booby trap to set off. He hit the ground, a small amount of fog misting around him. But nothing happened. I didn't hesitate to jump in after him. I could feel Tythian's cool gaze on my back, watching as we dropped in one by one.

I landed with a small thud, resting my hand on the dry soil as I scanned the area. It was stark, so contrary to the brightness and liveliness it once was as the humans went about their daily business. I followed Balzar curiously as he walked toward the iconic statue of their founder in the center. The glass tunnels were mostly intact, except one that had been smashed through with red staining the glass. Beside it was a dead man and wolf from what looked like a scuttle to the death, both of which had lost.

I ventured in the opposite direction. We divided in our investigation as I gravitated toward the residential area. Every step felt weighted as I scanned my surroundings, insensitive to the masses of bodies. I stepped over a detached limb and took note of the small fires that had been put out. My robe drifted behind me as I walked casually through the remains of the battle. They never stood a chance.

My hand hovered over my weapons, ensuring they were in quick reach if anything jumped out at me. It was out of habit. I was strapped with weapons, but none felt more deadly than the gold shine of my pointed claws that were already on my fingers. They were the very same weapons Chase's mother had used. I enjoyed their delicate clank as I taped the tips together lightly with a moderate hum as I censored out the irritating smell of the wolves' blood. There was something about their mutation which was displeasing to my vampire sense of smell. It was a mixture of off meat combined with an expired sour fruit. It left a twang in the mouth that was near insufferable, and I couldn't imagine how horrendous its actual taste was. The others amicably didn't make a fuss over it.

I pressed a button to open one of the doors to enter the glass tunnels. It opened without the need for a card. As Yolo insinuated the power wasn't cut off, and it was only limited in restrictive functions. I turned left down the tunnel. The eerie silence broke when Balzar stepped on a small mass of shattered glass—the crunch being the only awakening to my sensitive ears.

I exited another door entering the residential sleeping sector. It was a bloodbath. I glowered at the elderly woman on the ground, her throat cleanly slit. This wasn't just a recruitment process to infect other humans. This was also a purge to clear out who they deemed invaluable and a waste of resources. It was the reason why most of those who had been killed in this area were elderly. The humans had been just as ruthless as the wolves. I found irony in the detail of this human government having lost their humanity, no matter what way they justified it.

I traveled down the narrow dirt path surveying the two-story bunked sheltered rooms on either side. On my left an elderly man's body hung over the stairs, his body having clearly been dragged out, his face mauled, and his throat bitten into. These wolves were savage, and I wondered if they'd been trained to kill on command or on the night of the full moon had no control of their aggression. Maybe even beyond that, perhaps they were designed to always be like this.

Fire was different, and we were still unsure whether it was because we'd changed her by using my venom and mother's gift; or if the few wolves who had been hunted in the wild were defective in some way. There were so many unknowns surrounding her origin.

I suspended my next step, hovering my foot over a small teddy bear. I reached down and picked it up delicately with my golden claws. It had a few dirty marks, a small tear in its arm, but otherwise unharmed despite the havoc that had destroyed everything else around it. I thought of Titan. This childlike toy represented such innocence with only a few wear and tear marks that could be fixed. Maybe Titan would be the same if I or someone else could look after her and help reverse the damage that had already been caused. The trauma would remain, from what I'd witnessed in humans being saved from horrific circumstances and moved to Guild camps. But they found a resilience to survive. Because she was so young, perhaps she'd adapt more easily than the adults.

Balzar's whistle echoed throughout the tunnel. I looked over my shoulder, still thoughtfully hunched over the teddy bear. Yolo was at the end of the tunnel I'd walked through. He was looking between me and Balzar. He waved to summon me.

I tucked the teddy into the back of my pants and shirt, hiding it beneath the robe I wore. I took one last brief glance along the daunting dirt path. There were no survivors here. And nothing caught my eye besides the nature of every kill which was repetitive in its own way. Wolves went for the face and jugulars, and the humans went for the throats and chests. The cowards had attacked them in the dead of night when most of them slept.

Yolo waited for me at the founder's unaffected statue positioned centrally in the tunnels. We took a right toward Balzar and Tythian who waited. Their masks were stark as their focused gaze narrowed on the panel before them.

It was the same glass tunnel I'd made a note of when we first dropped in. Glass was scattered everywhere. The man had a bite mark in his torso and neck, where he'd evidently bled out. I assumed their fight originated inside the tunnel and by force busted through. The gray wolf had a sword in its chest with three arrows in its back. I followed the direction of the arrows to a woman's remains whose hand still held tightly onto the crossbow. The left of her body had been ripped apart. By the clothing she wore, it was evident she was one of the guards on the wall.

"I thought you said the security system was down," Balzar vexed. He clicked on the panel again, but the door didn't budge.

"It is. But maybe some were successfully overridden," Yolo said, enlightened. "Wait here, Esmore and I will open it from the inside."

"How tiresome, we don't have all day," Tythian scowled. Yolo ignored him in that way that Jenn would as easily have snubbed him.

"Just shout out if something happens," Yolo said far too casually, considering our circumstances. "It'll be interesting to check out from the inside what they might've overridden. From what I've gathered the cameras aren't working, but even if they can somehow highjack them that's what we have these for." He tapped on his red dog mask.

I wasn't well educated on the technology the humans used, but I couldn't assume that Cesar's sole intention for the masks and robes was only for this. As hunter's, we'd adapted to a more primitive way of living, and that was as far as my knowledge and experience stretched. But Yolo had been around just over three hundred years, he was turned when everyday technology was at its peak and never lost interest.

He circled the tunnel and darted right toward the direction and sector where the experiments were conducted. This section was only accessible with special clearance to privileged members. But if the security system was down, it should open without a hitch.

When we arrived at the door, Yolo had a mischievous glimmer in his eyes. He drew out a blood-splattered badge. "Apparently, one of the scientists turned out to be a defender of the good in the end, much to my surprise because I never liked Travis, but good for him." I didn't find his quirky joke comical. Yolo pressed the button, readying to use his card if it flashed red. Much to his disappointment, it opened. Which meant this side of the section, their worst part was fully accessible.

"Well, this should be a treat," Yolo muttered under his breath, no doubt thinking the same as me. Then what state were the experiments in?

# CHAPTER 7

YOLO WALKED THROUGH easy-going, though I knew the sword strapped to his back wasn't for ornamental purposes. I'd only ever seen Yolo fight once, but I didn't doubt his capability. I'd decided to keep my Barnett crossbow and sword at our lodgings and was strapped down with knives, daggers, and most importantly my claws. I cramped my fingers in an arthritic manner, prepared for the split second an adversary jumped out. Few of the lights were still on. One flickered on and off down the hall creating an ominous feel as we tentatively walked toward it.

Below the staircase was where I'd first witnessed Sydney's men being experimented on. It had also been where I met Whitney's brother, Charlie, who'd cruelly experimented on her and had since been killed by Tythian. In the same sector, further below was where Kasey and Kora had been held captive.

Instead of his custom heels clanking as Jenn, it was Yolo's lanky frame that shouldered the silence as we walked under the flickering light. The clinical rooms looked untouched, except for a few scattered papers that had landed on the floor where some might've tried to take their work with them. Yolo looked on with little scrutiny as he led us to the area that interested him the most. The section where Yolo frequented his daily rounds amongst the captive vampires and sabers. In those very cages was where I'd discovered Lincon. He'd been enjoying his highs from the sedations and gossip within the Human Compound.

We swept through the narrow halls, the first two doors parting for us easily. When we approached the third, the entrance to where they imprisoned the vampires, the door didn't budge. Yolo looked over his shoulder at me and stared. And stared and stared. I wasn't sure exactly what he was looking at until he tapped on the side of his head. Oh.

I opened telepathically to him. I was reluctant to use it with others. Chase and I felt about it in the same way. Between Chase and me, the fluidity was almost peaceful. With anyone else it felt evasive. As soon as the connection snapped into place, I felt the weighted pressure of his guard against my mind, despite welcoming me in.

*Sorry, I just thought you automatically knew when I was, you know, talking to you. It's just a theory but on this side of the door is where a small control panel is located. You know, the same one where we're given the sedation syringes and granted access into the room with the vamps. On the other side of the door, where Tythian and Balzar are, it leads to the main control room where we came through for our screenings. Maybe they've attempted to safeguard the control rooms somewhat.*

And then it dawned on me, and I halted him before he scanned Travis's card. *If you had a card for access, why didn't you try to use it on the door Balzar and Tythian were trying to open?*

I could sense the guarded amusement from Yolo. *Because if they knew I had a magic card, Tythian would've taken it from me, you know, big bro stuff. And I wanted to check down here first,* he admitted selfishly. I was wearily suspicious of his true motives. Yolo was still tentative as to how much of the compound he was willing to show his brothers. But it meant that he was just as secretive as the others. He seemed to be the least offensive of the four brothers I'd been forced to work with, and Chase's favorite by far. But even under the guidance and rule of Cesar, it didn't exclude him from being self-serving. We all had our secret objectives. I simply hoped his wouldn't jeopardize any of mine.

Yolo swiped through Travis's card. After a two-second delay, the screen flashed green and the door opened. The small hallway was eerily lit by one flickering red light, which was no doubt a part of their alarm system. Yolo hesitated, wary for an attack. When nothing moved, he stepped over the threshold and approached the door to his left for a second screening. He swiped Travis's card, and with the same time delay it opened. I watched him closely through the large glass window that separated our rooms. He wasn't acting suspiciously or rummaging through anything like a madman.

I briefed a curious glance toward the room that held the vampires who'd been subject to various experiments. My interest was piqued as to what they might've done to them. Had the humans abandoned them, killed them, or tortured them with the wolves? In my peripheral, Yolo sauntered over to the rows of refrigerated capsules. He pulled out a tray and raised one of the sedation needles so I could see.

*An utter waste,* he grumbled. He left the tray ajar and the fridge open. He walked over to the computer and started tinkering away on the keyboard. I couldn't fathom why the human government would want to so quickly dispose of this place when it already boasted such advanced equipment. Even if it were for the sole purpose of recruiting humans for their new experiment, surely it made more sense to keep this as a post. It was fully functional. Had they completely lost their minds?

*From what I can see,* Yolo interrupted my thoughts as I idly searched the decommissioned door and what may lie beyond. *Someone did log in and tried to override the system to close the dome. They were only able to override the first two main sectors, meaning clearance cards were required.* He squinted, scrolling on the screen that illuminated his mask. An offensive red flashed on his already red mask, denying him access. *That's bizarre though. The username who overrode them isn't one I'm familiar with.* His mind was ticking over on various theories. *I don't know this person.*

*Everyone has their secrets,* I replied soberly. *Could it be Walter?* I hadn't met the new commander who overshadowed Mr. Richard's rule in this compound, but Yolo had briefly told me about him. If he were in charge, surely he'd have access to everything. But Yolo didn't know much about his background, and it was highly possible he was the one who let the wolves in.

*No, he had his own, very similar clearance to Mr. Richard's. He would have access to most things, but whether he understood how to override the system is a completely other thing. He seemed more the military alpha type than tech-savvy. I've never seen this username before, and it's not very original 'GHOST.'*

A thunderous bang diverted our attention simultaneously to the unopened door. I tensed my fingers, suspending my clawed hands, ready to contest whatever was trying to escape. The echoing noise faded into an eerie silence as the tension built between Yolo and me.

He looked over at me, his sword already unsheathed. His red dog mask was still flashing with the red from the screen. It might've been one of the sabers, being free for the first time in years. Or a vampire collapsing against the door, desperately hungry to escape so it could find something to feast on.

I nodded at Yolo. Whatever it was, I was prepared to challenge it head-on. It only took him two taps on the keyboard, and the door panel flashed green. It opened slowly. Inside was pitch-black, aside from the blue glow of the ice capsules. Two vampires were still frozen in time inside. The blue glow was enough to illuminate the large brown eyes that stared back at me from within the dark. I heard the savage growl before I saw the small flash of white canines. The wolf lunged for me. Its mass propelled forward, its open mouth and canines drawing closer to my face. Its speed caught me off guard. I snapped its mouth shut, digging my claws into its muzzle as its hot breath flushed over my face. I grimaced under its stench, being slightly pushed back by its strength. I doubled mine, summoning the strength of my vampire to appear. My vision hued purpled and my fangs pierced out. Its wickedness washing over me like a much needed sigh of relief. I forced the wolf back into the room.

Yolo was already behind me and threw a syringe he'd gathered from one of the trays. He wanted me to sedate it. Not kill it. It helped me refocus instead of being over swept by my maddening power that wanted to rip it to shreds. Yolo emitted the reminder that this wolf could be just like those we were protecting in the cave. I caught the syringe and dove into the experimental boarding. The brown wolf scampered to its feet, shaking off the irritable pain of where I'd punctured around its muzzle.

Yolo cautiously remained behind me. There was a distinct difference between us. I had been bitten by a wolf and survived. As a full-blooded vampire, he wouldn't have the same luxury. I descended on the wolf, its speed surprisingly fast as it maneuvered around the syringe, equipped to its dangerous merit. Its thick fur acted as a barrier, as the tip of the syringe got ensnared, barely missing its neck. It barged me into one of the cages. On impact, one of the unlit lights dropped from the ceiling and smashed. As I braced for my balance against the metal cage, a clawed hand lightly brushed over my cold skin. A saber was attempting to latch its deformed nails into me, ready to draw me close and take a fleshy bite. I reefed my arm back, the sheer jolt knocking the syringe out of my hand.

The wolf seized the opportunity of my diversion. It leaped for Yolo, acute to his smell and accustomed to prey on the vampires. The wolf had never been after me, I had only been the obstacle. It was wired to attack Yolo. He snarled, backed into a corner with his sword held high, preparing for the impact. I scampered to my feet, with speed that outmatched my huntress self, I jumped on the wolf and plunged my nails around its snout, redirecting its face from Yolo. Yolo was frozen, his sword useless as he just watched on—stunned.

I reefed back the wolf's jaw with a predatory instinct, dividing it and splitting it in two. Its horrific yelp sounded off the remaining surviving experiments in their cages. Its furry weight crashed beneath me, immobile. My heart thrummed with exhilaration until my gaze reached Yolo. Through that red dog mask, I could see the anguish in his eyes.

"We weren't meant to kill it," he squeaked quietly. The vulnerability in his tone snapped me out of my exhilarating kill, and it dawned on me what I had done. I looked down at my bloody claws and hands. The mass of fur beneath me was no longer breathing as it pooled with blood from its deformed face. *But I saved you?* I thought, unable to speak the words. As the reality hit, I felt like I'd betrayed myself, as if it was Fire's jaw which I'd torn apart. I stepped back from the wolf, a moral war beginning to rile. But if I hadn't intervened, Yolo would've allowed himself to be taken down and possibly killed. Was I a hypocrite for lecturing Chase that we should save them when I just so sagely took one down?

"Sorry, Esmore, what I mean to say is thank you. I don't know what I was thinking," Yolo vocalized distantly. He was staring at his hands now, perhaps conflicted with why he hadn't moved. Had he been stunned and terrified? Was the sincerity of Jenn overriding his rational thought? Or was it something else altogether?

No matter how unpleasant it was, his lack of defending himself forced me to do what had to be done. Yolo was essential to our mission, to Chase, and even me. I wasn't going to let him be taken down so easily, even if that took away from my own merit. The minor claw marks in my arm began to heal. The room filled with the vile stench of the wolf's blood. I feared I'd never be able to scrub the smell from my bloodied hands.

"It might've been one of their normal wolves, like Fire," Yolo said, creeping around the wolf, devoid of the transparent emotion he'd shown only moments ago. "If it was a human left behind, it would've turned back already by now, not being the full moon, right?"

Yolo pushed past me to better evaluate the room. I wiped my bloodied hands on my black coat, disgusted that the stench so powerfully overrode my senses. Yolo peered down at a shredded white lab coat and picked up a name tag that had been thrown against the wall. "Courtney?" He looked back at the deceased wolf, its blood seeping onto the white tiles. The vampires and sabers surrounding him in cages rattled back and forth, frenzied by the kill.

"I don't understand," Yolo said, looking at Courtney's name tag and the wolf as if suspecting the same as me. Perhaps this had been a woman formerly and was now trapped in a wolf's body. Or maybe it was one of the wolves that descended upon them to inject this virus in the first place. "I thought after the full moon they turned back?" he questioned. This was uncharted territory, and maybe it was simply a coincidence. Maybe this Courtney woman had been taken and this wolf trapped or left behind.

The wolf had obviously bitten some vampires. There were gory imploded masses in the center of their cages. Those who had been spared now seemed more alive, reaching for Yolo as he walked past. They'd been smart enough to realize they were safer backed against the cage where the wolf couldn't reach or bite them.

"What do we do with the others?" I asked, looking at one of the malnourished sabers who was scabby and making ghastly thirsty whimpers at me.

"We should kill them, but if we do so and if someone loops back, they'll know someone was here." I looked at the wolf pointedly. They'd already know someone was here. "It's not the humans I care about knowing we were here. If they were smarter, they would've made this into a trap. What I'm worried about is who else might be watching us right now. But even with that said," Yolo twisted to better assess the saber who'd attempted to attack me through the bars, "I never much liked this room."

His firm grip tightened around the sword, and I stepped out of the way. Yolo set upon them with a viciousness I'd never seen him express. I turned, giving him this time and moment of relief as he challenged his own demons. I wasn't sure what was happening with Yolo, but whatever it was, he needed to release it within his own primal nature, and the caged sabers were easy for the picking. Or maybe I'd thought too harshly of his character, perhaps he was doing them a favor and freeing them in his own way. I leaned down to collect Travis's security card that Yolo had dropped during the scuffle with the wolf and let myself out, giving him his space. Only a few moments later he joined me. I glanced over his shoulder, the room was deadly silent except for the low hum of the backup generators supporting the blue glow of the capsules. He'd left those vampires untouched, forever leaving them to slumber.

He pointedly jiggled a backpack that radiated with an unknown coolness of what I suspected to be bottles and sedation syringes. "At least we're not coming back empty-handed," he said in a low voice as he slung the bag over his shoulder. "Let's go find the others."

# CHAPTER 8

WE DIDN'T LINGER around the Human Compound for much longer. We'd checked the screening room where evidently those who were on duty had been dragged away, along with the rest. Whoever hijacked the security in an attempt to close the dome had failed. And that unknown figure haunted Yolo for the rest of our expedition. He wasn't entirely his carefree self. Of all the brothers, Yolo was the one who still had playful delight glisten in his eyes, much of which I'd hardly seen the past few weeks. The brutality of recent activity was beginning to take its toll on everyone. I was grateful that Chase was still being light-hearted in what felt like a grim outlook. It felt like it was us against the world, compared to when it was only a few months ago that I was sheltered in my thoughts, beliefs, and tasks within the Guild. Ever since then everything had imploded.

We jumped over the wall and into the foliage in our grand escape. I looked back up at the wall once more, surveying its edges. I was looking for any hint as to where they might've gone, but there were footprints and marks everywhere. They doubled back over numerous directions so following them would be a nightmare. I had no doubt Tythian and Yolo had already assessed it prior to bringing Balzar and me here.

"Ladies first," Tythian said gentleman-like as he reached his hand out to me. I could see the malice in his blue eyes. How he must've hated being ordered to do things and teleport us because of my requests. I still owed him two favors. Knowing that, it must've been impalpable for him to be forced into service for *me*.

The nauseous wave of darkness swirled around me, and I was dumped at the front gates of the institute. Tythian vanished and returned, bringing back Yolo and Balzar one by one. I had to do a double-take on the explosive spectacle before me. The covens were in an all-out fight spread across the enormity of the front lawn. Fire's bark reached me through the gruesome sound of colliding bodies and struggling attacks. I scanned the crowd, magnetizing toward Chase who had a smile plastered on his face with his arms crossed over his chest, smug with approval. He was pointing something out to Cesar who was just as excited beside him with a lit cigar hanging out of his mouth.

They were perched on top of the roof, watching over the spectacle like it was a sport. Fire was right beside him, on the damn roof. "What on-?"

Balzar removed his mask and threw back his hoodie. He rubbed his eyes in irritation. "I'm starting to wonder if your boy and Cesar teaming up is a good idea."

"They're sparring," Tythian mumbled still hiding behind his mask. "I don't have time for this." And then he vanished, leaving us three to confusedly look over the vampires who snarled at one another. Tythian had yet again vanished to who knows where. The pair closest to us got into a scuffle and hurled one another over. The movement so quick I had to trace it with my purple eyes.

*The view's better up here,* Chase coaxed me to his side. I stared at him agape and confused. And why was Fire on the roof? I know she's a killer beast and all, but seriously, on the roof? I could hear his laughter through our connection pool into me.

The three of us made our way around the group and scaled the outside of the institute and onto the roof with little effort. It wasn't until we got closer that we noticed they were both holding guns. Chase had a singular pistol in his left hand, and Cesar had two.

"You look like an old westerner in some outdated movie. All you're missing is the hat," Yolo joked to Cesar. I removed my hood and mask, like the other two already had, the breeze a relief of what felt like a hard day out on the field.

"Right!" Chase beamed with excitement. "That's exactly what I said." Fire's tail wagged as she came to my side, pushing her head against the tips of my fingers.

"Cesar, what are you doing?" Balzar asked seriously as he brooded over the vampires with a technical eye. I could see him sifting through the crowd, surveying who the key players were. He was listing the strongest from the weak, both ally and possible foe. As I watched over them, as separate covens, I was certain they were equally measured.

"This one here," Cesar gestured toward Chase as a pillow of smoke blew out of his mouth when he spoke, "suggested we let them blow off some steam and get better acquainted. It wasn't a bad idea really. So as safety measures I pulled out a little scare tactic to make sure they don't go too far. Hey! You!" he savagely screamed. He aimed and shot. Chase covered my sensitive ears, but with little avail to blocking out its imploding force, especially when so close. Most of the vampires froze, startled and scared. One of the vampires dropped, screaming as he held onto his knee that wept black blood. After a few seconds, I realized the bullet wasn't pushing out.

"You're using silver bullets on them? Are you serious?" Balzar seethed. Two members of Jerimiah's elite team unsolidified from their gargoyle form to collect and drag the man away. I then noticed them surrounding the lawn as the security to keep it in check. The vampire who the man had attacked was holding her chest. Blood oozed from her wound where he'd gone to grab for her heart. She snarled at the vampire who was being dragged away and looked up at Cesar, nodding her appreciation before standing and finding a new sparring partner.

"We're not going to kill them of course, but it's going to hurt like a bitch," Cesar said, shrugging his shoulder and breathing out another puff of foul stench smoke.

"There are two simple rules," Chase cut in, removing his cupped hands from around my ears. His hands glided caressingly down to my hips so he could casually hug me from behind. His left hand that held the gun never removed his finger from the trigger. "No weapons or gifts to be used. And no killing."

"And if you get too daring, then well—you get shot and bleed out for a while as collateral damage," Cesar said, puffing his chest out and letting go a monstrous laugh. Cesar was unhinged, and I didn't know who was the worst influence on one another, him or Chase.

"You've got to be kidding me. You're both out of your minds. How do you think this is going to help camaraderie?" Balzar debated. "We've just been out investigating this wolf business for you and come back to you throwing nonsense."

"Watch your tone, boy," Cesar snapped on him. Balzar's body stiffened, and he held his tongue. Cesar's eyes averted back to the makeshift arena below. "Unlike you Balzar who gets special treatment to leave the perimeter, a lot of them can't leave this little nest aside from hunting in a restrictive border, and they're becoming restless. They need to spend some of their building aggression before it implodes."

"And besides," Chase added, "I thought you of all people would appreciate being able to watch over them and see what you had to work with?"

Balzar didn't like Chase speaking back to him, especially when it looked like for the first time ever Cesar and Chase were agreeing, worst of all in an eccentric way.

"Go join them, son," Cesar encouraged with not much room for debate. *There's a means to his madness,* Tythian had said about Cesar. He wasn't a stupid man and had lived far longer than most here. I imagined something so small as this was massively calculated, even down to the sounding of the gun going off. And I had to have more confidence in my familiar's judgment as well, no matter how bizarre the execution.

Balzar was hesitant to leave and whispered a fury of cold-hearted words under his breath. He jumped into the pit and shoved the first vampire he came in contact with, who just so happened to be one of Chase's members.

"He's such a down the line type of guy," Yolo joked.

"You were the bloody one who told me to turn him," Cesar chided back with a crooked smile on his face. He was pushing him, as I imagined he did all his sons. He knew their potential and capabilities. And he knew how it fitted into his inner circle best.

I caught sight of Clarissa who sat holstered on the fence, seemingly bored as her gaze dashed over the members. She was studying them, I realized, in the same way that Balzar did. Spungee was nuzzling his face against her. She continued to push him off until she'd had enough and backhanded him over the fence. He plummeted to the ground, landing awkwardly and whimpering. She didn't give him any attention, only enough to make sure no one was close enough to actually prey on him. He groveled back to her side, pretending to have an understanding and interest in the fight in front of him, mirroring her.

Clarissa wasn't an obvious fighter, with having Spungee as such a weakness. But still, she was a predator who prowled on the edges, calculating and formulating plans from the side. With Spungee always on the line to lose because of his easy vulnerability, she'd learned to rein in her temper if only slightly, and simply watched from the sides unless forced into action. Her dark brown almost black eyes snapped up to meet mine. Her long black hair whistled hauntingly in the shallow wind, my fingers still threaded through Fire's fur as I contemplated her. I didn't particularly like her, but could gauge she was an asset to Chase, especially when she'd founded this place awaiting his secure return.

From my peripheral, I noticed Connor and Deemori walking out from the trees. They didn't speak to one another and had a measurable distance between them filled with three sabers. Connor seemed unfazed by their presence now, adept to his familiars' gift. Others shadowed them, wanting to creep from the trees but deterred by an invisible command. They might've not spoken or even looked at one another twice, especially not in a lustful way—but they were always together. Deemori's long, oversized tee shirt was spotted with fresh blood. Evidence enough they'd just been hunting. Connor, the quiet embodiment of Tythian's sophistication, bore no droplet of blood. The two fascinated me in a way. I understood the pull of having a familiar and the desire to be with them in every way in every waking hour. I leaned into Chase, embracing his scent as it smothered me. How they had the discipline to ignore that was beyond me.

"How'd you go today? Did you find anything interesting?" Chase asked, squeezing my hips and pinching a small thrust against my black robe. He was cheekily pressed between my ass cheeks. I hid my smile, trying not to encourage his cheeky nature while others were around. He chose not to question my bloodied hands. He had access in my mind to everything that had already happened today. He sent love and warmth down the line with that underhanded cheekiness that only belonged to Chase.

"We'll wait and have a proper discussion about this when your mother returns," Cesar interrupted. He pointed his gun at a vampire, tracing his movement. Cesar was watching the vampire unfold into his primitive nature. He wanted to kill and be victor. Despite it, as if feeling the target on his back, he looked up at Cesar who dashed a wicked smile. The vampire stumbled over his next step backward and tripped. "Dang," Cesar mumbled under his breath as he lowered the gun.

"My mother?"

"I'm no fool, Esmore." His heavy gaze crashed with mine. "I know exactly what you and your brother have been up to." Yolo froze. "My two most spontaneous children keeping a secret cave of little wolves like a box of kittens hidden in a draw. You, I expected better from," he said pointedly to Yolo. "Though who knows who the instigator was out of you two." Cesar treated us as if we were children and instead of his wrath, he rolled his eyes and shrugged his shoulders at us which only irritated me more.

I went to argue with him, but he continued, unaffected by the pure rage that crept within me. I felt as if I was being looked down upon. Was he purposefully being condescending? Chase tightened his grip around my waist as if grounding me. He flushed through waves of calming bliss. It washed over my anger, simmering it down subsequently.

Cesar had been right, we were all tired, restless, and hungry—and I was no exception.

"Do you really think I wouldn't notice my familiar going amiss for more than a few minutes?" Cesar genuinely asked me as if he were offended. It was the first time I'd seen his irritation pointed in my direction. "And low and behold like daughter and mother alike, you both decide to support such a notion that could kill us all. But your mother's spunk is what I love about her most."

I kept my expression neutral, but I'd never considered my mother as 'spunky.' She had only ever been huntress—all critical and muscle.

"I've put the elite team on to guard them and Lydia in charge. Your mother's also concealed their cave and surrounding area so no one will catch scent of it. I don't agree with this decision, nor do I like any member of my team close to it, so we'll be discussing it over a banquet tonight."

"A banquet?" Yolo asked incredulously.

"Well, we have to feed these little beasties somehow, and I want to have a gathering with my *family*." The word left a distasteful tang in my mouth. "We can discuss all this political grief that goes alongside with it."

Cesar's gaze looked Chase up and down tartly. "And I suppose you can join."

I could feel Chase's humor and joy swell by the partial acceptance offered by Cesar. I rolled my eyes. *Now I'm scared of the encouragement you two might play on each other.*

Chase squeezed me tightly once more and smiled, nipping at my ear. *Scared I'll be the favorite, my love?*

I shook my head bemused and sent a visual of what it'd look like when I threw him off the roof. His laughter rumbled down our line, elevating me in the same way. I crouched down beside Fire, patting her matted leg. A shred of guilt bolted through me when she began sniffing my hands. She sneezed at the stench, and instead of turning her back on me she nuzzled under my palm, demanding another pat. A wave of relief passed over me, grateful she hadn't turned her back on me. She licked at my face with foul breath, and I pushed her away, revolted. "What did you eat today?" I asked, my stomach churning.

I felt someone's gaze intently staring at me. I eyed Clarissa who was watching my interaction with Fire studiously. Fire had been clearly ordained as an exception in the institute, and no one was allowed to touch her. It didn't mean she would be exempt from being targeted if someone tried to find an opportunity to take matters into their own hands. Yolo and I would have to come up with an immaculate case to be able to extend that protection over to the others. Yolo was staring at Fire intently as if thinking the same thing that I was. He wouldn't look up to face me as he studied the dry blood on my hands. Why had he frozen? Why didn't he fight back? We hadn't mentioned it to Balzar or Tythian either.

Feeling my uneasiness, Chase crouched behind me, his knees on either side of me, encompassing me once again. He pressed a possessive kiss to my cheek. I leaned into it, allowing its holistic power to calm me and release the tension in my body. When I looked back, Clarissa had diverted her gaze. Chase was endearing but also setting a gentle reminder. I was his, and that was to be prioritized, and by extension, that safety was projected onto Fire—theoretically.

# CHAPTER 9

T HE DEFINITION OF a banquet to Cesar meant being subject to uncomfortably sitting in a large room, seated marginally beside one another on seats where the fabric had eroded, and the peeling paint on the walls was a ghastly sight to the eye. Drapes had been eaten away by moths, a moldy smell clung to the air, and we sat in the dark, excusing a few scattered lit candles. A few paintings on the wall had either been torn down or were so thickly coated in dust that it was hard to make out their former images. And although Cesar had ordered someone to attempt to shake out what was once presumably a white tablecloth, it was still dirty. Cesar had reasoned that it hadn't yet been cleaned like other rooms in the institute, and for the most part this is where a lot of members from his coven rested. The reality was, there were too many vampires in one space even when this was just temporary lodging.

Chase rubbed over my thumb with an idle smile, finding amusement in my discouraging thoughts. We'd all arrived around the same time, Tythian being the last to have arrived. The four brothers, Cesar, Chase, Deemori, and my mother included. I'd brought Fire with us who was currently munching down on a bird in the back of the room, her growls loudly mauling over the feast Chase had given her. I was certain he was trying to get into her good graces by way of feeding her.

Deemori was here for no other reason than Connor not allowing her to leave his side. He'd become possessive and attentive to how the other vampires viewed her, considering Deemori belonged to no coven and he wouldn't officially claim her as his. My mother had been excused from her duty watching over the wolves, and the cave was currently being guarded by Cesar's elite team, Darcy, Jerimiah, and enforced by Kora and Kasey's projection so they wouldn't attempt to escape. They were the few I considered to have enough restraint to co-work together. Everyone within the room was uneasy for the reasons we'd been brought together, but also the activities we all wanted to return to.

Cesar and my mother sat on opposing ends of the table. My mother was to my left, and to my right sat Deemori and Connor. Across from us, Tythian, Balzar, and Yolo. Yolo was restless beside Balzar, flashing a glance up at Chase and me briefly, as if skeptical that we might be trying to pry into his mind. He was fidgeting with the wooden cross at his chest. It was evident he wanted this meeting to hurry and end so he could return to *them*, and the anxiousness wasn't unnoticed by Tythian or Cesar. I wanted to return to them just as quickly, but I knew far better than to let that show. We had to file a good case on their behalf, not show a maternal attachment to them. I'd already done that once with Fire, and it hadn't been in my favor. Weakness was always frowned upon.

Everyone, excluding my mother, had been given a glass of cold blood with another three pitchers in the center for refills. They'd all silently grimaced at the coldness of the blood. My counterpart as a vampire hadn't been awakened for long, but even I grimaced at its cool touch, much rather wishing it was hot and fresh. Cesar had made arrangements, no doubt through Tythian's teleportation to haul blood back to the institute. As for the covens outside, the perimeter to hunt had widened, but members were to hunt in groups for precautionary measures in case they crossed paths with the humans.

My mother gave nothing away on how she might've felt about everyone's 'serving,' but I wondered how bizarre this outlay was to her. Did she hate us because we drank blood? Hunter and vampires were after all, natural enemies. Did she despise her familiar in some way because of what he was too? Or, like me, did she have to come to terms with the extent of their love and what it actually meant? She too, had to love a monster and accept him wholly.

There was a light tap on the door, and Cesar summoned in the newcomer. A woman who I recognized as a part of his coven, but hadn't dealt with much, brought in two plates of hot food. The others watched on in amazement as she placed one portion in front of my mother and then me. Plated in front of us were chunky roasted potatoes and a cooked bird of some kind. She placed down a polished fork and knife.

"I apologize if it doesn't taste great. It's been a while since I've cooked or roasted anything," she said with a weary glint in her eye. She didn't want to disappoint Cesar or offend his familiar with her cooking. She pardoned herself as the smell wafted to my nose and my mouth watered. It actually watered. I looked up at the ceiling, momentarily in thought. *When was the last time I ate proper food?*

"I'm curious," Yolo said with his chin dipped in his hand that was propped on the table. He looked as if his mouth was watering as well. "Tell us what it's like. It's been so long."

My mother looked around the room and picked up her fork and knife, unperplexed by the gawking table. On cue, I did the same. "Does it really taste like nothing to you?" My mother asked solemnly. The room was uncomfortable with idle chat, though we'd fought through much together, the dynamic was amiss.

"It makes us sick," Tythian said, matter of fact.

"I'm kind of jealous, Esmore, that you can still eat even with your vampire side," Yolo admitted, looking at me longingly. Not me, I realized, but the imagery of what food tasted like. "What do you crave most, blood or food?"

I was already mid-bite as he'd asked. I rolled the hot food around in my mouth, savoring it. Although it tasted nice, nutritional, and hearty, there was a blandness to it that bleached my tongue. My body was mechanically accepting it, pleased that it had something substantial to function on, but I couldn't deny that it was underwhelming and didn't feel like it was hitting that certain spot or satisfaction the one other source could. I felt my mother's gaze on me, just as curious for the answer. Would she be disgusted in me if I openly admitted I had more of a thrill ripping into a living creature to quench my certain thirst?

"Both," I lied as I reached out for my glass of blood and swallowed a mouthful. The blood's thickness was like a syrupy sauce that rushed over the remainder of meat and washed it down. My eyes turned purple as my fangs slipped out, pleased with the relief, no matter how bitter or cold it was.

As if reminding them, they too reached for their glass and took a mouthful. My mother watched me from the corner of her eye as she cut into another piece. Self-consciously, I placed the glass down, denying my desire to gulp anymore and ask for another serving. Instead, I too, cut into another piece of meat. Chase's hand slid to my knee, washing a wave of calmness over me. I looked at him, grateful for his full acceptance of what I couldn't even yet fully and wholly claim without some kind of shame.

Deemori didn't touch her glass. She simply sneered at it with a distasteful grimace. I very much doubted the wild Deemori had used a glass in decades and was going to start using one now to be rewarded by cold old blood, especially when she'd just enjoyed herself a fresh hunt only hours before. The same three sabers that escorted her in the woods now slept behind her. All of them were once women, their ribcages sticking out as sharply as their elongated fangs that dipped past their bottom lip. Their hands, bodies, and nails were blackened with soot and years of unhygienic existence. Their hair was now barely wispy strands. When one stirred, Fire growled at them as if they were going to threaten her for the bird. I clicked singularly, and she stopped, still watching them. I couldn't let Fire step out of line or it'd only make the situation worse for both of us. For her, because of what she was, and for me because I was protecting and claiming her as my responsibility. She silenced, settled by my command, and continued gnawing on her bird.

This room was a mixture of oddity and natural enemies. From the most primal versions came Fire and the sabers to hunters and vampires, coven members alike. We were a group that years ago would've seethed at the thought of such an occasion. Yet here we were forced by the elements of survival and dependency.

"Right, no time like the present," Cesar announced as he poured himself another fulfilling glass. I continued chewing on the hot potatoes and meat in an attempt to enjoy it, but to no avail. Chase watched me from the corner of his eye and continued to pour calming waves over me.

A loud bang crashed through the door, and a dripping wet Lincon cursed and seethed as he waltzed in. He sloshed around in his wet shoes, flinging his long dress shirt onto the floor. His stark white chest was scattered with red wisps of hair. He glowed like a lightbulb in the night, so transparently pale.

"Sorry I'm late," he said, disappointed. He began removing his soaked pants. I looked away, disgusted in his crude nature as he let it all hang out, in the exact same manner I'd met him. When he noted there wasn't a chair for him, he opted to lean against the wall instead, feigning exhaustion. I didn't even want to know why he was so wet. The entire room was evidently confused and irritated as to why he was even here. There had been guards positioned outside the door, and I could quickly conclude his means of madness to get into here and what he might've done to them.

"This is a private meeting," Cesar gritted out pointedly, looking at me as if I were the one who summoned him. From my way of expression, it was obvious I hadn't invited him at all.

"Oh, yes I know that. That's why I didn't let those five follow me in," Lincon said, wringing out his long dress shirt, water sloshing onto the wooden floor in a loud, audible drip.

"Do you mean the guards?" Balzar seethed through clenched teeth.

"Oh, is that what they were doing?" Lincon hauntingly laughed. He stroked through his red hair, slicking it back. "Well, they weren't very good."

"This is private!" Cesar growled as if ready to stand.

"And I want to be here," Lincon argued with a taunting smile. "Do you really want to fight me on this of all things, Cesar?" The way he said his name, in such a provocative way, was familiar but also unsettling as if they'd had this argument many times before. Before Cesar could even stand, we'd all been encircled in Lincon's tricks. I gripped onto Chase. All sense of physical sensation and connection to him was gone once Lincon's illusions were in play. I wanted to break through to him, ensuring whatever terrors Lincon was feeding him wouldn't push him over the edge.

"Lincon!" I snarled angrily as pillowing snow tore over my face and ambushed my senses. "Lincon!" I could barely locate Chase's mind, the blockage from Lincon's gift tentatively pushing us further apart. I was worried for him, with Fier's disease active, I didn't know what triggers could cause Chase to lose control. Lincon was going easy on me with the barricade of snow, but I doubted he was encompassing the others with the same. And all this was to show his power, to defy the order about him, and the reason why I couldn't refuse his aid. None of us could overthrow his illusions. "Stop it now!" I desperately searched for Chase, my panic rising at the thought of him turning back into that *thing* and state I'd retrieved him in from Fier's Council.

The veil of snow dropped and ceased. The room came spinning back into reality, and I grasped desperately onto Chase, pulling his face into my hands and checking on him. He nodded his head, reeling from what he'd just witnessed. He was still with me. I spied on Fire, grateful she hadn't attacked, yet. "Stop!" I commanded her before she dared lunge at Lincon. Her hackles were raised, and she was ready to pounce. We'd only been encapsulated for a few seconds. And I'd caught her just in time because there was no knowing how Lincon would react. I trusted him no more with her than any of the others outside of this room. Especially when one bite could kill him, he wouldn't hesitate.

The rest of the room didn't fare so grandly. Lincon's illusions were too swift, even Tythian had been ensnared before he could teleport out. Cesar was on his knees, tears streaming down his face. My mother was solemnly panting into her dish, holding her chest, terror streaked on her face.

The smell of blood caressed my nose. I darted my gaze over to Connor and Deemori. She was rattled, snarling and gasping as she pulled her hand away from the broken wine glass she gripped. The glass was embedded in Connor's stomach. He tolerated no more than a grunt as he began to pick shards out of his bleeding stomach and shirt. His body pushed out chunks that sprinkled to the floor.

She seemed wild and frantic, slowly regaining her composure only to focus on what she'd done to him. She was pale and couldn't even manage words. He simply brushed it off like it was nothing and angrily glowered at Lincon. If he reacted, we'd be in the same situation again. Connor's defenses were equally offensive, but it wouldn't trump Lincon in speed.

"Now, I really didn't want to make a spectacle," Lincon said, flicking out his shirt, unperplexed by the most defenseless parts of his body hanging freely. "But, Cesar, when will you learn? Now carry on. Pretend like I'm not even here."

Balzar was frothing from his mouth as he slowly regained his consciousness and fixed on Lincon hauntedly. We could be playing this game with Lincon all day, and he'd be more than happy to participate. He was leering at the brothers, deliberately egging them on.

Cesar and my mother eyed one another warily. I had the sense that perhaps Cesar and Lincon had known one another formerly, or perhaps

Lincon was considered by all of them as the largest unchecked threat here. And for whatever reason, and for the time being, he listened to me. Well, when he wanted to, that's what made him the live wire.

"He knows about them," Yolo said in a low voice to Cesar, assumedly already knowing the first topic of choice for tonight's discussion. The wolves. And Lincon was as involved with that secret as we were.

"He can stay," I uttered and sat back down beside Chase, briefing a glance at him and then Cesar. No one wanted Lincon in this room, but if I stated and ordained I approved of his being here then maybe it'd keep Lincon slightly more in check. He'd feel as if I were on his team.

"Awww, Ezzie!" Lincon threw his hands on my shoulders, childishly. I bundled his fingers into my hands, crunching the bones tightly together.

"Don't touch me!" I snarled back, my purple gaze using the reflection of my glass to look back at him. He only parted a shallow smile, pleasuring in the pain. *Disgusting.* I released him from my grip as he disturbingly enjoyed the pain I inflicted on him. He laughed hysterically taking a step back, rolling his wrists in playful tease, starring at the hand he'd just been scorned by with pleasure.

*I don't like him,* Chase telepathically edged. None of us did. But he was a threat we'd have to worry ourselves with later.

Cesar growled his complaint but sat back down. He downed a glass of blood, pissed off. We sat there silently, calming ourselves. I could feel Chase's influence sweep over the room, subtly so no one would notice, but enough to take the edge out of it. Moments of silence passed as we watched one another wearily, waiting for Cesar to continue the meeting. Deemori sat uncomfortably digging her sharp nails into her thighs, one slow rake at a time, drawing blood. Connor noticed but did or said nothing to stop it. His stomach had fully healed, and he begrudgingly kept his cool gaze locked on Lincon. Balzar and Tythian were doing the same. They'd all been caught in his games, and none of them had yet figured out how to conspire against him. Their hands were tied, but their stares were enough to shoot down armies.

Eventually, the room somewhat settled as best as it could, considering how uncomfortable it was even before Lincon's grand entrance. My mother was the first to pick up her knife and fork and continue eating as if ignoring his very presence. Instead, his eyes glistened as if he'd been approved of.

"Seems like some of my spawn have been up to mischief," Cesar said as he downed another glass, still slightly irritated. The four brothers and I glanced at one another. It looked like Yolo and I weren't the only ones concerned with being caught as guilty culprits. I wondered what the others had been up to. Yolo knew better than to speak over Cesar, and I followed suit.

"We have a little nest of wolves in our area who are being fed, guarded, and dare I say nurtured by some guilty members in this room."

"What?!" Balzar snapped angrily, looking at me with rage filling his eyes. I tensed my grip around the knife. Chase's hand pressed firmly on my knee, reminding me I wasn't alone, and this was just a 'friendly' discussion. Balzar noticed Yolo's body straighten as if willing to take full responsibility and then he turned on his brother with confused rage. "Why?!"

All eyes rested on him. His casual demeanor had evaporated, and he was now poised femininely like Jenn Cadowalt, looking down her nose at the others. I wondered if even Yolo realized the two were becoming transfused or that his fabricated counterpart was so impartially influencing him.

"Hear me out. I think we can learn from these creatures."

"Bullshit!" Balzar snapped, pushing his chair back and slamming it against the wall, his fangs ejecting in a spurt of rage.

"Sit down!" Cesar retaliated not so much as having to move. His stare alone pinned Balzar. "You will listen." Tythian moved to collect Balzar's chair for him, amicably surprised the frail wood hadn't shattered. He positioned it behind Balzar, and through a quick glance, offered him a silent word of warning. Balzar huffed but sat back down, arms folded.

"As I was saying," Yolo continued, not unnerved by his brother's outburst. "These creatures were manufactured to eradicate our kind, yet from what we've seen, have no side effect on hunters if they're bitten."

"We only know that because Esmore was bitten once, but she might be an exception, as she is with most things," Tythian said coolly. He watched Chase wearily, who glowered back with a taunting polite smile.

"It's a risk," Yolo confessed. "The same goes for me being in such close quarters with them. I know that. One bite and well… we know what'll happen. But I know them personally and think they rein the discipline to not attack on emotion. And the only time we've seen them turn is during the full moon two nights ago. If the human is speaking the truth, then we can make sure to lock them up during the full moon."

"Son, is this more pity for your human friends or your inquisitive mind biting off more than it can chew?" Cesar asked seriously. "We can't take any of the above into factual account, and how do you plan on experimenting on them in any way without your gadgets from the Human Compound?"

"We're not experimenting," I cut in. The thought of Titan being experimented on bubbled a fierce instinct to protect her. Everyone's eyes were now on me. My mother laid her knife and fork down, her full attention on me. "Simply monitoring them. Seeing if we can use this to our advantage. If we can control them would they not be of greater gain to us when we fight against Oppollo and the Council armies?"

"You mean to put them into war, including the young ones?" Balzar asked sarcastically.

"Not the young ones," Yolo said, pulling his gaze away from me and focusing on Cesar. "But the adults were within the Human Compound's military. I'm sure their intel could be advantageous for us, and also if we can study them, then perhaps collectively over time, we could use wolves such as Fire in our favor. They're effective and would help level out a fight significantly, in my opinion."

"In your opinion? When did you turn into such a war hero?" Balzar mocked.

"The moment I pulled you from rubble and saved your life by having Cesar change you in a last-ditch effort to regain your honor," Yolo snapped. Balzar's knuckles turned white, and then a wave washed over him and his shoulders sagged. I realized Chase was sending a wave of remorse over him, manipulating his response. Or maybe he was simply amplifying it. But it was enough of a nudge to keep Balzar from spitting more snide remarks.

"They could turn on us sooner," Cesar countered. "They're too unstable and close to our nest." He swallowed a mouthful of blood. My mother was surveying him and how the others responded closely. "And besides, our main focus is halting the wolves being released from the human government. Not encouraging its spread."

"What if we could do both?" my mother interjected. Everyone's eyes swept to the end of the table. She wasn't uncomfortable as a roomful of vampires leered back at her. "I have a suggestion."

"One of which you know I don't like," Cesar said sweetly with a smile. My mother ignored him, and he let out a shaky breath, knowing she'd continue without his approval anyway.

"We take them to Dillian and the others, have them watched over by hunters. That way they're not close to the coven, where both are at risk, but we can still monitor and study them." She flashed me a quick glance. Titan would be safe, but if they were unstable, it would endanger the others. I quickly started calculating ways to work around that. "To counter the human government from releasing their wolves prematurely, I think we should notify the Hunter Guilds about the situation. Though they may not act on behalf of the human government anymore, they still monitor them. If they're watching them closely, I doubt the humans will move so freely like they've done in the past few weeks."

"Why would a group of hunters want to help vampires against humans, who they've vowed their life to protect?" Balzar tested. The very mention of hunters and the Guilds brought an unsavory tension into the room—a backhand to my mother and me, but one that couldn't be avoided.

"It's simple. Because the hunters don't want to be overthrown."

"That's ridiculous. The hunters would want this war to come to an end, they'd encourage these wolves to let loose to kill vampires."

My mother shook her head, and for the first time, plastered on a wicked smile. "No, because the hunters don't really want the war to end. They just want balance where *they* are not being overthrown. Where would that leave them? If vampires were vanquished entirely and the humans regained order. What would their purpose be? We as hunters," my mother said pointedly to me, "are not very flexible in our way of thinking."

"But you two are," Connor uttered, the first words he'd spoken this entire meeting. His crystal blue eyes were still watching Lincon intently.

My mother shrugged and leaned back into her chair, the most casual human I'd ever seen as if to make a point. "We were an exception. And though there are cases where few might stray, it's not an evolving sincerity within our kind. If anything, you could consider us as the defects." It was the first time I'd ever heard my mother title us as defective or anything less than what we were—warriors who had paid our time in duty only to be hunted down ourselves. But we were different, and although we had our personal reasons, it wasn't without judgment from our former Guild. Through the disaster of our Guild being over swarmed by sabers at Fier's lead, we'd been fortunate enough not to be the focus in Campture's eyes, although she'd certainly spared time for us. They still had to relocate, they couldn't put all their efforts into hunting down and collecting two fugitives, who as of now were heavily protected by their enemy.

"So then why would they listen to you? Your former Head Huntress will stop at nothing to chase you both down and kill you. We were there," Balzar said with sincerity in his wake as he diverted his gaze from connecting with mine. None of us had forgotten what they'd done to me when they captured me—especially what James had done. They'd pulled me from that nightmare, but they'd been too late. And I hated myself for not being strong enough to protect myself.

Chase winced uncomfortably, and I turned to pull his hand into mine. His eyes were closed as he uncomfortably shifted as if trying to erase a nose bleeding migraine. He was fighting it, the disease Fier had planted in his mind that was so sensitive to his emotions. And to the hate he felt for himself for being unable to protect me in that moment as well. *You're okay,* I soothed to him, trying to break through that tentacle-like wall that erected between us when it would flare. I only needed to afford a gentle nudge to get through to him. *We're okay. Stronger together, remember?*

He calmly interlaced his fingers with mine, reciprocating my touch. "I'm okay," he quietly admitted to the table, considering everyone as they watched him carefully. His eyes flashed open with an unreadable hardness, so parallel to his goofy expression. Only I knew how anguished he was by denying his expressions freely, especially when it was his most primal ones. Self-loathing. Hatred. Revenge. They ate at him within seconds.

"We don't go to *our* former Guild. We go to the head. They're based near the old city of New York. I've been there before by foot; I know its location. Vampires won't be able to come in, but if we can muster hunters, such as Dillian and the others, we'll have numbers on our side at least. The group won't be so evasive in size. We wear, as Cesar now mentioned going forward, masks and hoods so they can't see our identity. They'll see our fluorescent eyes and know we are of the same." This would mean theoretically, I would have to shift into my vampire self to exemplify my purple huntress eyes instead of my everyday gray, which put me at further risk if my mask were to come off. "We offer them this information and walk out. They'll have no choice but to act on it even if they don't believe us. Their own suspicions will get the better of them."

"We can't put Dillian and the others at risk like that," I said, calculating the risk involved. Why would my mother so willingly use them to simply make up numbers when it's been our sole focus to try and protect them?

"Daughter, it's your mistake to crowd them into a room and space where they can't act of their own accord. Though you might mean well, and as their Token they follow you, you've taken away their ability to act and fight for their own rights." My mother's words punctured my next breath.

"Are you saying I'm an unfit Token?" I snapped, pushing out of my chair, my temper quick to snap. My nails curled into my palm. My mother looked down her nose at me, that lecherous gaze she would often bestow upon me if I'd done something wrong as a child. But as she spoke it was gentle in approach. She didn't want to fight me but was merely making a point.

"They're hunters, Esmore, and like you once fought for them, they have the same right. They can make this choice. I'm not forcing anyone into anything. But at least they'll have a mission and purpose before they become rusty and stir crazy. A hunter without purpose is nothing. They're already following you blindly, at least give them something, if not at least the choice."

I didn't want to defy my mother, especially in front of the members in this room. We were partnered better as a stable front. It was logical. And when I pulled out of my wavering and uncontrollable emotions, I could see reason. I wanted to argue with her, to be right, especially when we had an audience. But I couldn't debate her as she looked down the table with such an oppressive knowing gleam. When I'd thought my mother had gone quiet within Cesar's coven and even up until this point, she hadn't gone meek at all. She'd been watching me and observing who I'd become, as a woman and Token, furthermore as a vampire. She'd been testing me, and I felt like I'd failed. Was that why she was speaking up now? Had I'd made too many wrong decisions leading up until now?

"And what makes you so sure they'll let you leave?" Tythian spoke down to my mother as if she were stupid. It hadn't gone unnoticed by Cesar as a prominent tap on the table made Tythian flinch. Cesar had put down his glass. He seemed more irritated by my mother's plan because there was no guarantee we'd make it out freely. Not that any of our missions within the Guild had ever guaranteed our lives.

"Well, there are options, but we have a backup if we can't fight ourselves out."

"No," Cesar grumbled, disheartened at the end of the table. "You'll take too much damage, and you don't heal like I do."

"What's he talking about?" I asked, confused, and not liking the sound of my mother being in harm's way, aside from the obvious one she was already putting herself into. This had been something they'd spoken about already in detail.

"Your mother and I share a combined gift, sweetheart," Cesar said coolly. "Glorious in all its form but it comes at a price. She wants to go in, and if it turns pear-shaped, use said gift to offer Tythian enough time to teleport in and take you and whoever else might go, out. However, it'll be taxing on her."

"What's the gift?" Chase asked, eyebrows furrowed in intrigue.

Cesar let out a hearty breath. "Not all gifts are a blessing. As I'm sure you already know, boy," he said pointedly to Chase, speaking in regard to the Descendant. "I killed a hunter for this gift, and although he could control it beautifully, in my hands and as a vampire, not so much." He dangled his finger over the table, and a tentacle crystal-like flake began to form on the tip of his finger, latching onto the table like a perfect crystal ball. It was beautiful, fragile-looking, but Cesar tapped against it with his other hand to prove a point. "It's near impenetrable. Beautifully crafted, but it has a downside, and he began attempting to tug out his finger.

"You can't remove your finger?" Chase asked, amazed.

"No. This is only a small one. Depending on the size of the projection it might take an entire limb if not more." With sheer force, Cesar ripped his hand away, the definite sound of his finger swiftly being torn away with it. His finger was still idly mounted atop the crystal sphere, black blood now oozing down its shell. Cesar cursed under his breath, grabbing part of the tablecloth to bandage up the finger. "That's going to take a wee bit of time to grow back."

I stared down the table at my mother who watched Cesar indifferently. It wouldn't scare her, a wound was the least of our worries, but I was concerned about how far she would go to make sure we came out safely. She was my mother after all.

"This all seems daring for a simple message," Yolo interrupted. None of them were surprised by Cesar's gift, and I wondered if this was the reason behind his one gift rule for his sons. So instead of being greedy and trying to gather as many gifts as possible, they had to choose wisely as a precautionary measure.

"Or necessary to keep the human government at bay while we focus on the Council. We don't have the numbers to stretch out and focus on both," my mother argued. "And this way with the help of the hunters, you'll have time to guard and study your wolf people."

That silenced the room. We were divided in opinion.

"Might I add a suggestion," Lincon spoke up. Cesar rolled his eyes over to him, clearly infuriated by his intrusion. Lincon charmed a smile and stepped forward as if that was approval to speak. "All of that dainty sacrificial stuff sounds right up my alley, don't get me wrong," he said to my mother, waving his hands about. "But what if instead of losing limbs over a pretty ice ball, you can use me." He plastered a smile in my direction. I avoided looking anywhere but his eyes. He was still swimmingly naked, his clothes lumped on the floor beside him.

"And why on earth would we want to use you?" Balzar gritted out, arms crossed over his chest.

"Well, you certainly had no issues using me when I helped you retrieve Chase and Tythian from Fier's Council. And if memory does serve correctly, I also somewhat saved Yolo's life. Remember, Esmore, when you were like screaming in anguish because you thought he'd been so cruelly unjust and murdered and you were unable to save him?" He waited for my response, his sarcastic tone deafening. "No. Nothing to say? Okay, I'll continue. What if you threaten them? Take me with you. I can remain on the outskirts and sidle up in Esmore's telepathy mind thingy. And if you run into trouble, you can threaten that an entire vampire army is outside waiting to ambush them, and if you don't come out unharmed, they'll slaughter them all. Esmore gives me the signal, and poof, just like that I can have them deliriously thinking they're overwhelmed by impending doom. It'll be easy to play with a few guards on the wall, assuming they have a wall and aren't living underground like some," he said pointedly to Cesar, laughing with self-appreciation at his own joke.

"You want us to bluff?" my mother asked, not buying into his taunts. And it was the only reason why we weren't leveled into another spiraling illusion. Thankfully my mother had halted the others retorting and feeding into his sensitive dig.

"Some of the best makeshift plans are ones created from utter bullshit," Lincon said, clasping his hands together and nodding his head excessively.

"And what do you get out of this?" my mother asked skeptically. "What makes you think we can trust you?"

"It's rather simple, and I've said it before. I follow Esmore. If I can be of assistance, then I'll lend my leading hand. And here I would've thought I'd proven that time and time again. I'm almost offended Esmore hasn't painted me in a better light."

"You paint your own picture, Lincon," I gritted out, still not turning around to face him. There was a gamble even in that. How much would Lincon have to gain from this? What was he really after? And maybe he'd leave us deserted. But it was another addition to this plan if we were to go forward with it. We wouldn't have to go straight to depending on our worst-case scenario to get out. And it would relieve pressure from thinking so profusely about what the human government was doing. I wanted to make sure the wolves were safe and that Titan was protected. And besides that, I had some favors to live up to. Oppollo had to be killed so I could repay Fier, only then would he relinquish this disease from Chase. Only then would we be free, or partially free to then worry about the others.

"Even if this were the plan of action, you're forgetting one thing," Tythian added, collecting his glass and having his first sip. When the attention of the room was on him, he continued. "Does Esmore even have the restraint to be in a Guild full of hunters without triggering or trying to eat them?"

The room fell silent, and all eyes were on me. Chase's thumb rubbed over my hand.

"Last time she said she could, she came back with a human she'd turned into a retard vampire. And she's even weaker now. Do you think it's wise to put a trigger happy vampire in that situation? Perhaps the plan is best executed without her?" Tythian said matter of fact. He was trying to put an obvious divide of doubt in the room. He was only pushing me further away from my former life of being a huntress.

"She'll be fine," Chase spoke up, rattling me. "I'll have her well-fed in no time before you leave," he said, pinching at my cheek. I pulled away, irritated. He was lightening the mood. Making the issue seem not as severe. "More importantly, the question is, will you be around if they need you, Tythian, or will you be teleporting in and out as you please, like you do of late?" Chase taunted that breath-taking smile once again.

Tythian tapped his fingers lightly on the table, assessing Chase. The room fell silent. These two who had worked together for so long in Fier's Council, knew one another more than most, and they were sizing one another up. "I'll be there. Whatever it is Cesar demands of me. I'm there."

Chase's smile remained, and the two continued to stare at one another smugly.

"Wait! Oh, my god! Does that mean I'm in?" Lincon squealed. My spine straightened uncomfortably at the sound of his voice. "Oh, my god, I'm in! Finally! I've been waiting to escape this shit hole since the moment we arrived."

I looked over my shoulder at him, and he bit his lip, cheekily smiling and pressing his finger to his lips to be silent. He shrugged, now acting casually, and collected his soaked shirt from the floor as if it suddenly fascinated him.

"So then do we move on to more pressing matters such as Tracey's Council and how we'll use that to our advantage?" Chase asked Cesar. Cesar considered it for a moment and sincerely looked at everyone. His gaze dropped to Fire who was now laid out on her paw, blood smeared on the fur around her mouth.

"No, from now on you and I will speak in private," Cesar said. Chase's eyebrows shot up.

"What?" Balzar growled. "But we're your—"

"And you will remain so. I didn't say you wouldn't be involved." Cesar was watching Lincon pointedly. "Sometimes, things change. And so, we have to adapt to our environment as well." Lincon beamed a smile. Whether it was because of Lincon's imposition, the discussion we'd just had, or another matter, Cesar locked up. The dynamics had changed once again, and now we'd be dancing around to our own secret objectives. Everyone was eyeing one another suspiciously as if we were all thinking the same. What was everyone doing behind closed doors?

What I found surprisingly interesting was that Cesar was still welcoming to engage and plan with Chase, despite neither of them being fond of one another. Maybe Cesar truly did depend on Chase's coven numbers. And likewise.

"In that case, shall we call this a night and agree on the above moving forward?" my mother asked, plopping another piece of now cold meat into her mouth. She waited for my response.

"We'll ask the others and take it from there," I agreed. This was depending on if Dillian and the others would agree to any of it. I looked back at the iced sphere that had solidified Cesar's finger atop of it. The dark blood had now drained around the sphere and puddled on the tablecloth.

"Then, this meeting is over."

# CHAPTER 10

L INCON LOITERED IN the room, sheepishly smiling at everyone who ignored him as we filed out through the double doors. The vampires who had been positioned at the door to ensure no one interrupted our meeting were left shaking in fear. One vampire was being jostled by their companion who defiantly slapped them across the face, telling them to snap out of it. Lincon breezed past them with a whimsical smile. They shifted uncomfortably and flinched under Cesar's gaze, scared of the reprimand they'd receive for failing at their task of guarding the door. I wasn't sure if they were more frightened of Lincon or Cesar.

"He got us too." Balzar acknowledged them as he grabbed one of their hands and helped them stand. The reality that they were still so shaken up meant that perhaps they'd been entranced in their own horrors this entire time. Members of Cesar's coven parted a clear path for Lincon to push through. We waited for him to bypass us, as ill impressed by his presence as the rest. He skipped through happily and out the front doors, where I imagined he would meet with the twins.

A few members from Cesar's coven snarled at us, toward those who weren't welcome. Chase, Fire, Deemori, and me. Connor glowered back at those who evoked stares and whispered ill things at Deemori. One of the vampires courageously tugged one of her sabers' back legs, evoking a yelp from her. Within seconds Deemori had already pounced on him, a scuttle breaking out behind us.

Chase and I walked ahead. For all the minor fights that would continue erupting in here, this one was the least of my worries. The vampire who'd antagonized her sabers was stupid for listening to its primal urges. And they were about to deal with the consequence from either Deemori who they underestimated, or Connor who acted as her personal guard. Either way, I couldn't see that particular vampire lasting it through another hour.

"Let's go out for some peace and quiet and enjoy some hunting," Chase mused, deterring my attention away from the outbreak scuttling behind us. "Do you want to go hunting, Fire?" he said in a sing-song tone as he ever so gently combed through the top of her head. He was still wary of her, but ensuring his claim on her was absolute, in case any of the vampires here were stupid enough to try anything.

Yolo brushed past us, steadfast in returning to the wolves. I wanted to seek them out just as quickly as he did, but was caught in the dilemma of prioritizing my thirst before we attempted to make contact with the hunters, and so I reluctantly let him speed past me, shouldering their safety on his own.

It'd been a while since I'd seen Dillian and the others. My mother's words of warning forced me to question if perhaps they'd already moved on and didn't need my help or direction as their Token any longer. What if they'd assumed that I'd abandoned them after my lack of communication with them these last few weeks? The thought twisted my stomach if they'd ever believe I'd betray them in such a way.

They were only a small part of everything I set out to achieve, but they were one of the most important. Dillian was still my best friend, or so, I hoped he felt so too. An uneasy paranoia wedge into my stomach when I thought about seeing him for the first time in weeks. Had my silence and turbulence of past events put too much strain on our relationship?

Chase squeezed my hand, pulling me out of my thoughts. *He's loyal, and so are you. Worrying will do nothing to change events, my love.* I grimaced at its stark truth. Worrying wouldn't change things in any way. But with everything that had happened, I'd felt I'd let them down. I could only be in so many places at once, and that wasn't a good enough excuse. I had to find a way, so I could prioritize them, as long as it didn't risk what I had with Chase. I was torn between the ideal way to secure their safety and how I could do it for each of them. I couldn't think past that.

There was something childish about running through the woods with Chase and hunting alongside Fire whose tongue hung out the side as she panted harshly to keep up with our pace. She wasn't as fast, but her sense of smell kept her on track with us. There had been a pile-on of chaos and unanswered objectives, but in this moment, like most with Chase, it was carefree and a frozen memory in time, reserved only for us. I let my vampire self hunt freely, unbound by my former hunter self's morals and judgment. Releasing that overpowering urge and satisfying my needs washed over me with a freedom I solemnly felt.

We stayed within the restrictive hunting grounds and perimeter we'd enforced on the covens, ensuring we lead by example, though it made food slightly scarcer. It'd only be a matter of time until we'd have to widen our hunting grounds or relocate.

"My bird's bigger than yours!" Chase laughed as he held a bird upside down by its legs. It was thrashing back and forth, still attempting to claw and peck at him. It latched onto one of his fingers, and he paled, mortified as it thrashed back and forth with a vengeance. I smiled, my fangs glistening with the blood from the bird I'd enjoyed moments before. I'd been silent as I climbed the rock and small crevasse it was nesting in. It wasn't much, but it delighted my palette far more than the roasted potatoes.

"You should have some too," I said, throwing the wastage Fire's way. Instead of eating it, she played with it, flinging it into the air and thrashing it around.

"I'm not a fan of birds if I'm being entirely honest," Chase said, poking his tongue out at me. "Call me a fussy eater." I could sense he was lying. He was trying to fatten me up, so my seemingly never-ending thirst would have the edge taken off, if only slightly. "I have a surprise for you when we return."

"That never sounds good," I said, slithering around him and embracing him from behind. I rested my head on the back of his long leather jacket. My hands threaded over his bare chest, entirely aroused. Being alone with him, in the wild, with my body thrumming with excitement for more blood was a sparkling aphrodisiac. I kissed the back of his neck, slipping my hand further down his chiseled stomach.

He breathed out a shaky laugh, flipping the position and slamming my back against a tree. His gray eyes sparkled with that passionate craze that frenzied me in the same way. He nipped at my bottom lip, playfully, teasingly to make me beg. I bit back with a smile until he finally caved in and swept his hot tongue against mine. His hips pressed into me, his very hard shaft making me weak at the knees. How this man drove me wildly crazy. Everything about Chase I wanted, his touch, his scent, his taste.

"Esmore," he grumbled through a heated kiss. I clung to his leather jacket, desperate to keep his lips on mine. He pulled away slightly, drawing my attention to the bird who was hanging upside down in his hand, near unconscious. He tried to focus, pulling away from the frenzy that encapsulated us whenever we got our hands on one another. "I told you, I have a surprise. And if we start fucking here, we're not going to make it in time."

"I don't care," I breathed hoarsely, grabbing a firm hold of his thickness. His eyes rolled to the back of his head. Seeing the satisfaction of my touch, exploded a heated desire between my legs. We needed to be naked, now. He wrapped his hand around mine.

"Esmore, please," he breathed desperately, hardly able to deny me. *"Trust me."*

"I don't want the bird," I protested, trying to dip my hand into his pants, frustrated that he denied me.

"You'll have the stupid bird," he shakily laughed. He bit into my neck, the immediate claim, stunning me in a feverish desire. My body sagged in an erotic solace. And as quickly as he bit me to stop me from moving, he pulled back, having thrust the bird into my hand while I'd been so distracted. I was mesmerized by my blood on his beautiful lips. I had the urge to smear it on his face, fascinated by the beauty of it.

He cupped my face lovingly. "You have such beautiful purple eyes," he said dotingly. My next breath faltered. I'd never considered that Chase could love something that was so entirely my huntress self. I knew he loved me, every inch that he could explore and then some. But the idea of my mother denying me because of my vampire self and then possibly Chase having issues with my hunter self was an insecurity not even I was aware of. The longer I stayed with Chase, the more seemingly undesirable emotions and issues were arising.

"Drink up, and we'll head back. Your surprise should be ready." He took a step back, giving us both space to calm down.

"I don't like presents," I grumbled still displeased he'd denied me.

"Says the woman who hasn't taken off my necklace since the day I put it on." He charmed a wicked smile as his calloused, dirty fingers rubbed over the blue gem tied around my neck. It was the matching one to his earring. I gave him a half-smirk and bit into the bird putting it out of its misery. It had been bigger than the one I caught. It tried to break free, but after the first few seconds, it was already too weak to fly.

Praying on animals didn't hit the spot entirely. But it was far better than the bland taste of the food I'd eaten earlier. Oddly enough, it had nurtured a certain hungry aggression within me if only slightly. I was becoming to understand my body. It needed both forms of nutrition and although it so heavily thirsted for blood—it needed normal food just as much.

I threw the bird toward Fire, who this time snubbed it, much preferring the one I'd caught for her. We could sense two grouped vampires in the distance, hunting much like we were. Chase flung his arm over my shoulder casually and began escorting me back toward the institute. Already the light-heartedness of the moment washed away and the reality of what was beckoning began to torment me. I had always known only duty and purpose, but in these small pockets of time, I wanted to be with Chase like this forever. He could so easily spirit away the upcoming decisions and horrors. And I considered what those terrors might be right up until we returned to the institute.

There was a scent that filled my nostrils and had my mouth watering. I couldn't place my finger on the rare scent amongst all the filthy vampires until we stepped into the main entrance. There, much to my surprise, were humans. Some were screaming as they were being toyed with and tried to scamper away. Others were entranced and dazed having already been bitten. I was torn by my immediate uncontrollable desire to pounce on them myself and my ingrained nature to save them.

*It's okay, just ignore it.* Chase tried shying me toward the staircase. But I couldn't look away, mesmerized by the thought of taking them for myself. Fire snarled and growled at the injustice. But was it injustice? I'd attacked and killed humans before. I very vaguely recalled the memory, but I did remember the taste and satisfaction. How could I pull away from this everlasting desire to devour the most delicious bait in the room?

Unlike the government soldiers, Fire didn't attack the humans. If Fire wasn't attacking and she literally was an animal, then surely, I could rein in my own desire as well. But even the purpose of her attacks seemed to hold greater merit than my own. Though every part of my nature tried to twist back into the room as we ascended the stairs, Chase kept a firm grip on me. It took me time, but I painfully retracted my fangs, losing my purple vision, in hopes that it'd deter my vampire self from trying to engage with them. If anything, the denial only made my yearning stronger. Chase practically dragged me up the stairs and toward our wing of the institute.

"My love," he gritted out, in slight amusement from the bone-crushing grip I had on his hand. "I told you I had a treat, didn't I?"

My mouth was so parched I couldn't even reply. I hadn't responded like this to Titan and the others. They were different, they smelt off-putting. And even my mother, though she had an enticing smell, I could take control and beckon my vampire self away. But with humans dangling under my nose, my most primal self aroused and I was fighting against a wave of pulsing black spots that were readying to take my vision and memory. *I was so thirsty.*

As we reached the top stair, I realized the smell only grew stronger. "Did you?" I could barely make out the words.

"Yes, my love, we have our very own human. I very much doubted birds and rodents would help take the edge off your thirst. I just thought the hunt might help you clear the mind for a little bit."

My vision went hazy, and he finally untwined our fingers, releasing me from my physical shackle. I burst through the door, unable to control myself any longer. A bulky man jumped out and tried to strike me with the wooden chair. My lips twisted into a wicked smile as my body pulsed with its predatory adrenaline. My fangs ejected as my vampire sighed its relief. Finally, it was a real hunt. And everything else went black.

# CHAPTER II

M Y MOTHER INSPECTED the bag full of masks and robes, indifferent, and zipped it back up. The hour before we met here was a blur as I came to my senses. Chase had tried to deter me from killing the human, but it'd been futile. I'd been too fixated on fulfilling my thirst and lashed out at Chase when he tried to intervene. I was equally revolted by my lack of control as I was satisfied by my craving being quenched for the first time in a long time. I couldn't look my mother in the eye, ashamed of what I'd done. I was self-conscious around my mother, as if she'd seen every bit of monster I'd become and forbade me.

"I've always loved school excursions. Well not that I've ever been on one," Lincon gleefully mused to himself. "But they were always easy for the pickings. Busloads of children at a time, just pretend like it's a tragic crash over a bridge and bon appetite, dinner and dessert."

"You're a terrible creature," my mother said, disgusted, with little fear of how he might react. His smile only stretched wider, complimented. Tythian seemed abhorred to share the same room with him, let alone having to soon touch and teleport him. Lincon wasn't commuting with us to Dillian and the others, but was on standby for when we'd teleport to the Head Guild. But first we had to inform the others of our plan and give them the choice to join us. If they were to deny the request then we'd return and reevaluate the situation.

I hadn't seen Dillian and Julia since they'd been entrapped underground within Cesar's coven. A lot had happened since then. I'd spoken to Teary and Tori more recently who had vowed their allegiance to me as their Token, but I wondered if reuniting with the others made my role redundant. As I was now, I had no right to remain as their Token, but that form of responsibility still felt heavy on my shoulders. If I were so easily thrown to the side… it'd crush me. It had been my prioritized task for so long, and I desperately clung to it, to my old life as best as I could.

"Shall we?" Tythian offered his arm out to my mother gentleman like. We grabbed hold and braced for the sickening swirl of being teleported. I was steadily becoming accustomed to the nauseating wave of Tythian's gift. As soon as he relocated us, he was swallowed by his amassing pool of darkness abandoning us.

Positioned in front of me was a small cottage that had been overridden by mold on its exterior. Teary's muscular arms constricted around the axe and splintered the piece of wood positioned in front of her, into two clean pieces. As soon as it hit the bottom, she raised the axe again, tension stringing through her body as she raised it to throw in our direction.

"Wait!" my mother adjured. Recognition sparked in her fluorescent orange eyes, stunning her just in time. She slowly dropped her arms, but not the firm grip on the axe. She swept a brief gaze through our surroundings ensuring we'd come alone.

"Lord al' mighty," she said. "Ye trying to get an axe thrown at the lot of ye's."

Tori rushed out of the cottage with sword in hand. Collectively, they would've sensed intruders. It brought me great pride watching their reflexes and defenses spring into immediate action. "Esmore!" he exclaimed. His short, buzz-cut hair had grown and was now a mop of dirty, sandy blond. I could sense Julia inside the cottage and Dillian rapidly running toward us from the outskirts of their camp. He'd probably been hunting or surveying the area.

"Well c'mon in, Dillian was hunting. Doubt he'll be gone for long now though," Teary rolled her eyes at our dramatic entrance.

"Hopefully ye got some news so we don't have to mope about here, my weapons are feeling rusty," she joked, and my mother charmed a small smile in reciprocation. It was bizarre watching Teary and my mother permitting themselves a moment of humor. I didn't know they were old friends, but there had been many secrets my mother kept from me in the Guild, possibly even now. I looked at my mother's side profile, her long blonde hair the same as my own. Her features were similar but not as delicate, and she was only slightly taller than me. She always looked tired with a resting scowl on her face from conditioning within the Guild.

I'd often looked up to my mother for guidance as to what I should become and surpass. And beside her, right now, I felt inadequate. It wasn't me who had gotten them here, it was my mother, cleaning up after my mess.

"Esmore." I turned to face the familiar voice that I'd been anxious to hear from for weeks. "You're okay," Dillian exasperated, sweeping his gaze over me. Only a few of his piercings had remained, there was grime on his face, and he looked leaner. His black hair had grown longer, past his shoulders where he now tied it up with a piece of loose fabric. I wondered how we looked to one another. Time had treated neither of us kindly, yet we were alive and had managed to make it this far.

Dillian awkwardly shuffled the crossbow that was slung over his shoulder. He stepped forward, watching me warily as if I might lose control at any moment. He came to a stop in front of me, looking down at me with an unreadable expression. Without Chase it was difficult for me to feel or decipher my limited emotion. But right now felt like it held an ambiguous importance. Dillian had always been special to me. He held his arms out wide, the gesture unnerving me.

"It's called a hug, Esmore," Dillian said in way of teasing me. But we'd never been huggers. Maybe Dillian but not me. I was compelled to close the distance between us, so I could selfishly enjoy the feeling of his warmth, alive and beating self. I awkwardly tucked myself into his arms, moving my face to the side so I wasn't so close and enticed by the beating pulse in his neck. His scent that smelt of wood, sweat, and survival allured me. I gritted my teeth, pushing the aroused vampire deep down. It was still subtly pleased by its previous meal and didn't overtly fight back. I released a shaky breath, truly settling into Dillan's arms. He was alive. We both were.

"Yea, you hugging feels just as uncomfortable as I'd always imagined it," he teased. Although he acted as the Dillian I knew, there was a strain and exhaustion in his voice and expression.

"I've missed you," I said uncharacteristically. I would've never done or said such a thing within the Guild. He seemed surprised as he pulled away to study my expression. I wish I could've hidden for longer so he wouldn't see such weakness. "I was worried you might've thought I abandoned you."

"It did cross my mind," Dillian admitted honestly, and that punctured a wound to my Token status pride. "But I knew deep down that wasn't like you. I was just worried you changed so much into... well you know, this vampire business that maybe you didn't even recognize yourself anymore. I mean, none of us really know ourselves anymore."

"I wanted to see you sooner," I admitted.

"I know, but then your vamp boyfriend got smuggled away, right? Your mother filled us in. C'mon we should join the others." He readjusted the bow again and led me to the small cottage. Had he ordinarily spoken to me like that or turned his back on me in the Guild, I might've reprimanded him for it later. But this was different. The hierarchy had changed. And the reality was that I might've not fit into theirs any longer, even if they did promise I was still their leader. Did I even have any right to be?

"Esmore," Dillian looked at me confused when I didn't follow him. I was different now, and nothing got past Dillian's eyes. I gazed out into the forestry one last time to make sure no one else was watching and followed him in.

Inside the cottage was practical and fabricated for warmth and survival. Julia was thrilled to see me. Dillian instructed her to calm and remain seated with the pelt wrapped around her. A small fire was burning in the corner of the room, on top of it a kettle which boiled a perfume of mixed herbs. A small section in the corner was outlined for a patch of vegetables they were lavishly growing. Julia's gift was helping them survive on the empty days if they couldn't find meat to hunt.

My mother sat close to Teary, the two seeming overly familiar. My mother waited for me to sit beside her.

"I'm assuming ye' don't have good news for us then?" Teary blatantly asked. Dillian's gaze shifted to me.

"We have a proposition for you," my mother began. Dillian seemed more interested in watching me and how I permitted my mother to lead the conversation. My mother had never been a Token, though she was one of the most talented huntresses within our Guild. And for once, I was too tired to speak, plot, and make our next crucial decision that might've involved them. I was making the most crucial mistake any hunter could afford, and that was doubt as to whether my mother's plan would work. It risked them too greatly, something we'd become accustomed to within the Guild, and yet somehow it now felt different.

"Remember the Head Guild in old New York City?" she asked pointedly to Teary. She nodded, knitting her thick red eyebrows together. "I want to go there and offer them some words of advice, and I ask you if you're willing to guard something until we can find you an establishment to integrate into properly." I still had my sights set on the human camp in the Antarctic, but there was little time to investigate it further until everything else had been dealt with.

"What do we need to guard?" Tori asked. He'd bulked slightly in muscle since I'd last seen him, but still had a chubby youthful face. He was now nearing the age of seventeen, his apprentice status would've been wiped away in a year's time within the Guild. He only had one more year of waiting until his gift awoke. And here he was, in the open, not wanting to return to his family but instead remain on this path that he thought was a great adventure. At what age would he properly understand all that he'd given away? Or maybe there was hope for him yet. Maybe we could return him to the Guild because he hadn't committed any crimes. Nor had Teary, but I doubted she would so easily change her mind. Her loyalty was profoundly narrowed down on me and my mother. But Dillian and Julian would never be able to return, convicted simply for their association with me.

My mother debriefed them about the human government, the wolves, and her plan to have a meeting with the Head Guild in an attempt to slow down their progress. The others listened intently offering very little away in reaction. Only Tori seemed to show his anguish and disgust as we mentioned the wolves and their origins. The others, however, were hesitant to give their opinions away. We as hunters had been fabricated just in the same light, only three hundred years ago. If anything, they probably pitied them.

"So ye' think it's a good idea to reach out to the Guild? How do ye' think we're going to get out? And what's stopping these wolf people from turning on us?" Teary asked. Her fists were clenched, bone-white exemplifying her anxiety around the situation. They should all be uncomfortable with this plan.

"From what we've gathered, and this is only theoretically; the bites are effective almost immediately on vampires. However, when Esmore was bitten there was no change. I have a theory that they originate from hunter's blood which means they might be ineffective toward us. But I have no guarantees. For now, they are fully conscious and human. And as for the plan of escaping the Head Guild, we'll be assisted by Tythian, the one who teleported you here; and Lincon, the vampire who helped Kora and Kasey escape the Human Compound."

"Kora and Kasey are alive?" Tori gasped.

"They were captured?" Dillian fiercely interrogated, jolting from his seat. Julia reached for his hand, but he pulled away flustered. Fury defined his usually serene expression. We'd all been prisoners at some point, but to have been taken by the very humans we'd vowed to protect was a slap to any hunter's face.

"Where are they now?" Teary asked, confused as to why we didn't bring them.

"They'd been experimented on," I confessed bravely. I waited until the new intel sunk in. "I don't think you're ready to see them and I don't think they would be ready to show themselves. They're... different now."

"Different how?" Dillian asked through a clenched jaw. Julia was rubbing her hand over his forearm, trying to soothe him in that nurturing way she was often ridiculed for within the Guild. There was no reason for me to lie to them. But I would be admitting to something that weighed heavily on my consciousness, where I'd felt I'd failed them. I knew logically it wasn't my fault and this had been the making of their own path, and even now they wouldn't accept my help. But it hadn't deterred my irrational responsibility for any member's safety. It was the last binding of the Guild I simply couldn't shake. All except one who I'd happily kill myself. *James.* I quickly deterred my line of thought, not willing to spiral into that seething hatred for him.

"They seem to be a mix of hunter crossed with saber."

"They were turned into vampires?" Tori paled, his mouth sounding dry.

"No, they weren't turned into vampires in the normal sense." I placed my Barnett crossbow on the ground, to properly settle in. The room felt too small for this conversation. I'd much rather beat out my pent-up physical frustration than have this conversation. Vampires could turn us, though they rarely did. Our gifts were the prize, and for that we had to be drained entirely. I'm sure it was the stories of nightmares Tori had been raised on. Well, we had all been raised on. "I don't know exactly what they did to them in there, but now they have elongated unretractable fangs like sabers. From what I've seen, they don't thirst for blood and eat as we would. Though personally, I crave both, so maybe they are at a cross between as well."

Tori flinched at my honesty and reality to my new existence. The casualness in which I now spoke about my vampirism unnerved them. There was no dodging around it. I was a creature, but one they still knew. If they chose to follow us, that was now their choice.

The room was silent. Kora and Kasey had always been irritating to work with, they were snarky, dubious, and disrespectful to my leadership of the team. But still, they were one of us.

"Why aren't they with us?" Teary asked finally. She was seemingly more adaptable to the change of events and allegiances than I'd even considered possible for a hunter.

"They're protecting the wolves now. But I don't know if they'll choose to come with them. They aren't what they used to be. They've changed." I couldn't articulate the words to best describe them and how their mental state had changed drastically. "Currently, Kora is self-mutilating, and Kasey seldom says much, and they have an attachment to Lincon, which isn't necessarily a good thing."

"Wait, the vampire you want to help us, and you don't trust him?" Dillian asked sharply.

"I don't trust anyone from there," I admitted. "Besides Chase." My wariness around the brothers was increasing, who individually had their own ambitions. And Lincon by far couldn't be trusted. "But he serves a purpose."

"And if he betrays us, we have a backup plan in place," my mother interjected. "But have no doubt, this plan has risks involved, as does most of our missions. Like every assignment we've been on, we can't guarantee your lives. But we wanted to offer you an opportunity to immerse yourselves in the fight, and into a Guild once again. This is your path, we acknowledge that. We're not here to make decisions for you."

"But you're our Token, Esmore. We listen to what you say?" Tori said adamantly confused. I wasn't sure if it was his naivety to the situation or adamant respect he held for me that confused him so much. But I seethed the idea of him blindly following me.

"I can't call myself your Token anymore. Though it gives me no greater honor, I can't lead you as I once did. I'm mixed in some dark business that honestly, I don't even know I'll come back from. But what's most important to me is your safety and protecting the humans whose lives have been taken from them because of this wolf virus. I want to ensure all of your safety no matter what. One of the wolves follows and listens to my command. I think they're misunderstood creatures and if anyone can help them, it's us. I want to at least give them a chance."

"There's something else you're not saying," Dillian suspected, knowing me far too well. I gritted my teeth. Damn him for being so perceptive. I swallowed, condemning my pride. They'd see me as weak for this.

"Yes," I admitted. "One of the girls, Titan, I want to protect. I am indebted to her father. I lost control, and I hurt him." The lie soured my tongue. "No. I killed him, I even stupidly turned him."

The others turned blanch white.

"You're siring your own vampires now?" Dillian said, disgusted. The accusation would've hurt had Chase been nearby. But I couldn't gather the strength to argue with him or defend myself. Still, with my mother in the room, there was a pang of shame and disgust.

"No, I did it accidentally and he came out defected. My familiar killed him so a maternal attachment wouldn't weaken me," I said, matter of fact. "I've done horrible things these past few months. I've killed humans in an attempt to regain strength to obtain my familiar back. And when I'd found him, he'd been tampered with. I will stop at nothing to enhance my strength so I can rectify the damage and those who placed it on him before it's too late." The honesty surged through like a weighted mass of water finally bursting through its withholding gates. For better or worse, I had to tell them this. I had to let them understand what I'd truly become.

"I'm a monster and can't decipher where this iniquity ends. But what I do know is I want to protect you, this little girl, and her people, as well as my familiar, Chase." I chose to withhold the information about my encounter with the Guild. They didn't need to know about the ugly truth of what'd happened during that time. I'd already told them the worst of it, that alone was off-putting enough. "So, in answer to your question, Tori, I don't feel as if I am fit enough to lead you any longer. I'm sorry."

My mother was watching me out of her peripheral. Her golden hair was coming alive in color because of the small fire that crackled in the room. She was either judging me or acknowledging her suspicions. I'd failed myself and team as their leader. Leading them had been the one purpose I'd latched on to since the disappearance and so-called death of my mother. And now I was no longer entitled to claim that as mine. Had I simply latched on to Titan and the others in compensation to still lead?

"I want to come," Julia said adamantly.

"Absolutely not," Dillian cut her off. "You're not a fighter, Julia."

"No, but she's your good friend and the woman who came back to save your life, and then mine so we wouldn't be separated. Despite her personal issues that I honestly can't fully fathom, I will always be indebted to her."

Dillian opened his mouth as if to argue but fell short. Julia surprisingly was strong in her own ways. An oversite perhaps in the Guild. She didn't have an offensive gift, but her mentality was that of a hunter through and through—no matter how weak she seemed because of her emotions and sentimental philosophy. And I was grateful to her.

"I have to be honest with ye,' Esmore. I don't entirely understand what you're going through. But I did promise ye' mother before she left, I'd watch over ye.' And that hasn't stopped. If ye' ever start yapping ye' fangs at me, I'll break your arms and tie ye' up, okay?" Teary said, crossing her arms over her chest. "But every action I've seen ye' take even since all of this happened, has been nothing but in attempt to help us, even when I personally put myself in this predicament by choice. Ye' might have a little demon in ye,' but it doesn't mean you're bad."

I sat uncomfortably, shuffling under their weighted measure.

"I mean, it's okay for us to help our Token too, isn't it?" Tori asked the others. And Julia nodded to him in a prompting manner. "I mean, Esmore, if I'm honest it scares me a little. Because you were already badass to begin with. But after you saved our lives and brought Fam's body back, I vowed I'd follow you. You were the only one who cared about him, even when we were conditioned not to express such sentiment. No matter what, I don't think you can be all that bad."

The room felt tighter as their words lingered in the air. I couldn't calculate why they'd been so accepting, other than blind camaraderie. I turned to Dillian, expectantly. I cared most about his opinion. Like I'd often done in previous raids and personal commitments, he had once been my only council. He seemed most reluctant to speak up, wavering the importance of this moment. Out of all of them, I needed his approval the most. He was the only one I needed to hear those words from, so this haunting restrictive belief that I'd failed them would levitate if only slightly.

He stared into the fire for a moment, watching Julia as she took the boiling pot off. "I never thought there'd be a day I'd be following you with vampirism and all," Dillian admitted. And I wondered if the same had happened to him, if he had turned, would I have killed him because it was how we were made? Or would I ignore that instinct, just as he had, to protect him? "But my goal is ensuring Julia's safe. So, if you need our help to get us there, then I have no choice." I could still hear the reluctance in his tone. The others had voted, and he could still decide to stay, but he wasn't yet abandoning me or giving up on me entirely. I would have to accept his small token of acceptance today and hope that I could prove myself worthy to regain his trust fully once again. A refreshing breath filled my lungs that I hadn't known I'd been holding onto. I was finally connecting with a piece of home, of my hunter state. No matter how small the inviting hand, it was a final offering on reconnecting with my old self. I wasn't entirely gone.

Teary clasped her hands together, her firm jaw clenched as she stared at my mother and me with expectation. "Right, so what's the plan?"

# CHAPTER 12

WE WERE A unified front with our long black robes and masks. I'd taken a liking to my iconic wolf mask because it embodied the vicious nature that lies beneath. My mother had been gifted a mask that looked like a rabbit, and the others wore similar designs, embedded with laughing and crying faces, all polished in white with rosy red cheeks. Their iridescent hunter eyes glowed eerily through the eyes slits, in a way that made them seem more ominous. Tythian teleported us to the outskirts of New York. This was uncharted hunter territory, and he was reluctant to step any closer.

It was my role to feed him visuals of where we were specifically, in case we needed him to teleport us out promptly. However, we only depended on that as a last resort plan. My mother and I wanted to hide our association with the vampires as best we could. We'd only reveal it if we were in a Pidgeon hole situation. Lincon was dancing in delight, hopping from one foot to another. He appraised the hunters cordially and asked me, "Can I have these ones too?"

"No," I snapped. I was apprehensive about what mischief he might get up to if I took my eyes off him for even one second. Tythian watched him warily from the corner of his eye, displeased with the role of babysitter. It was unsettling. Not even I knew what Lincon might do to

Tythian or anyone else for that matter if he started to become irritably bored.

My sword was strapped to my back, and my Barnett crossbow was loosely hanging at my hip, in easy reach. Alongside the knives and daggers hidden within my pockets and boots, was also the sachet of Chase's mother's golden claws I'd now adopted as my own. I ejected my fangs, the euphoric release coming out with a relieved sigh. It was nice to be free in this form. My sight glazed over purple with my huntress eyes, so I wasn't mismatching in profile as we prepared to descend on the city. We were on the edge of a bridge, its infrastructure still stable after all these years. I could hear rushing water below which was effectively hidden by the density of the mist. Scattered rusted vehicles were enveloped by the thick mist on the bridge. We'd have to be cautious with delicate footing to ensure we didn't step into any rubble on the broken road.

"There shouldn't be any sabers within the city but be on your guard just in case. This Guild has used the heights of the buildings to their advantage. So be prepared for the possibility of being ambushed from up top. I'll be taking us directly to the main center, where their headhunter should be, though I doubt we'll make it that far without being confronted by one of their groups. Remain calm and let me do the talking," my mother ordered. With no questions, we unified into our formation. Dillian and Julia were to the left, Teary and Tori on the right, and I followed the rear, hoisting my Barnett crossbow into the direction of the rooftops and open windows.

There was always an eerie silence when walking through one of the old cities. It had been torn apart in the wars against humanity and its remains engrossed by nature. But there was still an unnatural liveliness in the atmosphere caused by the ghosts and lingering presence of what was once a vibrant existence. Now it was the shell remains of bombings, loitering, desperate survival, and overgrown and populated plants. The towers had eroded, and some had even begun to lean on one another in decaying support. Metal beams kept their structure intact, but it wasn't fortunate enough against the natural disasters of nature as she plagued through.

Instead of hiding in the shelter of the forest like our Guild had, they'd opted to use the grid in the city to their advantage as a maze. It was orchestrated carnage. I wondered if their human camp was somewhere within the city as well or if it was a grave distance apart just as ours had been blueprinted.

I shifted my aim to my left, distracted by a flapping curtain. It reminded me of when my raid team last infiltrated San Francisco. On that day everything had changed. I'm sure the others noted the uncanny similarity as well. It was different now only in the sense of its mission and order. My mother was leading us as I protected the rear while simultaneously feeding visuals to Tythian. Unlike Yolo, there wasn't the option of two-way telepathy with Tythian. He was adequately guarded, only allowing the smallest of cavities in his shield so I could feed him essential images. If we did need him, I'd enforce a wave of dread, that was his signal.

Lincon, however, was an open book, and instead I was on the offensive guarding against him. I didn't want to peer into his unsightly mind, and I was certain he was doing it on purpose to unnerve me. I vaguely kept tabs on him, hovering over his scattered mind in case I would have to push urgency for him to play his part, of which he was eagerly awaiting.

We hadn't venture too far into the city amongst idle streets, when my mother halted us. An oppressive presence encroached on us. A group of ten hunters walked out from a small side street, unified by khaki pants and green shirts that somewhat matched the moss ridden building they'd crept from. Four archers made their advantage point known. They aimed their bows from above, positioned in the windows. I steadied my finger on the trigger. By quick assessment, three of them were still apprentices which meant they didn't have a gift to fall back on. Easy for the pickings. An unfamiliar weight sunk in my stomach as I sincerely sized them up as an enemy.

Only my own Guild had branded me as a traitor and turned their back on me. I had to remind myself that they would do the same if they knew what was hiding behind this mask. I targeted them, my finger resting on the trigger as I waited for my mother's negotiations to begin. I'd only be forced to move my hand if they did so first. I briefed a side glance at the others, to assess how readily positioned they were to oppose their own kind if this turned sour quickly. They were guarded, with weapons raised as if this were a standard mission. They hadn't hesitated.

Julia had dipped slightly behind Dillian as he expanded himself wider to cover her from the pointed direction of the archers. He side glanced me, his pink eyes eerily commanding. Julia was his focus, and their body movement gave that away. I'd have to compensate for his small giveaways if they targeted her because of it.

Stoically my mother stepped forward, challenged by the opposing leading huntress. Teary and Tori closed in the gap at the front, making sure we were a unified front. My mother met with their leader at a halfway point. Our eyes were the only reason why they hadn't tried to take us out yet. The African American woman who approached my mother wore a black eye-patch over her left eye. I imagined she'd lost it in a fight. Her expression was hard as she spoke to my mother. I could only see the back of my mother's black hood as they spoke. She peered around my mother inspecting our group.

I waited for a signal, any signal from my mother in the moment of suspense. My finger was lightly pressed on the trigger waiting for the small tell that they were about to ambush us. The woman scrutinized us, the slight wind that settled through the street, unable to push past her bush like wild hair.

They exchanged a few more words. I slowly allowed my hand to creep over my arrows, ready to draw string on the next one. The woman raised her hand in a signal, the other members following suit to put down their weapons. Much like them we pretended to lower our weapons, entirely prepared for the second anything changed. Either side would be dimwitted to let down their guard entirely.

My mother turned her back on the woman, an undisguised invitation for the woman to attack her as she met with our group. It was a test, but also a telling that my mother entrusted her life with her team and her own capabilities.

"We've been granted entry," my mother elaborated as she took her leading position in our configuration. I didn't divert my gaze from the archers even when the group of ten encircled us as 'escorts.' The eye-patched woman who led the front whispered to one of her members. They curtly nodded and ran ahead as a messenger. A brute of a hunter with green hair that matched his eyes flanked me. The short woman on his left was stiff in posture and purposefully swung her axe back and forth playfully, in an attempt to intimidate me. The brute of a man sneered an impolite smile. Had he known what was beneath this mask he might've seen the twisted smile with fangs that dared him to continue patronizing me.

We were guided further into the depths of the unfortunate city. It was just as badly shaken as the city of San Francisco and held the same lingering presence of walking through a mass grave. However, they'd at least gone to the effort to clean the bones and remains on the paths they used. The Guild had taken station here for over one hundred years my mother said. A relatively long time to maintain a Guild post. The city was engulfed in the appeal of being abandoned, but there were pockets in the towering buildings and even below on the grids that I could see numerous stakeouts. I wondered how long it took them to be rid of the sabers who once dwelled in this city, and how often stray vampires and sabers ventured in here none the wiser. I imagined hiding in the most obvious spot would be taxing in efforts to maintain its secrecy.

We were led further into the city where towering buildings encircled us. Their intimidating size was always a spectacle to see considering how different it was to our origins. We rounded the edge of a building, making sure not to fall into the concaved path. We were awestruck by the sheer open space in front of us. I readily scanned it's every detail, looking for any immediate danger. In the center of the grand open space posed a few stalls with foods, fruits, and oddities. Surrounding the secret establishment which was evidently their main quarters were towering buildings. Hunters were peering out at us from the windows. Hunters of all ages and ethnicities slowed in their task to a near still as they watched our group being escorted to the main hall.

It was singular level, built with a marble foundation. The six white marble stairs had chipped away in chunks from erosion over the years. Its extravagance was far different from the small tower office I was often reprimanded in by Campture.

Guards were stationed at the door, begrudging the eye-patched woman who'd escorted us here. The vampire part of me thrummed in anticipation, waiting, almost pleading to test itself against these warriors. It was an entangled mix of curiosity and stupidity. Some hunters crept out of side streets, and I kept an eye on those who peered down on us from the tall building at our back. The buildings shadowed coverage, and very little light seeped through the already cloudy day as if boxing us in metaphorically. For that I was grateful, so I wouldn't have to deal with the irritable sensation of the sun.

I had a sense that their numbers far outgrew the population of our own Guild. I wondered what Dillian and Julia made of this and if it gave them a glimmer of hope of being included in their former society. But even then, once they were identified it would only be a matter of time before their treason would be found out and they'd be strung up as examples. It didn't matter how far we'd strayed from our Guild. News would travel, and Campture's claws would find their way nestled into our backs once again.

The large wooden doors opened from the inside. The guard's jaw tightened unenthusiastically that we were being permitted inside.

"An impolite greeting, I would say to their own kind," my mother coolly said as she followed the eye-patched woman.

"Coming from the group who hide their faces and enter our territory unannounced," she replied with just as much potent sass. The hunters who flanked us dispersed, positioning themselves at the bottom of the stairs. The only two who followed were the brute of a hunter and woman with axe behind me.

I measured a quick scope of the room, sourcing out the exits, threats, and abnormalities. Washed-out dirty glass acted as the roofing in what I imagined to have once been crystal clear. Now with the built-up grime and overcast weather, it sheathed most of the natural light from coming in and unnaturally illuminated the room in a foreboding gray.

In the center of the hexagon-shaped room was a low wooden table with two empty leather couches on either side. Further past that, in the back of the room, were four large wooden tables, where two huntresses sat, tinkering away with metal objects in what I assumed to be archived from the technology era. The two women peered over at us with their red eyes before being distracted by their work once again. They feigned disinterested, but the sheathed swords beside their table weren't for ornamental purposes. They were merely playing a part to seem obsolete.

"This is unusual," a hearty voice echoed through the room. From our left, walked a well-dressed man in his mid-fifties. Like his underlings, he wore khaki pants, chunky black boots, and a green shirt that fitted to his body a size too small. His black hair had flecks of silver, and his daring fluorescent blue eyes beckoned our attention. There was something different about this hunter, something suave and alluring. I blinked once and then shifted my gaze to survey the room once again. It was then that I noticed Tori and Julia ogling at him, their guard entirely down. The two were susceptible to his unnatural charm.

"It would appear the leadership has changed since I was last here," my mother ordained, unsusceptible to the hunter's entrancing effects. I refused to look him directly in the eyes. Whatever his gift was it was coaxing and more potent when he caught my gaze. Dillian, Teary, and I shared a glance, evidently concluding the same. I directed my gaze to the right, signaling that we were to grab Tori and Julia and cover them against the wall where we could protect them if something were to break out. I didn't know the extent of this hunter's ability, but I was willing to gamble it was hypnotizing in nature. My mother, however, seemed unaffected by his allure.

"Well considering I don't know who you are and how long ago you visited, I'd say it's been more than six years," his musical voice sung out. Even his tone was coaxing. I kept the two who flanked me in my peripheral view. They were circling around us. Finally, the wooden doors behind us shut with an echoing clunk. We were locked in the room with six hunters, equally matching our own group number. This was either done strategically or they were foolishly underestimating us. There was something off-putting about the setting. Something in the room felt amiss and I couldn't quite place it.

"My team and I don't come to you in hostility. We've simply come to pass on a message of warning," my mother said, her voice calm and dominant. He seemed to take an interest in her which pitted an unsettled weight in my stomach. I internally constricted my vampire self that was so quickly ready to pounce and attack. I couldn't let its wicked nature take over. I adjusted my grip slightly on my Barnett crossbow, if only to try and focus on something momentarily as I counted to ten, to calm the temptation. So sensitive was my vampire side, wanting to flash about its presence and power.

"And who are 'your' people? I don't know of any Guild's who wear masks and hoods, especially bordering in our territory unannounced."

"Simply consider us a friend."

"No friend of mine is unwilling to show their face."

"Then perhaps you are too simple to have friends so great if you can't see past a simple prop," my mother said quick-tongued.

He cocked a smile, toying with her. He was different from the other hunters I'd come across; he was charismatic, in a race that was often poised. It was disturbing to think he might've been as estranged as us and was put into the leadership of the Head Guild. He perched himself on the edge of the closest couch. His behavior reminded me somewhat of Fier's right before he was about to chuck a tantrum. That antagonizing magnetic charm in full swing before he was to rain down his fury. I felt Dillian's hand wrap around my wrist, startled by the gesture, I looked down realizing I'd curled my fists so intently I'd started to draw blood from the tips of my sharp nails. I loosened, worried that I'd crush my Barnett crossbow in the process. The thought of Fier had made me lose focus momentarily. And nothing passed Dillian's eyes.

"So tell me, what's the message you'd like to converse huntress, I'm assuming?" He charmed an antagonizing smile. He was seemingly unguarded, but I knew better than to truly believe that. He was arrogant in status, confident in his gift and team who would protect him. There was something disconcerting about this situation. I could feel the presence of something lingering and couldn't decipher if it was a part of his gift or something else entirely. His iridescent blue eyes then slid onto me with interest.

I couldn't look away, didn't want to. Unlike the initial grasp he had on me, my body had shaken from the trance he was attempting to hold over me. My vampire self-sneered at his attempt. I'd been playing mind games with Lincon and Fier for some time now, and it might've prepared me for this hunter's evasive gift. I'd fortified some kind of tolerance to the nature of these gifts and tricks.

"Then why doesn't everyone in the room reveal themselves before we continue this conversation," Dillian said, resting his gaze on the empty spot beside the charming hunter who spoke. My mother didn't turn to face Dillian, but I knew he'd grabbed her attention by the way her shoulders tensed slightly. We'd all felt it, the presence of something off-putting. And Dillian had obviously felt its distortion as well. His gift and long vision sight might've been the only spectacle to be able to see some kind of variance around whatever he was staring at.

An older man materialized behind the charismatic guard. He was propped on the couch with legs crossed, watching us. "Some interesting eyes you have there, boy." His dry voice broke as he spoke. He looked to be in his seventies, still strong and amicable, but much like Campture, his prime days were clearly past him.

"Now there's the leader I recall," my mother voiced. Perhaps she'd had suspicions he was sheltering in his invisible form this entire time. Unlike Oppollo's phantom like ability, this hunter was only able to hide his visibility because if it were any more than that, Dillian wouldn't have been able to directly spot him. Which meant, physical blows could still strike him down.

"And if I recall that voice correctly, I know exactly who you are. And if memory serves correctly, you're a ghost," he appointed.

"It's nice to know I leave such a notable impression," my mother mused not denying her identity. And for whatever reason my mother decided to lead him on with that knowledge, I had to trust in her tact. Just because she gave away her identity it didn't objectify ours.

"It's okay, Sabe. You can step down," the Head Hunter said to the man with transfixing blue eyes. He stepped to the side so we could better view his leader. The charm he'd cast on Tori and Julia dropped, and they stumbled slightly as if out of a trance. Perhaps those who were weaker were susceptible to his gift.

"Thank you, Head Hunter, Michelle," my mother said formally to greet him. "We don't plan on staying long, and once you've heard us out, we'll take our leave."

The Head Hunter, Michelle hmphed. "And what makes you think I would want to hear from the likes of you?" I refrained from reacting to his outright disrespect toward my mother.

"Curiosity at least, because you know I'm not stupid enough to come here unless it was something that'd affect our entire race."

"Or you've come to feed us ill information to benefit whatever ghastly makeshift plans you're involved with these days. You must have so much time on your hands after fleeing your duty to frolic," he said down his nose at her. The glower reminded me of Campture. Were all the Guild leaders the same?

"You can be the judge of that," my mother said impatiently. Her rabbit-like mask had a smile painted on it, though her tone was far from friendly.

Michelle surveyed us and pondered, deciphering whether he should let his guards loose on us, or hear my mother out. The eye-patch wearing woman's gaze contently fell on me. She stared as if boring her attention through my mask and watching *me*. I doubted she or any of the others could because if they had they would've attacked the moment they saw my fangs. But if they'd encountered my mother before, maybe they'd heard estranged rumors of her daughter if Campture's influence reached this far. I dipped my head slightly forward, ensuring my hood was covering most of my hair and face.

"What is this vital news?" Michelle coaxed in snobbery.

My mother ignored the tone, playing the ever-formidable role of controlled huntress. It was eerily familiar to the same way I had once been—playing the part of subordinate soldier. "We've recently encountered a new experiment the human government has been working on. A virus of sorts that's transmitted through a wolf bite. It's fatal to vampires. However, if humans are bitten, on the next full moon they turn into these wolf-like creatures. From the very little information we've acquired, they're sent out to eradicate the vampire race, and they're willing to plague as many of their own kind in the process to make it happen. Although we personally don't cater to any one human camp, I'd advise you let your Guilds know and keep an eye on your human governments to ensure they don't make such a bold move any time soon."

Silence dominated the room as Michelle sneered at my mother with building anger.

"You came to tell us about a disease and spooky story?" Sabe released a deep belly laugh. The effective look from Michelle ceased his amusement. The eye-patch wearing woman watched my mother hauntingly unamused like her fellow companion. The man and woman who were once behind me juggled their gaze back and forth amongst us as if deciding who to take out first. They didn't even try to articulate this information because they were conditioned to follow protocol so closely. Don't think. Just do as told. I prepared Lincon and Tythian just in case this uncivil conversation turned for the worse.

"And why should I believe a traitor?" Michelle asked, finally standing. He cranked his head around Sabe who was reluctant to let us have a better view of him. "That, and I've heard many other countless things." His gaze then rested on me. "Had this been a formal meeting, you might as well have walked into your own execution."

"But being as wise as you are, you're fair in judgment, which is why you don't allow yourself to be guided by such rumors," my mother replied nonchalantly. His gaze didn't leave mine. He had suspicions of who I might've been, and I wondered what rumors he might've heard. What truths and lies unsettled him most? I had only been advised about the catastrophe I could wreak havoc on the world. But little did they know I didn't even have my heart beating in my chest to accomplish such measurable tasks. Did they know of my origins? That I was half vampire as well? Or had they been told worse, more creative stories that'd been expanded by Campture who so promptly wanted to capture me and use me to her own advantage. Or for all I knew to lead me here, to this very same room, in the hope of some kind of reward for handing me in.

"I dare say you were too cocky in your judgment," Michelle spat. "Cease them." I'd already unsheathed my sword before my mother calmly raised her hand.

"I wouldn't do that if I were you," she said, her calm demeanor unnerving. I alarmed Lincon, the push that surged through him an overwhelming sense of anguish. The first push was a signal to prepare. The second was to call upon his illusions. I halted at my mother's signal, not yet descending Lincon's illusions. But a part of me greedily wanted to fight, adrenalin already pumping through my veins. I wanted to test out these hunters who looked me over with a gleaming challenge in their eyes. "Do you really want to know?" My mother prodded, and I could hear the amused challenge in her tone.

Michelle stared at her, a condoning sneer crossing over his expression.

"Head Hunter," the woman who wore the eye patch spoke up. "Another time."

I readied myself for his leading command. He wanted this fight just as much as I did. My mother seemed unperplexed and was the vision of calm. Julia snuck tightly into the crook of Dillian as best as she could. For all her strength in words, she was a liability if we fought. But I'd seen her desperately fight for Dillian once, and prayed she had the same desperate fighting spirit that was engrained in all of us. I just hoped Dillian didn't do anything stupid or lose focus in the crossfire to protect her. Teary flicked open her lighter, readying herself to erupt chaotic flames into the room.

I couldn't identify who the eye-patch wearing woman was but for whatever reason, she was voice enough to make him think better of it.

Michelle grunted in displeasure. "Let us not meet again like this huntress, and let's hope your claim holds true. You already have enough enemies seeking out the very treasure you've brought under my roof." His eyes fell back to me. There was no mistaking it, he knew who I was. He'd heard rumor of my gift, and perhaps even past that of what I truly was. But unlike Campture who would've stopped at nothing to capture us, he listened to his member's advice. "Consider this my gift to you only once."

He flicked his head up in gesture, pardoning the guards to excuse us. The eye-patched woman escorted us out, walking closely beside my mother. I reacted in displeasure, eyeing those who herded us back into the main court. I directed the others out first, lingering at the back with my mother. The eye-patched woman gestured her gaze to the roofs pointedly at the armed archers. It was a telling sign that we hadn't entirely been pardoned. It was a ruse, and for whatever reason, this huntress was helping us. My mother drifted her gaze to me. I let out a small singular cough, signaling to the others to be on guard.

I didn't want to depend on Tythian and Lincon at the first sign of hostility. As hunters, we were trained for such events, and now that we were in the open, we had a better chance of making it out on our own. The others attentively changed their stance as they continued to walk. Even Julia followed suit, though her nervousness was a sure sign to have her targeted first.

They didn't attack us in the main center. Instead, the woman with the axe and the brute of a hunter with green hair and eyes led us toward where we'd first been received. The eye-patched wearing woman was inconspicuously directing our attention to the rooftops and small alleyways where hunters began to build in numbers.

Whatever their motivation was, they didn't want this fight breaking out in their main center. Probably aware of how much damage we'd cause and the bystanders who'd be hurt in the process. Or Michelle might've been chauvinistic in protecting his reputation to not turn on his own kind.

But my blood began to pound and thrum in excitement. These were hunters, people of my own make and kind, and yet my vampire self danced in delight, ready to let loose on them. Before I could rein in the overpowering shallowness of my anticipated victory—trying to focus on what was important, being the mission—the first arrow shot toward us and the hunters who lead us out of the city slung out their weapons and geared toward Teary and Tori on the frontal position.

I glided with ease, encircling the group and guarding Julia, who was already flanked by Dillian. I swiped my sword across two arrows, splintering and redirecting them to the side. I shot two in return. Both of which hit home, sending the screaming archers over the building to plummet to their deaths. Teary's flames erupted into a protective circle. The heat sweltered an immediate sweaty response. It gave us a moment to regroup.

"You three out," I instructed Tori, Dillian, and Julia. "Teary flank them." Julia and Tori were a liability. And the closer we got further out to the edge, the faster I'd be able to request Tythian to teleport them without eyewitnesses. Selfishly, I wanted Dillian to stay by my side and fight like we always had, but with Julia here as well he'd only be a liability.

The bulky hunter jumped through the flames, his skin peeling away effortlessly as it healed at an alarming speed. Teary met him head-on, her sword wrapped in flames as he clanked his sword against hers. She flicked him off and sliced through his arm easily, decapitating it, but just as quickly threads bundled it back to his body, re-attaching itself. He'd used it as a decoy throwing a knife aimed for her collar bone. She barely dodged it, the sharp piece slicing her arm. She jumped back, flanking the three who I'd instructed to move ahead.

Dillian was yelling and pulling at Tori, who seemed reluctant to leave us behind. My mother was fighting the woman who wore an eye-patch. I shot another three archers in the windows, aware of the ten hunters who now encircled us. The woman with an axe ganged up on Teary who lavishly swept her flames to keep her at bay. The woman flipped back, trying to reassess how to pass through them. The only one daring enough to engage with her head on was the brute of a hunter who seemed excited by the new challenge.

Teary crafted a large cascading firewall stretching over the street and between the buildings, allowing time for the others to run ahead. Confidently, Teary managed multi-tasking the erect wall and delaying the bulkier hunter for long enough while my mother and I sorted out the rest. Her beautiful, flamed wall acted as a barricade, preventing the others from being able to look back. A tainted smile stretched over my fangs. Now that the others couldn't see, I really could have some fun.

My mother was pre-occupied by the woman with an eye-patch who seemed to match her equally. Whenever others would intervene in their fight, the woman seemed to back off if only slightly. I didn't miss the detail. For whatever reason, she wasn't striking at my mother to kill her. And while my mother toyed with them, I was able to have my own fun, where no rules applied. They attacked us first. An uncharacteristic giggle crept out of me.

A hunter jumped out at me, his sword clambering to the ground by an unforeseen amassed strength. I sidestepped it. As soon as the tip of the sword brushed past me and tipped the ground, the cement obliterated. It wavered my footing slightly. *What a sweet gift. Such a shame it was too slow.* I pulled a dagger out of my garter and drove it deep into his thigh. He screamed as I wedged it into his muscle and hammered hard into bone, fracturing his hip. I rolled to the side once again, dodging the woman with an axe who now targeted me. I swept my feet around her ankles, buckling her over. As I rolled over, grappling a chokehold around her throat, I harpooned my sword into the chest of my former opponent when he tried to stand. He silently fell to his death with the low thud of my sword bearing true in its aim. The woman used my changed weight after throwing the sword to keel me over. She broke my grip and swung her axe, the clatter of it so defiantly hitting the cement in a desperate act to put distance between us. She groveled to stand. I flipped myself over and ran over to the man to reef out my treasured sword. I froze with my hand on the hilt, the blood inflating inside of my nose like a tempting treat. It ensnared me into a trance that promised delicious reward. The color of his blood was mesmerizing as it spread throughout his chest, his body desperately seizing and clotting. It could be mine—all of it.

An arrow swept past me, catching me off guard. I stumbled back, flicking out my cape, irritated by the way the arrow had caught in it. I reefed out a fresh arrow on my back and aimed my Barnett crossbow into the direction it came from, returning the favor. My mother had already knocked four unconscious, none of which were fatal blows. I realized she was holding back and a hiccup of pause seized my system. Should I be doing the same?

The pavement twisted up and around my ankles as a hunter manipulated the cement. I locked eyes with a beautiful huntress as she fixated on my capture. It twisted my ankle awkwardly, solidifying my leg into place. A robed and masked figure dashed behind her. They twisted her arms back and kneed her in the back. Slowly and cruelly, they extended their leg out, slowly but surely breaking both her arms. A defiant snap and pop entangled with her screams and the pavement that once fortified around my ankles fell away into its original form, freeing me.

I gazed into those familiar coral eyes of the twins. It wasn't Kora nor Kasey. No, this was Lincon amusing himself and alluding as a hunter. And though a rational part of me knew this was bad, and I might not be able to stop him during a rampage, an excited part of my darkness delved into the mischief and onslaught we might entertain together.

Lincon dashed through them swiftly, adhering to the guidelines of attempting to be at a hunter's average level. Though we could match vampires in most senses, our edge was our gifts. For any aged vampire, our strength and speed were lacking.

Three hunters encircled me, their abilities working in unison, as they attempted to land a hit on me. A miasma like smoke puffed around one of their fists striking for my face. I avoided it and enjoyed gliding my sword behind the knees of his companion. My hood pillowed around me, getting in the way at times so I couldn't see the aftermath of my results and landing strikes.

In my peripheral, a hunter was clambering into his belt for a blade, so he could aim at my mother's back. I swiftly pulled out my own dagger and threw it, dead center into the middle of his head. Lincon's eyes drifted from the dead hunter and threw his hands in the air. I'd obviously taken his next prey so he moved on to the next.

Teary's shriek snapped me to attention. With frightful speed, I ran to her aid, fortunate that her flames had dropped so I wouldn't be caught in them. The bulked man had her nestled in a chokehold, ready to bring down a knife. I slammed a wave of stricken fear into him. His mouth went agape as I manipulated his thoughts and pounced on him, bringing my sword across his face. The huntress with an axe barged him out of the way, so only his ear was amputated.

A swirl of miasma coaxed me, choking my airway. The hunter from behind advanced on me, and an array of trembles took over my body. I began convulsing as the estranged toxicity ran through me. Lincon gleefully swiveled through the hunters who turned on him, targeting the hunter who was poisoning me. A strong wind forcefully blew back our hoods, our masks holding strong as a new hunter approached from the sidelines. Lincon was blasted back. I dipped further to the ground solidifying myself into a ball, so I wouldn't so easily be pulled back by the winds. Teary gritted her teeth as her feet dragged back beneath her. Her flames flickered into near nothing as she tried to oppose the element's strength. I tried to grab hold of her, but she was thrown further back. My mother latched onto her instead, swinging her into one of the small alleyways that were blocked by the buildings.

An arrow shot from the rooftop, puncturing the hunter's shoulder from behind. His arm flung out, wavering his control of the wind. I pushed through the sweltering toxicity that clutched my body. I dragged myself into standing to advance on the hunter who controlled the wind. I curled my hands around his shoulder and pivoted him into a strong whirl, releasing him to splat against the wall. The defiant smack knocked him unconscious. But that wasn't enough for Lincon who pounced on his back, gliding a knife across his throat. I couldn't see his expression but felt the slow edged pleasure he tasted as he threaded the blade inch by inch.

I searched the rooftop for our savior. Dillian continued fasting his bow and shooting, never missing. His aim was more accurate with his gift, his keen sight a perfect balance for any long-distance fighter. Tythian had obviously already teleported the others. I took a wobbly step. The poison was still undeniably bubbling and thriving in my bloodstream. I growled angrily, pissed off that my body wasn't moving as I commanded it. Everything frenzied, my arms and legs included.

Flames overlapped behind us as Teary took the opportunity to erect another wall. My mother, Teary, and Lincon ran toward me, the flaming wall following her as others jumped behind the buildings to evade its potent burn. The brute of a hunter who had the ability to string his body together advanced on me, unperplexed by the flaming wall advancing on him. The woman with the axe and the one who poisoned me ran to the side, using the buildings as coverage.

I smashed the intensity of feverish illness into the bulky hunter, hoping it impacted him the same way I felt. Immobile and gritting against my own body. He took another step forward, pushing through my manipulation. I wobbled to stand, reaching for another arrow in my quiver but my body would barely move to my command. My vampire self thrashed back and forth within me furiously. Instead, I steadied with my sword still weakly holding it, preparing for when he reached me. The only way to kill him would be decapitation or piercing his heart.

A flamed wall slithered between us as a distraction as my mother grabbed my hand and dragged me into my first few steps to get the body moving. Realizing my legs were sluggish she hooked me over her shoulder. Lincon hooked under my other shoulder, and they began to race us through the city. Teary's erected wall steadied behind us as Dillian tracked us on the rooftops, jumping from each one to match our pace. The bulkier hunter had been held up in some way, but I couldn't see past the flames.

On the final building, Dillian jumped and soared through the breeze, when he jumped down from the four-story building the impact buckled his knees. Teary was already there helping him, dragging him to his feet and helping him stretch into the next few steps. As we rounded the corner, Tythian was there, waiting and not at all pleased. Teary tore her flames around us in case anyone could see the assistance we were accepting from a vampire. And then in the middle of the city—we vanished.

# CHAPTER 13

"BUGGER ME DEAD," Teary said out of breath as we plummeted in front of the cottage. Tythian had handled us so roughly that we'd all uncomfortably fallen. His blue eyes stared down on me, revolted by the necessity of his intervention. If it hadn't been for Cesar's orders he might've left us on our own. He bunched up Lincon's robe by the shoulder and teleported them out. Lincon's complaints vanished into thin air.

My body shook, my system overridden with a foreign toxicity it was fighting off. I tapped my throat, desperate to breathe. Dillian hunched me over, reefing my mask off. He was startled by my fangs, not having braced himself. I coughed, a splatter of blood coating his neck.

"Move," my mother said in her eerily calm tone, and pushed the wide-eyed Dillian to the side. "She'd heal of her own accord eventually, but let's speed up the process. Tori, look at Teary's shoulder," my mother ordered. Julia dropped beside Dillian, draping her arms over him in comfort as he watched on.

"It's fine." Teary slapped away Tori's hand. She had blemished and bruised marks around her neck from where she'd been choked, and blood was dripping down her shoulder. Her robe was tattered and torn.

It would eventually heal, but her pride would get in the way of receiving medical attention. She'd always been one to enjoy the pain and recoup process, to remind herself she had to be better on the next mission.

My mother loosened my robe and grabbed my arm, the connectivity with her gift in full effect. My blood felt like it was boiling as she tried to push the toxicity out. I snarled and lunged to attack her in response, but she pushed me back down firmly with her other hand and requested Teary's assistance to hold me down. Teary shoved her full force down on my shoulders, pushing me to the ground. Tori grabbed my legs as I thrashed back and forth trying to escape my mother's grasp desperately. I snarled and choked as my insides felt like they were boiling, fighting off my mother's intrusion as the toxins tried to thrive.

"Sweetie, I'm going to put you to sleep," my mother said in a surprisingly endearing tone that was so rarely used. I thrashed my head back and forth, not wanting to be put under. I could do this myself. I could… my eyes began to feel heavy; my body being over swept in a drowsy wonder.

*The city was inexcusably cold. A drift passed through pushing my unbound golden hair over my face. Slowly the pain began to fade in rhythmic waves. I felt tired and heavy. Pointed aches stapled and bound my body. I was in New York again. My thick dry eyelids could hardly stay open. My head rolled to my right heavily. My fingers twitched slightly as I noticed the nail embedded into my wrist that stapled me to the building. My other arm mirrored the same. My legs and stomach had been impaled to the wall in the same vile way so I couldn't move. The sound of my own choking breath caught me off guard. My gasps were desperate to flare my lungs into a rhythmic state once again. Instead, sharp spurts of air crashed in waves.*

*I raised my face up inch by inch. My stomach dropped as I looked across the center. On the opposing building, Dillian had been anchored in the same fashion. I tried to rasp out his name, but nothing escaped my mouth. I licked my lips, raw sandpaper texture brushing over them to only make them worse as we'd been strung out in the midst of the hot day. There were no clouds, only sweltering heat, and yet it was eerily cold. To his left, Teary had been pegged. Then Tori, Julia, and my mother strung up in order.*

*My body anguished as a lone cloaked figure walked down the street. They flicked a rock to catch and repeat. He was whistling a melodic tune, admiring his handy work. A loud gasp had my head twisting painfully to my left. Anguish and fear buckled me heavier into the nails as I tried to tug out of them. Chase. His black hair was covering his face as he hunched forward. I could make out the tips of his saber-like fangs. Tattered black wings were nailed to the side of the building alongside him. The wings that mirrored my own, the Descendant. I tried to reach out to his mind, but there was no response—only a thorny wall between us. The disease had taken hold of him and broken our fluid and nurturing connection.*

*My gaze rolled to the figure who was now looking up at me with interest. I couldn't make out any features of his face, it was a blur of darkness, nothing more than a cloaked figure here to paint my nightmares.*

*It pointed in the direction of a towering clock at the end of the street. It had been broken and shattered for years. "Tick, tock," they said. And the loud churning cry of a bell began echoing through the city.*

My eyes fluttered open. The roofing of the cottage was underwhelming in comparison to the open sky I'd just been suffering under in my dreams. I propped myself up feeling lousy and my body heavy but other than that, fine. My body wouldn't take long to heal from the toxins that were once raging. Julia was sitting beside me, a damp cloth in her hand.

"Oh, you're awake," she said, startled. Teary and Tori were resting in the corner of the room. Everyone had since removed their masks and robes. Julia went to dampen the cloth on my forehead once again, but I stopped her.

"That's not necessary," I said, irritated that I looked so pathetic in front of the others. Neither my mother nor Dillian was inside. "Where are the others?"

"Dillian's chopping wood and your mom said something about scoping out the area to place the wolf people," Tori replied.

"Ye got to give them another name, Esmore, wolf people just sounds, I don't know, tacky," Teary teased, trying to make light of the situation we were in. I had been their former Token, and yet here I was pathetically being cared for. I stood up, finding my balance easily. Looking at Teary's still raw throat and oozing cut, I gauged I hadn't been unconscious for too long. A couple of minutes at most. I touched my face, blotches of blood moist on my fingertips from where I'd coughed on Dillian. No, it hadn't been much time at all.

I left the others to tend to their wounds inside as I opened the pelt to the cottage and found Dillian chopping wood. His black hair was messily tied back as his pink eyes concentrated on his next strike. He knew I was there, watching him. When the piece splintered into two and he threw them to the side pile where an amounted mass would last them for months, I asked, "Don't you think that wood will last you a few months?" It was probably one of the few physical tasks they had to keep busy with while here to keep them distracted from the waiting game they had to play. He licked his lips and looked up at me, with underlying irritation though he tried to hide it.

"In case you missed it, during your fight, your mother and the woman with an eye-patch exchanged a note. So it would seem your mother is dealing with more plans than she might've been honest about, not that you were probably able to see that considering your state."

"What is that supposed to mean?" I asked uptightly. I tried to piece together what my mother's ulterior motives might've been. I examined the blows my mother and the huntress had exchanged. Her fighting was seemingly more of a distraction than fatal ambitious blows to my mother. My mother hadn't been fighting her to her full potential either. And if she'd used us in some kind of way to achieve a secret objective... I'd talk with her about it later.

"Can you still die? I've never seen you in bad shape like that before?" he asked stoically. His pink eyes were fierce on me as if he were shaking me physically for answers. I'd looked weak to him, vulnerable even. My fangs had retracted in my sleep, and my purple haze of my vision vanished. Now I was simply me, the origin of the Token he once knew. But a lesser version.

"I would've been fine. The part that makes me vampire means I heal faster." I shrugged and leaned against the cottage.

"But you can still die?" he confirmed. When I didn't reply, he scoffed and picked up another piece of wood to chop.

"It would be very difficult to kill me," I admitted. Oppollo had once plunged his grimy hands into my chest and found nothing. It was my mother's gift that kept me alive, replacing it with a temporary heart. Though if I were to be decapitated, then that would be an entirely different story.

"You know what! You thinking you're all badass and immortal has made you sloppy," he warranted.

"Excuse me?" I said, narrowing my gaze on him and crossing my arms. "Watch your tone."

"Or what, Esmore, you're going to threaten me? Chop me up? Eat me?" I sneered at the last comment, and he dropped his head in shame. "You throw yourself so easily into the fight without a care in the world. I watched you back there, it's as if you don't even care what happens to you anymore. That, or you have no control over your vampirism because that fighter out there wasn't the one I used to follow. You were sloppy and steered by reaction, not action."

I pushed off the cottage. "What, you think you're all noble because you're still a hunter? Because I'm something so ugly and mutilated that I can't fight anymore?"

"That's not what I'm saying," he muttered as he threw the axe over his shoulder, weary as I advanced on him.

"Then what are you trying to say?"

"I've made it very clear what I'm saying," he tempered.

"That you can't accept me because of the monster I've become?"

"That's your insecurity. I'm pissed off because my best friend just purposefully put herself in harm's way with little remorse for the consequence yet again. I've watched you do stupid things too many times."

"And they've always been to protect you and the team!" I spat back, infuriated.

"That wasn't for us or our team back there, Esmore. That was all for you!" he shouted over the top of me. I sneered at him and his daring insults. How could he! My mother's hand clambered down on my shoulder, jolting me in surprise. I'd become so wound up in my argument with Dillian that I hadn't even noticed her sneak up on me.

"I think it's time we start discussing relocating the wolves?" Her tone was warning me to stop. My fangs had slipped in fury, and my eyes were hazed in purple. I turned away from Dillian, so he couldn't see how quickly I now lost my temper. Shameful, especially when it exemplified all the points he'd just made.

I shrugged my mother's hand off, still irritated that she'd put me to sleep against my will. If I'd stayed awake, I wouldn't have to worry about evoking that figure which waited for me in the shadows of my rest. He was waiting there, always, his presence undeniable in strength, and always lingering, waiting to distort my memories or craft new ones that felt real.

The image of hunters staked to the side of buildings vividly crept back to mind. I wanted to swipe it away, but there was a lurching urgency in it. What if that happened and I wasn't there to stop it. What if Dillian was right, because of how I was now, I was a pointless fighter, losing my articulation and clever wit and giving in to this greedy side of me that forfeited its right to lead anyone.

But there was a bitter part of me that felt denied and rejected by him and even the others. They had no idea what I'd had to deal with the last few months, and though it made no difference, if they'd seen the things that I had or been corrupted in the same light, I'd dare them to come out a better woman for it.

"Fine," I gritted out to my mother, fortunate enough to have a break from them. I didn't need to prove myself to any of them. I just needed to make sure I could keep them alive long enough until I found a place where they'd be safeguarded. Then after that… well maybe these were the last few times we'd have together. Maybe after that they'd continue leading a normal hunter life as best as they could in a way they could shape themselves. And me… I would still be in the shadows, scurrying around for wild animals to feast on and trying to put this trembling war to a stop, if only long enough to stabilize my familiar. They didn't know what was at stake for me, so maybe I was going slightly wired and off-grid. But I certainly didn't have to justify myself to them. However, it didn't lessen the weight that pitted in my stomach. It still didn't feel right.

I shrugged out of my mother's hold, irritated by her as well. She lied to me, using all of us so she could pass a lovely little note to that huntress. With perfect timing, I felt Tythian appear in the forest. I walked to him, ready to return to the institute. I don't know why I thought it was such a good idea to come in the first place.

My mother lingered, and I could hear her say to Dillian, "She'll come around." I tried to ignore her, irritated that they were conspiring against me. A small fracture began in my logical thinking. My one true purpose I clung to was ensuring their safety, and yet the darker, more coaxing self, permitted me that it wasn't up to me to save them. That in fact, I could do anything I wanted, especially if they didn't care for my help. I shook the thought away. That wasn't me talking, no matter how angry I was with the others. I wanted to protect them. But it didn't mean I couldn't be mad at them.

# CHAPTER 14

A SCUTTLE OF noises grabbed my attention as I waltzed into the hallway, infuriated. On my right engrossing moans and groans were echoing into the hall, grabbing my attention. Only a few of Chase's coven members were sitting in the main hall room, so peculiar to the usual mass who waited for his order. I sensed my mother walking in the direction of the wolves and Yolo. I couldn't face any of them in my current state. I irritably had to admit to myself that even I was limited to such righteousness. I had to calm down.

"I wouldn't go in there if I were you," Clarissa called out, steering me into the direction of the stairs. Spungee was in the corner of the room beside the staircase, playing with a broken branch he must've dragged from outside. She was flicking underneath her nail, what appeared to be old dry blood. A small chunk of her hair was matted in the same substance. She'd obviously had her delicacy of the humans they'd been trafficking through here. Her black dress seemed untouched, always surprisingly clean considering her coven's living state. Another groan from behind the door captured my attention.

"Why?" I asked curiously. I could feel Chase's tug, summoning me. I also felt Fire's restlessness as she no doubt wanted to bust through the door to race to my side.

"You've pent up two covens of vampires, who hardly sleep and have energy and time to spend. What do you think they're doing in there, braiding one another's hair?" she asked with dry mannerism. "Though you do seem young, perhaps you're unaware of the fun play when it comes to an orgy."

I charmed a snake-like smile in return. "I seem to have plenty of fun to appease your coven leader."

"Until he gets bored. Don't think just because you're his familiar that in a hundred years you'll still be able to satisfy him alone."

I snapped, the last of my patience broken. I wrapped my hand around her throat wanting to ring the life from her. I wanted to see her beg for forgiveness to appease this anger inside of me that I couldn't entirely understand. She did nothing and simply stared at me with those doe eyes of hers that never really replicated any form of life. I slammed her into the wall, wringing her neck, trying to rattle her to action. Her inaction was making me even more furious.

"This world is new to you, heightened in all your senses," she said in a tightened monotone. "Give it time, it'll wear you down," she reproached her true meaning. Spungee cowered as he clicked forward, slowly trying to step in between us cautiously. He cowered on her behalf, his eyes wide and scared as he tried to aid his master in whatever way he could. Spungee's existence was a reminder of Sydney every time. And I felt a resemblance to Clarissa if Chase hadn't freed me from that path. I would've been worn down in the same way if I'd been anchored in such a way.

A few of Cesar's coven members were sniping remarks from across the room, encouraging me to rip off her head. I considered it, to appease my own anger but it wasn't because of Clarissa. No, she had very little to do with the emotions. And I certainly wasn't going to be pleasing Cesar's men anytime soon by giving them a show. I released my grip around her throat, still not entirely understanding Clarissa's motive to follow Chase. I eyed her, daring her to say something else. She thought better of it. My lip curled bitterly as I turned away from her and walked along the invisible line the gargoyles barricaded.

Chase met me atop the stairs and swept his gaze over my blood-soaked attire. My face was still dirty with blood, of which he'd know some was mine. My hands and neck were coated in hunter blood. His shoulders slumped. *Guess it didn't go so well then?* he asked politely.

I shrugged, plodding up the stairs. *It went as best as it could.* Fire ran down the stairs to greet me excitedly. It was hard to believe she was a wild wolf considering how she acted indoors. I had to remind myself of the viciousness in how she attacked the humans who'd stepped into our territory, that cardinal beast she'd feverishly turned into. And right now, just like my familiar, she was lapping up for attention and pats.

Chase offered his hand out to me, amused by my comparison. As I looked up, I noted how glorious he looked in his open jacket where his beautifully chiseled stomach was on full display, the dim lighting hitting his muscles superbly. I'd never grow tired of devouring him, and the prickle of Clarissa's words had set doubt. But would he ever tire of me? Was forever too long of a time, even for familiars?

"Are you okay?" he asked. I opened my mind to him freely, sharing the events of the day with full transparency of the hunter who poisoned me, knowing he wouldn't like it. He grimaced. "Let's get you cleaned up," he offered. As soon as my hands touched his, I felt a wash of fatigue run over me. I wasn't sure if it was me or him who felt the strain, but it was equaled out in measure as soon as we were together. He led me towards Cesar's wing, of which I was surprised he was permitted to enter. He casually led me into a private chamber. A claw bathtub sat idly under a large bay window with a small bucket beside it where I imagined they'd manually poured in water. Glass littered the ground, the window having shattered over the years. Chase raced around the room, quickly flaring a few candles alight with a match.

"You organized me a bath?" I asked, feeling even more depleted from the day and undeserving after Dillian's quip. Unlike the others here, I wasn't fully vampire which meant even I needed some kind of rest. It was a shame that when I did, I'd be greeted by another prisoner who toyed with my mind. The bath beckoned me in a way I thought was spoilt. I could feel the heat of it from here. He'd even boiled water, not that temperature control was an issue for either of us. But the wholesome act seemed considerate.

"I would give you the world and more, Esmore." He was stealing us another moment in time. It felt like these pockets of time were scarcely going to evaporate. The vivid memory of him being nailed to the wall beside me, in his saber-like form with his matted Descendant wings pinned unflinching, wounded me. What if that were real? What if I didn't make it in time to save him?

"I'm not going anywhere," he promised with a gentle kiss to my forehead. *You and I are in this together, remember?* he said in the most intimate of ways as he caressed our telepathic link and bundled me in a reassuring hug. Every wrong I might've done, or every fail I felt, I was reassured in Chase's arms. And I desperately had to find a way to defeat Oppollo so Fier wouldn't take him away from me. Today I had turned against my own again, and it felt like another punishment and damnation in my life as a vampire. It felt like the chance of retribution was slipping away and I didn't even know if it was something I was worthy of having anymore. This was my path, and the tethers of morals and justice were the only things holding me back from permanently claiming this power.

"Let's get clean," Chase cooed, pulling my sleeveless leather shirt over my head. As he reached for my pants, the hook of the small sachet drew his attention. "Oh," I said, forgetting that I hadn't yet spoken to him about his mother's claws. "Clarissa gave these to me. They were your mother's, apparently. Is this okay?" He twisted a sad smile.

"Who knew this whole time she had them. It's a crazy small world, huh?" He bundled the satchel in his hands and helped me take my pants off, not admiring my body in his usual sexual glower but in the way of someone who needed nurturing and love. I wasn't feeling my glorious self today, but the monster I'd become was truly and cruelly showing itself. I pushed back his leather jacket to the floor and assisted him with his belt as he guided his own pants off. Here we were, both naked, in the dim afternoon light, aware of one another's sins and raw vulnerability.

"Confession, I'm disappointed I couldn't find anything to create bubbles," he glowered. I shook my head with slight amusement in his attempt to lighten the mood. I followed his lead into the bathtub. I rested my back against his chest, lying on top of him as if he were my own personal warm blanket. He still held onto his mother's satchel, twisting it back and forth in thought. Fire laid by the door, uninterested.

"Do you want to talk about it?" he asked while unbinding my golden plait. I enjoyed the feeling of his fingers brushing through my hair and massaging my scalp.

"There's not much to talk about." I drifted wearily, lost in the touch of his fingers. I could feel his mind nudge against mine as if calling me out on my lie. He leaned over the edge of the claw bath, collecting a cloth and bar of soap from the bucket. He placed his mother's pouch down carefully beside the bucket. The gentle shift in his weight brushing his prominent muscles against my back.

"Dillian might've had a point, maybe you are being slightly reckless in your approaches."

I huffed in response, irritated that he sided with Dillian. He tugged the back of my hair lightly. "Hey, none of that," he said in his chipper tone, that I couldn't be angry with. "You know it's only voiced out of concern." He began to lather the soap into my hair, his strong fingers massaging my scalp in perfected motions. I moaned in bliss and could feel his cock twitch beneath me in response. I curved a promiscuous smile, delighted by the way he responded to me, even when he had no intentions of perfuming the room with sexual tension—yet.

I eased into him, depleting my simmering thoughts and feelings of being betrayed by my own kind. But I only had myself to blame. Dillian had always been honest with me, but I'd never seen him so angry like that, especially toward me.

"I don't know what I'm doing anymore," I admitted out loud. Chase could sense all doubts and moral uncertainty in some of the actions that I'd participated in. Some I had thought were essential, others I wasn't proud of. I didn't regret any of it though because it meant I wouldn't be here with him, but it hadn't come without its challenges. It felt as if some kind of mass power was trying to prevent our being together.

"That's kind of poetic in a way though, wouldn't you say?" he teased, pressing a gentle kiss to my shoulder before rubbing over it with cloth and soap. "And we're in this for the long haul, wifey."

I charmed a smile at how he took pleasure in calling me his wife. "Husband," I purred back, enjoying the blissful pleasure I felt beam down our connection.

"Let's not talk about today?" I rhetorically asked. All we were ever doing was planning, and it was Chase who was teaching me to indulge in these moments. Every moment we were together felt like stolen time because it was equally wasted time when I should be finding him a cure. I should be transpiring a way to extinguish Oppollo out of this world.

He yanked on my hair again. "I thought we weren't going to talk about hot and heavy." It was Chase, all of him that could unbind me in such a way. The calmness he swept through our bond, constantly brushing out the clutching knots preventing me from seeing and scheming with a clear mindset.

I peered over to the satchel on the ground. "Tell me about your mother," I said, changing topic.

"I'm in the bathtub, butt ass naked with the woman I think dirty thoughts about every waking minute, and you want me to talk about my mother?" Chase teased. I squeezed his thigh painfully hard, and he laughed. "Okay, okay."

I charmed a smile, easing back into him. He rolled the cloth over my shoulders and between my blades in small rhythmic circles.

"My mother would've liked you, in that hardcore, like to challenge you kind of way." He heatedly laughed. "Your mother reminds me a bit of her actually. In the sense that you know she has your back and loves you dearly, but will kick your ass if you do something stupid."

"My mother wouldn't fight me," I said honestly. We'd sparred in training. But we'd never fought even if we'd differed in opinion, it'd never turn into a physical confrontation.

"That's why I said kind of similar. I vaguely remember her when I was a child, and before she'd been turned. She was kind and nurturing. And against all odds even when she had been turned she protected me, but vampirism is a funny thing. It makes you a shell of what you truly were, devoid of the bright light. That's all I remember about my mother before she was changed." I stared at the ceiling, noticing the change in his tone. His humor was relinquishing to a sad lingering pain. I twisted in his lap to face him.

"You're not devoid of light," I answered his unspoken question. He flashed a small smile and began wiping away the grime and blood from my face.

"I know. But my mother had been. It was a barrage of events from the moment that vampire came into our life until he turned her. She became maddened with protecting me from them. And so, everything that derived from there was focused on acquiring more power. It wasn't until she crossed paths with Fier that she opened up to anyone's aid. At that point, it had only been me and her, and then…" I could sense his loneliness, in the way he couldn't articulate into words.

"And then it was Fier and her. And you were alone." His beautiful gray eyes watched me as if memorizing this moment and image. Like I, too, might leave him.

"I'm not going anywhere," I said, pressing my hand to his jaw. I collected the cloth from his hands, wanting to return the favor in the same nurturing measure. To show him in action and not words that I was here for him in every way. We held the same insecurities. Being alone in this miserable life. I sat up properly and turned in the bathtub to sit and face him. The water swished over the edges. We stared at one another, vulnerably and quiet. Sometimes things couldn't be presented in words, but the silent presence was enough to know we were there for one another. Entirely and forever. Relaying that message in the most intimate of ways as we spoke through our gaze. Everything we did, was for one another. And our own being was entirely attached to that outcome. Without one another, we'd be nothing. There would be no point. I began washing over his hard chest.

"I know that," he replied, watching my hand swirl on his chest intimately as I lathered the soap. "It's kind of ironic because between my mother and me, I thought perhaps I was the only one who still had morals or emotion of which I locked away for a very long time. That was until the Descendant took over and Tythian and her stopped at nothing to bring me back. Obviously, I didn't know about Tythian's association with Cesar's coven at the time. But either way, I'm grateful. It allowed me to see a desperate side to my mother, one that had stopped at nothing to bring the remains of her son back.

She'd always been so charming. Her and Fier were so fitted for one another in so many ways. They were able to charm and coax anyone into doing their bidding. There was a time there that we held no innocence. It's nice to be good for once, for you, Esmore. If you'd seen the things I'd done, I'm not so certain you'd look at me so lovingly."

My hand stopped running circles over his chest. I had for so long been caring about my judgment day and my worthiness of having Chase. Of having it all, power, safety for those I cared about, and a light at the end of the day where I wouldn't have to fear what might come next. And all along as I was trying to hide my demons from him, that he was so willingly accepting of, he was covering his own.

"There is nothing you could do that would make me turn away from you. Nothing," I promised him. His sad lopsided smile antagonized me to say more, to prove to him that I was serious. He ruffled his hair, distracting himself from the merit of his story and returning to his goofy self.

"But yea, she wasn't necessarily good. We wreaked a lot of havoc before we were even in a Council and so you could imagine the carnage of when we were entitled with authority in one. Those golden claws have sent a lot of victims to meet their maker. So I only find it fitting that you've acquired them. Hell has no wrath like a woman's fury," he joked.

I charmed a smile, suggesting that he sit on the edge of the bath, so I could wash his legs. He gave me a coy smile but still did as he was told. The water sank as he stretched himself over the edge of the bath. His semi-hard cock was at my eye-level. I tried to hide my smile, attempting to act indifferently. I rubbed the soap over his muscular thighs, running the wet cloth down his calves. Goosebumps ran down the trail as his cock twitched harder at my sensual touches.

"Do you ever regret leaving the Council?" I asked, moving to his next leg, trying my hardest not to be distracted by his cock that engrossed me so much.

"Never. Because if I were still there, then I wouldn't be here with you," he said. I looked up through my thick eyelashes. He was earnest. Sexy as hell. Fully erect and completely mine. I shifted only slightly, the water pooling around me as I did. I collected his hand, guiding his calloused fingers to branch through my wet hair.

I charmed a wicked smile. And so, I would show Chase, in ways that went beyond words, my action that would quench his insecurity and that I was here to stay. To be by his side as an equal, to serve him as a lover, and face whatever we had together head-on. I poked out my tongue, raking it up his hard shaft, shuddering at its delicate taste that aroused me. I could smell and savor his arousal, purely masculine and erect.

"Jesus, Esmore," he whispered as I teased him with my tongue lapping around the tip. I crawled closer again, the water splashing around my naked and feverish body. His grip firmed in my hair when I pursed my lips around his thick cock and pressed down hard, devouring as much of him as I could. His head pulled back with a hiss, and I bubbled with awakening, ready to please Chase in the only way I could. And so, I offered him pain, pleasure, and release in all the ways that his body begged me for. Because I understood Chase and his desires. And I wanted to lick every attentive part of his body, relieving my own stress in the process. I made my claim, over and over again.

# CHAPTER 15

C HASE AND I had been entangled in our own bubble of pleasure and rest, unbeknownst of what the outside world was doing. When we left the bathroom, I stopped dead in my tracks the moment I peered down the hall and saw Lincon exiting Cesar's room. He devilishly smiled at me, in the way that he often did when trying to encourage a question or response out of me.

My mother walked out behind him, leaving Cesar alone in his chambers. I purposefully kept an unreadable expression as Lincon walked past smugly, playing his little games. For what reason would those three need to be discussing things behind closed doors?

Fire growled at Lincon as he sauntered off. I brushed the tips of my fingers through her fur lightly, calming her. When my mother approached me, I conveyed my irritation effortlessly, especially after she'd exchanged a note with one of the members of the Hunter Guild who'd attacked us. "What could you possibly need to discuss with Lincon behind closed doors?" I asked. My mother raised an eyebrow in challenge at my tone.

"Not all things belong to you, Esmore. You already have enough to deal with, and we have our own," my mother reprimanded. She handed me the stuffed teddy I'd collected from the Human Compound and gave it to me fully stitched. "And remember that the things I do for you, even the conversations I don't have to tell you about, are in your best interest."

I gritted my teeth. "Like when you abandoned me at the Guild, that was what was best right?" It was a childish dig but one that was still raw and taxing on our relationship. Her secrecy had jeopardized my safety when she thought it was 'best' for me.

"I'm not going to continue going over this with you, Esmore. I told you I was sorry, and I believe it was the right thing to do at that time. As you have done and made decisions for others leading up until now—I had to do the same."

Chase tugged on my mind, halting me from riling and seething my rage on her.

*Your mother loves you,* he endeared. I felt ganged up on as if I were being reprimanded for being indignant. Why was everyone reprimanding me as of late? It felt lately no matter what I did, it wasn't enough. And others were starting to call me out on those fragmenting pieces.

"I'm returning to Dillian and the others. When I left, Yolo was settling your wolf people into their camp. I have a few more supplies to offer them." She nudged the oversized backpack on her shoulder. "Would you like to come and see them?" I was fuming that she wouldn't tell me any more about the secret meeting she'd just had, with Lincon of all vampires. And nothing good ever came when Lincon was involved.

Chase was filtering through loving thoughts, grounding me and stripping away the suspicions. I was almost angry at him for manipulating me in such a way. His face twisted in remorse. *I'm sorry,* I quickly said, grabbing his hand. He wasn't manipulating me. I understood that. He was only trying to help. He was trying to balance my over-sensitive emotions that I couldn't quite grapple with. I felt depleted. My mother's question was indirectly asking me if I was stable enough to be around others. They were both doing what they could for me, and I was getting defensive.

*It's a lot, Esmore. No matter what, we're always on your side,* Chase lovingly chimed in as he rubbed his calloused thumb over my hand. I curled my fingers into Fire's fur, embracing the small hand my mother was offering out to me metaphorically. She was bringing me back into it, instead of leaving me on the sidelines and away from Titan, Dillian, and the others.

"Yes. Please," I added, the manners always seeming foreign in approach.

"Already?" Chase whined, turning into his playful self and trying to alleviate the tension. "But I only just got her back." I twisted to him with a small smile and placed my hand on his jaw, rubbing those swollen lips I'd put to use in the past few hours. I'd braided his shoulder-length black hair into two plaits which he'd refused to take out.

"Stay here, look pretty and hold the fort, my love," I antagonized him. I pushed back one of his plaits that bunched awkwardly to the side.

A devilish smile broke out onto his face. "Well, it's what I was put on this earth to do," he said in a low manner of speaking as if shy. I slapped his chest playfully and kissed his lips fleetingly. I had to pull away or I'd be hot with desire to push him back into the private chamber to have him all to myself again.

Fire whined at my side, deliberately stepping in front of our path.

"Maybe she wants to come along?" My mother queried. I premeditated its risks. The humans would either be offensively frightened by her or it could click some primal element into their nature. This wolf stuff was all new and none of us knew entirely. Hunters and vampires alike had found their way to establish hierarchy and foundations. Maybe Fire could help them, and if not, I could always have Tythian teleport us out. We could at least try.

"Okay," I agreed. Fire's ears perked up, and she took her place between my mother and me. Chase grabbed my hand and swung me back into his arms for one more breath-taking kiss. Slightly startled, I looked up at him with a small smile creeping over my face. I was so profoundly indebted to him for being able to make me *feel*—all of this.

*Don't leave me for too long. You're forcing me to become needy,* he joked as his gray eyes pooled into me lovingly. I flushed with deep heat when he sent me an image of how I'd looked positioned between his legs and the part he'd liked the most.

"Ah-hem," my mother said, tapping her foot. Chase looked over my shoulder and boyishly smiled at her. He kissed my forehead and let me go.

Before I turned to my mother, I wiped the coy smile from my face. *Just be a good husband and stay out of mischief,* I joked when I turned my back on him. I felt the tremble of his laughter down our line. I embraced it, wishing I could capture the feeling and live on its high forever. So foreign were the times when I didn't feel overrun by the purging thoughts and malice that controlled my life and actions.

And all of that returned the moment we left the institute and Tythian met us out the front of the gates. He was hesitant to teleport Fire. He had no desire to touch the very creature that could obliterate him with one bite. So as a precaution, I muzzled Fire's mouth with my hands. He didn't seem to trust me with that task either, considering our mutual disdain for one another. But at my mother's firm request, he thought better of denying his coven leader's familiar. Tythian reluctantly teleported us out, murmuring under his breath that he was sick of being a chaperone.

The nifty thing about having an arsenal of vampires was the access to resources and building small cottages when necessary in mere hours. Here in the mountains, they'd built a second and larger hut adjacent to the hunters. Ceasar had ordered a handful of the elite twelve members on behalf of my mother's and Yolo's request. These were the few he absolutely trusted, and so I wasn't surprised to hear Balzar and Lydia led the operation. It'd been erected adjacent to the hunter's cottage.

The vampires had long been gone now, ensuring our association with vampires being kept secret. Cole had been against the unknown hunter who approached them fully cloaked and as a means of teleportation to a safer area. Tythian had been against impersonating a hunter and also touching the wolf people until Cesar enforced absolute command. And reluctantly he had to obey. It took Jenn some time to convince Cole and the adults of his group this was the best decision for them.

They'd argued suspicions that the hunters were trying to harbor them like we did into our human camps. After some convincing, they were equally curious about the small rebel groups of hunters who had no claim to a Guild and were willing to aid them. The truth was, they were confused and scared and though Cole didn't want to lead his people here, he'd smartly figured out that returning to the humans who did this to them, wasn't a favorable decision either. The only vampire permitted on camp, and much to Dillian's disgruntlement was Yolo, though his true identity was still hidden under the mask of wearing Jenn's skin.

The hunters and wolf people were divided into groups, all except Jenn and Julia who fluttered to cater for them. Tori and Teary watched coolly from a distance. Teary's wound had almost healed, not that she put a bandage on it to prevent possible infection. Dillian was studying them just as intensely while leaning against the cottage so he was only a fleeting movement away if anything were to erupt with Julia in its wake. She offered them a bountiful bowl of fresh fruit.

When we appeared out of the trees, making sure no one saw Tythian teleport us in, Cole rose from the log he sat on and charged toward me. Fire growled at him, showing fangs as she licked her lips. I brushed my hand through her fur, tugging on it lightly, silently commanding her to play nice.

"What the hell is that thing doing here?" he demanded. The commotion drew attention to us.

"This is Fire. And she is *mine*. She comes from the same place where your people originated. I thought it might help."

"No, her mutt-like kind is the type that forced us into becoming these things," he said, placing his hand angrily on his chest. I identified with that movement and feeling—the profound sense of a monster being in the core of your soul and belly.

"Cole," Angela said, creeping out of the hut in a panic. She froze at the sight of Fire and didn't take another step. She focused and drew her attention back to Cole. "He's shifted back again."

"Shit," he antagonized, prioritizing the situation first. "Just don't let that thing near us!" He ordered and dashed in after her into the hut.

I side glanced Tori and Teary as we slowly crept further into the camp. It was a clearer day, and so I took a moment to appreciate the mountains in the distance.

"One of te wee ones keeps shifting back and forth into a wolf," Teary said, approaching us. She looked down on Fire. "Will it hurt us?"

I nuzzled my hand through her fur in a show of her complacent nature, even if it were only temporary. "No more than I would," I dared say with an eerily dry joke. But even I didn't find humor in it. I searched the faces of the children who were huddled outside. Titan wasn't here. Shit.

I followed Cole, ignoring Jenn who was trying to grab my attention as she catered to the others outside. There was nothing Yolo could do for them inside and was assuredly staying away from the possibility of being bitten himself. I pushed open the door.

There, huddled in the corner was Titan who was being protectively shoved back by Angela. The tension in my body rippled away instantly when I realized it wasn't her who was being affected. Titan cried as she watched the smaller wolf in the corner yap and snarl at Cole as he slowly addressed him. His golden-brown fur was thick, and his golden trained eyes were focused on Cole as he approached. He yapped and snapped at him, warding him off. He was half the size of Cole, but those teeth were the intimidating threat. It might've been half the size compared to when the adults turned, but it didn't make it any less deadly. I looked on, confused. I thought they were only meant to turn on full moons. I thought back to the wolf I'd killed in the Human Compound. Yolo had theorized that it was one of the scientists, but we thought they were limited in shifting until now. Could it be a side effect?

"Shit." Cole stumbled back when the wolf lunged at him to take a chunk. Once Cole was warded off it cowered back into the corner. He stressed, "I don't know what to do."

"What's been happening to them?" I asked, looking around Cole to try and better look at the pup. My mother closed the door behind us so the other children might not be frightened by what they saw. Titan's head snapped up, only realizing now that I'd entered the room. Desperation filled her eyes.

"Ellie, please, he's my friend. It's Chris," Titan sobbed and tried to run over to me. Angela grabbed her, pulling her away from nearing Fire. Titan's eyes widened in fear as she realized the beast that was beside me.

"It's okay, she won't hurt you," I cooed to Titan. My mother side-glanced me. My maternal indignation felt foreign.

"I told you not to bring that thing near us," Cole seethed.

"Don't you think we have bigger problems," I said, striding to his side. The little wolf was backing itself into the corner of the hut, its tail twisting between its legs as it peed.

"He's scared," my mother said over my shoulder.

"No shit," Cole snapped. Fire growled at his imprudent tone, which only agitated him more. No wonder the little guy was scared, Cole was only making it worse. His stress levels were tentatively pushing through to the rest of them. Everyone in the camp was on edge. And although current events and change of environment were reason for it, his poor leadership was only making it worse. He had to get a grip on himself.

"Can't you turn yourself to communicate with him or something?" my mother asked him, reciprocating her contempt for him, making him feel worse because he hadn't yet done anything for the little boy.

"Well, don't you think I would've done that already if I knew how? It's not exactly an on and off switch, you know?"

"What happened?" I asked as I crouched to the pup's eye level. Fire was steady by my side studying him intently. The movement wasn't unnoticed by the others. I wavered my mind over hers precautious, just in case for any reason she was about to go rogue on me. I didn't pick up on any aggressive impulses.

"Titan and him foraged for mushrooms on the edges of the camp. Nothing crazy and they weren't far away. When he started shifting back and forth, Titan screamed. The hunters got to them first," Cole said as if hating himself that they'd gotten to them first.

"Why did you let them out of your sight?" I snapped at him.

"It wasn't that far, and I don't know if you realize this but a lot's happening. It was only like two seconds at most I didn't have my eye on them."

"I didn't ask for your crap excuses. You're meant to be leading them, not letting little children play around." I grabbed him by the shirt, trying to rein in my anger, contrary to my fist bunched up on his chest. "Titan isn't to leave your sight again; do you hear me?" He bared his yellow teeth back at me.

He scrunched his hand around mine, his face twisting in pure hatred. "Let go of me."

"Esmore," my mother quietly said. I diverted my gaze to Titan who looked frightened with her little hands over her mouth. Shame washed over me, and I dropped him. The little wolf tried to yap at my ankle, Fire intervened, snapping at him to keep him in place. I froze, certain she was about to go for his throat, but as soon as he cowered back into the corner she licked over her lips.

I put my hand against Cole's chest as he tried to intervene. "No. She's just putting him in his place," I said solemnly, watching them interact. The small wolf pulled his ears back, dodging her gaze as she lowered to his eye level, slowly crawling closer. When he'd completely submitted, she nudged him with her nose. She licked under his jawline and let out a small whimper noise.

With the sound of bone crunching and skin shredding, Fire shifted into a very real woman. My mouth went agape, and my mind blank as I tried to process what, or should I say, who I was staring at. Before me was a lean dark woman, no older than forty with white shoulder-length dreadlocks. Her left leg had a marred scar stretching over her buttocks. Those blue eyes mirrored the same as the ones I'd been looking into these past few weeks.

The small wolf mirrored her, the undeniable pain of bone breaking and restructuring, shifting into a small boy once again. The golden-eyed boy sobbed naked in the corner, heaving in panic and pain.

The woman who shifted from Fire's form spoke. "He ate some of the mushrooms, it's hurting his tummy." Her low voice was swirls of mystery and empathy. She turned her gaze to me, those blue eyes reflecting the same contempt look Fire often gazed at me with. My mother walked past me, tapping the bottom of my jaw to shut my mouth.

"I can help with that," she said as she aided the little boy and pressed her hand on his stomach.

"You're a—" I couldn't finish the sentence. For the first time, I was utterly speechless.

"You're one of us?" Angela asked desperately as if Fire was all the answers they'd been praying for, and maybe they had been.

My mind swirled with so many questions. Why hadn't she shifted sooner? Why did she comply to be mine? How was this even possible? How would this change things?

"I thought you were one of them, made from the lab?" I asked still stunned.

"I was a part of the first 'successful' wave they had, so to speak. Though I had no intention of shifting back into human form anytime soon, if ever. I much rather living as a wolf, it's easier," she admitted, and empathetically looked down at the boy who groaned about this tummy.

"Chris!" Titan screamed in joy as she ran to him, wrapping her arms around him. He jolted uncomfortable, naked and shivering from the unseen fever as my mother delicately used her gift on him.

Angela grabbed a long shirt from a small bag in the corner of the room, offering it to Fire cautiously. Fire looked at the shirt strangely, much in the same way Deemori had. She'd been wild for too long, that quipped gaze of hers distasteful that she had to return in her human form.

This was the levitation that Deemori wanted, to be the beast fully. In a strange way, they reminded me of one another.

"Why don't we do what we came here for first and we can discuss this later," Fire said, ignoring the outstretched piece of clothing being offered to her.

"Wait—" But she shifted back into her wolf form, dodging the offered shirt. I froze as she lost height but grew in size. Those predatory blue eyes glaring back up at me before she nuzzled her head onto the boy's lap who was now wrapped in a blanket. Titan hugged him tightly, adjusting the blanket so it covered him completely. She was wary of Fire but cautiously offered her hand out to the great white wolf. Fire slowly nuzzled her nose into the palm of Titan's small hand. A smile broke out on her face, and she scratched under her jaw.

"You didn't seem as shocked after we'd shifted," Cole scoffed with arms folded over his chest. I wanted to argue that it was entirely different. But to him it wouldn't be. I flicked through all the conversations I'd had in front of Fire and considered all the things she might've seen. I felt hot as I thought about only an hour ago as Chase and I passionately and explicitly made love in the same room as her. My jaw clenched.

"We should talk outside," I said to Cole, storming out of the cottage, overheated. My mother remained catering to Chris who complained that his tummy still hurt. Fire remained by the children's side, looking pleasantly tired as she yawned.

"I want to talk to you, privately," Cole demanded, catching hold of my elbow. I slowly twisted to face him.

"I wouldn't be grabbing her if I were you," Tori said as he sat on the ground sharpening his blades. "I learned the hard way." He charmed me with a boyish smile. Respectively, Cole was angry, confused, and a part of me genuinely wondered if he thought he could outmatch me. He'd seen my potential in the Human Compound, and even now I only showcased my abilities in a range of what a normal human could muster. If he truly knew of the monster that prowled beneath this skin, he wouldn't so daringly touch it.

He unclasped his hand adhering to Tori's warning, but his hard expression remained. His second, Ryan, watched us intently. "Fine," I replied. I looked Dillian's way, when our eyes connected, he looked away, embarrassed. Anger bubbled back to the surface, reminding me of the raw conversation we'd had previously. I led us in the other direction. That conversation and closure could wait. Cole signaled to Ryan that it was fine to enter the cottage. I led him into the outskirts of the woods. He was evidently scared of straying too far from the others because he kept looking back over his shoulder, hands content in his pockets.

"I think we should return to the compound. They might be able to help us, to turn this thing back or something through their experiments?"

I narrowed my gaze on him, infuriated by his cowardly tendencies. He would be willing to subject them all to being live experiments. Had he never seen the experiments that went on in there? This was the very thing Sydney was trying to protect them from, and he was willing to throw them into that, with Titan no less as well. "Would this not have been something you'd discuss with Jenn?" I asked, trying to keep this as a civil conversation. They were scared. I could understand that, but the leader I was hoping he would be wasn't shaping into form. Instead, he was breaking apart.

"She said we can't, that they'd experiment on us and we'd be worse." Which meant that Yolo hadn't told them the compound had been eradicated.

"Let me assure you that this is one of the safest places you can be. Those experiments you're talking about will only lead to further suffering and possibly even death."

"Being dead would've been better than this!" he gritted out angrily, throwing his hands in the air. I slapped him across the face, the deafening pitch enough to probably make his ears ring. He looked shocked.

"I couldn't care less what you wish upon yourself, but you need to get a grip on yourself and remember that you have children in your care."

"I'm not like him," he gritted out, adjusting his jaw from the slap. I wasn't sure if he was going to cry or scream. I didn't have time to deal with an unstable human with an inferiority complex.

"Like who?" I asked, not following. Had I slapped him too hard?

"Sydney. I'm not as strong," he said, deflated. He simmered down, his shoulders sagging in defeat. Oh. He wasn't like Sydney and never would be. There was something about Sydney that even I was drawn to, even when he was only human. This man would never level to the same caliber as him. But the fact that he idolized such a mentor meant they shared some qualities.

I saw potential in him as had Sydney once as well. Just right now, he was a broken man with no answers for his people. He wanted to be told what to do, and I had no doubt that it would only be a matter of time until he built himself up again and was able to guide them accordingly. Or so I had to believe that, and so did he.

"No, you're not as strong as Sydney. But what you need right now is to recoup, heal, figure this wolf shifting stuff out, and lead this small group of people. Going back to the compound is a coward answer because they'll only experiment on you further. Your life will never be the same. You need to stay, regroup and figure this all out. These hunters *will* protect you, giving you that time."

He weakly walked over to a tree, leaning against it. He huffed out a small mad man laugh to himself. "I don't even know why I'm letting you help us. Nothing matches up in your story. You're obviously something more than human. And even if your mom is a huntress and you're just normal, it still puts you at the advantage that Sydney always had over us. He might've been able to handle this, but we can't."

"What do you mean about Sydney?" I asked, curious. I crossed my arms in front of my chest, mirroring him as I too leaned against a tree.

"He was just like you."

"I highly doubt that," I replied under my breath. "In what way?" It was an odd curiosity that led me to ask more questions about Sydney. I would forever be indebted and poisoned by what I'd done to him. I'd been crueler than death itself.

"His mother was a huntress as well from a long line of them, and apparently, he was the first born to just be, you know, human. Completely normal. They threw him into one of those human camps, and when he was four his human father broke in and busted him and anyone else who wanted to follow. But Sydney had always been stronger, faster, more decisive, and surer of himself. It's because he had an edge. And the suckers still got to him." He hinged on a thought, his shoulders sagging further once again. "So, what chance do we have?"

I realized then he was not only a broken man, but someone who was still mourning the loss of his leader and friend. I had done that damage, and I faced him as if with no involvement.

"And now I'm in charge of his daughter's life!" He threw his hands up in the air. "And Angela. And the others. I knew something was up, that with new higher-ups coming in, something was shifting, but I didn't expect this. We're sitting ducks out here."

"Listen to me very carefully," I said, irritated by his weak descending spiral. Was he going to cry? Was this really the same wolf who'd shredded his own comrade to gain their alpha status? "You will train with the hunters, and you will teach these children how to be strong and effective killers." He grimaced. "You were already doing that. Now it's just not in the safety of inside your walls. Think of this curse as an advantage. It makes you stronger and more deadly to vampires. You can defend yourself."

"That's rich coming from the one who doesn't have this happening to her," he retorted back. I'd had enough of this self-pitying shit.

"You know nothing of my demons," I said angrily. Feigning to be human and equally on his level only made him arrogant and insubordinate. I had to manage myself and strength not to turn on him, to make him so scared of me, that he'd do everything I said. But that wouldn't help me here. I would have to show a 'softer' form of leadership here. If they knew what I was, it'd only make it worse. They'd never trust me. "If you're not up for the job, then keep walking into these woods and find your maker, eventually something will find you and end your miserable life. But those children stay and all those who want to live as well."

I walked past him, and he scoffed. "You only want to protect Titan. That's all this is to you." I stopped. "We all miss him you know. We all feel guilty about what happened that day and not being able to save him. Not even being able to bring back his body." He paused. "It's not your fault. There was nothing you could've done, that vampire was too strong. That's why we hate them. Because they prey on our strong and leave us weak ones behind simply to play with us."

I hitched my breath, scared it'd give me away. But I had been there. And it was me who'd turned on him. I marched forward, irritated by everything he voiced and stood for. I didn't need consolidation from a weak human of all things. I was making my dues with the demons of my past. That's why I had them here, in the safety of my hunter friends. But it didn't deter any of the shame or disgust I had for myself. It wasn't yet levitating any of the guilt. And though I might not feel it now, the moment I was back at the institute with Chase, it would flood over me in a desperate chokehold. And I never looked forward to that, but equally, I always looked forward to being with Chase.

On my way through, Dillian was resting against a tree, silently listening in. I locked eyes with his fluorescent pink ones. "The kids will stay safe," he promised. And I knew that he wasn't listening in to be nosy or intrude; but to take the place he always had, as my back up in case anything went wrong. Even if we had fought or disagreed, he always had my back. I nodded my head once.

"Thank you," I breathed out. His eyebrows perked up in surprise. He flicked a small smile.

"I'm sorry about—"

I stopped him with my hand, agonizing over my next words. My pride guarded me against believing such obscene things, and usually I'd find a way to reprimand my members in some way for speaking back. But, then what kind of leader was I, when there might've been some truth. Maybe I didn't know myself as entirely as I thought. And Dillian could see with those special eyes of his what I could not. "Your words struck because there might be some truth in them."

He slowly nodded, savoring the moment. "I've always got your back."

I offered him an uncharacteristic small smile. "I know, and I have yours." But it didn't mean I was ready to talk about all of this completely. I wasn't sure what I was doing with myself or while in battle. I didn't think the way I fought was any different, but I could admit I didn't have a handle on this vampire thing yet. But I never wanted to admit that to Dillian or he might lose faith in me entirely. And having him turn his back on me... I couldn't stand the thought.

I ventured back toward the hut, leaving Dillian to remain and monitor Cole. The hunters were watching them carefully. If one strayed too far then one of them would silently follow. I walked back into the hut where Yolo and my mother conversed. Yolo was now handling the bag.

"I'm assuming this is yours," Jenn said, pulling out the stitched teddy. Yolo must've recognized it from when I'd picked it up from the Human Compound. I curled my fingers around it and squatted in front of Titan. She was busily tucking Chris into the blanket. He was now comfortably sound asleep.

Fire rested on his lap, still eerily looking like an ordinary wolf. Her eyes were closed contently, but I could sense she was still awake. Her ear flickered slightly when I began to talk. "This is for you, Titan," I said, offering her the teddy. She looked confused by the gift at first and frowned. Her hand hovered out toward it, unsure if she should grab it or not. "Do you not like it?"

She shook her head. "I do, but I don't want to look like a kid," she said in a small voice. She couldn't look away from the teddy as it tempted her. I collected her soft little hand in mine and curled her fingers around it.

"You *are* still a child, Titan. And you can still be strong and have something comforting."

"But I have to be strong like you," she sniffled. She tried to hold in the tears, acting brave. This teddy resembled far more than a simple comfort toy. In its own way, I was attempting to hold on tightly to her child-like mind and innocence from the perversion of what had happened to her. If anyone was going to grow into this and learn the ways of mastering it, it'd be the children. Soon they'd forget about what they'd lost and hopefully, especially for Titan and her little friend here, Chris, they could use it to their advantage in the cruel world.

"You'll be even stronger," I promised, and tucked the teddy into the blanket between her and Chris.

# CHAPTER 16

THE DAY LEFT us fatigued, and the atmosphere in the institute was no better. Cesar, Balzar, and his elite team had been out for the day leaving Connor temporarily in charge of his coven. He met with another coven that he'd been having meetings with regularly in conjunction to teaming against the Vampire Council. Though it wasn't natural for covens to align, Cesar had made a promising pact with other groups, who shared information and strategy as to best push against the Council. It was their belief that if they didn't unite, over time they'd be forced to submit to the Council's rule or be taken out one by one.

When Cesar returned, he'd been fuming. The coven he met with was on the move once again, fearful that the Council had caught up with them and was closely monitoring their movement. Cesar would have to wait out the days to renegotiate whether they would continue to join us in force or if their leader chose it was safer to lay low. My mother decided to join Chase, Fire, and me in our wing while Cesar was in the process of destroying his chamber in wild fury. Guards were posted outside his doors to make sure he wasn't disturbed while he was in meeting with Connor, Tythian, and Balzar. My mother decided it was best to give him a little space before she approached him, and to give herself a few minutes of rest in the meantime.

"There's something I have to show you," I said to Chase as we entered our room. It'd recently been scrubbed and cleaned with an offensive chemical smell that burned my sensitive nose. The blood spillage from the human I'd messily devoured a few nights ago was efficiently gone. A weight lifted now that I wouldn't have to stare at the remains of my evil doing every time I entered the room. In the center on the desk was a small array of wildflowers in a vase, though they looked like they might've had better days. *Okay… Chase was trying to make this homely.*

*Are the flowers too much?* he asked slightly concerned. I shook my head, but admittedly it was the most feminine touch I'd ever seen in a room, and I was certain he had done it to impress me. So, I looked at them admiringly, appreciating his efforts. I clicked at Fire who trailed behind us into the chambers, expecting her to transform into the woman that she really was. She looked back at me aloof and walked away. I tsked at her. She was refusing to turn once again, and there was nothing I could do to change her mind.

"Fire can turn into a woman. More specifically, I should say Fire *is* a woman," I said, feeling like I was dobbing her in like a minor as I pointed at her.

My mother cozied into a seat in the corner, looking tired from the day's events. I fed through to Chase what I'd witness, and his eyebrows perked in surprise.

"Well, this kind of makes it awkward, considering all the times she was on your lap or even when she was in the same room when we—"

"Yes." I cut him off, embarrassed by the same thing. I didn't want to talk about it, especially in front of my mother. "But for some reason she won't shift now and introduce herself," I said pointedly. The wolf rolled her eyes and walked over to my mother, resting her large head in her lap. My mother seemed slightly taken aback but slowly brushed her hand through her fur. Fire contently closed her eyes, clearly enjoying the pats.

Despite our indifferences, I'm sure she had her reasons for not shifting. But it was also infuriating that she wouldn't prove my point, even though Chase could read my thoughts. I counted to ten as my father had raised me to do to calm the rising anger that too quickly took over.

"It might help us with the wolves at camp. Today was seemingly successful so my mother and I intend to go there every day to train with and monitor them. Maybe Fire can teach them what they need to know about shifting and surviving as wolves." I'd opened my mind and showed

Chase everything. How Fire had helped the young boy shift back into his human form. This was a positive contribution, even when he still wasn't so fond of the idea of the wolf people.

"We really need to give them another name. *Wolf people* is just, I don't know, creepy," Chase mused as he looked over at Fire. She opened one eye and closed it again, complacent.

"Well, I don't think their name right now is our priority," I grumbled.

My mother perked slightly with a sigh. "Cesar's tugging on our line," she said, deflated, and shuffled Fire off her lap. It was the first time I'd heard her refer to their internal connection and familiarity. Though they couldn't communicate as Chase and I could, I imagined they still held that undeniable link and tug that was sensitive to one another's movements and feelings. "I wonder how little of the room remains," my mother said heartily under her breath. And yet she still went when he summoned. Cesar was the opposite to the father who raised me. He had been kind, gentle, and caring. And my mother never loved him in that way, only as her best friend. Yet Cesar, who was impulsive, powerful, and slightly unhinged called to her. And although I didn't particularly like Cesar, I knew he'd never hurt her, and more importantly she'd never let him. So chaotic and powerful were my biological parents, and yet they couldn't have been more different in persona.

When my mother left, I faced Chase. But then again, Chase and I were so completely different and yet fitted the same. I was drawn into his embrace, the day of fatigue wearing over me as he began idly chatting about his day.

It was a day I too often hadn't seen. The sky was clear, and the mist had almost completely vanished. There was a glimmer of sun that irritated me, making my skin feel like it was crawling with tiny flames. It was durable, but uncomfortable. I rolled my neck, tapping on the wooden sword in a signal to continue our training. The wolves were absorbing their training with the diligence of what Sydney had left them with.

Cole jumped, always too keen to be on the offensive. I scraped my wooden sword against his, smacking it on his wrist and prodding it into his side. I then pivoted to sweep him off his feet. He lost his breath when he thudded to the ground. By now he'd have no left hand and lost both his feet in the literal sense. I looked down on him, in a smart-ass way that I knew would effectively stain his pride. Playing the role of Ellie was adaptably foreign. I had to ensure I not only kept my composure in all aspects as a human, but also try to mimic how a human might respond emotionally. For the most part, since training with them and Sydney in the past, I'd noticed that 'shit talking' and demeaning presence was often what was celebrated amongst the soldiers and motivated them to work harder.

I offered my hand. With a grumble, he took it and I helped him up. After our conversation the night prior, he'd changed his attitude. Instead of a broken man, I felt like I'd gotten through to him on some level. Instead of deciding to walk further into the woods and into his death where he could leave all this behind and cowardly abandon the others, he decided to step up. He'd never be the leader that Sydney was, but I hoped having him as a figurative role model would be enough to turn the odds in their favor.

Teary was training the children. Her ability to so comfortably nurture them when she herself never had a child was rather endearing. At over six foot herself, she towered over them but thrust the wooden swords she'd crafted for them with delicacy and encouraging words, somewhat softer than what we'd received in training at the Hunter Guild. The difference as hunters and humans was substantial, but I was hoping that with this new 'skillset' of theirs they'd maybe even adapt sooner than we would. They'd just have to tap into its power.

"Again." I motioned to Cole. He rolled his neck around for a quick breather. And then when he thought I wasn't looking, he pounced. His wooden sword crept close to my stomach as I easily blocked it. He deflected my sword, and out of curiosity, I loosened my grip, flicking my weapon through the air to give him an opening. He jumped at the chance, too eager and leaving himself wide open. I dodged him, finely pinpointing three muscles that forced his arm to drop. I roundhouse kicked his back, and he dove into the dirt head first. It was too easy. And that's why we were concerned. Were they ready for this outside world? Within the Human Compound they had barriers and traps on the outskirts. They could leave and quickly return. Here they were in the open, and they'd only be able to rely on their wit and immediate strength.

Fire watched on intently. Her eyes scattered over the children and the one on one training the other hunters were providing. Julia was the only one who was exempt from training them. Instead, she was stewing a meal and lullaby singing to her plants, of which I wasn't entirely sure if it encouraged her gift or was simply something she took pleasure from.

She'd always been an oddity within the Guild. Dillian was training closest to her, managing Ryan and Angela at the same time. In between rounds he seemed elated by her muse.

It was only months ago that he'd intended to propose to her, prior to our San Francisco raid when everything had changed. Now, he was waiting until they were stable and within a foundation before proposing to her. I hadn't the heart to tell him that Chase and I had secretly exchanged vows. I hadn't told anyone. It felt like it was a secret for only the two of us. And it was more for Chase's sincerity and being born of a different time. But for him, I was willing to do anything that pleased him, no matter how strange the notion seemed to me.

"Let's have a break," my mother spoke up. Everyone moaned their pleasure to finally be pardoned, rubbing their tired muscles. Cole angrily punched into the ground, his other hand still dropped to his side.

"Don't worry, feeling in it will come back shortly," I said, offering to help him up again. This time he rejected my offer.

"It's because you have that damn hunter blood in you," he sneered. I nodded in contempt. If only he knew to what extent. It wasn't *just* a flicker of strength I'd gained from my mother. Something he would never know. None of them would. Titan grabbed Chris's hand and dragged him over to the stewing and bubbling cauldron. In her other hand was the teddy I'd gifted her. None of the hunters had even broken out in a sweat.

Tori approached me. "Can we finally match?"

"You want to fight against me?" I asked, a little surprised.

"Yea, since like the day I met you. Even more so now." His blond hair was greasy from weeks not washed. I recalled our first time in meeting, when Campture had insisted he and his sixteen-year-old apprentice friend, Fam, join us on our raid. I was adamantly against it, and he despised my order. So much had changed since that day. Ever since, he'd been following me and watching me silently with the glowing respect of a mentor. I wasn't entirely certain I deserved it, but I couldn't deny his desire to learn.

"You know I'm limited as a human," I underhandedly said to him. The handicap would work in his favor, but still wouldn't be enough. The impairment would only influence my speed and strength. But any skillful warrior knew it was about wit and tact. Sheer strength was never enough.

"Making excuses already?" he asked with his boyish smile, picking up the wooden swords and throwing one my way.

"Finally, he's going to match against ye.' It'll keep him off my back for a few days after ye' give him a good ol woopin, Esmore," Teary said, smiling at my mother. She watched on with a similar encouragement. The others took a seat with their dish in lap, watching as an audience. It reminded me of my own apprentice days, and having onlookers watch from the sidelines. They would study us and assess who they thought possessed raw potential and would be permitted to leave the walls for raids and extensive military training. I had been one of the best. But even with that advantage, look at where it had ended me, everything I'd been taught and fed was a lie.

I waited patiently for Tori to make the first move. We walked around one another, waiting for our opponent to strike. I antagonized him with a few pretty swirls of my sword. It was enough to wear his patience thin. He pounced, coming down on my wooden sword and splintering it into two. He wasn't holding back. I raised my elbows as he kicked into my forearms as I blocked and I skidded back, my black boots collecting a slight dust about them.

When he plunged the sword toward me, I avoided it, twisting comfortably and open-palmed his hand, knocking him away and throwing him off. He tried to block, but I smacked the arm away, punching his throat. When his hand retracted to it with a hallowing gasp, I kicked the sword out of his hand. It flew through the air and into the distance of the trees.

I stepped back with an antagonizing smile. If he depended on sheer strength he would lose. Well, he would lose anyway, I just wanted him to extract some more wit before then. Still not recovered from my throat punch, he stumbled toward me, feigning left and undercutting a punch toward my stomach. I raised my knee, blocking the maneuver and pushed away his second fist aimed at my face. I deflected him, kicking his back and skirted him away. He took a few steps, frustrated as he took a sturdy breath.

His florescent blue eyes narrowed on me. And there I saw the man that he would be one day. The hunter who would one day make a spectacle of himself. He had top training within the compound, and his real-world experience would only strengthen that caliber. A part of me was almost proud, and if we had more time, I wanted to train with him firsthand every day, to make him the best he could be. I wanted to be there on his eighteenth to see the excitement of his gift awaken and what truly lay dormant within his core.

He charged at me with a loud grunt, impatient for his loss. Much to my disappointment, he'd given into his testosterone self, the one that focused only on evasive attacks instead of tactical approach. He was still a boy, no matter how grand a man he might become one day. I used the rock behind me for momentum, bouncing onto it and off for height. I came down on him, my leg suspended in the air and hardening the muscle ready for a bone-chilling strike that could cut through cement, even as a human with that particular technique. He was thrown off by it, dodging it and thinking he had the upper hand. I used it as a decoy as I grabbed the side of his shirt before landing. He gripped onto me, attempting to change the hold, but it was too late. I kicked into the back of his knee, dropping it and then kinking my leg behind his other as I pushed him down. He fell onto the ground, and I used his momentum to flip over, let go of him and come to a stand.

I looked over my shoulder. "That makes best out of three," I taunted him. He began to laugh, a surprising levitation to the tension we often felt if we ever lost in our own challenges at the Hunter Guild. He rubbed his eyes looking back up at the sky amused and pleased.

"Until next time, I suppose," he said with a shy smile, disappointed in himself but not seemingly surprised.

Fire let out a big stretch and yawn. She walked over toward the woodland, offering me one quick deliberate glance before walking away from the camp. I realized she was summoning me.

"I'll be back," I said to Dillian who was closest to me. He was rubbing his hands over Julia's arms lovingly from behind, praising her for her meal. I followed Fire for a few minutes into the dense mountains. I heard the breaking of bones and definite sound of her shifting. She gasped in a shallow breath, rolling her back and shoulders uncomfortably.

"You wouldn't believe how excruciating that is," she said as a way of greeting. Her dark skin glistened under the small amount of sunlight that drifted through. I stayed close to the trees actively avoiding it.

"Why didn't you shift before now?" I asked imprudently. Because of how abruptly she'd shifted last time before answering any of my questions, I felt like I had limited time now.

"Shift in the institute with two covens lingering." She furrowed her eyebrows in a mocking gesture. "You must be joking. The fewer people who know about me, the better," she said seriously. I admired the beauty of her tall, strong, and lean body. She was larger than Teary, a sizeable female warrior who held pride in her stance. The marring scar was identical to the one that contorted her fur's growth on her leg in wolf form. "And also, I prefer this form. If only you spoke wolf, I would never have to shift back," she dryly joked. If only I'd known that she was a woman sooner, I might've handled the situation completely differently. So much had happened since the day we'd saved her. There were so many opportunities and yet she'd remained hidden all this time.

"What happened?" I asked impatiently, wanting answers now. Even when I had beckoned her to shift once we'd returned to the institute she didn't, she either rolled her eyes or ignored me completely. "That day when we saved you. You were ready and willing to die until Chase forced you back with us. What really happened? Where'd you come from?"

"Yes, and your lover thought it was a great idea to lock us in together to see if you would kill me or not to prove a point, such an intelligent man," she mocked. The top of my lip twitched, used to baring my fangs. "Relax. I'm not offending your man. Let me assure you no one was more plagued by that day than I was. I honestly thought you would kill me which is why I didn't care about coming with you. I was so numb by the day's events that before I knew it, I was locked in a room with a—" She wavered her hand at me. "Whatever you were, waiting and hoping for my death so I could meet my husband in the afterlife. Instead, I was frozen in a room with you silently, as we stared at one another, two lost and amicable women at our wits end." She let out a small mad laugh and relieved the sigh. When I hovered over her mind now, I could feel the emotion roll off her blatantly clear. She was hurting and mourning all the same.

"The wolf that was with you, he was your husband?" I asked quietly, honoring it with the silence it deserved. Husband, mate, familiar, by whatever terms were used, I never wanted to know that loss because the suffering that emitted off her and into me was heavy.

"Yes," she said tiredly. "We'd been married for twelve years." I could feel her closing up, not wanting to talk anymore about the subject matter. So, I redirected the questions.

"Where did you come from?"

She heavily sighed to herself, her human form evidently uncomfortable for her. She shuffled from foot to foot, brushing her fingers over her skin curiously. Her movement wasn't fluid like a human, she'd for too long been in a predatory state and mindset, her movements even reflected that.

"We were found in our small human camp. We hid well for years until the day the human government found us. When they offered us liberation and security, we rejected them, accustomed to our own ways and comfortable with our ability to survive. We'd hardly seen any vampires for years in our land. And there was a gifted human of hunter descent that was able to savvily call to the animals. We used that as a way of livestock to get through for meals. We didn't need *their* help," she sneered. She looked away, disgruntled by the acid in her tone.

"And then what happened?" I prompted her.

"They did what they always do. They stole us. Took our babies, separated them from us, and took the adults to labs where a woman, no less a vampire herself, experimented on us."

"A vampire?" I said incredulously.

"Yes, a savage. She didn't let us rest, eat, or have warm clothes. Most of us died from the injections. It was horrible in there. They were extracting from hunters in there as well. And when the humans died off from experiments, they'd simply find more. Eventually, a small group of wolves was brought in, no stronger than we were. But over time, they became vicious. She orchestrated them in such a way that they became feral creatures and then one day, she let them tear into us. Most of us didn't survive. For those who did, well you've seen the aftermath." Her voice strained, ashamed. "She was creating monsters in that lab, ordaining it as the greater evil. In those final days, a few of us were able to escape, my husband and I included. We were hunted down, and by chance crossed paths with your people when we were found. The rest is history."

I absorbed this information, premeditating when I would tell Chase and Cesar. Who knew what other level experiments they were doing? Maybe it didn't just stop at the wolves? And who was this vampire that the human government was depending on? It infuriated me that they were so prejudice against the race and once depended on us killing their kind for them. And yet they were willing to use their support.

The children... how much more had Fire lost besides her husband? "Did you have children?" I asked, wondering if she had to make the decision to leave them behind or if she was still by chance looking for them.

"No. I unfortunately I can't bear children. It was my shame as a woman. But now I have a larger one to counter that so who's counting?" she said pointedly to me, hiding her own pain that she so nonchalantly shrugged off. I could sense her despair clearly, in the way I wasn't able to when she was in wolf form. She pined and longed for the ability to bear a child. The feeling was foreign to me and yet it so easily transfused into me that I was taken aback by it.

Her blue eyes struck me as she placed her hand on her stomach. "You can feel it can't you?"

"I'm not entirely sure what I'm feeling. If you hadn't received the message, without Chase, I very much lack in the ability to understand emotion."

She nodded with a shifty smile. "Yea, I've noticed, but this has nothing to do with emotion. There's a connection between you and me now. When you desperately saved me from those humans I'd attacked, I was ready for death. I was waiting for it. I will, at any given pleasure attack anyone who comes from that terrible place. But you saved me. With the combination of your venom and mother's 'gift' to resurrect me something happened to me when I was pulled out of the darkness of my peace." I felt guilty in the way she described it. Like I'd taken away her solace and the thing she'd wanted so badly. I'd taken even that away from her. I'd taken so much from a lot of people.

"I feel bound to you, Esmore. And in every waking hour, I feel persuaded to serve you, in whatever way I can. I don't know if I've been robbed of making that decision for myself because of some vampire ailment or if I'm indebted to you for saving me twice now."

I felt it, the small thread that was bound between us and I despised it not because I didn't appreciate her service, but because I had selfishly and unknowingly robbed her of the death she had so actively pursued. I had bound her to me out of desperation to not lose anyone else, especially what I once considered to be a gift from Chase.

She seemed to hold no resentment toward me, but it was another thing I would have to live with. The strangeness of our crossing paths did however bring a new hopeful element to our current situation. "Will you help the others learn how to live this life?" I asked. Fire knew how to shift controllably. How long she'd been in those labs I wasn't sure. Maybe even she was still learning how to control this new side of her.

But she did know more than them, and they would take all the help and advice they could acquire.

"I'll only do so if you ask it of me. But no, I have no desire to become anyone's beacon of hope. I'm simply going to count down the days until that woman finds me again." Fire was talking about the vampire who'd tested on them and I was so curious about her identity as well. She'd have to be stopped alongside the human government or who knew to what measures they'd aspire to. They would turn half the world into monsters if granted the power. "Whoever she is, she's a monster, and I doubt she will stop at anything, or any experiment for that matter. I hope, Esmore, after you have dealt with all you have and save your familiar from his curse, that you can rid the world of her too. If this virus extends over the years, there will be no going back from it. There will be no world or fighting, it'll simply be the remains of humans who shift uncontrollably on a full moon, hunting down anything that's still moving, or more importantly, undead."

Her skin and form seemed to irritate her, and without warning, she shifted back into her wolf form. I hissed at her, frustrated she'd decided of her own accord that this conversation was over. But I realized with Fire, I had no choice but to follow at her pace. She didn't care much for living, which meant she couldn't be motivated or intimidated in any way. She would simply do what she wanted when she wanted. And in that, I respected her more. She would be one of few who decided to fight by my side not out of obligation because I was her Token. But simply because. Bound or unbound. She was a woman of few words, but her actions spoke volumes. And that was a language I could understand.

# CHAPTER 17

TYTHIAN DROPPED MY mother and me at the institute's gates, not staying long enough to become witness to the ordeal that was breaking out before us. Chase was marching out of the wide-open doors, Jerimiah and Darcy flanking his side.

"What's happening?" I asked hurriedly, rushing to his side.

"Where's Cesar?" My mother asked, breaking into action as well.

"A group of four has been strung up on the edge of our hunting borders. And Cesar isn't here, he's still negotiating with another coven," Chase said rapidly. "Connor's in charge."

"You think the human government strung them up?" I asked, taking my place by his side and walking with him. He carried a long blade as if he'd pried it from the first soldier's hand when news broke out.

"No, I don't. It's not their style. More than likely vampires are behind this. Possibly another coven, if we've stepped close to their territory. You lot." Chase whistled to a large group of vampires who were sparring at the front. They hurried behind him. "Connor is holding base. I suggest you go in as well," Chase said to my mother. "I can't guarantee your safety with my coven." He was honest. Who knew what they'd do if the opportunity presented itself to turn on her instead. It was safer for her to be under Connor's surveillance.

"Fire, go with her," I commanded. It was bizarre knowing that the very same wolf I spoke to was a human inside. She growled her complaints but followed my mother anyway. I much preferred them having the safety of one another while I was gone and in Cesar's absence.

"This way," Jerimiah said, his rough voice awakening prompt action. I watched my mother safely reach the doors, inside Connor reined in order. Vampires were yelling at one another amongst the chaos. Was it Cesar's or Chase's coven that'd been made an example of?

It took us a few minutes to reach the border of our hunting ground. But there, as the spotter had suggested, four vampires were hanging by the throat, in thick chunky silver chains. Their limbs had been sliced off, and they were bleeding out. If they'd gone for the heart or head, they would've decomposed. That wasn't the message these vampires were sending out.

"It's fresh," Jerimiah said. "They would have no more than a ten-minute head start." He looked to Chase, waiting for his order. We couldn't spread out, we didn't know how many of them there were. They might've been waiting for us, drawing us out to ambush or they fled the scene after parting with their 'message.'

"What if I get an aerial view?" I suggested. Chase's striking gray eyes found mine.

"You shouldn't play around with the Descendant, Esmore, for something so trivial."

"I'm not playing," I growled out. "And this isn't trivial. We need to identify whoever these vampires were and return the message. If they think they got away with doing this once, then they will come again."

*I know that,* he growled telepathically. His aggression wasn't directed at me, but the reality that I might've not even been strong enough to use the Descendant willingly. The last time I'd awoken the Descendant I'd fallen to my near death, my wings tattered and broken. My only white wing had been tarnished into black to match the other. I hadn't seen them since.

Aware of the onlookers, Chase nodded. He trusted in me, ashamed of himself for having suggested otherwise. "Only to survey. As soon as you see something, you let us know straight away." He grabbed my arm softly. "We fight this together, Esmore."

"Yes," I breathed softly. My vision hazed purple as my fangs slid out, my vampire self gleeful to come out and play. With a bone-crunching force, I called upon the Descendant, a whirl of what felt like unlimited power welling in the pit of my stomach. I delved into its darkness and the bones and muscle in my back began to snap to make room for its powerful extension. Two great black wings protruded from my back. I hissed at the pain, the transformation so quick and immediate that it only punctured two precise holes in the back of my leather shirt to make room for my extended limbs. They weren't as beautiful as they had once been. They seemed tired and worn, and I was certain the only way to heal them was with time and blood. Like all ailments, I needed to replenish to my full strength once again.

Chase looked over them in bewilderment. Some of the vampires behind him gasped in surprise, taking a step back at their sudden appearance. Others weren't so astonished. Those who had fought alongside me once before had seen these wings already and the power I could draw from them. They were the same that mirrored Chase's, if he could ever learn how to control them without losing himself.

I pelted up once, the strange muscle motion aching already at the untrained movement. I thrust into the air, higher and higher, using my keen vampire sight to track activity below. Something caught my eye, and I harpooned in that direction. Wind pelted on my skin as I shot through the sky, my wings extending and riding over the waves in a way I couldn't entirely understand myself. I wasn't in control of this gift. The way the wings moved was in a way of their own, understanding a rhythm I knew nothing about. But I wanted to experience and master this gift and make these beautiful wings completely mine. I even wanted to admire the unbelievable ability to be able to fly, instead of straining to make sure I wasn't angling unnaturally.

I swooped closer to the dead treetops, smiling at the group of forty vampires I spotted. I fed the imagery to Chase, feeling his immediate response as they ran at full speed to catch up. I swerved to the left as a spear was thrown up at me. I wavered clumsily through the air, trying to control my spiral. My wings clipped the edges of dead branches before I harpooned myself back into the sky.

That one pillowing thrust came to an end, and I stretched my wings out wide, exhausted by their might. They flapped slow but powerful beats to hover me there, suspended in the sky. I looked out toward the horizon. Dusk was irritable as the remains of the sun bathed my skin. But it was eerily beautiful, amassed in its red glow. Below I could see the landscape of dead trees in some sections and barely thriving foliage in others. I unbound my satchel, and one by one pressed my golden claws onto my fingers delicately, as if savoring the smooth feel of each one. I had promised Chase I wouldn't act on my own. And being so high in the sky, with a fresh breeze, I decided with clarity that I would listen. Because if I disobeyed or stressed him out in any way, it would consequently affect him. It could egg on the disease in his mind. And I wasn't willing to risk that. I also couldn't act so alarmingly defiant in front of his coven.

I kept out of view, hovering over Chase and the others as they pursued them. They were so close, but meriting the distance to cover ground, they weren't fast enough. They had speed behind them but were too late. The group of vampires was running for a cliff edge. It was a dead end; except I had the sneaking suspicion they intended to dive into the water. I scanned the surroundings, the only way we could follow them was if we jumped too, and that would draw us out too far from our borders and territory. Maybe that's what they'd been targeting all along.

*I could hold them up, you only need a few extra seconds,* I telepathically said to Chase. I could feel his focus and fixation as he ran. He was enjoying the thrilling leg pounding run. It'd been some time since he'd given chase. My playful lover had turned into that badass scary vampire I'd first crossed paths with, who haunted and watched me from afar. He was reluctant, but I could feel the swell of his natural instincts take over, thrilled by the hunt. He didn't want to be disappointed in this pursuit either.

*We won't be long,* he replied. I curved a wicked smile, pleased that he trusted in me.

*Don't keep a girl waiting,* I teased as I leaned back and free fell toward the ground. This was liberation. It was raw, uncontrolled power at my fingertips, and I was idly playing in it, enjoying the wind that caressed my skin leaving goosebumps. My wings whipped around, the muscle movement jarring but effective on my back. But I didn't hold back my force enough. I'd really have to work on this flying thing. I smashed onto the cliff edge, parting a smile as the group of vampires screeched to a halt in surprise right before they could jump over. I'd anticipated them with perfect timing.

"Hello boys," I purred. The ground defiantly cracked beneath me, and my smile faltered. I jumped forward, skidding in front of them as the edge of the cliff broke off behind me, shattering from the impact. It was a rather flattering display of my strength.

They were startled and only faltered for a moment before decreeing that I was one singular woman. I flashed my fangs at them in a polite smile.

"Get her!" one of them shouted, awakening the rest into action. They gargled a camaraderie cheer. I jumped in with my delicate golden nails slashing at the first vampire's face and dodging the oncoming sword that glided past my back. I only had to keep them entertained from jumping over the cliff edge.

Rustling echoed from behind as Chase led his group of vampires into their mass and overpowered them. Darcy and Jerimiah were quick to flank me, making sure to intersect any others who raced for the edge. Some of them balled up attacking Chase's coven who gleefully sprung to the opportunity of slaughter after being in lockdown for so long. They attacked with an array of weapons. Cries and screams encompassed the cliff edge and echoed into the valley below.

Chase flicked his sword, spluttering dark blood onto the ground. He pivoted around another, his footing slowly approaching me as if we were in our own pleasurable dance.

I drove my claws into a vampire's chest, erupting his heart inside by squeezing it so tightly it exploded. I ripped out the tangible leftovers as the black mass of his decaying body dropped. A vampire ran between us, jumping over the edge and into the water. I went to give chase, but Jerimiah put his hand in front of me, stopping me. In my stead, he dove over the edge, solidifying as a gargoyle midair so he dropped faster. He splashed into the racing water, speedily reaching the vampire and fighting him in splashes as they stretched further down the valley and into the distance.

I swept a vampire's feet out from beneath her as she tried to run past me and over the edge. As I did, Chase dove down on her, piercing his sword into her chest. We looked at one another, a smile pressing on our lips in heart-pounding erotic pleasure.

I shoved back the vampire who dared try to attack him from behind. I punched his nose, breaking it and roundhouse kicked him. He took a few wobbly steps back. Darcy kicked up one of the spears that had fallen onto the ground, grabbed it, and pegged it into my vampire's chest. We all worked in perfect synchronicity.

With a small final gurgling noise, he combusted into a black mass. The vampire behind him skidded to a stop, realizing he was the last of the forty and now surrounded.

"Don't kill him," Chase said and the others compliantly submitted. Two of them pinned his arms and legs back so he couldn't fight against them.

"Who sent you?" Darcy asked, collecting the same spear from the decaying dead vampire. He didn't even bother wiping it off before he started dragging it along the vampire's chest, leaving deep trailing cuts in swirling motions. The vampire whimpered as he gagged in disgust from the other dead vampire's blood and remains mixing with his. "I'll give you only one chance," Darcy growled and slowly tilted the spearhead in harshly, dragging it around in luxurious circles.

"I don't know. We were just told to come here and make a statement, or we'd be next!" he said desperately, "That's all we were told!"

"From what coven?" Darcy asked in a coaxing tone that didn't match the character of who he usually was. He was usually light-hearted, and now he was cruel and wicked. The switch in his nature so undeniable that I admired it.

"Will you let me live?" the vampire begged, his chest rising and sinking in panic. He was so frightened of death that we didn't even have to use silver on him or various tactics of torture to pull the information from him.

"Sure," Darcy said. "Now tell me, who's coven you come from." He pressed his spear in further, close to the vampire's chest, black blood oozing around the tip. His body continuously tried to heal from the wound. He thrashed back and forth, the others only holding him tighter and snickering.

"Demetri's coven!" He sobbed and begged. "I'm from Demetri's coven!"

Darcy turned to Chase. They both shrugged. Neither of them was familiar with the name, but maybe Cesar would know whose coven it was that would dare patronize us.

"That's all then," Darcy merited and walked to the cliff edge. Chase and I followed him as those behind us tore the vampire apart. "How far down stream do you think he went?" he asked curiously, trying to block out the screams of the vampire behind us.

"Not too far, but it'll take him a while to get up here," Chase said somberly as we looked at the valley that stretched in height and length.

"Shall I go collect him?" I asked, fluttering my wings. A wicked grin sparked on Darcy's face. Now he looked like the goofy redhead and freckled child he often acted as—nothing like the menacing version I'd seen only a moment ago.

"Please do," he asked more pointedly to Chase.

"We'll clean up here," Chase offered, looking over the decaying bodies. "We'll throw their bodies into the water so there's no trace. I'll speak with Cesar. Looks like we might have a little side mission to venture out on." He grimaced. The others were excited, and though my vampire self was elevated that we were finally able to have some fun; a foreign coven attacking us wasn't something we could overlook or let play out for too long. And what made it worse was that someone else was playing puppeteer behind the scenes.

I kissed Chase on the cheek as a gentle parting and jumped over the edge, glorifying in the harsh muscular beat of my wings. My back ached in its new way use, but I knew in time, with a little bit of training and restraint, I'd perfect this skill like any other extension of my limbs and body. I swept over the river and closely reached out with my finger to lightly dance over its rapid waters. I found beauty in the valley and amassing rock around me. After a minute of searching, on the bank to my left was Jerimiah.

He was swatting off his black leather pants, uncomfortable by their saturation. I swept in left, pushing my wings hard against the wind to halt me. With little control, I plummeted into the rocky edge. It wasn't enough force that I hurt myself, but it was enough to be embarrassed by and clumsily enough to scratch down my arms. As if upset with the way they were being handled, my wings shook themselves off, an entity of their own. I pulled myself out from the rock face, raising a hand to Jerimiah to let him know I was okay and didn't need help.

"I've come to pick you up," I said.

"Not with that kind of driving you're not," he said dead serious. I stared at him in slight disbelief that he'd unknowingly made a joke.

"Did you get him?" I asked.

"Yes, they came from Demetri's coven. Whoever that might be." He shrugged and checked the few pockets he had for his weapons. "I'm not particularly familiar with the covens on this continent."

An idea sparked in me. "You know I could use you to help me in training as a weight to strengthen the muscles in my wings," I joked. He was mortified. "I'm joking, Jerimiah. Now let's catch up with the others."

"With all respect, Esmore. I feel slightly emasculated if I allow you to carry and fly me."

I grinned, liking the sound of that.

"But if we do, we'll get there sooner. And it's most pressing that we do," I teased. He grimaced, conflicted by his pride and responsibility. He looked at the wall I'd accidentally demolished and forfeited.

"Fine." He grimaced to himself, and I couldn't help but find amusement in the dig to his male pride. The more time I spent with these vampires, past their inhumane nature, I was discovering hidden personalities and humor. There was still a spark of life in most of them. I'd been so hindered by the idea of losing myself entirely and I was beginning to realize that maybe there stood a chance I wouldn't totally hate what I was becoming. Like I had today, I could have fun with both hunter and vampire alike. For the first time, in what felt like forever, I was satisfied by the day.

# CHAPTER 18

CESAR FLIPPED THE wooden desk in his chamber. It splintered all over the floor. I wondered how many of those he'd destroyed in his lifetime. Recently, his temperament was untapped as the stresses began to vex him. Lydia shifted uncomfortably beside him. Even after following him for so many years and previously being his lover, she was still cautious around his angry disposition. My mother watched on in silent contempt from across the room where she sat. The rest of Cesar's elite team was stationed outside waiting for their next order. Lydia was the only one permitted inside because she was one of the best at identifying members in covens and councils alike.

"Why wasn't anyone guarding the human?" Cesar bellowed, infuriated. The human we'd imprisoned downstairs had been killed during the commotion. After Cesar's absence and the attack on his members, Chase's group that handled it left a chaotic gap in the institute. And it left Connor to manage the restless group as well as securing the safety of my mother and Fire in Cesar's room. Meaning whoever had dared kill the prisoner had slipped into Cesar's wing which was even more alarming.

"I thought you had men posted outside!" Cesar narrowed on Balzar and Lydia. Both of whom had left with him to the foreign coven.

"We did," Balzar said blatantly and looked at Lydia pointedly. She uncomfortably fidgeted.

"I'm sorry, Cesar, it was an oversite. I thought when we swapped shifts and when Connor was in charge, he'd put someone on it in the meantime."

Connor snarled at her implication of him. Lydia raised her hands defensively. "I mean no offense. It's no excuse. This was my fault. I'm sorry," she said frightful of the consequence. Cesar snarled, kicking over a piece of the splintered wood. Not only had his meeting gone terribly wrong, but he also lost four men who'd been used as a message. On top of that, there'd been a fault in his guard leading to his prisoner being taken out in his very own wing. Everything was going particularly bad for Cesar today, and he had every intention of taking it out on the others.

We'd informed Cesar about Demetri's coven attack, and Balzar had been the one to find the remains of the human we'd kept prisoner. He'd been the bearer of bad news and taken on most of the brunt of Cesar's fury. It was messy. The moment we were attacked on the outside and dealt with it accordingly, our groups went into disarray and started fighting one another. It took Deemori's sabers, the gargoyles, and remaining members of Cesar's elite group to break it up. It'd been a mess. We were walking a very fine line of this entire estate erupting into mass implosion. Chase and I shared varying thoughts but concluded on one thing. For it to have been done so efficiently, it meant that someone within our very walls had done it. Someone poised enough waited for their moment to kill the human, or someone was stupid enough to risk their immediate satisfaction during all the havoc. Connor and Deemori remained silent in the darkly lit room.

Cesar's room was larger than ours in space, but was positioned on the second level with only one singular window that had been covered by a sheet. A few candles were lit offering it the same ominous glow of their coven located in the tunnels once before. The bed was grander than ours too but looked untouched. The most monopolized section was the very couch my mother now sat on, sipping on freshly boiled and cooled water. Fire sat by her side just as depleted from the argument.

The small click of the door grabbed our attention. Tythian walked in, adjusting his well-fitted blue dress shirt.

"And where the hell have you been?!" Cesar seethed, kicking the splintered pieces of what was once his desk. He ascended on Tythian, his rage palpable. Connor flinched in the slightest as Cesar walked past him. He'd considered defending Tythian until rank overshadowed the brothers and they seemed to shrink into the darkness further.

Cesar wrapped his hands around Tythian's throat. Tythian's icy blue eyes slid onto his leader, inactive to argue or fight him. Tythian had been the one to teleport Cesar and others to their coven meeting. Once their assembly had ended, he'd returned them to here. But if he wasn't with Cesar the entire time, then where had he vanished? He'd been aloof a lot lately, and it hadn't gone unnoticed. Cesar's grip only fastened around Tythian's throat in rage, as if it were his fault that all of this had happened. At any time, Tythian could teleport them out, change the dynamics of the situation, but even then, I wondered if his gift would work so greatly against Cesar. I'd only seen Cesar fight once, and that was briefly. But I perceived that others in his coven feared him, for what I imagine to be good reason.

"Cesar," my mother called out from behind him. "We need to find a solution instead of pointing our stubby figures around and playing the blame game."

Balzar's jaw unhinged in shock by the way my mother spoke to him. Connor side-glanced her unimpressed. Lydia was uncomfortably standing beside Deemori who had lost her long shirt in the commotion. She wore the shirt as frequently as Fire seemed to wear her human skin.

Cesar's cold gaze drifted to my mother, and she equally matched it. I mimicked the others, looking away and staying clear of being involved in their inner conflict. Tythian was still suspended in the air limply, his feet not touching the ground. Chase was holding back a laugh. I shot him an exaggerated look, effectively telling him to keep it in check.

Cesar dropped Tythian, letting him slowly slither down the door. He adjusted the collar of his shirt. "I was gathering more masks and robes as you'd requested."

Cesar grumbled under his breath and made his way to the center of the room. It felt oddly empty without Yolo being here.

Cesar sighed heavily, childishly pushing aside the splintered wood on the ground with his foot as he spoke. "We've got multiple issues here. I thought the Council would wait a little longer to make a move, even if by a few weeks. Demetri's coven isn't a threat. But the message is." He stroked his beard. "We need to act fast as well. Demetri doesn't lead an aggressive coven. They're smaller in size, and he keeps to himself for the most part, which means someone has forced his hand to send us a message and we have to reply."

"Don't you think we should try to align with him instead of turning on him?" Balzar asked.

"No, because he's already made a decision to make a move on us. He's intimidated by whoever forced him to make a move more than he is us," Chase said with a grimace. His playful nature had vanished. "My name and coven are new so maybe they'd be willing to take the risk and comply to whoever it was that forced his hand, but if he knew it was Cesar's coven then he deliberately made a choice. You do have a reputation," Chase admitted somewhat coy. He might've never faced him previously, but if Cesar was one of Oppollo's descendants, I had no doubt he had a name for himself.

"So, we locate and wipe out Demetri's coven to send the Council a message in return? That we shouldn't be underestimated, and it'll buy us more time. Or they'll come down harder on us, but either way, they'll make this into a habit. They're baiting us," Balzar said. I was certain there were more interworkings and components Cesar was considering. Though Balzar often led the elite twelve into fights, this wasn't his standard mission. This wasn't his tier, it was Cesar's, an old war. We would have to either stand against them or relocate again. But how often would we continue to relocate, like Cesar's ally mentioned today? But even if we did oppress them, for how long would that last?

"We will challenge them, but not just yet. We need to refocus and deliberate Tracey's Council. Wiping out Demetri's coven is a given, but we're being watched. It won't be enough just to wipe out their coven to make a point in our strength and numbers, which we'll need to do or the attacks will continue. But we need to gain leverage over their members and Council. It's time for you to negotiate with Tracey. We need to start finding leverage on the inside of their Council," Cesar said to Chase. We'd discussed it briefly before. That Chase, Tythian, and I should go to Antarctica and either manipulate through their ranks or convince them to side with us and against Oppollo. But no one knew how long that'd take, and I didn't want to risk the time gap and distance from Dillian, Titan, and the others any more than necessary.

"But the wolves—"

"Are nothing but yours and Yolo's interest," Tythian cut me off. Chase grabbed my hand, calming me into silence. There was a time and place, no matter how ignorant I thought Tythian was. "Cesar's right. We need to fall into action. We were forced to relocate from our old coven because of Thomas's betrayal." He offered Lydia a pointed look, and she uncomfortably stared at the ground, ashamed. After he'd been exiled, he offered himself to Fier's Council. They had no choice but to relocate. "And now our location has been found out already. We can't keep relocating at this rate. It's important we start getting numbers behind us or a seat at the Council ourselves at least. And the weakest Council to target is Tracey's. She has nothing to lose. Oppollo forced her into the Antarctic and her members are struggling. We use that to our advantage and negotiation."

"Do you really not think she'd know it was us who slaughtered her group those months ago?" Lydia reminded the group.

"No, I don't. You did a clean job did you not?" Tythian asked pointedly to me, Balzar, and Lydia. "No one saw, and there were no survivors. So she would've been sitting on her icy throne this entire time, simmering on the doubt of her fellow Council. It's an easy priority. We can get in."

Everyone silenced thinking about this new tactic. They'd been discussing it for some time, but the stresses of acting now was pushing everyone into a narrow-minded field.

"The wolves are important as well," I reiterated to Tythian. He filthily looked at Fire.

"The human government and their experiments are a new element, but we can't let it drive us from our original course of action. And that is obtaining a seat at the Council and opposing Oppollo." Tythian sneered.

"And if we have numbers, these wolves who effectively oppose vampires then—"

"You will not have time to build an army from wolves!" Cesar angrily spat. His desperate outburst caught me off guard. "My daughter, forgive me, but you do not understand the poison of this war. We are being targeted. *You* are being targeted. We don't have time. These wolves are nothing but a distraction that we can face at another time."

Calming waves washed over me as Chase stroked his calloused thumb over my hand. I wanted to pull it back, feeling betrayed by him. How could he side with Cesar? Why wouldn't he stand behind me? But he only sent me loving thoughts, and in his vision and goal, I was his only focus. My safety was his largest concern above all.

Cesar looked defeated. "Please understand, Esmore. I've been fighting this for a long time. Why do you think you found us hidden behind a wall of sabers and underground? I have lost good vampires to this fight and war already, constantly being cornered by the Council. All of the covens have been. Why do you think I had Tythian infiltrate Fier's Council and Yolo in the Human Compound?" Chase watched me wearily, conscious of his contribution to hunting down the covens under Fier's order. "This upcoming Council meeting is for certain going to erupt in chaos. Oppollo want's utter rule and he will rid any objection to that." He looked at me pointedly. Me. I was one of those threats to him, known for a gift in which I couldn't even use.

"It's not just your gift he finds threatening, Esmore," my mother spoke up as if having heard my thoughts. "It's what you stand for. You're not anchored to any one species or side. You can rally against him in a way that no other has been able to do before."

"That, and he tried to kill her once and failed," Balzar said dryly. I felt like there was much unsaid in my mother's words and I didn't entirely understand her foreboding tone.

"Fier had hoped to overthrow him by this Council meeting," Chase said idly. His voice was strained as he tried to push away the toxic thoughts he had of Fier and how he'd violated him. Fier was the only one who could rid him of this disease. We were all racing against time. Oppollo had to be wiped out so Chase wouldn't have to suffer anymore. And the only way to do that was an all-out war. Coven verses Council.

"Which he needs us for," Tythian said in a monotone, undoubtedly angered by being caught once by Fier as well. "Cesar's right. We need to advance on Tracey's Council. The longer we wait the worse it could be."

"We sort out this Demetri coven to counter any other attacks, and focus on rallying other covens, while you focus on Tracey's Council for an in on the Council table," Balzar reiterated. Everyone seemed in agreement but me. My irrational anger bubbled over, the vampire sneer taking hold. Chase clamped down his hand on mine, pulling me back from lashing out. Yes, I was coming from a selfish place, but I needed to make sure the others were and would always be safe.

"I can't just leave them," I growled to Cesar under my breath. "They might be *just* hunters to all of you, but they're *my* team. I've put them into enough danger as it is."

"Stupid girl, can't you see everyone is in danger!" Tythian snapped, uncharacteristically. Chase and Balzar stood in front of me protectively. I barged through them, ready for this fight—begging for it. Cesar's large frame towered over me as he blocked my path. He looked down on me with a hollow expression.

"Perhaps I have spoilt you too much," he said, absent of any emotion.

"Or perhaps she needs time to adjust, she's an eighteen-year-old girl," my mother said as she stood from the corner of the room. Fire's growl and piercing blue eyes seemed to glow from the dark. "And she's been dragged into a war we've all had more time to prepare for."

Cesar deflated. I was offended and mortified that my mother suggested it was because of my age or lack of maturity to grasp the situation. But at most, I wanted to kill something or someone, so sick of being pushed back and forth in this never-ending fight.

I whistled once, calling on Fire. I just wanted to run and hunt and not be around anyone until I fully calmed down. I was about to snap at any moment, and it would only prove their point, which infuriated me all the more.

"Esmore," Chase said from behind, trying to grab my elbow. I pulled it out of his reach, storming to the door and waiting for Fire to join me before I slammed it shut, leaving them in the darkness of their ridiculous meeting.

I stormed down the stairs, barging through vampires who didn't dare move out of my way fast enough.

"Oh, Esmore," Lincon chimed with the twins depressingly trailing behind him. "Am I missing another meeting?"

I barged past him, knocking his shoulder and throwing him into the twins. He laughed hysterically before I picked up speed and ran, wishing I could turn into some kind of physical beast like Fire, instead of being controlled by it from within. She ran beside me, keeping pace with me.

I felt Darcy and Jerimiah follow me, not so closely, but enough to reiterate that I'd never be alone. Only secure and told what to do like their little girl. I was imploding and had to ensure I was far enough from Chase where my emotions wouldn't affect him from the disease Fier tainted him with. My vision went hazy as I allowed myself to finally give in to the temptation of letting the beast out and tiring my pent-up rage. I either submitted to it now, or it'd be only a matter of time until it took over entirely.

# CHAPTER 19

I
T WAS MY mother who found me, limply folded against a tree from exhaustion because of my rampage. Fire looked equally as tired. Those few hours had been a blur as I scuttled about devouring prey and destroying anything in my path. When I'd awoken from my outburst and sat against the tree, I studied my hands and fingers that were smeared with blood. My blood. My nails had peeled back and were already sowing to heal. The surrounding trees had unnatural claw marks in them from where I'd taken my aggression out. A few had even splintered and keeled over from the impact where I'd used my fists instead.

I had been somewhat aware of Darcy and Jerimiah following me. They had kept their distance and ensured to redirect vampires who were hunting to specifically stay clear of me or return to the institute. Fire had never left my side or got in my way. I was tired. Frustrated. And dare I consider—fragile.

"It's not their fault you know," my mother said as a way of greeting as she trudged through the mud after a full day's rain. Her brown leather boots sloshed as she approached me, her robe the same that we'd worn when we visited the Hunter Guild.

"You didn't help my case by suggesting I was acting like a child," I said bitterly.

"Esmore, my love, you are a child of this war. And your blind loyalty is what will be your downfall." She stood across from me, looking down on me as Fire brushed her nose into the palm of her hand in greeting. I sneered at the gesture. Obviously, Fire wasn't above picking sides.

"We're all children of war. If we weren't, none of our kind would even exist. And my blind loyalty is why I was selected as a Token. To lead a team and have their lives in my hands, I can't so quickly throw that away even amongst all of this madness."

"Yes," my mother agreed. "And it's no negative attribute in a leader. But in this fight, it is because there is so much more to be lost. And trust me when I say, even though you feel like plenty has already been taken from you, there is always more to lose."

"I know that," I grumbled, annoyed by her tone that made me feel as if I were a child being taught an important lesson. I knew what was left to be taken, and I was so desperately holding on to it, trying to protect it. And because of that I was being turned on and reprimanded for it. I wasn't the one leading covens or armies. I was a pin-up of what I *might* represent. And though I did not doubt their beliefs and understanding of this war were better than my own, I was being pushed down by this pressure of being told where I needed to be and when, especially when I felt divided by place. Beside the remains of my hunter team and the wolves that they'd promised to protect, who I'd promised to protect. And Chase. It just became further complicated from there. I lifted my knees to my chest, staring at my blood-stained nails. And then there was this thing inside of me. The creature that always lurked in my inner shadows, waiting to be freed. It was greedily becoming louder and slowly unhinging my huntress beliefs and programming. I was certain it wouldn't be too long until it unnerved me completely into a state I'd never be able to return from.

"I want you to return to the New York Hunter Guild with me," my mother said. I snapped my gaze on her. Was she spiraling into insanity as well?

"I'm not so certain we have the same recollection as to how they tried to kill us last time?" I asked dryly. "But then again, you were the one exchanging notes and plotting out ulterior motives, so what would I know."

My mother let out a small sigh, irritating me in the way she seemed condescending. "Esmore, do you recall what I'd first said when we were reunited? That I'd been busy putting things into place to ensure your safety. As does Cesar and everyone else, in the grand scheme to ensure most of us make it out of this fight alive, and also *you*."

"I'm no more important than anyone else!" My vision hazed purple, and I barred my fangs at her. My outburst infuriated me only further. Both at her and me. I was so sick of being suggested as so precious and fragile. Fire peeled back her own lips, growling with her canines on display. She might've vowed to stay by my side, but it clearly didn't deter her from having an opinion of me. My mother's orange eyes bore into me, unimpressed. "Don't look at me like that! I can't stand your judgment! You did this to me! I am the creation of your doing! So, don't you dare judge me in disgust!"

"I'm not judging you because of what you are. I'm judging you because of your inability to control your temper," my mother gritted out, attempting to remain the face of calm. She had always been like this, in control of herself and the room she walked in. She was as awe-inspiring as she was lethal. And above all she had the tendency to ensure she was always right.

"Oh, I don't know, maybe it's because a certain mother removed my heart, I lack in emotions and so when I'm close to my familiar, I'm bombarded with an intensity I can't entirely understand. So maybe that has something to do with my unsuspecting temper, oh, as well as throwing in I'm dealing with newly founded vampirism all in a few short months."

"And how long shall we keep playing this loop?" My mother sneered back. "I apologized numerous times. And it was for your greater good. Even I didn't understand the consequence of what would happen, but at least it'd keep you alive. You say you're not important. Who knows, maybe not? But what I do know for a fact is that you are *my* daughter!" She erupted, surprisingly. My mother rarely had outbursts. "And whether you hate me for the rest of your days or not, I will still do everything in my power to keep you alive. And make no mistake, I will do what I can to keep the others secure and alive as well. But you, Esmore, are my priority."

The dense air between us filled with silence. The sentiment of family was frowned upon in our kind. We were guarded in nature. We weren't to show displays of weakness, even for our own blood. I'd seen harsher parents, who only reproduced to give back to the Guild an aspiring heir. Some became supportive of their children, and whispered such endorsement in the shadows, scared they'd be reprimanded and thought of as deteriorating if heard out loud. Here my mother and I were, having a discussion I never thought I'd be a part of. We were the same. I'd learned most of what I knew, following her lead and guidance, in complete awe of the necessity she was within the Guild. And now we were both lost, playing at a war that was bigger than us, and always had been, all in the sake of protecting those who we loved. And we were engrained with a natural response to dive into a situation head-on, sacrificial even. We were both at a loss and it embarrassed me to be so childishly taking it out on her.

"I don't want anything happening to you either," I said more gently. "I thought I'd lost you once already." Although I had doubted Campture's words and was in denial about my mother's death. The reality was she was absent, and I never thought I'd see her again. Was that not enough reason to believe that she might've been dead?

"I know," she admitted in a small voice. Fire nuzzled her head under my hand, waiting for her privileged pat. Fire's greatest disappointment was she could never bear a child. The sentiment wasn't lost as she silently mediated my mother's and my argument, trying to find closure as best we could in a world that had been foreign to us for so long. We'd both adapted, it was our nature. We were warriors and survivors. But it didn't mean that either of us knew the answers. And like to like—we both stood tall, announcing our thoughts with conviction as the hunters we were, unwilling to let our own inner tremble show. Simply, my mother was better at it than I was. And I was already slowly losing to an inner battle I'd unknowingly been fighting my entire life.

"The reason we went to the Hunter Guild wasn't entirely because of the human government movement, though it played a part. The woman who led us to the meeting with Sabe, the one with the eyepatch; her name is Louise, and she has the gift of foresight. Her and I once trained together, before you were even born, as members of Guilds exchanged training quarterly. She clearly warned that I would give birth to a child, one who had the ability to both heal the world or destroy it. That you would not be what we are as traditional hunters and would be pursued by all legions once they found out about you. I dismissed her, thinking she hadn't yet trained around her gift properly and that she was mixing fantasy with delusional thinking. And I never thought twice about it. Not until after having met Cesar."

"Where you let the vampire woo you over, and I came to be," I bitterly mocked, still so anguished over the detail that the man who raised me and I'd loved wasn't my father. But in every way, he still had that honor. He guided me in ways that my mother hadn't. So much had happened these past few months and it was only now that my mother and I had the briefest of encounters to have this conversation. Not about warfare or our next step and impending doom, but a relationship that was broken, where it once thrived. And the reasons for my mother's actions and how it impacted me.

"No one tried to fight against it more than I did. A vampire, truly." She looked up with an anxious sigh. "I hated myself and tried to kill him on more accounts than I'd like to admit. He was a monster, an obstruction to everything I'd been taught." My stomach twisted, her words all too relevant to when I'd first met Chase and how hard I'd tried to fight my compulsion of curiosity and need for him. "But there he was. An unnatural and in explainable pull and desire to claim him. I fought it, Esmore, I truly did. And even after the days were done and we'd entangled in one another's company, I was revolted by myself in the way that it was the first calmness or vulnerability I'd truly felt in my life. I pushed away, and he pulled. I ran, and he tried to chase. But he was burdened with a coven and was already on the run from Oppollo so it made my departure all the more easy. Well, that was until…"

"Until I came along," I said for her. She nodded curtly.

"That was when I recalled Louise's prophecy. I was burdened throughout the entire pregnancy, scared of how you would come out, what you would be. A mixing of hunter and vampire was unheard of. But no one on record had my gift either. I was relieved when you were born. No abnormalities, a little baby girl with bright purple eyes, who looked more like me than her actual father. And so I raised you with Tyler like a normal huntress. He had fears it'd change, but I wanted us to move forward with normal lives as if it'd never happened. Until your eighteenth. That's when it all changed. When your gift immediately turned on you and started naturally attacking me, for the first time ever in my life, I felt terror. It was as if an amounted pressure from the years, unknowing if you had vampirism erupted suddenly then. And I knew then that darkness would inevitably call to you and you were bound by that destructive nature. I did the only thing I could think of at the time.

I took your heart so you couldn't use your gift, and hid it. That's when I found Cesar. And here we are. I reached out to Louise because although I mocked her gift, she told me the day the movement was upon us, she'd help us. Apparently, the future can often change, and so she said she saw many outcomes. But that we'd need the hunters. Not all of them, because they would sooner kill us for being traitors. But those who believed in this changing of times and weren't bound by the mold we'd been placed in and no longer believed in our methods and dealings with the humans. I gave Louise that note, to suggest a meeting place and time. That being tonight."

I sat there, absorbing all of this. "So how did you know she would still help us, after all these years?"

"Much like what everyone else is doing, I had to take a gamble in order to call on allies. Esmore, what's coming frightens me." I was agape. It was the first I'd ever heard my mother admit that out loud. "Everything is a risk. Much like Cesar is rallying covens, this is how I can play my part. A back-up of sorts in whatever way it might benefit us. If I'd known what Cesar and I had truly inflicted on you I would've been better prepared."

My mother looked exhausted, her usually vibrant, glowing skin taking on a dull complexion. Her blonde hair that was plaited similar to mine hadn't been washed in weeks. This was taking its toll on everyone. Seeing my mother so openly look vulnerable in front of me struck through a bravado to protect her, just as much as she was me. Just as I was selfishly trying to protect the others as my priority, hers was me, and I couldn't mock or deny her that right.

"I still don't like the idea of infiltrating Tracey's Council," I confessed.

"I know. None of us are keen on the idea. But it's important. We're hiding in the shadows for now, but we can't stay here for too long or that's how we'll get taken out."

I rested my hand on my chest, where my heart should've beat instead of a synthesized form from my mother's gift. So much had happened that I'd never considered what it might be like to have that back in my chest, to be equipped with such a gift that could be used for mass destruction. If my gift had the ability to splinter away at any moving creature, whether dead or alive, perhaps that was the answer to defeating Oppollo. "Maybe my heart and power are the only way to bring this to an end?" I looked up at her solemnly. Only my mother and Cesar knew where my heart was hidden. I felt violated that my gift, my true identity as a huntress had been taken without my knowledge or permission. I'd overcome and compensated for my lack of magical ability. But I finally understood why my mother had done all that she had leading to this point.

"Maybe," my mother said quietly. "But if you lose control like you did on the first night it activated, it would be catastrophic and a beacon to those who are hunting you down." It also challenged the greater question, my most important purpose of living. Even if I managed my gift, how would Chase handle it? We were in this together. The moment I received my heart and gift and we were intimate, my gift would be transferred to him. With his mental state and the disease that was eroding within him, could he cope? Would it completely undo him? It wasn't just a matter of if I could control it and anyone within the vicinity survived.

I stared at my dry bloodied hands. I had to figure out a way to vanquish Oppollo with these bare hands of mine. But how? "What are you hoping will come out of this meeting with Louise?" I asked. "We can't exactly waltz back into the center of New York, and I don't want to subject Dillian and the others to that again."

"I don't intend on taking them. It'll be just you and me this time. Well, and of course a few security measures, on behalf of Cesar's demand. We'll be taking his elite team in case the meeting goes wrong. And Lincon."

"Lincon is never a good idea," I warned her, surprised she was willing to include him.

"Lincon and Cesar have history. He doesn't trust him nor like him. But the stray vampire you collected from the Human Compound isn't exactly insignificant in this grand war either. He's been around just as long as Cesar has. He knows of this old war between vampires. It was never about humans against vampires. It'd always been the vampire's playground. Oppollo just had one intention and that was always to conquer, when he'd unified the Vampire Council and basically took control of that, he moved on to the next species which was humans. They'd both been there for that, personally. And the reason why he's coming is for the reason that he came to the Hunter Guild in the first place. In case something goes wrong he can fortify the illusion she's outnumbered. Or unless she has turned and brought a team to kill us, then we use brute strength in return. So what do you say?" My mother offered her hand out to me. There was still so much I didn't understand. And hearing of Lincon's and Cesar's history should've alarmed me more than it had. But I'd gotten used to everyone having their own secrets and history. And I had to trust my mother and her conviction.

I accepted her extended hand, and she pulled me up, resting her hands on my shoulders. "I do love you, Esmore. Maternal care is foreign to our kind, but I have it. Somewhere deeper than just being a huntress, I'm aware that you are my only child and I would kill or hunt anything to ensure your safety, no matter how old you are."

I placed my hand on my mother's, slightly uncomfortable by the gesture but felt like it was necessary. In ways that we couldn't naturally share our emotions and thoughts, I hugged her instead. The gesture far grander than how I might've stumbled to articulate my response. So instead all I said was, "I love you too. And we'll all make it out of this alive."

My mother's warm embrace tightened around me. We would prepare for the fights ahead of us as best we could with the clear vision of being victorious because there was no other option. Only death, and it wasn't one any of us was willing to claim.

# CHAPTER 20

I N THE DEAD of night, when the quarter moon was at its peak, we waited at the outer edge of the old city of New York. The fog unified a wall of sorts where we couldn't peer into the city. My mother and I waited in the open, with robes and masks on. I was still certain Cesar had an ulterior motive as to why he was enforcing everyone who left the institute to wear them. I wasn't convinced it was only for the purposes of concealing our identities and unifying us in such a way, but I followed suit. I acknowledged that Cesar had been playing this game of war far longer than I had. And as the brothers suggested, he had his reasons for everything, no matter how peculiar they might've seemed at the time.

My mother and I stared intently into the mist, waiting, depending on this meeting to happen. Fire was at my side. It was a brief discussion as to whether I should bring her. But I wanted it to be out of the question, from now on she was to go everywhere with me. It even brought Chase some relief to know she would be there at least in his stead. Lincon, Tythian, Balzar, and Cesar's elite group were hidden behind us, deep in the overthrow of the night within the trees. Balzar was leading the elites, a task he was honored to take.

I lightly clanked my golden nails together, concealing my hands in my long robe. We were strapped with weapons, but like any meeting of negotiations or exchange of information, we had to look unarmed. Louise of course would act the same, and I had no doubt she would bring others—if she ever came at all. Or maybe she'd come with half an army. That was the gamble we were playing with tonight.

In the distance, Louise's fluorescent green eye appeared amongst the depths of the fog, as other colored and bright eyes appeared in the same way. Their silhouettes slowly dawned on us as they approached, splitting the fog into two. There were only six of them. My nails clambered defiantly against one another. The others being faces I recognized. The tall brute of a hunter and woman with an axe followed Louise. The same hunter who'd poisoned me, much to my surprise. Beside them was Sabe, who I adamantly thought was setting us up. The charismatic hunter, who had appeared to be Michelle's advisor, surely wouldn't be daring enough to turn on his own Head Hunter? I wasn't familiar with the other man, but I'd made sure to engrain his face into my mind in case this went the wrong way.

My lips peeled back, revealing my fangs instinctively, even when hidden behind the mask. This would be the supposed group who would turn on their own, the Hunter Guild, just as we had? Or they'd be the wiser to turn on us now. All we were riding on was a prophecy based on twenty years ago, a note passed from my mother, and my mother's conviction that this was the right measure to take. Of all those elements, the last was the only one I had any faith in. But I wouldn't lower my guard even for a second, thinking that there could possibly be so many others like us.

"Trinity," Louise called out to my mother then looked at me. "And you must be, Esmore." I dipped my head in response. Her gaze descended to Fire with piqued interest, though she didn't seem surprised by her. I wondered if she'd already seen this meeting in advance or associations with wolves in general.

"It's smaller than I thought they'd be," Sabe said with a charming smile. Fire growled in reply. I delicately relinquished one of my hands, slowly placing it on Fire's back that came to my hip. My movement was deliberate so my gold nails would catch their attention in a way of warning.

"Would you like to see how small she is up close?" I asked dryly. I could feel my mother's warning glare.

"You once said you could help me," my mother said to Louise. I could sense Balzar and the others restless behind us. Ready and desiring to attack. How they'd love the opportunity to take down a group of hunters as a treat.

"I did, and I can forewarn you that our discussion here will be limited. Let's just say some of those who are guarding your backs aren't entirely trustworthy, and should they overhear our discussion, then it'll be a chain of events that won't benefit either of our goals."

I hovered my mind over the vampires behind us, identifying if anyone reacted to her statement. Some seemed focused, others curious, and mostly angry that they couldn't attack unless given the order.

Irritation. It was Tythian who overshadowed the rest, annoyed. From what I gathered to be from teleporting us once again. Lincon was jittery, like usual, for a fight or some form of entertainment to break out.

"And are you saying all of yours can be trusted?" I asked.

"How dare you," the bulky hunter sneered. "We're not the one's fraternizing with bloodsuckers!"

"Enough!" Louise silenced him. Sabe flashed another brilliant smile at me, purposefully trying to antagonize me. He rested his hands casually in his pockets. "Despite his words, we're all here for the same reason. There are others like us across the continent that are outsourcing another way from what we've become. From what I've seen, your involvement is essential to that."

"We want to see the fangs," Sabe said impatiently. "We want to witness with our very own eyes this mix breed that Louise has told us so much about."

"She's not taking her mask off," my mother said coldly. I side glanced her. Considering she was the one conducting this meeting, surely, she'd know this would come into question.

"No offense, mother duck, but we have a right to see the truth of this before we put our lives on the line for it," the brute of a hunter said.

Louise shot him down with an effective glance.

Sabe sighed. "All we're saying is that we need some kind of evidence. All we can see is hunter's eyes, and please forgive us, Louise, we trust in your gift, it's never led us astray. But this isn't something we've seen or heard of. All we are asking is for a little evidence."

I hovered my mind over my mother's. I tapped on her mind in an attempt to communicate with her. She slowly drew open to me. I was exposed to her raw emotion and inner workings. I took a second to rebalance myself, an avalanche of her thought processes and personal mechanics rubbing on me. The intimacy of speaking with someone in their mind was overpowering, alluring, and felt perverted all in one.

*I could just show them my fangs,* I said to her. Cesar and my mother had their reasons for ensuring we didn't show our faces. So, I could make sure to not show them entirely. As much as I didn't want to be submitting to their demands, this is why we were here. And I would be requesting the same evidence if I were in their position. *Or maybe even my wings, they seem to be impressive.*

*Only your fangs, nothing else that might identify you,* she strictly replied. It was then I realized the hiding of our identities came from a place of fear. I pushed into my hood, lacing the strings to my mask around my fingers and pulling gently. I pinched my mask up, making sure to cover the upper half of my face, and flashed a striking smile. One of them gasped.

"Do they actually work?" Sabe asked smart-ass like. I couldn't see him, but I could picture the smile on his face.

"Would you like to test?" I asked. I lowered my mask again, so I could see through the eyeholes and tied the mask back up tightly.

"Surely this isn't all the evidence you need?" my mother ordained.

"No," Louise said. "But it's enough for now. You won't see us for some time. We're not needed yet." She walked toward my mother. I ensured my golden nails were sparkling elegantly in preparation. She offered my mother a folded handwritten note. "As I said before, we can't speak here. Your company is a larger threat to you than you know." She looked at me pointedly. "You're being watched."

Surely, she didn't mean in the literal sense right now. She lingered with note in hand and suggested my mother open it only when she was alone. The air was tense as she approached my mother and offered it. Both groups were guarded and ready to attack at a moment's notice. But they amicably exchanged the note.

"The road ahead will not be kind on you," Louise said to me, her one eye focusing through my mask as if she could see all of me. "Fight the darkness that eats away at you because if you don't, you *will* lose those you care about most."

I grimaced at her words, offended that she thought she knew me or the extremities of the nature that lie beneath.

"We're done here," Sabe said, waving a hand over at me. "See you guys around, maybe." Louise lingered briefly to take one last look at my mother before following her group. They ventured back into the mist, alert as they turned their backs on us.

I caught Lincon by the back of his leather jacket, yanking on him and slamming him onto his back. He seemed dazed by my reflexes.

"No! We were meant to have fun!" he said, throwing his legs and arms in the air. "I thought we were going to get into a fight! And I was so good last time! Please, Esmore, just one?" he begged sincerely.

"No," I snarled. Fire snapped her jaws toward his face. He cackled, not frightened in the slightest by her being so close to his throat. It infuriated her only more. Where other vampires within the covens stepped well clear of her, understanding that only one bite could be their demise, Lincon flirted with the thought of danger.

Perhaps it was Lincon she'd described as the untrustworthy one. Or any of the vampires behind us for that matter. I didn't trust any of them more than the next, and I'd become complacent with my company. But so many of them had proven to take care of me when I was incapable of doing so myself. Of what gain would they have to turn on me now? I reefed Lincon up by his collar. "C'mon, we're going now."

It was an underwhelming and aloof meeting with very little in detail. I side glanced my mother who had already pocketed the note. Whatever was on those pages were surely the answers my mother might've been hoping for. But I honored that we might've gained nothing at all from today. We would still have to work with what we had now.

An ominous, prickling sensation threaded on my skin, and my mind felt hazy. I detached from my mother and fixated back on the mass walling of fog to enter the city. Someone was watching us. The image and reminder of my previous dream came into manifestation sporadically. The scene of us all nailed and strung up on the side of buildings. This was that same presence.

"No," my mother grabbed my arm, having already sensed my curiosity intending to veer me astray.

"Someone's watching us," I whispered.

"I know."

"It feels like the same presence that's been haunting my dreams and distorting my memories," I said quietly, hoping very few others would hear. "I need to find out who or what it is."

"This isn't about only you, remember?" my mother said and tugged my wrist lightly in the direction where Tythian waited for us. "It's not a risk we can take today."

"Your mother's right," Lincon grumbled, mocking her feminine voice. "We should go."

"Since when do you listen to reason?" I asked, kicking up dirt at him as he still laid on the ground. His cackle echoed through the trees. Something didn't feel right about this situation.

"I listen to reason when I know the odds aren't in my favor," he solemnly said. Had I hit his head too hard into the ground?

"Esmore, please," my mother begged. "Leave it for another day." Fire rubbed against my leg, encouraging me to move back to the group. This had been a part of my mother and my conversation. And I adamantly swore my best to listen instead of following my selfish notions. I needed to trust in her and stop acting of my own accord because it did affect everyone else. What if it put the others in danger? It was difficult to subdue my curiosity and turn my back on my nature that would often run into harm's ways for answers. But I'd also promised Chase I'd be careful, and if he were in the same circumstance, I'd want him to listen to reason as well.

I agreed with my mother. Tension rose in my stomach every step I took away from the looming presence that called to me. My mother's urgency was real, and I was the first to be thrown into Tythian's arms to be teleported.

There was equality in our discussions, but I was still being kept in the dark and prioritized into safety first.

# CHAPTER 21

I'D BECOME ACCUSTOMED to the secrecy within the institute and aired the same mystery around myself. It was only a matter of time until all those bundled secrets and withheld information would collapse on us one way or another. For Lincon to have so quickly closed up the way he had only piqued my curiosity further. There had been a presence looming in the mist. Not part of the Hunter Guild but something entirely of its own entity. And both my mother and Lincon sensed it and warned me away from it. We'd all made it back safely, but it meant whatever the presence was that tormented me in my dreams was now catching up to me in my reality. Or maybe it'd always been there. Whatever it was I had my suspicions that Lincon most definitely knew what it might've been, and perhaps even my mother.

Chase and I were summoned to Cesar's quarters shortly after we'd only just arrived. Chase had been snuffing rising tensions in his coven as they became restless and took offense to his accusations that someone within the institute had killed the human prisoner. It was an inexcusable felony. No one seemed to know about it or stepped forward.

I tapped on Cesar's door, waiting for the beefy vampire to call us in. Inside, a small circular table had been organized in the center of the room. My mother was already sitting beside Cesar and Tythian. Two chairs remained available for us. A small, murmured gasp in the corner of the room grabbed my attention. There hidden behind a small Asian themed paper screen was a human weakly dazed and gasping. Their wrists were bloodied. My fangs ejected, climaxing at the thought of burying myself deep into his pulsing wrist. Chase grabbed my hand, pulling me by the waist and into him as he guided me toward the table.

"A little discourteous, wouldn't you say?" Chase said with an iron grip as he led me to the table. I grappled at the strands of my control, desperate to try and focus on anything else but the delicious meal in the corner of the room. Chase was crashing calming waves over me and helping me fixate on the warm glass of blood in front of me. My hands were trembling beneath the table. I flashed a quick glance at my mother, ashamed of my impulses, but still unable to keep my gaze from shifting to the corner of the room.

"Oh, come now, it's one tiny human. Surely the great daughter of Cesar can control herself if only slightly," Tythian said in a dry, sarcastic tone. My mother was evidently uncomfortable as she pushed her glass of water away. Chase as a way of distraction hoisted the bottle of wine he'd brought.

"Well, I didn't figure out who killed our prisoner yet, but I did find a very good, aged wine in the cellar that I thought we could try." He raised a suggestive brow, cooing the others to join in. His other hand was still firmly planted into mine. He placed it on the table, intentionally drawing their attention away from me.

*You can have my glass too, Esmore,* Chase offered as he pushed his wine glass filled with freshly squeezed blood beside mine. *You're okay. Just focus on me.* Cesar hadn't commented on my impulses before, but I was starting to have the impression that after this recent 'message' received from Demetri's coven, he couldn't cater to my personal needs or desires. I was no longer his 'spoilt child' as the others had once called me.

I wondered where Balzar and Connor were, considering they were usually a part of these meetings. But supposed after the outbreak in Cesar's coven, after he so grandly put a few of his own vampires on display in an attempt to draw out the culprit, they were needed to simmer out the tension he'd brewed.

When we returned, Cesar's elite team had been put into place, full force to calm them down and ensure they didn't provoke a fight with Chase's coven to try and relieve their own tension. It only needed to be a small spark to create a deadly outbreak amongst them. Fire sat in front of the Asian screen where the human was huddled behind. Every time my eyes darted over to it, she lifted a lip and growled quietly, as if in warning that she'd attack me sooner than let me dive in for that human.

I readily accepted Chase's strength and calm waves, deterring from the thirsty vampire within that clawed at me from the inside to escape. Cesar took a tempered swig of his wine glass. "Put that wine away, boy," he chastised.

"And here I thought the Paps was starting to like me." Chase rolled his eyes, making idle chat at me. He was drawing the attention for himself, as always, so they weren't as focused on me as I noticeably reined in my urges.

"Ever the smug one, Chase, even when we need to be serious. That quirk of yours will get you killed one day," Tythian commented, raising his glass to his lips.

"Enough of this macho business," my mother interrupted. Her gaze avoided the corner of the room where the human was shallowly breathing. "Let's just be done with this conversation." Her glare was ineffective on Cesar. He still hadn't entirely simmered from his last outburst.

"You need to go to Tracey's Council and see what you can manage," he said devoid of emotion. He assessed his glass and licked his lips impatiently. "Let Yolo manage the little wolf pack while you do your duty."

Chase opposed his hand to Cesar. "Just to make one thing clear, she doesn't have a duty and will do as she pleases. The only way this goes forward is if she agrees willingly." I was overwhelmed with the love Chase held for me. He agreed that we had to go to Tracey's Council, but he still wouldn't stand for someone speaking to me in that manner. I swallowed hard, unwilling to open my mouth in case it enticed me even further with the intoxicating smell of the human. Instead, I swiftly grabbed my glass, downing the lukewarm fresh blood. It took the edge off only slightly.

"Listen here, boy, you may run a coven, but you're still in over your head if you think—"

"Well, firstly I think I'm a much better negotiator than you. After all these years you still haven't learned how to play nice." Chase tisked.

"Interesting, considering you're the bannerman for bringing together other covens."

Tythian swirled his glass. "You seem to live in a mindset of time and luxury considering the ticking time bomb you have in your head. At any point you could go saber, and then *we* will lose the advantage to having your coven as an asset. And that binding is simply because of who your familiar is to us."

Chase snaked a smile, but I pressed my hand to his. They weren't threatening him. But it was putting a lot of unnecessary heated pressure if I continued to act like their adversary. My mother had asked me to become more compliant for all of our sakes. And so I wanted to offer my willingness. To put down my pride as a Token, and do what was needed of me if it'd help Chase and the others in the long run.

"I'll go," I gritted out. The taste and smell of the human danced on my tongue. Chase's hand stapled my hand to my knee, ensuring I stay put. "But I need to make sure the others will be okay. Beyond only Yolo's protection."

"We can't spare any more guards into your secret little oasis," Tythian sneered. He'd been growing even more bitter toward me these last few weeks. And I realized as his immaturity was gleaming through, I had an advantage to keep my cool.

"Those are my terms," I replied. "If I'm to endure going to whatever place with *you* of all people as well, and risk others safety in my absence, then you bet I have a small condition to be adhered to."

"Tythian," Cesar dismissed, stroking his beard. Tythian flashed an angry glare my way. Gone were the days where he could have his say every time and his bidding be twisted to his beg and call. Those days were behind me where I fell for his manipulation. I had to put my people first. *Our people,* I said to Chase. His coven included who could swarm around and protect him when he needed it. We had to be ready for the offensive, so we weren't caught off guard like last time, and divided once again. At least in Tracey's Council, we'd be able to go together.

"Fine, discuss it with Yolo. But let me make this clear, daughter," Cesar's endearment wasn't sweet, but as sharp as a blade that'd just been forged. "Yolo cannot be there forever playing nurse and scientist. This divide has gone on for too long. Either the wolves can reform to our bidding, and the same for your hunter friends, or they're on their own."

"I promised them safety."

"When your focus is divided, it'll draw our enemies closer to your vulnerabilities," Cesar belittled. "Take this little attack on the inside as an example." He wasn't angry at me directly but his inability to yet find the culprit.

"What about Demetri's coven?" Chase asked. The question snapped Cesar out of his feverish grumbling. My mother daringly put her hand over his. His gaze fastened on her as if repulsed. But his body sagged under the touch, and he curled his thumb over hers slightly. He'd lived too many years as a vampire that could savage villages at a time. And my mother so daringly brought him back to something more humane. The balance between the two was remarkable to watch.

"I'll send out a group in two days' time," Cesar acknowledged. "Find out who sent them, and then wipe them out as a returning favor and message. I'll focus on that while you focus on how to deal with Tracey's Council. I'll leave that up to you two boys since you've already dealt with her within Fier's Council."

"And what shall we do about the little one's heart?" Tythian asked casually. We all froze. My mother was the first to tilt her head in interest.

"*That* is of no concern to you," she emasculated.

"Well, of course it is. If we're to use her as an example of what we can bring to the party, don't you think we should at least be able to put her power on display? Or did your hunter friend inform you not to say anything in her little note?"

"Watch it, boy," Cesar snarled, turning on him. "I've had enough of your cockiness these last few days."

Tythian's blue eyes rested on us one by one. He scoffed and stood up. "Well, I suppose this meeting's done. I'll excuse myself." He teleported across the room, taking the human with him. It was bittersweet. I'd wanted the human for myself, but relief washed over me as the temptation had finally been removed.

"What did the note say?" I asked my mother. She side glanced Cesar, still holding his hand.

"Not much, only to keep you safe and alert to the dangers around us, yet she didn't specify much other than that." I could tell my mother was lying. If it had been anyone else, maybe it would've slipped, but I could identify the small telling of her lie by the twitch in the corner of her lips. I took a restful breath. I decided to leave it. I would trust my mother and the reasoning behind her secrets. Perhaps she couldn't say because the one who couldn't be trusted sat across from me. I stared at Cesar, making him somewhat uncomfortable.

"Well, if that's all, I'll prepare for tomorrow." My mother and I would be returning to Dillian and the others, and I had to think of what I'd say. How I'd shape a story and forge a partnership between the wolves and hunters for longer. I needed to ensure their safety, and check up on how Titan was fitting in. It was an oasis of sorts. Because of my mother's gift of concealment, they wouldn't be smelt or heard by any vampires passing by. But it still wasn't enough for me. I needed to find extra security in a community they could live in comfortably and with purpose.

"Well, at least we'll finally get to go on an excursion together," Chase said, breaking the tension in the room. He swept the bottle back up, pardoning us and treating it like a beacon of hope.

*Something still doesn't feel right about all of this*, I admitted to Chase. He pressed a kiss to my temple, interlacing his fingers with mine as we walked outside.

*I know, but we'll have each other. No more distractions, Esmore. When we go into Tracey's Council, we go in together and focus on the objective. Do what you need tomorrow to find temporary closure. I don't know when we'll be coming back.*

I grimaced. Two parts of me were tortured over the idea of leaving the others. But I had to stand in line. The conversation with my mother the previous night weighed on me a lot heavier than I'd realized. For all of us to make it out of this, I had to finally start abiding by their world and the complexity of this war I'd only just stepped into. I had to submit to the pressures around me and the command that knew better, even if it didn't sit well with me.

As we walked through the main room and to the top of the stairs, Darcy and Jerimiah following us closely, Chase stopped and drew attention to himself. "Who's daring enough to take a swig out of this bottle?" he asked his coven, and some stupidly cheered and agreed. Darcy's expression paled as he drew back further toward the walls. I rubbed my hand through Fire's fur, grimacing at the thought that this was what I was staking my drastic hope on, in keeping Chase safe if I weren't here to do it myself. And some of them were just as bad if not worse than him. But his coven would serve a purpose. We all did.

# CHAPTER 22

THAT NIGHT, I tampered with the leisure of stretching out my wings. The Descendant was calling to me and not in our customary way where I'd depend on my gift in a desperate struggle of survival. It was elevating to summon my wings, and the extension of power it flooded me with to enjoy its beauty and stealth purely for me. Although it was exhausting and painful to manifest them, it did little to take their glory away. Flying was something I could become accustomed to, although it was draining to use untrained muscles; the gravity of the moment was breath-taking. When I flew, bare-chested in the night to avoid shredding apart another of my leather shirts, I was liberated and free. I was separate from the madness of what was happening below, and soaring in a stifling silence that was uniquely mine.

I made sure to stay within our perimeter. Darcy trailed as best as he could in the treetops, trying to ensure his role in 'keeping me safe.' Jerimiah stayed behind with Chase and Fire. He'd been conversing with his coven for some time now in a macho barbaric way vampires did.

A figure in the distance grabbed my attention. It was a woman with long blonde hair and a flowery dress. The woman was walking rather peculiarly, slowly and in clear sight. If she'd been a spy or intruder, she would've been better at hiding herself, surely. I swooped lower and circled in an attempt to get a better look at her. The closer I got, a rising vile lifted in my stomach. My curiosity came to a stifling halt when I recognized the face. *Whitney.*

I dipped in the sky, having forgotten to beat my wings, the moment startled me as I regained my poise. When I looked back down, she was gone. I dove for the ground, sweeping to a halt as I landed not so delicately on my feet in the same spot that she'd been standing. The bottom of my wings sagged to the forest floor, scraping up the dirt and few dead leaves as I surveyed the directions she might've run into. Nothing.

Darcy burst out of the trees, elated to have finally caught up. "Did you notice anyone else here?" I asked. Had he sensed her as well, or was I mixing memories with fragmented and confused present time? Was it happening again? Was I just seeing ghosts?

Darcy shook his head, refusing to make eye contact with me or even look in my direction. I was charmed by his innocence and decency after having lived all these years. He still wasn't daring enough to look at my bare chest. Searching once more, I concluded that my demons were haunting me, and my conscience was creeping up. I was being followed by both Whitney's and Sydney's ghosts, even in fragmented instances. I wondered if I didn't have my emotional bond with Chase, whether the trail of guilt would still consume me.

After finally stopping, my body sagged in an exhausted heap. As enchanting as flying was, I was still untrained and needed a few hours of rest before the next few days. I still wasn't fully recovered, nor would I be for years. I needed to balance my healing process, just as Chase nagged me about. Even though I'd said the same for him.

When I returned to our chambers, I swooped in on the arch opening near the bell and in front of our door. Chase was already waiting there, pouring some of the ill tampered wine on the floor for Fire, gesturing for her to lick it up if she wanted some. Her eyes dragged over to me, unamused.

"Wow," Chase exaggerated, placing the bottle on the edge of the bell. It was a different one to the one he'd acquired hours before. He took in the mass of my black wings, sending admiring waves of appreciation through me. I was beautiful, a vision and everything more in his eyes. I felt self-conscious almost tucking them in slightly, aware they still looked tattered and worn after their last great fall. But they were functional and in the process of healing. "Esmore, they're beautiful. You're beautiful."

He approached them gently, reaching his fingers out to brush past them. His touch was an eager electrical current that tingled along their bone and down my spine. I shivered, oddly aroused by the sensitivity of them. He too felt it, his expression changing into an entirely different curiosity. My wings drew out more, wanting to be touched by him again, craving the sensational urge that overpowered me in a spectacularly different way. As his fingers brushed over them once more, I felt the pang of sadness wash over him. He was remorseful that he couldn't manage his own Descendant. That it would forever be hiding inside of him, unable to spread its wings in such a way where I could touch or embrace.

"Hey, we'll get there one day. Soon we'll be flying together," I promised and cupped his jaw. He charmed a delicate smile and took my hand in his.

"I'll give you everything of me, but sadly that's something I don't think I'll ever be able to offer." He doubted our ability to trump Fier, and destroy the madness in his mind. He was so openly admitting that he feared he might lose himself entirely, and that I might not be enough to bring him back. Utter insanity. There was no way I'd let him slip through into becoming a saber so easily. It wasn't an option for either of us.

I opened up to him, the imagery and sensory of flying alongside its liberating freedom. "That will be us one day. I have no doubt." We were frequently and openly bouncing off one another, when one doubted the other showcased their strength and support. And I was okay with this dance and raw vulnerability we committed to one another. Both of us were damaged which was what made us entirely whole to be together.

He was frightened of what would happen in the coming days when we went to Tracey's Council. He believed it was the right thing to do and if it were just him, he'd be appeased with it. But because I was going as well, it was an obvious weak spot. One that we'd ensure we showed no one.

"We're going to be okay," I promised him again. My wings naturally curled around him, extending to reach out and tuck him into me. He found amusement in the action.

"I can kind of understand what Jerimiah was concerned about, it is kind of emasculating." He laughed at the size of my black wings, cocooning us together. "But I can't deny the allure of these either." His eyes diverted to my bare breasts. He greedily cupped them, admiring them with a boyish smile. His delicate ego about the size of my wingspan now gone.

"So simple-minded," I purred, stepping further into his palms.

"You know how it is," he shrugged, rubbing his nose along my neck and shoulder. I arched into him, begging for him to take a bite. His fangs slid into my supple skin, driving a wave of sensuality through my core and pitting in my stomach. My heat pulsed for him in ecstasy as he kissed the spot he'd marred and licked over his delicate bite. He grabbed my hips and pulled me into him, teasing me with his length that had already hardened. My nipples were cold and pointed, wanting to be lapped up in the motion of his tongue.

"A-hem." My mother's voice broke our tension. I froze, hiding behind the wall of my wings. I felt a heat blaze across my cheeks. Chase popped his head out of my wings.

"Oh, well if it isn't my mother-in-law," he said cheerily. "Now might be a slightly bad time." I hid my face in my hand. "You see your daughter and I are—" I grabbed hold of his cock firmly, submitting him into a silent squeak. Clenching his length was agony as I was torn between the embarrassment of the situation and my desire to fondle him more.

"Esmore, dear, I'm looking for Tythian. I think it's time we returned to the hunters and wolves."

Chase's smile widened, despite his jarring pain. His hand rolled over my hips and down to my ass as he sent me image after image of all the things he'd like to do to that ass. I couldn't win against him. I pressed my lips to his, aggressively pushing my tongue against his and claiming him, flashing back all the challenging positions I wanted to put him in return. As he grew more excited in my hand, I flashed a wicked smile and gathered all my control to step away, my wings still covering his evident arousal. He was flushed by the distance I'd put between us and now had to face my mother once again. A defeated smile spread across his face. He raked his hand through his black shoulder-length hair nervously. His smile only grew wider as he found no words. I loved when I could make him speechless.

"I'll just go put a shirt on," I said. Chase folded his long leather jacket in front of him, walking away and making sure to hide his length from my mother.

"Make sure you're back before dinner time," he mused, pecking a kiss on my cheek. "Or more specifically dessert," he growled into my ear, begrudgingly that I'd ended our fun and games. I'd be making sure to lap him up as much as possible before we had to 'pretend' to be uninterested in one another at Tracey's Council. I'd been hoping there'd be more time so I could rest, but patience was not a virtue for the wicked.

# CHAPTER 23

I T TOOK US some time to find Tythian. He'd been hunting, for the first time in… well, since I'd ever known him. We still weren't on talking terms but silently agreed we had to work together for the sake of our common goal. But it didn't mean we could put our differences aside. We loathed one another from the first time we'd met, and he tried to break my neck, and I attempted to put my sword through his chest, until even now when we'd been forced to depend on one another so frequently. He would always hang over my head the favors that I owed him and hate me furthermore because Cesar orchestrated him to be my personal chaperone. And on top of that, I would forever be burdened with the guilt of Whitney's death, having taken the one thing Tythian adored most in the world. There would be no reconciliation between us.

Abhorred, Tythian teleported us. Swirls of orange and red were an eyesore, and smoke overruled my senses. The cottages were up in flames, and the mixed smell of enticing hunter blood and the rotting waft of wolves tainted my nose. Burning flesh bombarded my attention toward the first cottage as I tried to fumble into action and make sense of what was happening. Teary's limp and pale body laid at the entrance. Two precise vampire bites were nestled on both sides of her neck where she'd been savagely bitten into. Ringing in my ear began as dread enticed my reality. It threw me off balance, elongating the effort in every step. I had to move. I had to reach them.

Fire ran off, giving chase to something that darted in the woodlands toward the mountains. I stumbled into the door, pushing it open and raising my hand to the drastic flames that swarmed at me. In the blossoming smoke, Tori, Julia, and Dillian laid limply on the floor. There was a light, fleeting beat and desperate breath from Julia as she choked on the smoke unconsciously. I couldn't sense a heartbeat from... "Dillian," I squeaked.

Blood was everywhere, the scent alluring and hazing my instincts to drag the remains of Julia instead of protecting them. My mother reefed me back by the shoulder, pulling me out of the entrance to the cottage. I retaliated clumsily, and she flipped me over onto my back, having already anticipated my attack. The loud thud and crackling of a beam falling from the flames startled me long enough to focus on her orange eyes that peered down on me. I focused on that sharp gaze, using it as my pillar to dig myself out of the instinctual beckoning to drink from Julia's struggling, desperate body. Dillian and Tori, they weren't... I dipped my head to the side to look at Teary. Her pale body was unflinching as well. My mother grabbed my cheeks and angled my face back toward her. She was ruthless as she snapped my attention back onto her.

"I'll get them out. Find the others," she ordered. I was at a loss, her words and command drawing in slowly until I could decipher the action she wanted from me. I nodded, allowing her steady self to shower me in strength. In a time like this, I couldn't lose control. In a time where Dillian... Dillian... sickness crashed over me. *He couldn't be...* and he wasn't the only one. I scurried to my feet desperately. I had to get to the others.

"Titan!" I shouted. Tythian remained still, silent in his disposition, calculating. He teleported in a flash of enveloping black. "Yolo!" I screamed out. Where was Yolo?! I came across Cole and Angela's bodies first, their heads decapitated. It looked like they'd been guarding the entrance to the second hut that was being wildly ravished in flames. The small teddy I had once gifted Titan was abandoned in front of it. Bile rose from my stomach and into my throat.

I opened the door, the remains of two dead children and wolves who'd been savagely shredded apart. The blood was so fresh, sending the abominable scent to dance on my tastebuds. I gagged. This had only been recent. Fire's howl cried out. I floundered out of the hut, my legs wobbly crossing over one another as I tried to focus on her whereabouts in the woodlands. Those children in there… it wasn't Titan. She might still be… Dillian… Teary… Tori… Julia… I looked over at Teary's recently drained and unflinching body. My mother had already dragged Julia and Tori out of the flames, racing back in to drag Dillian out.

Fire howled again, a clear calling to me. I followed her grieving cry, desperately hoping she'd sniffed out Titan. I ran into the darkness of night and far away from the smoke and flames that were wildly licking the dry and dead debris around the camp. The pillowing mist around my ankles concealed the wolf I tripped over. I tumbled over the dead wolf's body, looking back at it only momentarily. It was Ryan's wolf form. *It's not Titan.* I hoisted myself, avoiding the second dead wolf on my entangled path as I followed the thread that linked me to Fire. They'd all been killed. Only Titan and Chris's bodies remained to be found. *Please let them be alive.* I sent a silent prayer to Sydney, if his ghost truly were haunting me, or even if it was just my make-believe insanity creeping on me, I was throwing intent into the superstitious belief that maybe he was protecting her in whatever form he was taking.

Fire's howl echoed throughout the woods, an elongated cry stretching out in urgency. When I reached her my wobbly leg's felt weighted as every step forward became a struggle. Everyone's faces became a crashing wave of weight. Dillian… his name continued to encompass my mind and weigh on my body every step I took further away from the campsite. My best friend. My… I choked, a desperate surprise of locked non-physical pain. My body was shaking with an unexplainable symptom.

Fire's white fur caught my attention in the black of the dark night. Hidden in a crevasse were two shaking and frightened wolf pups. I dropped to my knees as the weight finally amounted on top of me. "Titan," I whispered so desperate to hear her response. So anguished to know that she was safe and alive. I couldn't lose both of them… I couldn't lose any of them. And yet… a single tear streaked down my face, improbably strange as my body shut down and moved of its own accord. I couldn't understand what I was feeling. Simply I knew that there was a desperate struggle that was so finely tangled in the survival of these two wolf pups and the unfathomable regard that the others had…

Fire shifted into her woman's form. Her beautiful dark skin illuminating in the night. "Whoever it was, they'd only just made it out."

The air was sucked away from us. Tythian teleported in with Jenn's limp body sagged over his shoulders. His expression hardened on Fire. "Don't!" I yelled, stepping in front of her protectively. Fire shifted back into her wolf form, her identity exposed. Tythian didn't say anything, his expression only tormenting over the truth of what we'd been hiding. Fire had been a secret.

Jenn's unconscious body was limp with a twisted neck. If it weren't for Yolo being a vampire, he'd be dead. It wouldn't be long until he'd wake up again once his body revived, which meant this attack hadn't been orchestrated long ago at all. Tythian fixated on the two small pups that huddled closer together, too afraid to creep any further out.

"What do they know?" he asked inconspicuously.

"I don't know. I just found them, but we have to take them and the others back. Now! Guard them!" I said to Fire. I called upon the Descendant blowing a swirl of wind beneath me as I took to the sky, desperate to find any traces of who attacked them. The area was scarce, even a few animals of the night dared to venture out. The fog shallowly hid the ground but not enough to conceal someone entirely. It was completely barren. I desperately torpedoed through the sky. They couldn't have gotten far. I searched aimlessly, eyeing for any movement as my thoughts desperately barraged over one another.

But they were gone. The remains of who could've done this forgotten and forever a secret in the mountains where they'd been hidden.

Fire's howl sang out to me again, I looked back at the black billowing smoke and licking flames that began to spread loosely on the trees and plants that'd begun to thrive in the area because of Julia's gift. Just as her presence had aided them, it as quickly turned them into a victim of the violent element. Fire's consistent song desperately sung out to me, and it'd soon call upon too much attention if she continued.

There was no one here as if they'd vanished as soon as we'd teleported in. If we'd only been minutes sooner, we could've been here for them. I could've protected them if I'd come back those few minutes sooner instead of training my wings and messing around with Chase. Or maybe if it hadn't taken us so long to find Tythian. So many thoughts began to loop on replay.

This isn't real. This can't be real. I refuse to believe it's real.

I swooped low, Fire's vibrating tug on our thread compelling me toward her. They were all gone. Only Tythian and Fire waited for me. I marched toward him, grabbing his arm and not daring to look back at the wolves' bodies, who I'd promised to protect and failed.

The nauseating swirl and teleportation took us back to the institute where chaos had erupted once again. As soon as Chase was in my reach, I was crippled by the propelling mixture of emotions. Rage, desperation, shame, loss. I choked on it like a poisonous pill expanding in my throat. I clutched at it, certain something had to be in there to cause this suffocating notion.

"Esmore," Chase cried out, lunging over the steps to reach inside the main hall. I ignored him, trying to push away from the wallowing emotions and thoughts that terrorized me. I followed Fire's lead into the main teaching room, where we'd once tortured the humans in. I burst into the room, my mother, Cesar, and the brother's presence swirling around me. Titan and Chris were still in their wolf form, huddled and cowering at the three sabers who watched them with curiosity.

My mother was working her gift on Julia, having already propped her head on a pillow. Jenn gasped, her form shifting back to Yolo as he grabbed for his neck and rose, clawing at Balzar who pinned him down.

"Yolo, you're okay!" he snapped. It took him a moment to focus and pat over himself.

"The children!" He leaped up, suddenly aware of the room he was in. His grave expression and gaze swept the room as I did.

"Esmore." Chase desperately clutched onto my shoulder, sending through waves of calm. But the more he tried to manipulate me the further I pushed into hysterics, especially when I stared at Dillian's unbreathing body. His nails dug in tighter, forcing blood to trail down his fingers. *Esmore,* he tried to desperately reach out to me telepathically. I slammed down on our link, insensitive to his grappling thoughts and desperation as the smashing waves of intolerable grief consumed me. *They can't be... I promised to keep them safe.*

"Esmore," Deemori warned, creeping closer to me. "You're pushing him to the edge." Her words swam past me as I could only gravitate to one thing. I took three steps forward and concaved over Dillian. His neck had been marred in the same way that Teary's and Tori's had. *Vampire.* Tears streamed down my cheeks as I hiccupped. My tears turned into a desperate flood that drew toward the floor. Alone, I was so alone. They were the last of my team. All that I had left to cling on to my former self as a Token Huntress. And Dillian was my best friend. We'd do and had done anything to protect one another. We'd sacrificed our own lives for the other on more than one occasion, and this time, I'd been too late. A slow, drawn-out wailing began, broken by hysterical tears and grief. At some point I realized it was me as I desperately wiped away the tears and hid my face in Dillian's soot-stricken shirt. Dying, I felt like dying. It should've been me in his place.

This had been my promise. "I'm sorry," I sobbed. "I'm so sorry!" Chase heaved me up by my shirt. I snapped on him, rolling us onto the floor and raising my fist. It was like a snapping escapade that followed, he retaliated, the kindness in his eyes vanquished and replaced by the feral nature that was mimicking my own. But while I was dampened in my grief, he'd been enthralled in his inescapable toxic rage. He snarled at me, and I leaped matching him, protecting the others… even though they'd…

I was as equally as mechanical in my fighting. We tore at one another's clothes, and before anyone could grab hold of either us to separate us, we'd burst through the doors and smashed over the railing, and plummeted into the main room.

The covens crawled out in interest as they watched on. Chase's eyes were dilated, fixated on me. Unlike last time when he continuously tried to escape, I had his full attention now. The wetness of my tears continued to stream. I couldn't think straight. I couldn't contemplate how to call him back. I so desperately wanted to return to the others. My heart ached and lurched as I realized I'd failed yet another. I'd failed Chase as well. The gargoyles fell upon him, locking him into a hold. Darcy pulled me back, redirecting me to focus on the others instead. I was only making the situation worse by fighting back. Onlookers surrounded us to watch the display of all things that were wrong in our inner workings and failures.

I couldn't be here for him now. I was the one who'd pushed him over the edge. And as much as I wanted to scamper to him and tend to him, to kiss away the poison that was devouring his brain. I was only fueling the flames, wallowing in my urges to commit, and silence my pain. How could I show my face ever again, after having failed everyone? If only I could vanish. My spiraling only continued to propel me further into the depths of a desperate and unsalvageable beast. It festered on my pain, eating me from the inside, where I was truly trapped.

Tears continued to flood as I watched Chase desperately fend them off, not as my familiar but an animal. I couldn't turn my back on him.

But I had to. I was doing this to him. Our closeness and link was killing us both from the inside. Darcy's nudge reminded me that I hadn't moved. I was simply staring emptily.

I took one more wavering look, apologetic and ashamed furthermore to what I'd done to my familiar. We were both monsters, unable to fight against the inevitable. I brought death and Chase would only be another victim to that, but a slow and suffering one. His hand reached out for me as he tried to lunge for me again, his snarls and vicious expression devoid of my lover and husband. My hand gravitated to the lock of hair I had bundled in my leather pocket, thinking of our vows and union. We were one another's strength, but also weakness.

I turned my back and leaped onto the next level, ignoring the snarls and taunts that echoed behind me from his coven members. Clarissa sat atop of the stairs, shaking her head at me disapprovingly as I walked past and gravitated back into the room and to Dillian's side.

The room was grave. The wolf pups were frightened of Yolo who'd just shifted from Jenn and into an aloof looking male vampire. They'd only allowed Fire near them. They hid their faces in the corner of the room, too scared to face the vampires who were at their backs.

I dipped my forehead to Dillian's cold one, murmuring apologies to him. Tori and Teary... even they wouldn't hear my sobs or cries that I hoped would bring them back. I snarled weakly at the firm hand that pressed on my shoulder. It was Cesar, attempting to console me. I sobbed harder, so desperate to take these last few months away that felt like they'd amounted for nothing. Tears dropped onto Dillian's face as I wished and prayed for him to take another breath, an act so desperate it would've been frowned upon in the Guild. The Guild... I hated it, and I hated them! If they'd never chased Dillian out, this would never have happened. They should've been living their lives happily and together. They should've never been subjected to this life that I'd inevitably dragged them into.

"I'm sorry," I pleaded for his forgiveness. All of their forgiveness. Even Chase's for what I'd done to him. I opened my thick eyelashes, my site hazy from the tears that continued to well. I wiped at them fiercely, so exhausted and humiliated by how my fierce warrior self must look in front of the others. They had to bear witness to this imploding lack of control.

A blur of black grabbed my attention. I wiped at my tears, enough to clear them temporarily as I dipped my finger into the mixture of Dillian's wet blood and… "Venom," I whispered.

"What?" my mother asked. She'd finished attending to Julia who now slept peacefully, wrapped in blankets on a makeshift bed on the floor.

"Venom," I repeated louder. "They're—"

I allowed Cesar to lean in closer, unable to bear the shredding hope and misfortune that was playing on my mind.

Cesar took a brief glance and looked over to my mother. I searched her expression.

"Esmore, this isn't what they'd want," she tried to say with reason.

I blanched. Dillian and the others could… live. Not in the way that they knew now, but they would still be here. Was it okay for me to want to keep them in such a way? Would they change? Did I truly want them to suffer in the same way I had, unable to find control in my wicked mess?

"Esmore, we should—"

"No." I don't know who did this or why but I clutched at Dillian's body defensively. A flashback reminded me this was the same way I'd desperately held onto Sydney. "They could live."

"Esmore, they're not living. Don't make me explain sense to you right now about their mortality," my mother begged me.

"But they would be here. All of them."

"Not all of them," Cesar announced. "The Scottish woman is dead. She's been completely drained. And the meek-looking one wasn't turned. Only the two boys."

My hands fastened around Dillian in a flash of new hope. The thread between Chase and I continued to thrash back and forth, alarming me that everything was wrong. Would I be damning Tori and Dillian? Yet the thought of burning their bodies… I couldn't do that to them. What if they wanted this, a second chance, a new life?

"Esmore, you know this is wrong." My mother eased into my peripheral. "This is the greatest taboo as a hunter."

I blinked, abashed by her reasoning. Yet it was okay for me to live a life like this, lurking in the shadows and hunched over animals and humans, craving their life essence. I didn't want to damn anyone, but they were still so young. Surely, they'd want to face this decision themselves. We'd been taught and raised that being turned into a vampire was the biggest horror and abomination of our kind. But what if it wasn't?

"You won't have long to decide. Hunter's don't take long to turn," Balzar said gently.

"What was it like for you when you turned? Are you happy it happened?" I asked Balzar, seeking the right answer. I so desperately wanted to keep them with me, only a small hesitation was preventing me from committing to that. What if they hated me for it?

"Eh," Balzar was caught off guard, "it was different for me."

"No, it wasn't!" I snapped. "You were a human who hated the vampires and were fighting them. You hated them just as much!" I yelled. I was clutching on to an unforgivable act in the hope that another unforgivable act would counter it. Even if they hated me for it, at least they would be alive, sort of.

"I don't know," Balzar said honestly and uncomfortably looking around at those who watched him. "I don't think any of us truly love or hate this form, we simply exist, Esmore."

I searched the others anguished as if looking into their eyes would give me their answers, and in a way it did. Cesar was seeking revenge on the vampire who'd turned him and killed his human family; Connor hated all humans for what they'd done to him and his family in his human life seeking dominance and death on all humanity; Deemori was seeking liberation by losing her sanity and becoming a saber herself; Yolo was pining to be reunited with his familiar and slowly morphing into her in a sickening way, and Fire was bound to me because of my selfish act prior to keep her by my side. No one was *happy* in this life.

Tears trailed down my face as I realized I'd already taken so much from them. Tori would never grow to the age where he could experiment with his gift; Dillian would never marry Julia; Julia would never have the family she always dreamed of in a community that she supported; and Teary would never... she was just no more.

I wasn't the only one losing friends here. I searched my mother's eyes, despairing. Her calm demeanor and pained expression mirrored my own. "What do I do, Mom?" My bottom lip wobbled. How could I make that decision for them? What would Dillian do? I was certain he would've let me go. But then again, he'd been watching me now even as I was a vampire. Maybe they'd adapt just as I had. Or maybe they'd hate me for not letting them die an honorable death. That of a hunter, like many had died before.

"Esmore, I think you know what to do," my Mom said, nodding her head in approval. It wasn't up to me what monsters should be able to live and die. I looked over at the two wolf pups huddled in the corner and Fire who nursed them. Her blue eyes gave no inclination as to what she thought I should do. "Esmore," my mother pleaded. "You know what to do."

I searched Dillian's face desperately, reaching out to his dead mind, desperately wishing he could tell me what I should do. "Dillian, I don't know what to do," I begged, looking for any inclination other than the desolate one that continued to swarm me. "Just tell me," I begged, embarrassed, shaking him, desperate for him to wake. I just needed a sign.

Giving myself over to superstition, no longer able to maintain the strength for logic, I could only remain so strong after so much loss.

A defiant crack broke the silence in the room, and Tori's body twisted violently. I was going to vomit. It was already happening.

"Esmore, they won't be the same," my mother urged.

"Keep the one with the eyes at least, it'd be a waste to let his gift die. We could use him," Tythian said to Cesar. I snapped on him, so angry that was all he could think of. Cesar held me in position, his iron grip keeping me in place. Maybe that was my sign, I'd asked and begged for them to reach out to me, maybe this was how.

"Maybe they could be," I replied to my mother. "I could help them and teach them how to be like this."

"Esmore, your mother's right. They won't be the same," Yolo gently said. "None of us ever came back the same. Can you say the same for yourself, truly?" My hands were shaking, I didn't want to make monsters or decide who lived or died. I only wanted to slaughter our enemies, fixated on the task of killing everyone who stood in our way to protect those in this room, even if it'd cost me my life. But it was never meant to cost them theirs.

Julia stirred in the corner of the room, startled by the conjuring of Tori changing. We only had minutes to decide. Her eyes fluttered open, and she panicked, still startled by the events that put her in an unconscious state. She jumped against the wall, her chest rising and falling in dread. My mother tried to calm her.

Julia's gaze fell on Dillian, and her lips parted. Her shaking legs carried her over, but my mother halted her, protectively not letting her step any closer. Dillian's foot twitched.

"Is he alive?" she asked me, the wildest I'd ever seen her. She was still delirious, only able to focus on Dillian's limp body.

Her wild fierceness shook me if only slightly enough to answer her. "He's turning, unless we..."

"No! You cannot let him die!" she yelled at me. "You said you'd keep us safe! He's not allowed to leave me!" She howled. My heart thawed and splintered as I thought of Chase downstairs. I wouldn't give up on him, even when I was devoid of the answers or spirit on how we might make it through. I'd never give up on him, no matter what creature he'd become. And he would do the same for me. The quaint Julia was no different to that. But she didn't understand it all either. She was just desperate not to be left alone. More than ever, I resonated with Julia. I didn't want to be left alone either. And that made us selfish. But we had a choice. And Teary didn't. So many of those in this room didn't have the choice. Nor had I. But we'd united in a sick way to support one another.

"Esmore!" Julia screamed at me in pure rage as she tried to break free of my mother's iron grip.

"If we don't end their suffering now—" My throat bobbled, praying that Julia would be my out and excuse not to end them. "They won't be the same," I warned her. But I knew she wasn't thinking that far ahead. And I didn't want to either. I'd become so depleted, and the thought of another loss was too much. It weighed too heavily.

"Esmore, please!" She sobbed, breaking down into my mother's arms. Julia was weak and crumbling, unable to save him, just in the same way I had been. But right now, I was the one who could either stop this change or not.

I looked back down at my best friend, his face was pale and spotted with dirt, blood, and soot. Dillian for so long had been my everything. And that would never change. My throat bobbled as I caught on my words. "I'm sorry. Please forgive me."

# ORPHAN

*We are the orphans of the old world.*
*Submerged in taint and born afresh in this new conditioned place.*
*There is no rest, nor will you find peace.*
*Only a fragment of you shall remain;*
*And the memory of what you might've been;*
*And the cruel devastation of what you should've died as.*
*I am sorry.*
*Forgive me for the sin that I have enforced.*
*Because I was too scared to be alone and an orphan by myself.*
*Sorry for the recklessness of my behavior and my selfish act that can never be forgiven.*
*We are the same.*
*And I hate us equally for it.*

# CHAPTER 24

BANG! MY BODY was immobile. I'd stopped flinching at the repetitiveness hours ago as I stared into the darkness. The fresh dabble of blood flared my nose. I focused my vision if only for a second to witness Chase bounce back from the impact after slamming into the bars, all of which were plated with silver. He was a mess and had knocked himself out more times than I could attempt to reach out and into his mind to counter him.

I dragged my legs closer to my chest as the emptiness devoured me from the inside. Dillian and Tori were beside him in their separate cages, trying to fight one another through the bars long enough to not be burned by the silver. They screamed barbarically as soon as they touched it, untrained and innocent to their newfound weaknesses. And then they would dive for me, slamming at the bars, just as Chase had done once again.

My grip tightened around my legs. I was as still as the gargoyles who guarded the cells. Darcy was solidified inside the room, and Jerimiah was atop the stairs. They hadn't shifted since I'd taken my rightful position here. The swelling darkness of the room was swallowing me whole, and I wished it'd already taken me. I'd been driven into a corner of guilt, loss, and despair, strangled by the interlacing I had with Chase and Dillian. It was maddening me, and I sought refuge in that pit of swelling darkness.

I just wanted it to be over, and the grieving for the loss of my lover and best friend taken away. I was unarmed and completely stripped to my core in self-repugnance. I'd done this to them. For those who I cared about most, I'd failed them not only once, but in their passage to an honorable death as well. I'd given a hand to craft them into monsters, and now even I was unable to reach either of them. I simply didn't have the strength, too stunned to conjure any effective plan.

The rosy prick of Chase's mind was intimidating and closed off to me. Even when I had pressed against it, banging into it so hard it splintered my mind with splitting pain, I made no budge. I simply leaned against it for hours, in a silent prayer that it'd devour me whole instead.

Dillian scratched at the floor, attempting to dig his way out. His hands were a bloody mess as he screamed, animalistic in frustration. His eyes had dulled to a dark brown, so sinister in comparison to his once lively fluorescent pink. His lips were curled over his newly ejected fangs that he'd been unable to pull back since he'd first tried to attack Julia in the room upstairs.

They were starving, all desperate to escape and devour whatever they could get their hands on. Not only had I done this to them, but I'd also been the one to deny them the privilege to quench their thirst. We'd caged them, cornering them as animals instead of liberating them as the warriors they were.

All three of them scrambled into a frenzy when another scent wafted into the room. Darcy didn't shift out of his gargoyle form, though I knew he was taking in every detail. For the last few hours, I had been their sole attention. I wanted to melt further into the wall, so the newcomers wouldn't see me. They would once again bear witness to the crimes I'd committed. Or worse, they'd try to reason with me and pull me out of there as if I wasn't deserving to be locked in the cell with them. I remained still, encompassed by the swirl of complete and echoing darkness that I'd pitted myself into. There was no end to it, and I was comfortable sitting at its core, eaten by the beast that it was, hoping that it'd draw me out of this misery. Praying that it'd take us all to a better place.

"Esmore," my mother gently said. I didn't acknowledge her. She wasn't alone. Julia and her scent created mania on the other side of the cages. I narrowed my hearing on the dripping pipe in the back of the cellar near the wines, trying to escape into this room further. It was calming, entrancing, ever going and never to stop, not until someone fixed it. If anyone knew how.

Julia dipped toward Dillian. "Dillian," she gasped. She pressed her hand against the bar, hope filled in her eyes that she'd reach him. Tears spilled over her cheeks as she weakly smiled. As if her nurturing aura and smile would be enough to pull him from this chaos, if only for a second of recognition. Any sign to show her that he was still in there.

He weighed back on his toes, crouching as he watched her from the back of the cage. He was silent. I watched on, in the hope that Julia could bring him back. I tried to focus a thought of purity or emotion that might calm him further. I stumbled over his mind, offering a wave of calm manipulation. But the emotion was repulsive as I skimmed past it, unable to sincerely preoccupy him. The effect shattered within seconds and triggered him.

He charged at her, busting his forehead on the silver-plated bars, and was propelled back. She tripped and stumbled back, wailing hopelessly in fright. Drip. Drip. Drip. The water continued to soften the silence. I wondered why she was the only one who wasn't turned or killed by the vampire that attacked them. Was she a prisoner in her mind just as I was?

Chase's arm was outstretched through the bars, sizzling in pain in an attempt to grab hold of her. Dillian turned on him, squabbling through the bars that divided them over the 'prize.' Tori had begun to cower and shake in the corner, more in tune with the hierarchy of members in the room. The apprentice now looked so young and small in comparison to the man he should've been. He would be the hunter whose gift would never be realized. Though Dillian still had his gift coursing through his veins, I wondered if its ability would be just as potent, or if he would even have the will to use something that might remind him of the life he had before. Their hunter's eyes were gone, vanquished like the flame of their life.

Julia whimpered into her hands. My mother rested a hand on her shoulder in an attempt to offer some form of comfort. I don't even know why I'd tried to help Dillian. How did I expect to muster any kind of emotion to pacify them when I was so transfixed and held down by the weight and toxicity of my familiar's mind and my personal undoing? The flame that once flickered in me was gone. I was detached not only from Chase who helped steady these emotions that spiraled out of control, but also the pending purpose I had. Everything else seemed irrelevant. I couldn't even remember what my purpose of saving the wolves was. Perhaps if I'd focused only on Dillian and the others they would be safe. Had I selfishly done it to rebuild my sense of moral and jeopardized the others because of it? I'd always considered myself as superior, one of the best. A Token. And here I was, crippled by the torture of sickening empathy that had no end, alongside a committed fury to unleash on myself.

Chase lowly growled at Dillian, his fangs fiercely outsizing Dillan's. I couldn't reach any of them. My knees couldn't be dragged any closer to my chest, and I simply wanted to curl into a ball, become smaller, and morph into the wall my back was pressed against.

Julia stood up in a fit of fury. My mother grabbed her. "You did this! You said we'd be safe! You said we could still be happy! I believed you!" Her every word crippled me further. I could see the hatred in her beautiful huntress eyes, behind it her nurturing and giving soul, spitting hate and vile on me. To blame me for this inexcusable act of allowing them to be turned. She'd wanted this. But I knew it wasn't the right decision. And I wanted to use her as an out so I wouldn't lose them either. But she had every right to hate me. All of it was true. "You ruined everything by bringing us to these vampires!" Julia had never erupted in such a way, her spirit too tender to be so confrontational. But I had stolen Dillian further away from her and for what? Myself? It felt almost like a similar punishment that I'd maddened my familiar in the process. An eye for an eye.

My mother began dragging Julia away, briefing one more glance my way. I could feel Darcy's attention on me as they passed him and so I only shriveled into myself further. I followed the link into Chase's mind that was so abruptly cut off from me. It was like having my oxygen siphoned from me. I'd become so accustomed to him being there, and now, it was nothing but darkness. I nuzzled myself against it, despair tensing my body. I would do anything to feel that warm love he always threaded through.

*I'm sorry, my love,* I confessed, aware that he couldn't hear me. *I know this isn't the end. But I just don't have the strength to pull you out. Forgive me, for I am lost.* The last time I'd pulled him out, it was from a place of love and unrelenting desire to have him back in my arms. Now, I didn't even want myself back, and I could feel that prevented me from having any real effect on dinting his prison.

I waited for his response, but nothing came. My essence stretched out over the prickly thorns that conjured sharp pains in my mind every time I skirted them. I found myself seeking them out, brushing past them to feel that suffering. I just wanted to feel anything that would punish me for my inability to save them. And I just wanted to be closer to Chase even if it meant I'd be conditioned behind the same walls as him.

*Forgive me,* I breathed into the darkness. I smothered myself against the wall, content with being lost in our minds together, the ultimate sense of silence where there was no pulse on the other end. I wanted to be with him. Even if he were in madness, at least we'd be there together. A very small part of me knew I had to call upon strength to free him, but this ebbing darkness only grew thicker and more commanding. I was on my knees, having prayed to a superstition that left me crippled in belief. How did I ever think I would navigate my team or Chase to victory? How did I ever assume I was superior? I was nothing but a mutant in this world, having damned myself for losing faith in what I'd been raised on as a hunter and not being able to entirely convert into the world of the new. Stagnant. I was drifting, and because of my inaction and wrong-footing, I'd hurt those I'd loved.

My mind thought of Titan, who I'd so desperately tried to protect. And what would she do when she found out I was the reason her father was dead? Would she so quickly run into my arms, thinking of me as her savior? Or would she see the true monster that I was that could only hide in the shadows? A phantom that shouldn't be seen or hurt. If I were to truly give myself to this new world, I would have to become exactly that. I couldn't beat the dark, so I would have to morph into the non-existent shadow.

I grew tired on the other side of my link to Chase, being a masochist devoted to the pain and suffering of banging my mind against the wall that tore between us. Blood dripped out of my nose and down my face, the warm liquid a reminder that I was still in the present room. It wasn't enough to become nothing and vanish. I just wanted to be in the sickening madness with them, where I should be in their place. *I'm sorry.*

I was shivering in the cold. Only seventeen and caught in a wild storm in the afternoon. Drue had orchestrated us to take shelter and wait out the vicious weather in a small cave we'd come across. The memory was accurate, except I was alone and relinquished of the warmth I'd ordinarily have huddled amongst my raid team. I trembled, weak from the chill in the air as the storm swept past, still splashing about close to my leather boots. I shook as I tried to rub myself warm.

No one else was here, separate from the memory I'd had, or maybe this was the same.

"I'm growing tired of these unimpressive attempts to distort my memory," I said to no one, yet feeling the presence of something lurking. The figure hadn't shown themselves, playing with my mind for weeks now every time I drifted off to sleep. Instead of being so entirely consumed by the dream, as I had in the last, where the others were nailed to the sides of buildings and all the ones before that, there was an odd clarity and focus in this self-sabotaging darkness that continued swirling around me. When I didn't have the strength to fight, it all seemed clear because nothing would change, and I was still trapped here—alone.

As if unamused by my lack of participation, I felt the shift in this meeting place, or whatever it was. I closed my eyes, the pain imploding as someone else was attempting to attach to me. I was familiar with the presence. Although I pushed back weakly, not wanting to talk to him of all people right now, he pressed on through, the pain skyrocketing. It was a satisfying punishment in return.

"Shivering and cold, how glum from the little golden bird I staked a bet on," Fier said as a way of greeting. I was disgusted by his very presence that tarnished everything it touched. The other had left, whoever or whatever it was. Perhaps my lack of curiosity bored them. "Trouble in paradise?"

I curled my lip slightly, with a small snarl being all that I could muster in effort. *He* had been the one to do this to Chase. If it hadn't been for Fier, this trigger would've never been a curse. But the true punishment had been because I was too late to save him.

"Wow, they really broke you, huh?" He took a seat beside me. He was flashing his nails about, examining them. "It's painful isn't it, the loss of your familiar. The oh so desperate desire to peril with them is overbearing." There was a touch of tenderness in his tone. From what I imagined might've been him reflecting on his own familiar. I said nothing. Fier had lost Chase's mother, and yet he still dared to torture him in such a way.

"If you had truly loved her, you wouldn't have ever laid a finger on her son." I was too weak and cold to fight him, depending on my words as the striking force that would irritate him.

Fier clicked his tongue. "True, I certainly wouldn't have gotten away with hurting him if she was still around. Then again, she would've never allowed him to run away with a hunter of all things. Though I must confess, one of the things I loved most about her was her vicious ambition that might've even outweighed my own. If she wanted something, she would stop at nothing to get it. So, despite it being her son that I've used as leverage, she might've quite enjoyed my cunning plan."

The storm picked up in force, the sound of thunder crackling over the gushing rain. I couldn't make out anything past the cave entrance, it was blanketed in fast-moving motion.

"Have you given up entirely?" he asked, cleaning underneath his sharpened nails. "Just say so. I can end him now just as easily. He's still holding on, but I can just crank it up so he erodes into full saber, and that should take you down with him, isn't that what you want?"

My lip curled again agitated by his condensation and threat. It was true that Chase's current state was waging on me. I couldn't tell the difference between my self-torture or his. I was left fragile and weak, engrossed in the beauty of committing to the darkness entirely. To fight against that felt so heavy, so jaded to attempt to even lift my body. So broken was he. So tortured were we.

"Or you can live out your purpose and rid us of Oppollo. Consider this a courtesy call," he said and stood up. "I have no desire to fight you as you are now. It'd be embarrassing. You're either useful to me or not. And if you're not, then our leverage dies. It's your choice. But if I were you, I wouldn't be waiting around."

Fier stepped into the opening of the cave and vanished into the rain. The moment he stepped away from our connection and created distance, it felt like the first time I could take a breath. And now I was alone, shivering in this darkness, with a decision. I had fought all my life, and for the first time, I wondered what else it might cost me if I were to give up completely. I'd already failed those I'd vowed to protect. Wouldn't my disappearance only help them? But a small part of me, my inner huntress who vowed to protect and the sincerity of my love that was devoted to Chase; argued. Reminding me that we all had a purpose, and I would be Chase's only saving grace. My purity was our only leverage. But I'd never felt so disconnected from it.

A hard slap to the face dazed me awake. The raw throbbing evoked my gaze as I wrestled the person's shirt out of reflexes.

"Oh! There she is," Lincon said with a cruel smile, his stinky breath flushing my face. A small ring in my ear continued as I opened and shut my jaw.

"Did you just—"

"Slap you? Yes. Now, if you wouldn't mind, could you tell this certain little cement figure to pull his prod out of my back." Behind him, Darcy had a sword pointed at his back, directly behind his heart. It took me a moment to gather my thoughts. "Though if you want to prod something else back there, I wouldn't be against it," he said enticingly to Darcy. I loosened my grip on Lincon, awakening to the reoccurring noises of Chase, Dillian, and Tori. My head throbbed after the amount of invasiveness to my mind.

I released Lincon, not entirely sure why I was still holding on to him. How many days had I been in here? I sent out a wave of calmness over them, trying to get my bearings. The slap had jolted my body awake. Dillian and Tori were susceptible to my influence, but Chase had a strong tolerance, and his thrashing remained.

"Wait. What?" I said to no one in particular, still trying to reel back from the shocking hit that woke me. I didn't want to be awake. I didn't want to be here for this. I wanted to vanish, just like they had.

"No, no, no," Lincon said, grabbing me by my leather shirt. "Before you dip into your self-hating and self-mutilating ways, which by the way looks utterly boring on you, and trust me I'm usually into these sorts of things; might I make a selfish request?" He shook me, slamming me hard into the wall. The physical act far more effective than I would've liked it to be. The monster within me was becoming aggressive, unable to suppress its natural urges to fight.

Freckles of memory were arising of people checking up on me. People checking up on them. Humans being brought in to suppress their appetites if only in the slightest. Flooding of memories that I hadn't been here entirely for. One-sided conversations with my mother and Balzar. Even Clarissa had dared come down studying Chase and me for a few minutes before returning upstairs. I didn't want these memories or days returned. I wanted to go back to that cold and dark place where I was alone.

"Leave me alone, Lincon," I said bitterly, wanting to vanish back into my hole.

"Your eyes are pinning on me, Esmore, I know you're awake. If not, at least your beast is, and that's exactly the part of you that I want."

I hadn't even realized my fangs had slipped, and my vision hazed purple. Only a reminder of the hunter eyes and coloring that were removed from Dillian and Tori. How would they ever forgive me? I tried to fold back into myself.

"Oh, no you don't," Lincon said, grabbing my throat and dragging my back along the cemented wall. I didn't even bother clutching at his grip, forfeiting any defense. My beast within me struggled with the sedation, fighting against me as I pushed it down limply. I didn't want to fight. It raged within me, furious that I'd let anyone throw me around in such a way.

"Sooo, your Daddy Dear is up to something, and I think it has to do with Demetri's coven. And I want in!" he said giddily. Darcy was still poking his sword into Lincon's back, waiting for my signal. Jerimiah had pounded his way down the stairs the moment my feet were suspended off the ground. I flirted with the idea of Lincon being a real threat. Maybe if I denied him, he'd really do it. Maybe it could all end here. My inner beast raged and thrashed back and forth, trying to ignite the tethering flame that I'd simmered out. Maybe it was best. My gaze glided over to Chase who prowled in his cage back and forth on all fours, primal in his nature of being a saber. But could I really leave him like this? I was the only one who could bring him back.

"Hello?" Lincon was clicking his fingers from side to side in front of my face. "Okay, let me put it in sad person terms that might evoke some reaction from you. Maybe you could have an all-out fight and let that burly grizzly beast out and test how good you really are? Instead of being all like 'poor me, I'm the worst, I suck,' you can be awesome like me and unleash, and if you're not that great, you die! Win, win."

I glowered at Lincon, his appearance and smell offensive. He could manage to go on his own. Lincon always did what Lincon wanted. Whether Cesar said he could join or not wasn't up to me. He'd go on his own accord anyway.

"Let her go," Darcy growled. I was fading in and out, fighting to stay conscious as he crushed my windpipe. I closed my eyes welcoming it, ready for the darkness that would drift me into another place.

"Let's go about this a different way then." Lincon let go. I slithered to the floor, irritated that I was still conscious. My beast was raging within me, scratching so painfully on the insides that I thought something might claw its way out of my stomach. My hand instinctively went there, as if compacting it from the outside would sober it from its intoxicating rage. My eyes were wavering back and forth in purple as I fought against the instincts of my huntress to be in control and the beast within, my vampirism, wanting to claim and be victor, to strangle and fight. I suppressed it further, making myself sick. The pain it caused was delicious all in the same sense. This was the suffering I wanted, and I could only obtain it by turning on myself. Only I could enforce this punishment.

Lincon's gaze landed on Chase, crippling him. Chase concaved into the cement, his nails clutching at his head in pain as Lincon began his illusions.

"Lincon!" I screamed, lunging at him. He swiftly moved and released his mental hold on Chase. I smashed against the cage, having clumsily jumped at where Lincon had been. My legs were wobbly, my strength evaporated with my will to keep fighting. Chase pounced at me, digging his nails into my shoulder and reefing me against the cage. The silver burned us both as he plunged into my shoulder, messily trying to ravish me.

I tried to pull out of his grip, but his will was far greater than my own. Darcy seemed torn, unsure of what to do. He'd never oppose his coven leader. But nor was he in his right mind. If the others saw him as he was now, it would ruin his credibility as their leader. For how long would they protect him in this state before they thought it was better to turn on him? My blood oozed over my shoulder, slickening my leather sleeveless shirt.

I dipped down and reefed out of his grip, stumbling forward. Unable to bear the pain of the silver any longer, he jumped back. I looked at him, really looked at him for the first time since we'd been down here. His mouth was marred with my blood. His hands already so filthy and bloody from trying to get out. I looked down the line of cages at Dillian and Tori, who were still mindless creatures. They'd told me this could go on for years, or maybe they'd come back momentarily if their thirst could be slightly quenched. Tythian was finding and importing humans daily. But not even a slither of their former self had returned. The one and only time Julia had been down hadn't been enough to spark an ounce of recognition from Dillian.

"You're a vampire, Esmore. It wants to quench its bloodlust just as much as my own, simply for fun. If you have something to prove, prove it in the only way you know how," Lincon cooed. "Or let your huntress self, who is so 'noble' lead you into the path of self-destruction."

"It's this vampirism that wants to sicken me, not my hunter self," I clarified in defense. I didn't even understand why I was explaining myself to Lincon of all vampires. Or why he was even trying to involve me in his schemes. I'd turned my back on my ways, thought I was adapting, and this was what had happened in consequence. This was the misdeeds accumulated into one.

"Oh no, Darling, a vampire does not wish for death, even if it's what they truly want. Its nature is to survive and thrive. Or let's put that to the test, shall we? Throw yourself into this fight and see deep down how badly you really want to die. Prove me wrong and be reckless in its wake. And if you've already given up, why does it even matter?"

It all mattered, that was the problem. And I was ensnared in this inability to help anyone, and least of all I wanted to help myself. I looked down at my open palm. How many lives had I taken with these hands to protect those I claimed to love? How many lives had I taken in the name of what I thought was right? Or selfishly how many of those did I kill, simply to appease this darkness within me. So wicked was its kiss, a living pulse and entity that wouldn't let me out of its grasp.

I could feel Deemori and Connor descend the stairwell. "Leave me alone, Lincon," I said in a lowly growl. I didn't want him riling or trying to drag me into his deluded fun and games. This was serious. My familiar's life was hanging loosely in my hands. I wanted no part of living in this world, let alone attempting to thrive in it once again. Look how far that had gotten me.

He sneered at me, his usual goofy mannerism toward me turning into the rotten creature most saw. "You'll be seeing me soon. Of that I have no doubt," he tempered.

Deemori and Connor paused at the bottom of the stairs, making way for Lincon. Connor was already standing in front of her, protectively. For the first time, she didn't bring her entourage of sabers. Perhaps being considerate of how it might've stimulated Dillian and Tori. They weren't like Chase. She couldn't help them; they were waging through the natural process of having just been turned. But Chase was in a new and dangerous alienation.

She was wearing a long-oversized shirt. When she'd been turned, she was frozen in time around the same age as Tori. Mentally she had never been stifled, the wise gleam in her eye of an ancient. I wondered if it would be the same for Tori, whether he too would become accustomed to his frozen physical state, never yet an adult. And there was no greater pain than a hunter having not realized their gift. I was an example of that.

She wanted to help Chase, and maybe as it were now, she'd be a better help to him than I could be which only sullied me further. I nodded. When Chase had alluded that we find her before we rescued him from Fier's clutches, I wondered how clearly he prophesied this would be our future. That because of my instability and our link as familiars, he would be bouncing in and out of this state, gambling until he could come back no more. Connor, following her everywhere, briefly looked at my upheaval. He looked like he might want to say something, but his near-mute tendencies would make no exception this time. He was a man who embodied suffering. It was his drive to kill humans that kept him going. Would replicating such a pinpointed focus get me through?

"Esmore, I can calm him for some time, if you'd like to rest?" she asked. That gleam of ancestral wisdom echoing her every word.

I moved to the side. Not because I wanted the rest, but in the hope that she could help him more than me. Connor's icy blue eyes remained on me until the screams and chaos erupted in the main hall. Connor ascended the stairs with lightning speed.

Darcy stood in front of the stairwell blocking us in. He shifted into his form. "It's Lincon. He's throwing a fit before he leaves." He was reluctant not to join the chaos himself. "It'll be over soon, I'm sure."

But with Lincon, I was never too sure on how long his glowering moods would last or who he would take down in the process. I'd forfeited the leash the moment I'd declined to come with him to fight in this next little war he wanted to wage.

"There you are," Deemori cooed to Chase, enticing him as a lowly and groveling creature. He seemed to calm, despite the screams that echoed the hall as Lincon tortured them on his way out. I brushed past his mind and slammed a forceful wave of shock into him. The screams stopped, startling him momentarily. If he continued, I'd have to ascend the stairs.

Silence… I monitored his mind, gauging his location as he made his exit toward the forest. Eventually he had disappeared. I sighed, exhausted. I hadn't entirely lost my grip on his leash. Yet.

# CHAPTER 25

I T WAS ABHORRENT to watch Tori and Dillian fight amongst themselves, squabbling over their meals. Three humans had been brought down, and I watched on as they screamed and cried, their life messily being taken from them. I couldn't look away. I was fighting my natural urges to steal the prey but also protect them. I sat in a steely disposition. My appetite had completely vanished. The further I pushed my beast down, stifling it into non-existence, the more bile rose in my throat. Because of Deemori's presence, Chase was quick with his. He didn't play with his human in the same way the others were once he'd drained his. The others, however, were clumsy and messy. Blood spilled from their cages as they learned to navigate their fangs and ability to feast.

It was horrendous, as I realized it mirrored what I myself had become. They were hunched over and flicking the humans about. They were learning to tease and taunt them, an entirely different personality from how I knew them. The man Tori had been offered was twice his size and yet with a few head slams to the bars, Tori knocked him out and happily sucked on his wrist as if he was having a light snack in the corner of his cage.

I'd noticed that Tori's behavior began to change slightly. The more he fed, the less aggressive he was becoming. He wasn't as bothered by

Dillian who often antagonized him and tried to pick a fight. But the drinking seemed to only spur Dillian on, further propelling him into belligerence.

When they fell silent, I watched on hoping it'd be the moment clarity would sink in and a part of their former selves would awaken. Darcy enthused some took only a few hours to come back and some weeks. Worst-case scenario—years. When they awoke they craved and knew only one thing. Blood.

With Deemori maintaining her grasp on Chase's mind, he'd pacified. The calmness that over swept him eased me slightly. He was grimy and bloodied, unfocused as he stretched back and forth from standing to crouching. His jacket was coated in blood and mud from the disgraceful bedding he'd been spending the nights in. I wanted so badly to take him to the bathing chambers but felt guilty for not being able to do the same for the others. Deemori ushered him to sleep as easily as a few cooing noises that entranced him to dipping onto the floor.

She opened the gate. I tensed, waiting for him to erupt, but instead, he was left in a pleasant stupor. She weightlessly dragged the dead human woman by the arm. "Would you like to go in with him?" she asked quietly. It was a sober thought; to touch and be with him, but it wasn't enough to stir me from my spot on the floor. I didn't want to hold him in his current state. How could I caress such a fragment of him that he himself would entirely despise? I shook my head and reveled in the numbness that had taken over the past few days.

"Esmore, you should eat, go outside, or something," Deemori said. I curled my knees into myself further, hiding from her opinion. I wanted to waste away until they were back within my grasp. Even when asleep, Chase's mind was glorified in its thorny guard. I couldn't penetrate or hear anything past our link, exposing me to a loneliness I hadn't felt since the moment our bodies became one and we commemorated being familiars.

Jerimiah stormed down the stairs, his frame and height taking most of the small entrance's space. "Esmore, more vampires have been spiked on the outskirts. This time it's our coven members made an example of."

Dillian and Tori backed away from him and further into their cages, clearly intimidated by the hierarchy of his power. It was the quietest they'd been these past few days. I didn't want to speak. My throat felt too dry, and I felt too exhausted. A lump was at my throat, weighing down my ability to conjure words. When I ignored him, and he refused to move before receiving an answer, I glumly rasped out, "Hasn't Cesar dealt with this problem?"

Jerimiah shook his head, uncertain as to whether he should look at only me. But he briefed a glance at Chase who was passed out, lying on his back with his arms and legs stretched wide. He looked peaceful and utterly vulnerable. If he wasn't there to lead the coven, then I was supposed to take his place. I understood that, and yet leaving this small crevasse where I could watch them, waiting for their return compelled me to stay. I was so anchored to them that the thought of physically moving from this spot made me feel nauseous.

"Esmore," Darcy said gently. "If you believe Chase will come back to us, then you have to take charge in his place. We'll watch over him." It was pointless trying to hide further away from them. I couldn't morph into this wall anymore than I already had. They saw me. And as ignorant as I was to my responsibility, sickening myself in the process by pushing my will and raging beast within down, I acknowledged that the only thing keeping me going at this point was Chase. He was the last remaining reason I hadn't allowed myself to surrender to the depths of this chaotic mindset. If I forfeited myself, it would leave him in that place forever. And if I didn't have the protection of the coven to guard him, if they were to turn on him because of me and my absence in his stead... it was redundant. I wouldn't let that happen.

I pressed against the wall, my legs tender and sore from being in the same torturous position for days. I anchored into that festering anger inside of me spurred to continue each and every step of which I counted. It took my eyes a moment to painfully adjust to the brightness when I reached atop the stairs.

"Stay with him," I ordered Jerimiah who was halfway up the stairs behind me. I needed to do this on my own. I needed to guarantee that they'd be safe and looked after even after I left the room. I didn't need them playing bodyguard at a time like this, even if it was under Chase's orders. Jerimiah was reluctant, and I turned my back on him not leaving space for argument.

Blindfolded humans were steered toward the cellar by Lydia. Their smell aroused my inner beast, and I stifled it with the same squashing control I'd been using on it these past few days. It'd been the most control I'd ever had over it. I wanted to feel this burn and suffering from not quenching my thirst. Those humans were for Dillian, Tori, and Chase and only them. She seemed surprised by my exit.

"Esmore, you've left the cellar?" she asked, confused. "Shouldn't you be with Chase?" I ignored her not at all in the mood to explain myself. She was the only one who seemed disappointed that I was leaving his side, even momentarily. She watched me as I walked past, biting her lip as if to say something else. "How long will you be gone?"

"They won't bite," I hissed under my breath, but loud enough for her to hear. I could sense anxiety in her mind. Perhaps she was sensitive to the idea of being in a cellar filled with vampires, none of which were her coven. But even then, I expected more from one of Cesar's elite twelve.

I could sense Julia, Fire, the wolf pups, and my mother in my wing of the tower, furthest away from the commotion below for which I was grateful. I didn't want to have to face any of them right now.

My throat felt dry, and my body was tenderly sore. All my muscles tensed and constricted with every step I took. The institute's noises bombarded me after finding refuge with the dripping water in the cellar for so long. I coiled into myself, ignoring as much as I could on my way to Cesar's chambers. I walked past the bathing chambers Chase and I had tenderly enjoyed only days ago. It filled me with the sense of a grave loss. Even then I had felt as if I were going to lose him at any moment. And now here we were, because of what I had done. My finger trailed his locket of hair in my pocket, and I savored its feel. It was my reminder as to why I kept walking now. I had to take the lead for Chase while he was absent. I focused on the weight of the blue gemmed necklace around my neck that he'd given to me when I'd first infiltrated Fier's Council. Everything about me was smothered by Chase, and yet that disease in his mind still prevented us from speaking to one another. I was just too numb to fight and was running on fumes of strength and will to live as I reached Cesar's room. Without knocking on the wooden door of Cesar's quarters, I entered, revealing Cesar, Tythian, Yolo, and Balzar intently talking over a map.

"Esmore," Yolo gasped, surprised. I didn't look in his direction. I had no desire to speak with him. I didn't want to talk to any of them, particularly.

"How's Chase?" Balzar asked, unexpectedly interested.

"Ooof, touchy subject," Lincon said pushing past me, having come from nowhere to look at the map. Cesar scrunched it up and hid it behind his back. Lincon placed his hands on his hips. "No fair!" I was abashed by his entrance. He just appeared out of thin air, ever acute to any confrontation that might soon to be had.

I didn't want to be a part of any of this. I wanted to simply be back in the cellar, away from the commotion of the outside world and left to rot in my punishment. "What's this I hear about Chase's coven being spiked? I thought you sorted out Demetri's coven?" My voice was raw and quiet, devoid of any emotion or ambition. I was a shell of my former glory.

"You need to focus on staying with Chase and bringing him back. We still need him for Tracey's Council," Tythian said matter of fact. His existing and patronizing manner flared the last of my anger. Tythian was one of few who could pull it from me so easily and so that pointed savageness was quick to surface on its own accord.

"*You* have no right in telling me what to do," I hauntedly replied. "None of you do. This concerns my familiar's coven. What right do you think you have of keeping me out of the loop?"

Tythian sneered. "Look at you, honestly, you can hardly stand, let alone fight. Why don't you stick to the promises you've already made instead of causing more trouble for yourself?" Tythian lashed out.

"Is that what this is about?" I had two promises yet to be kept with Tythian. One of which was to kill Thomas, Lydia's brother who had betrayed us and joined Fier's Council. The second was to kill Fier because he'd killed Whitney. Was this why he'd spited me so much, because it all wasn't moving to his agenda or time schedule?

"Guys, this really isn't the time," Balzar interrupted. They all infuriated me so much because they all had their own agendas, and yet I was told to act like this or be in this position at their mercy. My will of freedom had been lost the day we'd joined Cesar's coven. I knew logically I never had such freedom initially, but irrational anger and anguish took over me. It was the only spark of life I'd had in days, and it was so quickly to form in my most apparent language. Rage.

"Either you let me go with your big killer party or I'll go on my own."

"Well, not entirely alone of course," Lincon said, pointing at me as if I were crazy.

"You don't even know where you're going," Tythian snarled, aggravated.

"No, but I'm pretty certain all I have to do is make some noise and something wicked will come this way," I replied dryly. I stared at Cesar who stroked his ginger beard thoughtfully. Yolo had gone quiet, unable to look at me, ashamed and disheartened in the same that he wasn't enough to protect the others.

"Esmore, it's under control. Balzar will be preparing and leading a team to deal with this. You are far too important to send out on a whim party," Cesar remarked. My inner beast vexed, ready to show each of them what I was truly capable of. Every part of me had been born and crafted to lead. And I'd already led his elite team before, all of whom survived. Balzar looked uncomfortable. Usually, he'd be ecstatic to be positioned at the head.

Something didn't feel right. They were meant to send out a team days ago, so why now were they sending out an elite team? All of the brothers remained here in the institute, so who had he sent out that failed so miserably, if anyone at all? I doubted this was simple turf wars. Someone was sending a message. I switched off, snapping myself out of my automatic calculating agenda. I didn't want to guess, plan, or strategize. I just wanted to be put in the center of a fight. I wanted to either entirely deny myself all privileges of this creature inside me or be devoured whole by it. And then the beckoning of being with Chase eluded me once again. The rage that so quickly swept over me was quickly vanquished into the longing to only be in the cellar with the others. It was our resting place. I lost all bravado and quickly succumbed to my miserable and selfish desires. I didn't want to fight. I didn't want to feel or do anything.

"Fine, I'll tell Chase's team it's being handled. Just sort it out," I said in a way to excuse myself. Lincon's mouth was agape at how easily I'd accepted my fate. Arguing with Cesar, especially while Tythian was in the room was pointless. I was certain Balzar knew more, and I would wait for the moment I could corner him. Until then, I wanted to hurriedly return to the others. They were safe here, in this institute. The spikings were happening on the edges of our territory, a threat, but not so directly that they were daring enough to walk to our front door. My head was all over the place. There was a silence that I found peaceful. And then my default of controlling and articulating an advantage in every situation. I was whiplashed by the constant struggle between the two.

"Lincon," Cesar ushered him to stay for a moment. I paused, reluctant to switch my curiosity off. I kept walking. It didn't matter. Everyone had their secrets and ambition. And I didn't have the energy to involve myself.

"Esmore, wait!" Yolo called out behind me as I stepped outside the room. Within a flash he was in front of me. "Esmore, please, I don't know what happened. You have to believe me."

I stepped past him. All my rage and fury narrowing into hatred toward him. I wanted to blame him, but it was my fault for not having led them to safety sooner. I'd become complacent, and it cost them their lives. I vowed to destroy the vampire who'd done this to them but even now, I couldn't build the strength to advance in any way. I was just so empty.

"Esmore, please!" he shouted out from behind me desperately. As I walked along the main corridor, nearing the staircase, I was ambushed by snarls and mutters. The voices of Chase's coven rose in fury, blasting me for being an 'ill mate,' 'a parasite,' 'a mix-breed,' and 'inactive ruler.' I kept my head high. I'd suffered similar scrutiny within the Guild for my dull eyes and lack of gift. I let the darkness swallow me whole again and drifted away from reality. I just had to put them at ease long enough until something was done.

Lincon had already caught up, blabbering about something to himself like always. When I reached the staircase atop the great hall, Clarissa was waiting for me, blocking the exit. Outside I could sense a few of Cesar's elite team, who I had no doubt was soon to be rallied by Balzar on their mission. I doubted Cesar was willing to gamble a large loss in numbers. Especially when Chase's coven was in disorder and lack of leadership to ensure they didn't turn on the rest of Cesar's coven. The tension in the room was palpable. Something about the situation didn't feel right, but I disregarded that instinct, fostering the idealism of the lie I was about to tell his coven.

Clarissa sneered as I approached her. "It's nice of you to finally show up. Shall I continue governing in your place or are you actually going to do something about the vampires who are spiking our heads?" Some of the coven members egged her on in spurts of enthusiasm.

"You have a lot of audacity speaking to my little queen like that," Lincon growled in warning. The word 'queen' ran a shiver down my spine. How revolting. And it always brought me back to my time spent with Fier.

"I'm speaking to you, Esmore," she said and stepped directly in front of me. I'd been jealous in the way Chase could depend on her with his coven, and even now she was more favorable in this position than me.

"Cesar's coven will be rid of them tonight. We will remain to ensure Chase's safety." The words didn't even sound authentic or convincing. I didn't know what I was doing, my head a jumble in a way I'd never known before.

"Should you not take some of our men instead of depending on them?" Clarissa demanded. "Now is the time to lead in his place, instead of running away," she pushed. My top lip curled. Yet I couldn't deny running away was what I was doing. I couldn't leave them, my body so entitled to stay with them until they were better—if ever. And if they didn't improve then I'd waste alongside them.

"Oh, honey, none of that!" Lincon interrupted. "Do you know how much effort it took me to drag her out of that little dungeon? So, let's not chase her back into the sinkhole."

"And what of Chase? How does he fare? You haven't given us anything," she angrily asked on behalf of everyone. His coven was watching intently, waiting for the verdict. It was a surprising loyalty they'd adopted toward him. But I wondered how long it'd last until one of the airheads in here would think with their brute force and desire to gain his title by challenging him. Would Clarissa stand in their way or step to the side. And the same went for even the gargoyles that were positioned in the center of the foyer, acting as a protective barrier between the two covens under Jerimiah and Darcy's order. How long would their loyalty last?

"He'll be okay," Balzar said, taking a few steps at a time as he came down the stairs.

"No one asked you, buzzcut," she hissed.

"Well, no one asked you to block the staircase either, and yet, there you are, in all your gothic dread," he retorted.

"Oh my, your flirting is so outdated," Lincon snickered, barging Clarissa out of the way. "There are my two girls," he said, summoning Kora and Kasey inside. It was risky considering they weren't part of either coven and still hunters even if mutilated. Kasey glowered at him. Kora was sketchy, watching everyone and looking like easy bait that could be preyed upon. The fang that she'd shattered in her mouth hadn't healed. And I was under the impression that it never would.

"Your coven failed once boy, I wouldn't be getting smart," Clarissa replied.

"Who said we failed?"

"In the way that you haven't done anything yet." She pressed an empty smile. Spungee was clicking slowly toward her, his neck twitching. One of the gargoyles stepped between the two with lightning speed. These two always bickered and grew tired of one another quickly. And I wasn't in the frame of mind to deal with them today. Let the gargoyles deal with them in the position that they were granted.

"You stay and ensure his safety, no matter what." It was the only form of direct order I could give. What did they want from me? How much more could they take? They despised me and for what I'd done to their leader, so why still have adequate control around the formalities.

"You stupid bitch!" Kasey broke past and lunged for me. I was startled by the outburst. Kora quickly projected a barrier between herself and the vampires who were tempted to pounce on her. I toppled over, allowing Kasey to have the edge, welcoming her fury as the punishment no one else had yet dared to unleash on me. My beast was furious that yet again I was letting someone have the upper hand. She punched my face.

"You let them turn!" The pain of her fist colliding with my nose was glorious. This was the punishment I deserved and so desired. "You failed them!" Balzar grabbed her by the shoulder and threw her off. She skidded into the masses of vampires. Lincon tsked at them in warning. If they dared touch her, they'd be welcoming havoc with him. He charmed a coy smile at everyone's hesitation. Oh, how they feared him. And they were evidently confused that his favored 'queen' had been hit and he allowed it.

"At least get up while his coven is watching," Balzar addressed me, reefing me up from the ground. My nose began to crunch and heal slowly.

"How can you live with yourself?! He was your so-called best friend! Nothing but death and disaster follow you!" She spat at the ground.

"Twin one, bad," Lincon reprimanded Kasey by flicking her nose. She slapped his hand away, furious. "Don't make me choose, you know Esmore is my number one. Now, run off and play."

Lydia walked down the stairs, her appearance drawing attention. "Ah, I just fed them," she said. "Maybe you should check up on him?" I felt empty. Once I'd been so full of spirit to lead them, and now, now I was nothing. If I remained in the space with Chase and the others, I'd only spiral further into that dark place alongside Chase. I wanted to go back and commit to that suffering. But if I did, I'd only nail in Chase's fate. It was hard to fight and find my way when I didn't have the will or strength any longer.

"Lydia's right," Balzar said. "Maybe you should cool off for a moment." He hugged me. My body went rigid at the sentiment of an unworldly attempt in comfort. It didn't suit either of us, until I felt his hand slither behind my back and slip a piece of paper in my back pocket. "There's only so much time." He released me, flicking off the exaggerated feel of my touch.

"What, no!" Lincon grumbled. "Aren't we going to fight too?!"

I ignored him, nodding my thanks to Lydia as I ascended the stairs. Vile words were whispered amongst the coven and room. All the energy I'd mustered to leave the cellar felt spent. I couldn't even remember how I'd convinced myself that coming out was the right thing to do as I followed that disastrous link and returned to Chase. I tried to ignore the ominous feeling that something wasn't right. I just wanted to be left alone—away from thoughts and responsibility.

I blatantly ignored Cesar's door and the curiosity of what schemes they were conjuring. Let them play their power games while their coven was distracted below, unsettled by another spiking. I unfolded the piece of paper Balzar had given me. It was a map with a few markings as to where they were heading. Black ink followed the river and canopies where we'd intercepted the members of Demetri's group. Balzar and his team intended to go downstream the river and in a small blotch on the page was where their suspicions were of where the coven was based.

I crumpled it back into a folded piece and shoved it into the back of my leather pants. I grazed my fingers delicately over the blue gem of Chase's necklace tied around my neck. It was unusual for Balzar to go against Cesar. And now I knew how to get there. But putting in the effort to actually go… to leave the others… I shoved down the patronizing part of me that began calling me a coward, a true vision in all its rage and pity of how much I'd fallen. And I wasn't sure what part was loosening on me. Was that my vampire, or had my huntress even given up? My entities were splitting, leaving me with a hollowness.

My feet stopped in front of the bathing chambers. My eyebrows furrowed slightly, confused why my body was working of its own accord. There was a coolness that seemed to emit from the room and behind the closed door. Before I knew it, my hand had already stretched out and jarred it open. It slowly opened with a creak that seemed to echo in its slow draw. The darkness of the night was spilling into the room. Hauntingly, my steps gravitated further in. Something was in this room.

The small moan of the floorboard was my only signal to dodge. A black shadow jumped out from behind the door. I stepped back, raising my arm to divert the sword that struck at me. I'd missed it barely, but it still cleanly sliced through my flesh, my blood flicking to the ground. It wasn't a shadow, it was a vampire wearing a black robe and mask, similar to the one's Cesar had provided us with. I realized with total clarity it wasn't one of our own. *Assassin.*

My body moved on reflexes, with stupor, retracting from the sword that so swiftly was striking and slicing at my chest or any other openings that might stun me long enough. The blade sliced past my face, finely sprinkling a strand of my hair onto the floor. I swept low, flicking their feet out from beneath them. Instead of falling to the ground, they flipped onto their hands and somersaulted back. I grabbed the bottom of the claw bath, flicking it up at them with a burst of strength. The bathtub collected them mid-air. They flicked it off, the tub shattering into the side of the wall.

Yolo opened the door, stifled by the noise. "Es—" Yolo was caught off guard by the assassin and jumped back before they struck at his heart. I took advantage of the distraction and jumped, catching under their arm that held the sword. I popped the shoulder out and flicked the blade to the edge of the room. It clattered on the floor. Yolo lunged for them with an aggressive snarl. The assassin kicked him back and grabbed my back, flicking me over their dislocated arm. I oomphed as my back hit the ground. I rolled to the side, his foot barely missing my face as he tried to stomp it in. The wood beneath his foot crumbled where my face had once been.

He flicked out his arm, a quick fix to his dislocated shoulder popping back into place. He ran for the window, but Yolo blocked him, dodging the few hits that would've been the end of him. Yolo was able to smash one good kick into his knee, buckling him momentarily. I grabbed behind him, collecting his underarms. Yolo busted in his other knee. I could hear the scraping of Fire's nails drag along the wooden hallway. I yanked on the line that Fire and I shared. She'd already sensed the danger and made no error as she glided through the entrance.

"Fire!" I summoned her. I twisted slightly, giving her a clear opening as I pinned back the vampire. She lunged for his throat, ripping out his jugular. But it wasn't the wound that would kill him. It'd be the bite.

He gurgled as I put my knee into his back buckling him further to the ground. Fire's mouth was marred in black blood as she snarled and threatened him. His throat attempted to slowly heal, but I could see the festering rapidly begin. He'd implode within minutes.

"Who sent you?" I demanded, tightening my grip on him so he couldn't move. Yolo pushed back his hood and reefed off the mask revealing a twisted and scarred face. Yolo's face paled as he looked at the vampire with only one eye and severe scarring and twisted burns on his face. His lips had mostly been melted together, except the one singular fang and few teeth that poked out in a permanent sad smile.

With his throat torn and body that started to convulse from Fire's bite, I tried to push myself into him telepathically. But he wouldn't link or obey. His gurgles and squirting blood splashed at Yolo's bare chest. He moved his wooden cross so it wouldn't be dirtied.

"Esmore, he's not going to tell us anything," Yolo said in a small voice. All the fury I'd bundled up and pushed down awoke, and I tried to keep it at bay. I felt like I was boiling over. They were here. And so close to the chambers where Chase and the others were being kept. The very same chambers where the human had been assassinated. Cesar suspected it was an inside job, but maybe someone had navigated to let them in. Either way, no one else had sensed the assassin's presence. It was dumb luck that Yolo was looking for me. And it could've been seconds too late until Fire had felt the desperation in our line. The assassin could've made his way to the chambers in a small space where the others so weakly were locked up. My body shook with fury, and I was suddenly aware of where I had to be.

I delicately placed my fingers on the assassin's neck, slowly and brilliantly twisting his head off with satisfying content. The mass of his body decayed onto the ground. I dropped his head onto the pile, my vision hazing purple. *They had lied to me.*

# CHAPTER 26

C ESAR HADN'T SENT the others out on a mission to simply send a warning message to a coven disputing territory. Someone was terrorizing us, and they'd been only a short distance from where Chase and the others were being kept.

"What happened? I heard a noise," Jerimiah was a second too late to watch the demise of the assassin who'd just broken in. He saw my sullied hands and the decaying mass in front of me.

"Guard the doors to the chambers and make sure they're protected at all times," I ordered. "There was an assassin amongst our midst."

"But how, this place is fully guarded and concealed?" he asked, confused.

I hurriedly left the bathroom. "It's concealed by Cesar's gift but not if someone guided them in. That and whatever kind of vampire it was, it didn't have any presence. This wasn't just any assassination attempt. The vampire was trained and near undetectable."

"And what will you do?" he called out behind me. Fire was by my side, snarling in displeasure very similar to my own discontent.

"I'm going to do what I do best." My body was acting on its own. I was still devoid of any intrigue or thought process as to where my actions might lead me. All I knew was that I had to protect Chase and the others at all costs. This assassin had been too close.

"Esmore, wait! What are you going to do?" Yolo tried to hurriedly follow me. I ignored him. Had he been in on this too? Known of what was really happening? But how could he when most of the time he was with the others? What if this assassin had been the one to do this to Dillian and the others? But by way of the uniform robe and mask, I had an instinctual feeling there was more than one.

Goosebumps trailed up my arms as I pushed the fury down, trying to punish my inner vampire that tried to spring to the surface. I wasn't ready to confront it, terrorized by its failings previously. What was I even going to do now? The link to Chase beckoned to me like a sinking sandpit, compelling me to brief its edges once again so I could spiral with him. But one leg pressed in front of the other, ascending my staircase and ignoring all the taunts made by Chase's coven on my way. I slammed a hard alert to Lincon, beckoning him to come my way. He would get his way after all.

I stormed into my room, startling Julia who had been ushering the wolf pups to sleep in the bed. My mother had been guarding the door. "Esmore." My mother sprang into action following me. I ignored her, pacing across the room to reach for my garter. I strapped it around my thigh and started gearing my daggers. "Esmore!" she said harshly. My body stilled, having been conditioned to listen as a young child. But not anymore. Had she known?

"An assassin just breached Cesar's wing," I said blandly as I darted back and forth in the room, collecting my things. Julia gasped from the corner of the room. Titan began rubbing her eyes. As soon as she saw me she sprang to life.

"Ellie!" I shuddered under the name and fake identity. Worst of all, I didn't want to see her. I ignored her, pretending like I couldn't see or hear her. I blanked her out with the others.

"What?" My mother seemed shocked. "Cesar will handle this. I saw them send out a team a short time ago."

"Who very well might not return because Cesar's been a bit vague with the details." My hand paused at the hood and mask. Did I have a need to wear this anymore? It was only to mimic them wasn't it? Was that why Cesar had forced us to wear it? Though Balzar and the others had worn theirs. And for whatever reason, Balzar had given me the directions to follow them if I so desired, ignoring Cesar's orders. I fanned it out and over my shoulders.

For once, instead of grumbling my complaints about the robe and mask, I felt as if I were armoring myself. Hiding further into becoming the non-existing phantom I wanted to be. I was still being pulled in the direction of Chase, ever begging to be in his presence and spiral with him. But I couldn't bring him back unless I did this. I was evoked by something that needed to be awakened or let fate decide my future. I was equipped with daggers strapped to my leather pants, one inside my boot, my sword strapped to my back, and my golden nails readily available in my satchel that hung at my hip.

"Esmore, I won't allow you to go," my mother ordained. "Let Cesar deal with this." She stood in front of the doorway. I collected my Barnett crossbow and looked at her deadpan. Her size and experience might've once bullied me into submission, but no longer. I wasn't a little girl, and I was sick of listening to everyone else's orders. I'd tried and look where it got me. I had to follow my instinct and action. I knew no other way.

Fire backed off, remaining outside the door. "Don't make me use this on you," I said coolly to my mother, raising my crossbow.

"You're going to die." My mother crumpled in fury and despair. "That was the note from Louise. She foresaw you being killed by Oppollo's assassins."

The air stilled in the room. I was being rash and rebellious, the very things Dillian had negatively dictated I was being. But I was compelled by it. Finding an ending either by Chase's side, spiraling into nothingness with him and my guilt of what I'd done to the others, or pretending to still die as a hero. At least there would be an ending. As Lincon had dictated, maybe I needed to challenge myself this once.

"I've never feared death," I said honestly to my mother. "What cripples me is failing to protect those I've vowed myself to." My gaze inevitably drew to Titan. "I never wanted this pressure or destiny crap. That's your story, not mine. And if she's right, then so be it."

"Esmore, I won't let you leave," she said, hardening herself. I could feel Lincon's lingering presence. He was positioned slightly ajar from being seen.

"Then I'm sorry, mother," was all I said and slammed a sense of approval into Lincon. My mother went into a haze. Not a screaming or terrifying purge but one that forced her into succumbing to his illusion.

This was something I had to do. They had been so preoccupied with trying to keep me safe that it risked everyone else in the process.

I strapped my Barnett crossbow over my shoulder. Where I would often braid and tighten my hair, I decided to leave it loose, my blonde curls blanketing over my shoulders. It was different, necessary even in the way I was attuned to myself. Julia had been pulling back Titan, making sure she didn't step any closer. I ignored them. I briefed one glance at my mother as I closed the door, apologetic for using such a cheap trick on her. They had all once called me reckless, and maybe they were right.

I was damned if I followed their orders and I was damned if I didn't. Lincon whistled to himself, impressed with the coldness of my attitude. Fire followed. I looked into her icy blue eyes. The black blood around her mouth was still wet.

"I can't ensure your safety," was all I said. My voice sounded so distant. As if trailing to find a way it could drag me out of this life entirely. Like how I couldn't be told what to do, I would no longer try to control the actions of others. They were all permitted to do as they pleased. My robe flapped over the skirting of the spiral cemented staircase as I hurriedly walked down them.

"I want you to order Kora and Kasey to stay, together they'll be able to put a barrier up," I said to Lincon.

"To keep the assassins out?" he asked curiously.

"No. To keep everyone in."

Cesar was squaring me as we entered the main hall. I gazed at him, pushing down the hungry beast within me that lashed out. The covens silenced with an appreciation for the tension between us. Lincon walked ahead of us to locate Kasey and Kora to instruct exactly what I'd just said.

"We have this under control!" Cesar said with the bitter anger his reputation upheld. My actions were undermining him, and that was out of his jurisdiction. I descended the stairs, my robe skirting on each step. Chase's coven gathered closely at the line that divided the two covens. Clarissa was watching on in curiosity. Tythian was standing beside Cesar, smug as he stood. Finally, he would see Cesar disappointed in not him, but me.

"Esmore, please," Yolo urged. I didn't blame him for running to Cesar. He had to inform them of the assassin that had entered our space. But I wasn't willing to put up with this nonsense any longer. My body was moving of its own accord, taking me from this place to the next and whatever lay beyond that. I tried to ration my thoughts, siphoning out of the eroding and magnetizing pull of returning to Chase. I wasn't strong enough to pull him out. But maybe in doing this I could find the will to live again, to find that purpose that was tied in with my purity. The purity that would help him dissolve the toxicity in his mind. If I couldn't do that, then there was nothing left for me here.

Maybe if I could prove that I wasn't the strongest or even all that important, they would let me go too. They would stop buffering me from this cruel reality of so many who wanted to kill me. Because of it, so many were being hurt and killed on my behalf. Or maybe in its aftermath, I'd be closer to a destination where I'd understand how to trade places with Chase. Maybe the act in fighting itself would ignite my desire to continue on and regain something, any piece of me that was willing to fight, if only for the others.

Chase would do this for me. I allowed that to be my guide. And so, I would let that reckless nature thrive with the intent to re-spark something, anything, in my desperate plea to reverse everything that had happened these last few days. This was the truest form I knew and acknowledged. It was all I could do to re-stitch one notch on all that had already become undone.

"I forbid you from leaving!" Cesar's voice bellowed through the room. I stilled, just as I had with my mother, except unlike her, who I loved, I had no kind words or fair departing. I twisted on him.

"*You* have no control over me. *You* who lied to me!"

"Oh, for God's sake, you wouldn't have cared anyway, you were moping in the cellars," he barked back.

"We trusted you." I fixated on squashing down the anger that was bursting at the seams. It created a stomachache as I pushed down on my vampire, cutting off its oxygen and right to breathe through me. I wanted and chose to be this empty vessel. "And now Balzar might not make it back alive because those assassins are trained for this. How wicked of you to have kept that from us."

"Don't be daft." He crossed his arms as a few of his coven muttered amongst themselves. Yolo flinched uncomfortably. "It's a simple coven, Esmore. They've been sent out to simply kill a weak coven as an example. They'll be fine."

"Then you should have no issue with me going as well." I turned my back on him. Fire snarled as he went to take a step. Connor fixated on her and Lincon made his presence known, swishing his finger back and forth. If Connor dared to use his gift on her, Lincon would intervene. Perhaps Cesar genuinely thought Balzar and his elite were enough to take out the assassins. Or perhaps he wasn't willing to admit he misjudged the situation. It was already too late because his team was gone. Tythian could stop them, and yet Cesar chose for him to remain. He could do as he pleased and I would do the same. *Like father, like daughter, no?*

"You need to stay here, at least for your familiar," he grumbled angrily, trying to remain collected.

I addressed Clarissa. "The cellar and my wing are to be guarded at all costs. If any of them attempt to turn on our treaty, then effective measures are to be taken."

The life that sparked her only minutes ago had ashed out once again. She gave me a complacent nod.

"Are you threatening me, girl?" Cesar asked from behind. I twisted, my mask blocking some of my peripheral vision.

"No. I'm enforcing my rule," I said ambiguously. "If it's me that they want, then it's me that they'll get. Just pray that your blood is as mighty as you claim it to be." I was certain that Cesar wouldn't break into a fight within the institute, especially now that he'd removed a handful of his best warriors and would be trapped inside with them. Not that he knew that yet. I took satisfaction in knowing that Tythian would be trapped for once in this miserable life as well.

"Let's go." Clarissa and a handful of vampires guarded my back, so no one could intervene with my exit. Kora and Kasey waited at the institute's gates.

Kasey didn't so much as look at me. Kora seemed meek as she wavered a tense glance between us. Lincon patted them on the head one by one. I felt the barrier go up as soon as I stepped past the entrance of the institute's gates.

"How long can you hold it?" I asked. Kasey looked away, ignoring me, so ignorant that she refused to answer.

Kora was mousy but still said in a small voice, "Maybe an hour or two tops. We've never managed one this size before."

"That'll have to do." I faced Lincon who had already put on a long robe and mask that smiled from ear to ear. I shook my head, not even daring to ask where or why he even had it. He obviously suspected I'd change my mind and sneak out. Ever the puppeteer he thought he was. "And, Lincon, drop your hold on my mother. Let's go."

I hovered my mind momentarily over the link between Chase and me. I glided down it smoothly until I was infected with the harshness of the wall that kept me out, but also sung to me to obliterate with him. This was the only way I knew how to act. I was deteriorating faster than I knew how to keep up with my thoughts. And so, I decided to run with the momentum of the first action I'd been ensnared by, besides self-mutilation or torture, in punishment for the crimes I so heavily felt I'd committed.

I rested my mind against his, assured that if we were in reversed roles, he would do the same. I couldn't let Balzar and the others go into this unaware of the full force they might be greeted by. If I could help, if only a little to take their attention away from this institute, then I would. The thorny prickle of Chase jabbed at my mind, but I pressed harder, envisioning that Chase was on the other side. *I don't have the strength to pull you out right now, my love.* How could I when I'd lost my strength to fight for even myself. *But this much I can do.* I caressed the sharp edges of his mind, requesting his forgiveness for my recklessness and putting him in that state in the first place. *If I can do only one thing for you. Let it be that I fight.*

# CHAPTER 27

*A* HUNTER WILL *always find themselves in battle. They discover who they are and their capabilities at their most basic instinct—and that is to survive.*

It was one of the first classes Campture had ever taught us herself. I was only six at the time, staring up at the chalkboard wide-eyed and in admiration of the strength the warriors had carried and the legacy of their stories. I'd watched them leave the Guild gates but very rarely saw their return. Often, they'd come in the brink of night or in a way that very few would see them if they came back with less than they'd departed with. No one mentioned or spoke about the aftermath. After the fight, or after the war. No one spoke of those who lost their lives, or the open wounds that marred the warrior and slowly hardened them or broke them into an irreparable undoing. No one dared to raise a hand and ask if there was any other way. The days of mastering peace and negotiation were over the moment the humans betrayed the treaty with vampires. Three hundred years later, we were still cleaning up their mess, in a never-ending war that was far greater than what we'd been taught. We were told only one side of the story, and many of us died under the pretense of honoring that. And there was certainly no pep talk for those who wanted to give up. You either died fighting or lived only for the next. There was no honor in walking onto an off the beaten track.

It didn't take long for Lincon and me to track the others. I'd followed Balzar's detailed map and spotted them running along the riverbank, close to where I'd once manhandled Jerimiah. Lincon and I descended the cliff wall. When Balzar spotted us he halted his group of forty.

"Esmore?" Lydia asked, confused. Balzar made an effort to complain, but I knew he wouldn't have given me the details to follow him unless he thought less of Cesar's plan. He was doing it for show.

"Walk with me," I said, inclining him to the back of the group. Lincon took his stride at the front badgering Lydia as she tried to concentrate on navigating the team. We dropped back from the group.

I gently tapped on Balzar's mind, a suggestion of permission to speak to him privately telepathically. He wore the same horned mask he'd been wearing, but I didn't need to see his expression to feel his reluctance to open up to me. "We were attacked."

Those three simple words snapped him to attention. His mind coherently opened up to me. *What? When?*

*As soon as you left, an assassin wearing a mask and black robe came through Cesar's chambers. I encountered him by chance. Yolo and Fire helped me take him down.*

*Shit, that was a lot faster than I thought they'd make a move,* he admitted deep in thought.

*You knew?*

*Well, of course I did. They're after you. They're Oppollo's assassins. Their group is renowned amongst the covens as 'cleaning up his mess' and doing his dirty work. Why do you think Cesar forced us to wear these masks and robes in the first place?*

*To hide our identity.* I knew there was further reasoning to it, but couldn't place my finger as to why. But after witnessing the masked assassin I had suspicions it had something to do with them.

*Yea, well that and Cesar was trying to throw Oppollo off our trail. He knew he'd bring his best down on us. So everywhere we went, all places all over the countryside, we were to wear these. To confuse others who might've been following us but to also throw him off. If his 'group' were seen here, there, and everywhere, it'd create talk and friction within the other Council's. They'd question him and his motives. It might've also put doubt in his mind about his own men as well. But obviously it didn't work as well as Cesar had hoped.*

*Why doesn't he face us head-on instead of sending assassins?* I queried. If he wanted us gone so badly, then surely he was a man to take matters into his own hands. That was the impression I'd gotten from the only chance encounter I'd had with him.

*Because Oppollo has to be careful of how much attention he invests in us. The Council meeting is coming up soon, and I'm sure he's focusing on that. We're nothing but a thorn in his side. But one he wants removed immediately.*

Both times vampires were spiked it was a momentary distraction and chaos in the institute. It'd been a distraction from their real objective, and that was getting inside. The only way the assassin would've known where I was specifically was if someone was helping them from the inside. *Someone from the inside is helping them.*

*No shit, Balzar grumbled his complaint. You'd been in the same spot for days now, wallowing in the cellar. It was a keen target on your back. If you hadn't been pulled out even during those few minutes, he would've come for you just like he had the human.*

I didn't think much of chance encounters or luck, but I was indebted that I'd crossed paths sooner with the assassin before they reached the staircase. Though I doubted the assassin would've made it past Jerimiah, Darcy, and me, the conditions could've changed under the 'what if' principle. We were locked in a small space, and there were too many variables that could've gone wrong.

*Why did you betray Cesar and give me a map? You know you're probably walking into far more than just a rival coven, don't you?*

"Of course I know that!" he said out loud, grabbing Lydia's attention. He seemed embarrassed and looked at the river. *The truth is. I thought you had the right to come if you wished. I know Cesar and your mother are trying to protect you. But the way I saw it, you were pretty down in the dumps for fucking up in protecting the people you loved too, and I didn't see any other way of pulling you out unless you could redeem yourself in some way. I've seen you fight, Esmore. I know it compels you just as much as it does me. The things we can't place in words, can only be found out there, in a life and death decision. And if we get killed… well, it was all for nothing anyway, wasn't it?*

I side glanced him, suspicious of his ease in putting it into words. Lincon had said something similar but in a maddening kind of way.

*Just don't ever tell Cesar I helped you,* he quickly added.

*You don't view me like the rest, do you? Like some fragile thing to be protected?*

He scoffed. *Fragile is the last thing I'd label you as. But I know what it's like to feel like you're fighting an already losing battle. I respect Cesar's decisions, and I follow him because I genuinely believe he might be one of the few to stop the Council from moving in and eradicating the covens. But, his grudge against Oppollo makes the operation a little too personal for my liking. On the other hand, if we do nothing about it now, then we're all doomed. I know what I'm fighting for and I almost feel sorry for you because you've been forced into this battle without so much as an opinion. A spoilt little brat, but stuck in a cage, and the only fluttering moments you've had have devoured you. So this may end up kicking your ass. But at least you had the option to come.*

Balzar had been the one I once hated the most. And yet strangely enough his observation and opinion of me resonated somewhere that I kept buried. He might've been right, or he might've been wrong. But I was willing to stake my life to protect him in this fight. He knew what he stood for, and despite his rough exterior, he was fair to everyone who wanted to stand a chance and fight for what they believed in. I found refuge in that.

The small remains of the town that Demetri's coven dwelled in was sanded down by years of harsh weather. The homes and buildings were either torn apart or stripped away. Alcohol glass bottles littered the streets alongside the remains of human bodies who'd begun to erode and fester with small parasites. To my left, beside a building with the signage 'library' was the remains of what looked like a furred mammal. I couldn't begin to decipher what it might've once been because it'd been drained and mauled apart so badly. Fire lifted her nose as if disgusted by the insulting smell. My mask did nothing to block the putrid invasive stench of the town.

Our robes pushed against the low wind that howled down the empty streets. It had long been abandoned, but there was an ominous ambiance that raised the hairs on the back of my neck, forewarning me that we were close to something. My mother's words echoed, *You will die.* I'd already thought so many times that it would be the end for me, and instead of fearing it, I became desensitized by the notion. The further I crept away from Chase the more I was able to think clearly. I wasn't as oppressed by the chaotic harshness of his mind escaping into my own, unbeknownst to me.

The group split into two, one led by Lydia, and the other by Balzar. I followed his suit, hanging back with his group. Lincon drifted off with Lydia. And even amongst the tension of the situation she begged Balzar for a 'swapsies,' pitying herself for having been stuck with him.

We rounded a small corner store that had been blown out years ago by an explosion. I took the rear of the group and kept my hand on the hilt of my sword, ready for any change in our surroundings or oncoming attackers. There weren't many places they could hide. The town had been destroyed leaving very little for coverage. Fire flanked me as if we were separate from the group and ensuring she had my back in case we were ambushed.

Balzar squatted, and the rest of the group followed. I lowered myself to Fire's level watching the other group's backend disappear behind a street of abandoned homes. Balzar instructed us to move on, so we did, following each and every edge like it'd set off a trap. The town was empty, and there were no signs of any recent outbreaks or carnage. We had no waft or inclination of where Demetri's coven might've gone. The river on the town's outer edge was what guided us from one end to the other.

It was only when we reached the town's tail end and began resurfacing into the bushland that we noticed recent tracks. We followed it, being threaded through the bushland some more until we paused on the edges of a large establishment. It looked to have once been a small sawmill with numerous cargo containers and a profoundly large warehouse. Scattered on the edges were small, constructed metal offices. Atop and mounted on the roof's metal sleeve to the warehouse were three vampires, chained by silver, gasping and moaning in pain. That was already a grieving sign that Demetri's coven had been compromised.

Balzar's horned mask twisted over his shoulder, his green eyes summoned me forward. I silently walked through the group, Fire close to my side. "It's too quiet," Balzar confided. "And there are no guards."

I could sense there were others inside. I inspected further, hovering my mind and sweeping over them. They varied. Some were frightened, leading me to believe they were a part of Demetri's coven. This was a sacrilege punishment within their own coven or they'd been bested easily by Oppollo's men who were using this coven as the bait to draw us out.

We searched for an opening; any tell as to where they would ambush us from. The space was open and barren, luminous in comparison to the trees we were hiding amongst.

A twig snapped, directing our attention to the swarm of members who approached us slowly. They wore masks and robes. Fire growled as they approached us slowly, sounding my alarm. I scanned over their minds, none of which resembled any of the members of Lydia's group.

I sent a wave of panic into Balzar's mind. It stifled him for a moment, and he looked past me at the dark-robed figures that were advancing on us, slowly as if it were to their advantage that we'd mistake them for our own group. More robed figures advanced behind me. More than the members we'd come with. Well, at least there would be no delay in our ambush. I opened the small satchel plating my fingers with the delicate golden nails I'd become accustomed to.

Balzar tapped his temple, indicating for me to tap into conversation. I slid into connection with him, shifting into the wave of his consciousness and ignoring it as best I could.

*I'll lead the team on the left, and you lead a team to counter the few advancing near the water,* he instructed as he slid on his metal spiked knuckles beneath his robe. I wondered if Lydia and the others had been approached in the same manner or if they'd verged off into another direction entirely. But I couldn't think about their safety now, and had to believe in their ability to dig themselves out.

We weren't outnumbered, but they had the element of surprise, or so they thought. My eyes hazed purple, my vampire swelling in the breath of life it was given as I brought it forward. Now would be the moment I could finally express everything that needed to come to the surface. To break from my compelling attitude that was dragging me down alongside Chase. I thought of Dillian and Tori who were trapped in their cages like animals. If I ever wanted to seek any kind of revenge on those who'd done that to them, I'd have to live past this day. I had to break free from my shackles before I could alleviate them.

I gathered the last of my strength that had so easily seeped from me these past few days. I would dance on the battlefield in the most instinctual way I knew. Balzar threw a few hand gestures, and our group prepared. My vampire was thriving beneath the surface, thrumming for the fight to come. But I couldn't even manage the creeping smile that would usually occur. I had to re-spark it, anything that would give me the will to live. Something had to awaken, and I was certain I would only find that in a fight. In *this* fight. If all went well, I would send Oppollo a message in return. To not think so simply of us, and to never return again unless he brought his army.

The dust and mist swept up around us, as all at once we burst into our separate directions. Six followed me alongside Fire who matched my speed. As soon as we burst into action so did the others, having realized their ruse was up. We charged them meeting at the muddy water edge of the river. They'd descended the cliff edge on the other side, leaping over the water. Their robes suspended in the air as they did, the sun silhouetted around them, hiding the expressions on their unchangeable masks.

Fire leaped for the first one, latching onto its arm and reefing it to the ground. The member screamed, perplexed by the shuddering pain that ran through their arm. I splashed ankle-deep into the water meeting the first masked figure who sized me up. They weren't coy about attacking first. I dodged their sword. Their movement was intimidatingly fast, striking, and deliberate. A small whistle shuddered around their blade as it passed me.

As the vampire's foot lightly touched the ground, they'd already sprung up kicking my sword out of my hand. The movement was so swift it reminded me of when I challenged Pac in our spars back at the Guild. I rolled to catch my sword, but the swiftness of the vampire was already on me. My body burst into alertness, unable to think of any tactic other than staying alive. His foot with a spiked edge on the back of his boot came down on me. I caught it with both hands, digging my sharp claws into their foot and swung them, propelling them back into the side of the cliff. *Don't think, just act.*

The mass of the rock crumbled around them. I briefed a glance in Fire's direction, catching hold of one of my daggers and propelling it toward the vampire she'd challenged. The vampire caught my dagger, so acutely aware of their surroundings. They harpooned it back toward me. I stumbled back and toward my sword. I balanced the hilt on my foot and flicked it up to catch. The vampire Fire had challenged wasn't yet imploding, and I worried about how long she could hold her own against them. These were trained warriors—an elite team. A gurgling scream sounded behind me, and the waft of rotting vampire followed. One of our own had already been taken out.

The vampire I'd thrown into the cliff edge pushed away the broken rock that had crumbled around their impact. They dusted themselves off as if to make a point to me that it barely hurt. All that marked any damage on them was the few holes in their robe. I took a few steps back reassessing them. They tilted their head slightly, as if doing the same to me. Through the mask I could see beady brown eyes studying me. We might've not been outnumbered, but the others were certainly becoming outmatched.

I briefed another glance in Fire's direction. Her bite was finally taking hold on her opponent. No matter how skilled these vampires were, they evidently hadn't yet heard of the wolf bites which could be to our advantage.

An explosion detonated around the sawmill, the remains of one of Balzar's members toppling over in it. He screamed, the top part of his body blasted away from the rest. The ground rattled from the explosion. My opponent was already using the distraction to their advantage. I vaulted twice to the side, grabbing one of the daggers in my garter and pegging it at their mask. It sliced past, fractionally grazing it.

I assumed it was a male by their build, and they were a few inches shorter than me. I tried to calculate how I could use that to my advantage. I was again on the defense. He pounced. Their knuckles glazed past my throat with such purpose and fine precision that I felt my throat constrict just from the speed of their handling. Their other arm jabbed their sword toward my stomach. I jarred my hip, narrowly missing it. I savagely bit into their arm, ripping off flesh and pulled back as they went for another stab.

My vampire self was so infuriated by the disadvantage. I was holding myself back, and I didn't know how to unlock it. How to be on the offense instead of the defense. I was in such a static haze that I thought I'd only multiply my clumsy steps. I spat the patch of skin and blood on the ground in distaste.

The vampire Fire had challenged was now screaming wildly, raking at her arm where the wound had festered. I used it as my distraction. I sharpened the intent of panic over my opponent's mind, freezing him into a confused stupor. It was the slight I needed for the advantage. I propelled forward, gliding my sword along his, enough to angle his wrist awkwardly and plunge my sharpened nails into his wrist and reef it off. His hand and sword went flying. In return, he splintered a curved blade down my face, the mask only blocking it partially. Its fine metal struck down my face and eye. I held in my grit, the blinding so powerful that my Descendant birthed itself, communicating only with my vampire now.

My black wings sprouted out of my back, cocooning around me in a swift sweep. My wing backhanded him across the dirt as I clutched at my wounded eye. He skirted in upheaval toward the small sawmill, triggering another explosion. When parts of his body showered to the ground it was nothing but sludges of decay.

My mask split into two, toppling to the ground, revealing my face. Blood oozed down my face, marring it as my blinded eye slowly began to heal. Only three remained of the six I'd brought into this fight. They were struggling to fend off those who were equally matching the elite, if not overpowering them. Another explosion went off, shifting the ground beneath me.

Black robes caught my attention in the distance. Five vampires were being dragged to the back end of the warehouse by a group of eight in matching black robes and masks. My vampire tugged on its ounce of control. It didn't want to think and to simply act. And I embraced it, susceptible to its pull now that I'd already allowed it an ounce of freedom. I wavered my mind over those who'd been captured. Lincon and Lydia being two of them. Lincon's mind was offering waves of bemusement. Did he purposefully let himself get captured?

I snarled in fury, the opening of my mouth allowing my blood and own taste to spoil my mouth. I spat onto the ground, furious with him. Fire caught my attention. There was a gleam of warning in her eyes, as if she'd already known what I was going to do. My eye was beginning to slowly heal as I savored the power that licked at my lips.

I reached out to Balzar, *Lydia and the others are inside. I'm going in to retrieve them.* Balzar was so preoccupied with staying alive that he couldn't argue with me to do otherwise. The others couldn't make it past without possibly detonating the bombs. But I could. Fire ran at me, snapping and snarling, aware of what I was about to do.

I wouldn't chance her coming in with me. This was about me indulging in the extreme power I had furling within me, ready to splinter out. I had to awaken and unleash to gravitate to something, any principle I'd been raised on or even anew. I just needed to find myself. And this recklessness was the only way I'd find that. If not, I'd die trying. I'd never felt such total clarity.

I thrust my muscle and wings, propelling me into the sky. My robe flapped between my shoulders, caught between my two spread wings. My hood was fastened around the crown of my hair, keeping it bound despite the wind that tried to tug it out.

A large ceiling glass window was mounted beside the three foreign vampires who screamed and cried at their bloody limbs that were burning as they slowly roasted in the irritable sun. I clutched onto my sword and hoisted myself to hover over the glass before plummeting into the warehouse boots first.

The glass showered around me as I sunk to the dirty floor. My wings flared, trying to block the hailing pieces of glass that dusted the room. Lydia and the others were rallied in a line. In front of them, three robed vampires watched on as the others sprang into action against me. Huddled in the corner were the remains of what I imagined to be Demetri's coven.

The first vampire advanced on me, and so I began the dance that I'd learned as a child. Either they died, or I would. I studied his stance and bronze knuckles, similar to the ones Balzar used. He was a hand-to-hand fighter which I could use to my advantage. I rolled my shoulders, my wings stretching, ready for the avalanche of attacks. Another vampire circled me, two gleaming knives in their hands. They circled me with anticipation. I kept an eye on both of them, the one behind me proving difficult to see while my other eye was compromised.

The one with the brass knuckles made his first move, a brut who clearly favored one leg. I dodged two of his punches, assessing his limp leg. I rolled to the side before the vampire behind me slashed at my back. I blew my estranged hair out from my eye where it had begun to get matted and twisted in the wet blood that dripped down my face. The vampire with brass knuckles had a severe wound prior to being turned, and that was his leg, a weakness I could use to my advantage. I only had three daggers left in my garter.

With one huge sweep, I catapulted toward the vampire with the knuckles, torpedoing toward him. The vampire with the knives tried to jump on my back as I propelled toward their comrade. I halted with ease of my powerful wings, the force sweeping a mighty breeze their way. The one with the knuckles went flying into the back of the warehouse, whereas my focus had been on the one with the knives.

I grabbed their wrist, so they wouldn't be blown away with the same momentum and pulled them toward me. I sent a wave of dread over them, stunning them and leaving them wide open. I thrust my golden claws into their chest, ripping out their non-beating heart through tattered bits of their robe.

Glass shattered around me as I used my wings to protect my face and swerved out of the way. Fire busted through the secondary glass window on the roof. I huffed, infuriated she'd followed me. Her keen sense of smell would've enabled her to avoid standing on the bombs, and she'd followed me into certain danger even after I'd told her not to. However, I found comfort in the camaraderie. She would protect my back and had every right to fight, just as much as I did. It was pointless now to argue with her. She'd already made up her mind, as had I.

She snapped and snarled at the next wave of vampires. I flexed my fingers around the handle of my sword, advancing on the limping vampire with brass knuckles. His mask was pure white, with no painting or expression.

I dodged a dagger that was thrown from behind, shortly followed by Fire lunging at them. Her snarls echoed behind me viciously as her canines tore at their robe. My vampire self only spurred me on, viciously striking at the vampire with my sword. So savage was my internal beast, letting loose to be the victor. The masked vampire was fast, brilliant even. But every step I made cornered him further against the wall, all in anticipation to use his weakness against him. The moment there was an opening, I cut through his good leg. My sharpened sword resisted going through bone. One more strike and the cut would be clean. The muscle of my wing busted into his face, slamming him against the wall. I slashed through again, cleanly chopping off his leg. His gurgled scream brought a smile to my face. As he leaned unevenly and buckled under his weak leg, I spurred my sword from groin to throat, opening him in two.

A vampire threw a thin dagger into my right shoulder, forcing my grip to slacken on my sword. I dropped it, and my wing sagged losing all strength. My sword clambered to the ground. I twisted behind and used the vampire I had near killed as my shield as tiny daggers were thrown toward me. After six precise thuds and one sinking into his heart, I dropped him and reefed the paralyzing blade from my shoulder.

I ran into a litter of metal sheets and crouched behind the pile, shielding myself from the daggers that tinkered along them. I rolled my shoulder back and forth as it came back into use now that I'd taken the dagger out. I looked across the distance of the room where my sword was.

To my left, I saw Fire doing the same as me, hiding behind scrap metal as one of the vampires began to convulse and feverishly claw at their ankle where Fire had bitten them. Her icy blue eyes connected with mine and there was an understanding, the link between us forming a collective advancement of what to do next. I flicked up one of the sheets and threw it flatly across the space that came between us. She jumped in the air protected by the metal sheet. The vampire who'd thrown fine daggers at me had done the same to her. I threw another sheet so he couldn't possibly touch her. She landed at my side, barely able to catch her breath as I flicked the next metal sheet up and used it as a momentary shield as it curved in the air.

By the time the vampire circled around the sheet, I was ready for him, collecting another sheet and slicing it over their wrists and stomach. The metal sheeting was blunt but grazed enough of a wound to give Fire time to jump onto my back and maul their mask, shredding at their face.

A scuttle broke out amongst the vampires who'd been wrestled to the ground. Lydia and the others tried to break out of their silver bindings. I rolled over to collect my sword. A vampire who I hadn't noticed dropped from the ceiling and dove their claws into the tops of my wings, puncturing them. They slid their sharpened nails along the brim of my muscle and plunged them deep into my neck. I realized then that they were going to decapitate me with their bare hands.

I imploded, life or death being my only answer. I slammed them against the wall behind me, shattering my wings from the impact by how savagely I thrust us back. We broke through the wall, falling into the dirt outside. The blinding sun irritated my skin, and I reefed myself up and out of their grip. The weakness of my wings was able to slap them across the rocky terrain. They triggered a bomb, their limbs splintering apart as it detonated.

The blasting threw me back into the warehouse. Wood splintered and compiled around me. Fire yelped as I was thrown into her, skidding us both along the ground. We wobbled to our feet, the ringing in my ears badgering me back and forth. Blood pooled from Fire's ears as she shook her head, trying to focus. Only four of the robed figures remained. My vampire swarmed back and forth with indignation because its strength had been taken away by my temporary imbalance.

"Bring that one to me alive," the vampire who stood in the center demanded. The other's scuffle had only lasted seconds, two more of them were killed as an example. Now only Lydia, Lincon, and one other remained still bound and helpless.

"These seem effective enough," one of them said somberly, and pulled the pin to a bomb and threw it our way. My vision wavered, but I was able to collect Fire in my arms and jump to protect her. The blasting burned my back and wings, propelling us into the metal sheets.

My body roared with pain, my ears bleeding from the surreal siren from the blasting. Flashes of my memories brought me in and out of consciousness. The most apparent memory being when Chase first dove into the rubble and blasting of the bomb to save me in San Francisco. I'd sacrificed myself then to protect my team, and I would do the same over and over again. How many times since then had he saved me? But there would be no chance savior now. My body ached with relentless pain, but I thought of him, and all the memories we'd shared. It felt like a cool balm, replacing my burned and battered body. We had been taught we'd understand our truest form on the battlefield. And as I looked down on Fire's shallow breathing body beneath me, a tiresome belief swept over me. But had it all been for nothing? All of this? Why was I here?

"I said alive!" the vampire in charge said angrily. I was dragged by my tattered wings, being pulled backward. "Keep the mutt alive as well." Fire snapped at the two members behind me, but her edge was off, every bite as she incoherently was backed into a wall.

I was brought to my knees beside Lydia. One hand was firmly placed on my shoulder as silver was slithered around to bind me. My wings flexed, pushing them away for a final fight. But I was pulled away by memories of Chase once again. That's when I realized Lincon was using his illusions on me. My head rounded weakly to where he sat beside me with an apologetic smile.

"You traitor," I said viciously, though my words came through as a slur. He said nothing, shrugging, and looking forward. My back overheated with insufferable pain as my wings laid limply trying in vain to flair. But they were unresponsive, the nerves in them dead.

"What a commendable effort," the vampire in charge said and addressed Lydia who shook with fear.

"Please," she sobbed. "I did everything you asked of me."

"What?" I said weakly, unable to see her as one person because my vision went hazy. I was seeing doubles of everything. The blood coursing through my veins worked rapidly to heal, but the bombarding of Lincon's illusions were suffocating me in an attempt to put me in a stupor.

Lydia looked at me with hatred in her eyes and tears streamed down her face. "You did this! All of this! If it weren't for you my brother wouldn't have been exiled, and your stupid bitch of a mother wouldn't have taken Cesar from me!" She sobbed pathetically. "She's the one you want! I brought her straight to you!" she screamed desperately as if my being here had all been a part of her master plan.

Another vision of Chase, pushing back part of my hair and smiling up at me as we laid in bed together. He was laughing at something I said, and I felt frustrated that he found my serious nature comical.

"Take her now! She's what Oppollo wants, isn't she?!" Lydia screamed, unnerved by the silver that bound and drained her. The only reason why she wasn't screaming was because all of Cesar's elite team had known pain beyond redemption. But even then her tears eluded the knowledge that she was suffering.

"We don't care for some washed up vampire who's a part of Cesar's coven," the masked figure said crouching toward her. She looked stunned and confused.

"I don't understand, she's who you've wanted all this time. Oppollo wants her." Her eyes and skin were uncharacteristically blotchy as she sobbed hysterically. Her fangs were weakly pressing against her bottom lip, producing bubbles of blood.

I sensed confusion in the room. "You are the golden huntress, the one fated to turn on him. And so you shall die today," his voice was muffled beneath the mask.

"Wait!" I screamed, confused. Wasn't it me that they wanted? Another wave of Chase's beautiful imagery lofted over me. Chase was standing in the moonlight, basking in the cold water of a river we once bathed in. His hand was outstretched, welcoming me in to join him.

"She's right there!" Lydia screamed, her shackles binding tighter as she tried to break through them. "She—" The vampire delicately placed his fingers on her face as if ushering her into a cruel sleep.

"Traitors die," he said with cruel intent. She went still as if something had suddenly dawned on her. He unsheathed the sword at his front and sliced the silver blade through her face, cutting it into two. Her body piled onto the floor in a decaying mass. I choked, so shocked by how quickly it'd all happened.

"What about these two?" The robed figure behind me asked. Lincon was unusually quiet. The robed figure assessed us and looked over to the few huddled vampires who were bound and tied in the corner of the room, shaking in pain and fear—the remains of Demetri's coven. Fire was snarling and trying to push off the weighted chains that had been placed around her neck and tied to the roof. One bad stir and she'd hang herself.

The robed vampire in charge looked at me and crouched at my eye level. "You've done well," he praised. "Oppollo will be pleased with your contribution of bringing the golden huntress to us. You will be rewarded. Both of you," he added to Lincon. I looked up at him, stunned. Why was he praising me? Wasn't I the person they'd been looking for?

I couldn't think straight through Lincon's bombarding illusions, so I acted on reflex. I threw my head back and head-butted him. I could hear the crunch between his nose and my forehead through the mask. Blood dripped down his chin from beneath the mask, and I could sense his dark humor in the act.

"Leave them and let them be returned to their coven where they can still message us. Let them go empty-handed now that their prayer for hope has been killed," he said, kicking the decaying corpse of Lydia. "We leave now!" he ordered. The three remaining vampires flooded out the door. From the broken hole in the wall, I could see more robed figures dart outside, and past the warehouse we were in. They were all leaving—All but one, the leader who stood in front of me now.

I was confused and drained. The robed figure tipped over and sat in front of me cross-legged. I kept Fire in the corner of my eye, finding the strength to reach for the small dagger in my boot. The ringing in my ear had come to a near stop, and I could feel my skin itching together. "Well, that was my best performance yet," the man said theatrically. The tone stifled me. The Lincon beside me vanished dramatically into a pile of smoke. "Would you not agree?" The man removed his mask. Lincon's bright blue eyes sparkled in pleasure.

"What?" He hissed at the silver that plated around his fingers as he tried to untie me. "Lincon?" I asked, looking at where he had once sat beside me and was now standing in front of me.

"Always a bit slow on the upkeep, aren't we? I knew you'd come in guns blazing, but I didn't think you'd try to ruin my best performance yet?!" He glowered. "Right now, they're under an illusion that they're being led back by their good old commando sir. In a few seconds, Balzar will counter him and 'kill' him so to speak, and look like a league of hundreds of vampires are outnumbering them. They'll run back to Oppollo pleased with themselves because they think they killed the real you. I'm clever, am I not?" I was stunned. This whole time, it had all been staged? The scraping claws of Fire grabbed my attention. As soon as Lincon had snapped the chains apart I scrambled to her, my wings limply dragging on the sullied ground behind me.

"You're okay, you're okay," I said as she whimpered, strung up, near choking. I stiffened my hand and sliced the gold of my nails through the chain that bound her. She fell to the floor and into my arms. "You're okay," I said, placing my hand on her head and retracting blood. She shook my hand off, watching me warily as if to say she would be okay. She licked my face, the affection surprising me.

Everyone in this room had witnessed Lydia being killed, except they'd all thought it was me. What they saw was the unearthly reality and now whispers of my murder. I thought of my mother, who ordered me to stay because Louise had foreseen my death. I wondered if this was what she had seen, mistaken for someone else taking my place.

I was bitterly weak and confused by Lydia's treachery. Had she been working with Oppollo? Her interest in me being with my familiar right before the attempted assassination made the crime perfectly clear. I'd come here to awaken my own strength or beliefs, or anything. And instead, I'd only rattled a cage of lies and deceit. I'd still been too weak to help the others, and if it hadn't been a setup, then I would've failed the others with my own two hands. And worst of all, I hadn't awoken anything that would dare be strong enough to bring Chase back. I had failed in my own right, to reignite that nobility or raw desire to slaughter. I still felt stiflingly empty.

My mind spiraled as I wobbled to stand, trying to take in everything around me. Balzar burst open the door, panting dramatically with a hooded figure chained and gagged over his shoulder. "Is everyone okay in here?"

"Well, as best as we are ever going to be," Lincon mumbled. "Now, it's time for me to have some actual fun." He giddily tapped his fingers in delight. "We can't have any witnesses, can we?" He walked over to the remains of Demetri's coven who shook in fear.

"We won't say anything we swear. We didn't want to be involved. We didn't—"

"Sssshhh," Lincon ushered with serenity. "This isn't about what you want. This is about me and what I want. And that is always fun." I looked away, blocking out the painful screams that followed as Lincon began to torture in his most creative ways.

Balzar was covered in blood. He still had severe wounds that were stitching themselves together, but the majority of the blood was not his. Only a handful of the vampires who'd gone into battle with him had come back alive. "C'mon, we better get out of here too." He shuffled the cloaked figure over his shoulder, repositioning his weight.

"Who is that?" I asked cynically. I'd been left out of the intel, having been given near to nothing, and I had no doubt that a lot of the efforts were to capture this sole vampire as well. A well thought out plan that could've gone terribly wrong. All those times Lincon and Cesar had silently whispered to one another had all been for this. So did Lincon press for me to come, so I could bear witness to the masterplan and big reveal of his involvement?

Balzar looked depleted. "This was one of the real reasons we came today. It was an extract mission, to take prisoner Oppollo's right-hand man." The one who Lincon had impersonated and who they thought was overpowered and killed during their retreat.

"You lied to me?" He hadn't entirely lied to me, but he withheld the truth. Yet I had no energy or anger toward spiting him. I still felt as if Balzar had been one of the few who offered me my right of freedom and gave me a choice. And maybe he thought I'd be the right amount of distraction during his operation. Had he feared coming into this by himself? Did he doubt the percentage and ability to be able to pull off such a major mission? And why had Cesar sent with him so few men? If anything, I pitied Balzar who was so engrained to follow his orders and missions that he'd been forced into an unlikely outcome. And for that he offered me to fight by his side, assuming I could tip the scale. He was one of few who actually *saw* me.

"I was earnest in what I said. But you had your mission, and I had my own. If you had known everything that was to happen, it wouldn't have gone as successfully. You're not the only one who has plans of their own, Esmore."

My words fell short as a familiar tug yanked me to attention. My battle-scarred wings reacted on their own, propelling me weakly through the broken glass on the roof and toward the river. My wings flapped limply three times before I weakly dipped toward the ground, scared another beat would break my already healing wings.

I retracted my wings, the painful crunch of bone morphing into my back. I ran through it, using the pain as the fuel to my fire. The link swallowed me in adoration as I let it guide me toward him. My only. My everything.

In the distance, Chase and a handpicked fifty vampires ran toward me. Tears pelted down my cheeks as relief flooded through our bond. "Chase!" I said, throwing myself into his arms. He wrapped his strong arms around me, catching and spinning me. My body ached with every movement, but I relished in its feel. He nestled his head into my neck, entranced by my natural perfume.

"Esmore," he whispered desperately. "You idiot. You big idiot," he repeated hopelessly, every word washing a sense of relief through our line. "I thought I'd lose you."

"I could say the same for you." I pulled back, my shaky hand embracing his tight jaw. Those beautiful gray eyes shone back at me, weeping with relief. "How?" I squeaked.

"I don't know," he anguished. "But I heard you. All of it, and I knew you were about to do something stupid. And I just fought my way out to stop you, but I was too late. Why, why did you do that?" he pleaded. He brushed his calloused thumb over my cheek, searching my gaze for my answer. Instead of me finding my way to him, he'd unbound himself to come and protect me. I was embarrassed and ashamed that I couldn't help or bring him back. I rested my forehead on his.

*Because you were gone and I wanted to be with you. I was too weak to bring you back, Chase,* I confessed, ashamed. *They were in our home.* I nestled into him, embracing the warmth of him. Of everything I thought I'd lost once again. The thorny walls that kept us apart were gone. I could nuzzle my mind against his, embracing everything that was calm and loving about him. *I did the only thing I knew how.*

*It was reckless, Esmore. Too reckless. Promise me, you'll never do it again. Please, he begged.* I pressed my lips to his, his breath filling me with the first spark of life I'd felt in days.

"You would have done the same." His eyebrows furrowed in anguish but he kissed me back desperately. He didn't deny it. He couldn't lie to me. He and I were the same. So separate in our thinking but the same in our actions. *They had been in our home.* I had nothing else to give but sit outside their cages, and they still dared to try and take the last of my pieces away. They still tried to destroy all that I had to try and heal.

"I love you so much," he said, kissing me passionately and desperately. We kissed through broken breaths, yearning to touch one another everywhere.

I kept hidden, deep down, far away from where even Chase could catch the thought that had he arrived, he would've been too late.

# CHAPTER 28

CESAR ROLLED HIS fingers on the end of the table with a light, considered tap. My mother was at the other end. The four brothers, Chase, Lincon, and I, filled the remaining seats. The dining room was still torn apart with old canvases and washed-out paintings barely hanging on the walls. Unlike the pleasantries of last time, there was no blood to be shared. Connor was evidently on edge, with the absence of Deemori who had decided to go hunt without him.

When we'd returned to the institute battered, bruised, and exhausted, my mother ran down the stairs and hauled herself at me, sweeping me into a hug. It'd been the same when I was sixteen and went out as an apprentice on my first raid. Tears had sprung in her eyes and then she slapped me. Then hugged me again. I was so mixed with emotion by the response that I hugged her in return. But it was short-lived as we both uncomfortably pulled away from one another. She warned me never to run off on my own like that again or use one of my vampires or tricks against her. And then she vanished into my quarters as quickly as she had come down. I hadn't seen her since, until now.

No one in the room was particularly happy that I'd threatened and locked them in the institute. Privately, Balzar admitted it was rather impressive. Lincon was thriving in the tension of the room, amicably proud of his contribution to the mission.

From the start, Cesar and the brothers had organized that it would be an extraction attempt to pull out Oppollo's second and turn Lydia over. What they hadn't anticipated was my involvement. Though without my distraction of breaking into the warehouse I wondered when Lincon would've so easily slipped into the role and pretense of being the robed figure who we now held prisoner in Cesar's private chambers.

"You're a bad influence, boy," Cesar grumbled his complaint toward Chase.

"She's always been like that," my mother debated, pissed off and proud all the same.

"It was reckless," Yolo reprimanded with his arms crossed over his chest.

"But I guess all is well in the world now that darling Chase is back to normal," Tythian seethed. I snarled at his tone.

"Tythian, buddy, give us some time to rejoice, huh?" Yolo said charismatically, making a joke of the moment.

"It was reckless, anything could've happened between the covens while she was gone. And if you hadn't broken out of your diseased mind then we could've all been in danger," he chided back.

"Aww, he's unhappy because he couldn't teleport out." Lincon laughed at him. "Poor baby." Tythian stood up, threatening and baring his fangs. Lincon charmed a wicked luscious smile, tantalizing him to act on it.

"Enough!" Cesar yelled, not fond of being locked down and bested by two young female huntresses. After an hour of holding the shield, Chase convinced them to relinquish their barrier. When anyone tried to advance on them afterward, Kasey immobilized them. They had been two silent figures amongst all the schemes, which favored Lincon and me to use them as a trump card.

I wasn't certain why Lincon so desperately wanted me to be pulled away into the fight, but he had been right in some regard. The act of fighting was what I'd been manufactured to do. While I was driven to the point of madness with Chase trapped in his own mind, I would've inevitably spiraled further. It wasn't for me that he had done it, he wasn't so selfless. But his desire to be seen and rewarded by me was a driving force I didn't entirely understand when it came to Lincon. For whatever reason, he'd attached himself to me. And it was a striking fear to have someone so close and dangerous at my disposal. Or eventually it would lead to a knife in my back. His sparkly eyes were still torturing Tythian, daring him so desperately without words.

"There's no point in being so hostile toward each other when you're departing for Tracey's Council tomorrow," Balzar said pointedly. Tythian folded his arms over his chest, irritated.

"You still want us to go?" I asked Cesar, surprised after besting him he still entrusted us partaking in this peculiar mission. I wasn't ignorant to the scheming he'd been crafting behind Chase's and my back, and I wondered if that further stemmed into what we'd be doing at Tracey's. My only rescuing calculation was that my mother would never allow for something that she thought would be life and death for me. This mission would be risky, yes, but something they all deemed necessary.

"It still needs to be done. We need to start turning heads on the Council table against him before their next Council meeting. I'm certain Oppollo will solidify his dominance there, and if he has them all working together, then the covens will be the first to be turned on, maybe even before the hunters and human government."

"And what of the wolves?" Tythian asked poisonously. Chase brushed his knuckles against mine beneath the table, sending a wave of calm over me. Every one of his touches and signals, I embraced dearly, not ever wanting to take them for granted again. With Chase in his right mind once again, I could make sense of my own thoughts. Had he not been able to get himself out, I don't know what I might've done or what state I would've come back in. Perhaps I'd engross myself into the same trenches I'd barely survived, waiting until I rightly died by his side. Death had never scared me, but that way of thinking and allowance of deteriorating in such a way did.

"For now, the human government's been quiet. After their 'extract' of turning on their own and taking them from the Human Compound, we haven't heard anything from them since," my mother reported. "I think for now while they're being closely watched by the hunters as well, they might lay low for a while which will give us time to focus on other things."

"I meant the other wolves," Tythian gritted out. Cesar gave him an effective look, not to speak to his familiar in such a way. "The ones we house upstairs."

"I'm looking after them," my mother said, no-nonsense. "Is that a problem?" He stared her down at the end of the table, savoring the direct challenge.

"Alongside Yolo who will be studying them," Cesar added. The room fell silent. "And while we're all here, let me make one thing clear." He narrowed his gaze on me. "You might be my daughter, but you are never to pull a stunt like that again, if you do, I'll be coming for his head." He pointed at Chase. Chase stretched his arm across me, so I wouldn't rashly cross the table.

"Don't make promises you can't keep," he said with a cheesy grin. "Now, if you'll excuse us, while there are a few more hours to be had, I'd much rather spend it alone with my familiar."

"And what about me, while you're gone?" Lincon looked at me wide-eyed. Had he a tail, it would be wagging as he lapped up the little attention he was being given.

"Do what you do best, Lincon," I said bemused. "Wreak havoc on those who jeopardize my ideals."

His smile stretched from ear to ear. "Goodie," he said, eyeing each of them daringly. His gaze lingered on Tythian longer than I would've liked. It wasn't a threat per se, but it was a reminder that while we were gone, there would be laws and people in our place to protect that of which we valued most.

I laid in Chase's arms, swimming in his masculinity. The claw bath that I had once flipped on the assassin had surprisingly survived, been restored, and the room already cleaned. We laid in there scrubbing the last few days of filth off. I stroked my hand back and forth over his forearm, content as I laid on him. I thought back on the conversations we'd had in this very same room and the desperation I'd felt that I was going to lose him. I had in a sense.

There was no true relief in this moment because we had been torn apart because of my unraveling and inability to remain composed. I had put Chase into that state yet again, and there was no way I could ever apologize enough in actions or words.

"Hey," he said delicately, massaging my shoulders to try and wake me from my thoughts. "We're in this together. You need to stop thinking like that."

I twisted to face him. My eye had completely healed now, my face seemingly untouched by the viciousness of today. His rolling thumbs eased the tension in my back, and somewhere deep down I hoped it was helping massage out and restore my wings. "How can you be so calm after what I've done to you?"

"You didn't do anything to me," he replied easily.

"I'm serious, Chase. I lost you because I gave in to my emotions."

He grimaced and rolled his hands thoughtfully over my arms, drawing cold water over them. "Esmore, I'm living in the now. And tomorrow we have to face one another as if we've never laid eyes on each other in this way. I never want to take a second with you for granted. Emotion and all."

I huffed in irritation, more alienated and annoyed about what was to come tomorrow. I'd be propped up and prized as the one who got the upper hand on Oppollo. Because of that, it was up to us to convince Tracey and her Council to turn against him, all while I'd be subject to denying my bond with Chase and watching some princess vampire ogle over him.

Chase laughed to himself. "Esmore, it has to be done. And you know nothing is going to happen between us. Though I do find your jealousy rather sexy."

"It's not that I think something is going to happen," I grumbled my complaint. "It's just your mine, end of discussion." I crossed my arms. He wriggled his fingers under my arms, trying to tickle me. The water splashed as I tried to knock him away.

"And you are mine," he said light-heartedly. "And I don't like it anymore than you. But if you do it well, we can be out and done with it in no time." He twisted around me so he could press a gentle kiss to my temple. I leaned into his touch, comforted but all the same still grumpy.

"Will you see the little one before you leave?" he asked. I thought about Titan and Chris, ashamed of everything that had happened. I could hardly face Dillian and Tori once again. How could I possibly face two children who I'd wronged so badly? I wasn't their hero or savior. I was a confused woman, selfishly trying to salvage the only redeeming qualities of myself before I was completely taken over.

"No," I said and leaned into him as dead weight, allowing myself to be overcome by his masculinity. He didn't press me any further, instead, brushing his fingers up and down my arms, running a light calming shiver over me as I rested my eyes, dejected from the day. I fell into a solemn sleep.

I didn't so much as search for him, but Fier made his intrusion known, just as he had the last time. We met in the same rainstorm, the two of us sitting beside one another under the cave, except this time I wasn't cold. In the living, I was comforted by Chase's warmth.

"How unlike you to be so welcoming to my intrusion," he said, disgusted in the dirty sloshes of water that flicked on him as the rain hammered. "Good to see you got a happily ever after. I'm surprised he was able to pull himself out of it. Oh, how cute love can be." He sighed romantically.

"A word of advice," I said, feeling far superior in this situation as he tried to bait me. "You have a traitor amongst your midst."

It went without saying at the meeting that Lydia didn't have the connections to reach out to Oppollo herself. But her sure connection was her brother who fled to Fier's Council after Cesar had exiled him, and through that, Fier's Council, who was obliged to work with Oppollo and all other Councils. It set Thomas up with mysterious connections and the ability to undermine Fier. It wasn't Lydia who planned all of this out, she was simply a puppet to her own brother's workings. And that subjected Fier to a possible leak in his personal goals of overthrowing Oppollo, depending on how much Thomas knew.

"What are you talking about?" Fier aggressively asked. It gave me great satisfaction passing on this information because the demise of Thomas served me as well. What happened to Lydia should've been avoided. She had been caught betraying her coven, but had she not been so open to her brother's manipulation she might've remained loyal to Cesar and the brothers. The hit the elite team took today was massive. Five of their members had been taken out as they went against a handful of Oppollo's best. That was the consequence of raising so much as an objection to Oppollo. I was quickly beginning to understand that. And how quickly he'd webbed his way into finding us. But without Lydia offering that intel, Cesar's gift should be enough to conceal our whereabouts for a while. The brothers also hoped their cunning plan worked and that Oppollo was under the impression I was a dead woman for some time.

"Thomas was in communication with Oppollo's Council through his sister, Lydia. She betrayed us, and so she was beheaded in my place. So, you might start hearing rumors that I'm dead and Oppollo is the victor."

Anger flashed on Fier's face as the wind picked up speed. His frustration was pelting the rain faster and heavier. "I'll kill him," he snarled. I hid the smile. He was too easy to antagonize. And I would finally have Thomas's head, as promised to Tythian.

"So maybe before you come and check up on me and how we're doing on this end, you should worry about your own Council. You would think you'd have learned from the last time you were betrayed, Fier."

His hand firmed around my throat, and I charmed a wicked smile. "Don't get cocky, girl."

"I could say the same to you," I mused back with confidence that Fier would never kill me. Would never try because despite all his strength and might, he was depending on me to end Oppollo's reign. He tarnished my familiar's mind, and I'd never offer him a shred of remorse. I looked forward to the day where I could wrap my hands around his throat instead, enforcing pain beyond his wildest dreams in place. For all that he had done to me and my familiar, he would pay. These check-ups, and mockery of my progress now festered to spur me on. I'd already lost most of what I had to give and tried to protect. Now all that could stray was my mind.

I reefed myself out of our connection, not missing the moment I felt the familiarity of the presence who usually lingered to delude my dreams and memories. They were watching, as they had been these past few weeks, but for once they allowed me to have my well-earned rest. I still hadn't fully healed from my battle with Oppollo. And like the others had said, it would take me years if not lifetimes to, but all I could do was that which I knew. And that was to fight, even if I didn't have the strength to fight for myself anymore. I would fight until I fell to my knees, in the direction that Chase thought was best for both of us. He would be my moral compass in a time where I couldn't even admit to him, that I'd already given up.

# CHAPTER 29

"WE MIGHT AS well start calling you reckless huntress instead of Token," Darcy joked. The reminder of my former role and name overshadowed a stark atmosphere into the already dark cellar. I had been sitting across from Dillian and Tori now for an hour. Neither of them had changed. Chase was with his coven, communicating the next phase of our transition and things that had to be done while he was away.

"I don't know why you follow me," I said dryly, trying to craft the same humor as him but falling short.

"Well, we kind of like you," Darcy said sheepishly and looked to Jerimiah for confirmation.

"Darcy always had a thing for bad girls," Jerimiah mocked.

"Shut up! It's not in that way!" He blushed and looked toward the staircase in case Chase overheard.

I offered an insincere smile, resting my head on my arms once again, watching my two fallen hunters as caged animals. I watched my best friend pace back and forth, like an animal, shattered and overwhelmed that this was still reality.

"But seriously, Esmore, it takes courage to do what you did, in the sake of making sure they were safe. That Chase was safe," Jerimiah reiterated. I appreciated his efforts in consoling me. And that he was one in few who understood I'd turned to action the moment they'd stepped into the institute, even if it cost me my life. And it saddened me by how much Chase wanted me to live and thrive, and I still wanted to waste away in this cellar with the others. The moment Dillian and the others were attacked, a final piece of me broke. It was something I don't think I'd ever truly understand. And thoughtfully, the only place I ever found answers was through the act of fighting.

Yolo walked down the stairs. He'd cleaned himself up after our confrontation with the assassin. He took his seat beside me, watching them as I did, silently. Jerimiah and Darcy left the room, hovering atop the stairs to give us privacy.

"Do you think Oppollo's team did it?" I asked, offering Yolo a thread of forgiveness. I couldn't hate him anymore than myself for not being there to protect them. I was showered in grief. Never would I hear the thick accent of Teary again or see the wolves group in a way that they could survive themselves. And the hunters who remained would never be the same. I had this void to fill to avenge them, and yet the self-starvation impacted my focus greatly. I didn't even know where to start looking for the mastermind who'd done this to them.

"I don't know," he said honestly. "But I doubt it. No one else knew where they were, except for us, unless some vampire stumbled on our location randomly. But even then, I would've sensed them coming toward us. It's like they came out of thin air," he said, disheartened as he played with the wooden cross on his bare chest. It was the item he carried to remind him of his family and catholic upbringing, in a time where people believed in a higher being and better place.

"I really am sorry, Esmore. I wanted all of them to find a place where they could be safe," he said earnestly. I believed him, his sadness mirroring my own. I had been left with the dangerous choice of whether I should let them die or let them be turned. And now, I wasn't so sure I'd made the right decision.

"Let me ask you a question." I angled my head toward Yolo, looking at him for the first time since he'd entered. He was handsome, in the way most vampires were. But there was always something different about Yolo. He carried the same playful nature as Chase, but the part that kept him pure and sincere was what I thought to be shifting into Jenn so many times. "Had you the choice to turn Jenn, would you have?"

He blew out a dramatic sigh and toyed with a small smile. "Yes. And I might've regretted it every day, having taken the choice away from her. She didn't want to be turned. But had I been in my right mind, instead of killing her completely, if only I'd turned her instead… I would've rather her hating me a thousand years but still being here, than her being gone entirely." Anguish marred his woody brown eyes. And maybe I would live that very repercussion as well.

"Here," I said, stretching out and collecting the wine bottle beside me. I'd taken a few swigs that had left my head swirling. I drank the barbaric tasting liquid as punishment but also enjoying the slight buzz it gave me. It was of course under Chase's recommendation.

Yolo kissed his wooden cross. "I think I'll be needing the big man for this one." He lightly laughed as he took the bottle to take a swig.

"Esmore." Tori's shaky breath snapped my attention to his cage. There in the darkness, a weary awareness had set across his face.

"Tori." I pushed off the wall and toward the cage where his hands met mine. He flinched away from Dillian who tried to attack us between the cages. The dead body beside him hadn't yet been removed from the cell. He looked down at it in horror.

"What's happening to me?" he asked, frightened.

"Sshh, everything is going to be okay," I said, clutching his hand. He looked too young to be facing this reality. He was scattered as he tried to understand and come to the reality of his past few days.

"Something hurts. It hurts all over," he said, his other hand stamping out across his chest. He was set into a panic. Dillian lunged for the bars, smashing into them. He rebounded and snarled in a crouching position, his fangs for show. Tori's hand stretched over his neck as if the terror and memories were returning to him now. "Am I?"

"Listen to me," I said, holding his head and forcing him to look into my eyes. "Everything is going to be okay." He began to shake as coherency came forth. I sent a wave of calmness over him to assist in handling the panic he was stricken with.

"Am I?" he asked again. So innocently to what I thought he might've been like when he came too. I thought he'd be savage, completely taken over by the soulless creature he'd become. But instead, as if worse but a saving grace all in its own, he was nothing but a scared and lost boy.

"Tori... yes... you've been turned." His expression went blank, and he faced the reality of the dead woman beside him. His hand slowly rose to his mouth, pricking at the tip of his newborn fangs. I forced him to look at me again. "Tori, listen to me. As your Token, you'll be okay. Okay?"

"I can never go back, can I?" he said shakily. "To the Guild. I can never be a hunter again?" My stomach lurched, and I could sense Chase noticing the prickle of change in my demeanor. Had he thought that somehow, even when following Teary and the others? That still vowing to follow me he would've lived the end of his days in a Guild?

I shook my head, apologetic for not having forced him to return to the Guild sooner. Tori had never committed any crime, other than being an innocent bystander and following what he thought had been the right thing to do. And instead, it turned him into this.

"I'm sorry." I dropped my grip from his. What more could I say? How could I fix him in the reality that everything has been taken away from him? And how would I face Dillian when I was to tell him the same. Tori was overwhelmed, the moment of his consciousness evaporated into his gnarly beast as he lashed out at me, striking his nails down my chest. He'd hidden within himself once again, inside the beast that would be suckling on his soul, cooing him that he'd protect him and show him the right way, when really, it was ensuring its own safety. "I'm sorry."

Yolo placed his hand on my shoulder. "Esmore, he'll come back too. The start of it, the changing, it takes a while," he said apologetically and offered me the half-empty bottle. I starred at Dillian for the remaining few hours I had, wondering if before I left, I'd have to face him in the same light. If I'd have to explain to him what he'd become and the future he'd become fixated on wasn't possible. How would he react when he realized he lunged for Julia? How much would he hate me? I spiraled into a private agony, hiding it from Chase as best as I could. There was nothing I could give, say or do to right this.

I hugged Fire in her human form, her beautiful body having fully healed after our last battle. The connection I had with her was second to that of which I had with Chase. When my mother had revived her with my venom running through her veins, we were compelled to one another, to serve one another in a way that felt like until death would us part.

"I want to come with you," she grumbled her complaint. Fire was reluctant to shift out of her wolf form, especially in front of Tythian and Chase, even when we were behind closed doors. Chase's jaw unhinged as he saw the beautiful woman manifest, cruelly with broken bones and shredding skin to take human form. But she carried the weight and pain, accustomed to it. Like me, she might've even welcomed the pain as punishment.

"This is one place that you can't. I want you to help my mother and Yolo with Titan and Chris." I knew that with the three they'd be protected. Whoever had ambushed them once wouldn't be so daring to do it a second time, not in the presence of two covens who were enforced to protect them. They might've been reluctant to do so, but I was certain they feared the wrath of their coven leaders far more than the decency of making a point. Lydia had been made an example of, as much as it shattered the bound trust in Cesar's coven.

"You want me to play babysitter to the wolf pups," she grumbled.

"I want you to play the part of protector while I'm gone, with the most valuable things I have to claim," I said, pressing my forehead against hers. The intention of Dillian, Julia, and Tori included. "I can full-heartedly only trust you with this." I trusted Yolo and my mother. But there was an unbreakable bond between Fire and I that couldn't be replicated. She was in part me and I her. And she had staked her life for me numerous ways, in the same way that I would do for her. She was a woman of the same age as my mother and yet I didn't look at her in such a light. She was my given warrior and sister. One who Chase had randomly plucked in the midst of chaos, thinking himself smart, and in fact, he'd given me yet another gift that could never be replaced. "Please."

She looked at Chase and eyed Tythian wearily, her upper lip curling. She trusted him less than me. But she didn't need to warn me twice. My mind was already made up.

"Just make sure you return safely and soon. Both of you," she said pointedly to Chase. "Oh, and this nickname 'wolf people' sickens me. It sounds like we worship dogs or something," she said light-heartedly in her thick accent.

"Do you have a name you'd like to be called by?" Chase asked her.

"Yes, call us werewolves. It sounds spookier and fiercer." Her white canines showed as she smiled. I nodded curtly.

"Werewolves it is. We'll be back before you know it," I dared to say, hoping it to be true. But the reality was I didn't know what would wait for us on the other side of Tracey's Council or what would be expected of us. She nodded, and with the bone-shattering noise of her shifting from skin to fur, she transformed into a werewolf. Her snow-white fur was clean and fresh. Her piercing blue eyes fixated on us as we departed.

Chase offered his elbow to me. I appreciated his finely sculpted abs that protruded courtesy of his open leather jacket. I took it in, receiving a small kiss in reward. He became greedy and pressed his hand gently around my throat, claiming my tongue with his. It would be the last moment and kiss we could tenderly offer one another. I embraced his scent, warmth, his everything because soon I would be denied the ability to claim him as mine. In Tracey's Council, we would pretend to be nothing but comrades, dispersing rumors of being familiars and playing a part I thought would be most difficult to me.

"Disgusting," Tythian said, flicking a small piece of dust from his dress shirt. It didn't stop Chase's hand from gravitating toward my ass with a prickling smile as he grabbed it.

"Oh, Tythian, I owe you one less favor," I said as Chase all but mauled me with kisses and inappropriate groping that forced Fire to look away.

Tythian scoffed. "And how do you figure that?" He'd enjoyed holding every favor over my head, as the rope that he soon hoped would noose around my neck and hang me.

"Thomas is dead," I replied, returning Chase's faithful and smiling kiss. "Now, all I owe you is Fier's head."

Tythian was silent for a moment. Probably measuring how I would have gained information about Thomas being deceased. "You will always owe me far more than just a few trinket favors," he said unsavory. I ignored him, focusing on Chase. My everything. I'd even had to hide his locket of hair and blue gemmed necklace. Removing the staple of them and claim on me, made me feel empty. I understood there was a reason for this because we'd have to act in such a way. That it would be like before we'd ever met. I would be cold to him, and he was simply carrying out a mission that would influence and assist his coven. But it saddened me to think that this one thing in the world that was truly mine, could so easily be masked. And that was what Chase would have to do.

"You know it's only temporary," he reminded me with another gentle kiss to the lips and then temple. "And this is for our future."

"Don't pretend like you're so forward thinking now," I joked. "But keeping my hands off you will be the hardest part."

"Oh, I know," he challenged in that purr that aroused me. "And it'll push me to my limits as well. But we have to do this, for everyone's sake." I nodded, grazing my nails down his beautiful chest and stomach one more time. "After everything we've been through, Esmore, we've always come back home and into one another's arms. This will be no different."

I smiled, hiding my lack of confidence that I didn't share with him. I surrendered to a part of myself that I'd lost in the cellar while I was down there with them, praying to a superstition I'd never believed in. I never thought I'd embrace Chase the same way, or at all. And so, I gave part of myself away, not able to deal with the hurt. And I was scared that if he was so quickly taken away from me again like all the rest had been, then I would offer it my final piece—completely empty.

"It's time," Tythian said, aggravated by how we fooled. I foreboded all that could go wrong but instead pulled back my shoulders and let Chase's gleaming smile lead my way. No matter how fake it might've been. He was sincere in the love we shared, but even he couldn't predict how this would turn out. It could be fruitless, or as Cesar predicted, it could be so much more.

At this point, all I understood was that a rumor would start about my death. And it might've prevented some from seeking me out momentarily, but it would only last so long. And I was subjected to what rumors and stories they'd heard of me, and of a power I couldn't put on display if Tracey asked of me, or of what the world expected from a huntress who was born half vampire.

I gently pressed my fingers along Tythian's forearm, disgusted that I had to touch him. We were swept into darkness with the nauseating stir of Tythian's teleportation. The cool brisk of snow and ice came into form as we were blanketed in white.

# ABOUT THE AUTHOR

Kia grew up in the Darling Downs Region in Queensland, Australia. Graduating High School, she pursued a career in freelance journalism. In 2014, having always had a passion for writing fiction, she decided to follow her dream of becoming an accomplished author.

Now living on the Gold Coast, Australia and travelling every spare minute she gets, Kia is constantly searching for new inspiration for her writing and filling her heart with adventure, one country at a time.

# OTHER BOOKS BY
# KIA CARRINGTON-RUSSELL

### Mad Hatter Vampire Prince:
A PREQUEL NOVELLA TO THE TOKEN HUNTRESS SERIES.
CAN ALSO BE READ AS A STANDALONE.

Kyran Klaus is the prince of Grand Klaus, his reputation honoring him the title of the Mad Hatter Vampire Prince. Crazy, deadly, lustful, and utterly bored with life.

Sasha Pierce is one of a kind. Having been experimented on by her mother as a child, she's become a human weapon who's looking for answers beyond the walls where her kind aren't enslaved to vampires.

When the Mad Hatter Prince takes a sudden interest in Sasha and her work, she scarcely begins to cover her tracks and hide her secrets. What she doesn't anticipate is being a pawn in his most sinister performance yet.

Disturbingly Wicked! This novella is not for the fainthearted. Lust, Gore, Wit, and Malicious Humor. Prepare to be deliciously tainted.

## *Token Huntress*

Being born a hunter, Esmore has been raised with one purpose, to hunt and kill the vampire race that destroyed the world as it was known. At eighteen, Esmore's a Token Huntress in her Guild, surpassing her mentor's expectations of her, despite having no magical ability, like all hunters before her.

During a raid in the once iconic San Fransisco, Esmore's team is ambushed, and a mysterious vampire that she is drawn to captures and takes her to the Vampire Council as a prisoner. Her captor- Chase, a lethal, immortal, sexy, and charming vampire who will stop at nothing to claim her as his familiar.

While in captivity, Esmore learns information that makes her question everything she's been taught.

Now in the year 2341, Esmore fights for her survival. But who exactly is she fighting against? The very people who nurtured her, or the evil she's supposed to hate?

## *The Shadow Minds Journal:*

In this world, there are creatures lurking in the shadows. As a child, I once played with them. As a teenager, I began to fear them and became victim to their attacks. As an adult, I now realize that no matter how much I try to escape the grasp of this world, I was inevitably born into it.

Now reborn as a Guardian in the year of 2986, Vivian Lair must uphold the treaty between Angels and Demons on the human world and city of Shabeah. Contracted to seven demons who she can shift into while taking direct orders from the Underworld Lord, Haymen, it wasn't exactly her ideal rebirth. Involving herself with the Angel of War, Gabe is even worse.

Still fighting those who try to possess her during her sleep, Vivian must now record and try to hunt the Volv through the Shadow Minds Journal. Now stuck between the hatred and lust of two of the most powerful entities in all worlds, Vivian is involved inevitably in the upcoming conflict.

*Blood. Lust. War. She must kill before being killed.*

## *My Escort Collection:*

A collection of the Best Selling contemporary series that includes: My Escort, My Exception and My Expectation. Clover is personal assistant to Debra Coorman, the merciless boss of Candice fashion magazine. The bright lights of New York are dim for Clover, who is tormented by a work schedule like no other. Debra is relentless in her determination to demean Clover. For once, Clover dares to play Debra's games, and intends to prove her wrong at the next glittering event. With mixed emotions, Clover contacts a male escort, Damon. If his velvet voice over the phone is anything to go by, Clover knows her money will be well spent. But when Damon appears at her door, something unexpected happens. The taunts and the games begin. Who is truly going to win at this game?

## *Aroused: Taming Himself*

"Remember my name because you will be begging me for more. This is my promise to you."

Meet Hayden Zilch: entrepreneur, sports manager, investor. Cocky, tantalizing, and an utter womanizer. He is a man who loves pleasuring women. He can show you a world you have only fantasied about.

So what happens when this sex-mad womanizer decides to finally find The One?

Starting off with a list of five women, Hayden sets out to learn the difference between lust and love. His adventures have him laughing, crying in pain, and begging on his knees as he battles to tame himself. Can Hayden really control himself around these five beautiful temptresses?

*Taming Himself is the first in this five-book series which tells the story of Hayden's search for both love and pleasure.*

## *Phantom Wolf*

*A book that is so dynamic and can pull my emotions free so easily is a 5 star novel.*
★★★★★ *- Paranormal Trance Reviews*

Sia is a Phantom Wolf. Neither dead nor alive--and rotting from the inside--she is on the edge of her curse. Once a Phantom Wolf has been created, they hunt their blood pack and slaughter all their loved ones. Except for Sia, who woke years after her death to find herself rampaging through the land on a lonely path.

She continues to run from the rival pack that hunts her because she is a Phantom Wolf. Attracted to a scent, Sia finds her old best friend, who is now a grown woman. Having once saved Keeley, Sia takes the role of protector yet again, despite Keeley's involvement with the mysterious Alpha, Kiba, and his kin brother, Saith. An ambush separates the pack and the four of them blindly fight the new warriors that attack them: desperately needing to find out where the attacks are coming from, as Sia has vowed to protect Keeley. But at what cost?

Now being chased, Sia finds herself conflicted by the mortal and spirit world while trying to protect her kin. Sia must confront her fears, as well as the human lover who killed her many years before. It is not only survival Sia contends with, but her own façade that must be broken so that she may find peace within herself once more.

## *The Three Immortal Blades*

Contains the entire Award Winning Collection. Karla Gray is an ordinary young woman that is taken from her mundane life into a world of blood lust as she begins to struggle with a unique ability. Karla is a Shielder; an exceptional fighter born with the rare ability to project a Shield for protection. However, Shielders are not the only kind that possesses such a talent. The Shielders battle a war that has been raging for centuries against Starkorfs, who harvest humans and Shielders alike to obtain a near immortality. Alongside the charming Lucas and selfless Paul, Karla must unravel the purpose of her curse and battle an unknown presence manipulating her thoughts; a mysterious woman who may be dormant for now, but has every intention of possessing Karla- mind, body, and soul. Within this new reality that Karla faces the search for the Three Immortal Blades begins.